SPIRAL

Titles by Bal Khabra

COLLIDE

SPIRAL

SPIRAL

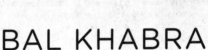

BAL KHABRA

BERKLEY ROMANCE

NEW YORK

BERKLEY ROMANCE
Published by Berkley
An imprint of Penguin Random House LLC
penguinrandomhouse.com

Copyright © 2025 by Bal Khabra
Excerpt from *Collide* copyright © 2024 by Bal Khabra

Book design by George Towne

Library of Congress Cataloging-in-Publication Data

Names: Khabra, Bal, author.
Title: Spiral / Bal Khabra.
Description: First edition. | New York: Berkley Romance, 2025.
Identifiers: LCCN 2024022433 (print) | LCCN 2024022434 (ebook) |
ISBN 9780593818282 (trade paperback) | ISBN 9780593818299 (ebook)
Subjects: LCGFT: Romance fiction. | Novels.
Classification: LCC PR9199.4.K4727 S65 2025 (print) |
LCC PR9199.4.K4727 (ebook) | DDC 813/.6—dc23/eng/20240517
LC record available at https://lccn.loc.gov/2024022433
LC ebook record available at https://lccn.loc.gov/2024022434

First Edition: January 2025

Printed in the United States of America
1st Printing

PLAYLIST

TAKE CARE | Beach House

WASH. | Bon Iver

FALLEN STAR | The Neighbourhood

WILLOW | Taylor Swift

SATURN | SZA

RYDER | Madison Beer

CRY BABY | The Neighbourhood

MATILDA | Harry Styles

BE MY BABY | The Ronettes

WHEREVER YOU GO | Beach House

MOONLIGHT | Chase Atlantic

STARGIRL INTERLUDE | The Weeknd, ft. Lana Del Rey

BE HONEST | Jorja Smith, ft. Burna Boy

LET THE LIGHT IN | Lana Del Rey, ft. Father John Misty

FADE INTO YOU | Mazzy Star

REDBONE | Childish Gambino

EVERYWHERE, EVERYTHING | Noah Kahan

REAL LOVE BABY | Father John Misty

LOVE GROWS (WHERE MY ROSEMARY GOES) | Edison Lighthouse

FOLDIN CLOTHES | J. Cole

You are a light in this world,
don't waste it on those who can't see it.
Find the people who can.

ONE

ELIAS

TORONTO THUNDER'S GOLDEN BOY KEEPS THE ICE COLD AND THE WOMEN HOT!

Being a rookie in the NHL is as bad as you expect it to be. But being a rookie in the NHL who's constantly in the media and hasn't scored his first career goal is even worse.

The hotel lobby has a selection of magazines to choose from, but the one on the coffee table has my name on the cover. It's a blurry picture of a woman leaving the nightclub, with me right behind her. The rare time I could be persuaded to celebrate a win is when they catch me with a woman. If they bothered to do some research, they'd know the woman is Brandy, our team photographer. I had offered her a ride home, and didn't expect someone to snap pictures.

Avoiding parties and outings isn't something I do intentionally, but it's difficult to celebrate something you had no part in. I prefer going over the games and analyzing my mistakes to find what's preventing me from getting that first goal. So that's exactly what I have planned for tonight.

Except we're in Dallas, and I'm still waiting in the hotel lobby for my room to be ready. Despite knowing not to, I take a closer look at the magazine, and read the smaller headlines.

IS WESTBROOK LOSING HIMSELF TO FAME? ANOTHER BAD MOVE FOR TORONTO?

"Mr. Westbrook?"

I drop the magazine as if I'd been caught reading something illicit and head to the front desk. When I thank the concierge for the key, he shoots me a not-so-discreet wink that confuses me. Ignoring the weird interaction, I head up in the elevator to my room. Sliding my key card in the door, I waste no time heading straight for the shower.

The hot water unravels the tense muscles in my back and the thoughts of the stupid magazine. Steam wafts out of the shower behind me as I wrap a towel around my waist and run another through my hair. I've been dying to get into bed and turn on the game highlights, but I stop dead in my tracks when I see what's in my bed. Or rather *who* is in my bed.

What the fuck?

Clutching my towel, I take several steps back. "Sorry, did I get the wrong room key?"

I didn't. I'm sure of that since my luggage is only two feet away from me. Suddenly, the concierge's wink makes sense. The woman's long blond hair falls in waves around her face, red lips and perfect teeth forming a smile. She's lying on the king-size bed in one of the hotel-provided robes with half-eaten snack wrappers from the mini-bar strewn across the covers.

"The key seems perfect to me." Her mischievous smile as she sits up makes me uneasy.

"I'm not sure who you're looking for, but it's definitely not me."

"Trust me"—her eyes map every inch of my torso, lingering on the wet droplets slipping down my abdomen—"it's definitely you, Eli."

If this is a prank, I'm killing my teammates.

"I thought you'd want to celebrate tonight's win," she purrs, taking a step toward me.

The only reason I'd celebrate is if I scored, and that hasn't happened yet. I take several steps back and toward the door. "I'm sure you can find someone else who's interested."

Her brows jump so high I can tell she's never been turned down.

My refusal doesn't have her putting her clothes back on and leaving as I'd hoped. So I turn and walk out. In the hall, naked except for a towel, I head straight for a neighboring room. Aiden and I are only a few rooms apart since the rookies are paired together, and I'm hoping he's still awake.

Aiden Crawford, my best friend and teammate, isn't like me. He got his first career goal the moment he stepped onto the ice in our very first game. His second goal came that next night with an assist by me. Since he's joined the Toronto Thunder, he's been nothing short of stellar, and I couldn't be more proud. But Aiden's not one to throw a party for each goal. His ambitions extend beyond a single game, a drive he's had since he led us as captain at Dalton University.

So right now I'm hoping he's also bailed on celebrating, because hotel guests are walking in the corridor, and one has taken a particular interest in my half-naked state. If they recognize me, I'm sure cameras will start clicking.

"Aiden!" I knock harder than I should, earning even more looks when the elevator opens to a new batch of hotel guests. *Fantastic.*

Mid-knock, the door swings open, and Aiden eyes me with curiosity. "What's wrong?"

Before I can explain, the reason for my escape strolls out of the room, scanning the hallway for me. "That is." I gesture to the girl and barrel my way inside his hotel room.

"Again?" Aiden chuckles, closing the door. I see the phone in his hand, with his girlfriend, Summer, on a video call.

"Hey, Brooksy." She waves at me through the screen, and I wave back, clutching my towel a little tighter. Although, Summer's probably immune, since she's seen way more than she signed up for when she and Aiden started dating earlier this year. We've become great friends, and there's nothing I wouldn't do for her.

"You need security, man," Aiden says. "I'm pretty sure those people in the hall took a picture of you."

I sit on his bed and drop my head back against the headboard in defeat. All I ever wanted was to play professional hockey, but now it feels like the dream is slipping through my fingers. The extra attention and opinions wouldn't bother me if I could shake off the pressure to perform. It's a weight that conveniently snatches my ability to do the one thing I've always been good at.

"Did Eli just virtually cockblock us?" Summer asks.

Aiden shrugs and smirks at his phone. "I'm still down if you are."

I groan. You'd think them being in a long-distance relationship would give me some reprieve from the PDA.

"I think I'll pass." Summer laughs. "Have fun at your sleepover!"

I drop my head in my hands. "How am I supposed to focus on playing when I know this is the stuff that's hitting the headlines first thing tomorrow?"

Aiden tosses his phone on the nightstand and gives me a pitying look. One he does every time something stupid like this occurs. "This is some pretty shit luck, man. I can't believe people are buying into the 'golden boy turned playboy' narrative."

In an unexpected turn of events, a video posted by our team went viral. I had hesitantly agreed to film a day in the life of an NHL rookie, and the fans loved it. I'm not sure if it was the bloopers they found endearing, or maybe my workout routine was just that inspirational. But as soon as the media knew what the fans wanted, they became hungry for more. And when I was two games in with nothing on my stats sheet, the criticism started pouring in. They credited my draft to my parents' connections and discounted my talent, all within a few days. I went from being the endearing rookie to the rich playboy whose only goal is to get laid.

"It's my fault. I should have turned down the extra press when I had the chance." When our social media team approached me with ideas for more content, I could have said no. Thinking it would benefit my image rather than dampen it, I stupidly agreed.

"They would have talked you into it regardless. They need eyes on the game, especially with the ratings dropping last year."

I sigh. "'Pretty boy hockey player who can't score for shit.' That'll be the next headline."

"You've had plenty of assists. Trust me, you'll get the goal too," he assures. "Just find something that lets you breathe. Something that takes away the pressure you're feeling."

"Easier said than done. We can't all have a Summer," I mutter.

He smiles. "True, but the media only leaves me alone because of her dad. He'd shut that shit down before they tried anything."

Summer's dad is in the NHL Hall of Fame, and we were all pretty starstruck when we met him at our last Frozen Four. "Maybe I should date him," I suggest.

Aiden chuckles and tosses me an extra pair of his sweats. "Good luck with that."

When I'm changing into the sweats, my phone vibrates with a text from Coach. It's his sixth reminder about tomorrow's event. We have to be ready for bidding since the team is auctioning dates with players.

"You going to the fundraiser tomorrow?" I ask Aiden.

"It's mandatory. The whole Thunder organization is going to be there," he says.

Great.

OUR FLIGHT BACK to Toronto this morning was more uneventful than anticipated. No new headlines and no more surprise visits from fans. The hotel even apologized for letting the woman upstairs, but they couldn't have known since she introduced herself as my fiancée.

Apparently, she attends every game, whether home or away. Her
dedication to the cause would be commendable if it wasn't so creepy.

The collar of my dress shirt suffocates me as we enter the venue.

"Relax, man." Aiden nudges me to stop pulling at my collar. "It's
only a few hours, then we can head out."

"You're only saying that because you're not the one being auctioned off."

The auction happens every year, and since the older women in the
crowd are the ones bidding, our PR team thought it would be great
to throw me into the mix. That, or it's a bit of hazing for a rookie.
Aiden got to bow out by using his girlfriend as an excuse.

"I got your back, but just know you'll make someone's grandmother very happy." He grins.

I roll my eyes just as Coach comes to stand by me, his presence
alone raising panic.

"Westbrook. A minute." He gestures toward the bar.

It doesn't take a genius to figure out what this is about.

When I join him by a table, he places his phone on it, revealing
an article and a photo of the girl from last night leaving our hotel in
a robe, and my face under yet another headline.

TORONTO THUNDER'S ROOKIE IS OUT FOR THE COOKIE.

Seriously? Are they hiring an intern to write these?

"I don't make a habit of reading this shit, but when the GM questions why my rookie is seen covering more magazines than he is
covering the ice, I have no choice."

Crap. The general manager, Marcus Smith-Beaumont, is the
hard-ass of hard-asses. If he's heard of this, I'm sure I'm the talk of
the board of directors—the ones who decide whether I'm worth the
advance they've paid me.

When I first got recruited, I had heard a rumor that he was
against my draft to the Thunder. It isn't a norm to draft two players
from the same college in one year, but it's not exactly groundbreaking
either.

"There are a few articles from this month alone if you want to do some light reading." His words come out less angry than they should. I'm single-handedly tainting the rookie image, and the organization can't be happy about that. "Another scandal and another game without a goal. I don't know how many press meetings we can control if things like this continue to surface."

The bartender offers a drink, but I refuse. "It's all fabricated. I have no idea why they're spinning it this way."

"Because you're popular. That social media video of you went viral, and the people want more. It's great publicity, but not great for your career if you become the next playboy."

"That's not who I am."

"I'm sure, but the only perception the league cares about is the fans'. You need to pick up your game and keep your hotel rooms empty."

I run my hand through my hair, feeling a headache forming. "I understand."

"Get that first one out of the way, and I can downplay the press we're getting about you. Don't make the organization question whether they should have signed you. You're a strong player, Eli, I can vouch for that, but I can't do it unless you back it with some proof."

He takes the drink I had refused, downs it in one go, and walks off. The echo of his advice and a fading clink of emptied glasses circle my mind. The pressure is overwhelming.

If I stay in here another second, my head might explode. I don't stick around to find out, and bolt for the double doors, signaling to Aiden that I need a break.

And maybe a solution to all my problems.

TWO

BROKE BALLERINA.

It kind of has a ring to it.

"Auditions will be held again in the spring. We do not need any more background dancers." Aubrey Zimmerman barrels through the rotating glass doors in a flurry.

Next *year*? That's an entire dancing season gone. Another year older. Another stack of unpaid bills. Another has-been.

Broke, washed-up ballerina.

Not so catchy.

"Mr. Zimmerman, I'm here to audition for the swan queen."

Either he hears the desperation in my voice, or my statement is so bewildering that it stops him in his tracks. My focus lands on the back of his balding head, glistening in the sunlight. He isn't old in terms of years, but he looks rough for a thirtysomething-year-old. I guess that's what years in this industry do to a person. Some days, I feel halfway there.

When he turns, his lips tip in a curve that makes me tilt my head to assess it. But then the sound that comes out of his mouth drops my shoulders.

Aubrey Zimmerman is *laughing* at me. "The swan queen? You've stopped the artistic director of Nova Ballet Theatre to declare *yourself* as the lead for *Swan Lake*?"

Well, when he says it like that, it sounds laughable. But even with the disdain dripping from his words, I stand tall. It took me three hours to get to this audition. *Three*. The man sitting next to me on the bus had a cold that I'm sure I caught when he sneezed on me. As if on cue, a chill runs down my spine, though that might be the product of Zimmerman's icy gaze.

"Yes," I squeak. I hope my posture is doing enough for my confidence, because my expression has dropped into the depths of hell.

He chuckles. "When I start taking orders from nobodies on the street, I'll let you know. But thanks for the laugh. I really needed that today."

Zimmerman answers his ringing phone, dismissing me as he mutters something about never holding auditions in the crack of Ontario. Huntsville was the only city with an open audition because auditions in Toronto are invite-only, so I arrived two hours prior but had to wait in the line that wrapped around the building. By the time I made it to the door, they ended auditions early. They didn't bother offering the rest of us another audition time.

Irritation flares in my gut as I watch his retreating figure. His bald head and straight-set shoulders burn into my memory. At least I'll have a new silhouette for my sleep paralysis demon.

A few passersby give me pitying looks that only make my plight worse. It's the same look I got inside from the director's assistant.

Nothing seemed to convince her to let me audition, not even the recounting of my dreadful commute and definitely not my childhood story about my love for ballet. It's the story that got me booked in a winter showcase last year, and I hoped it would work again. Except that showcase was performed at high schools and colleges. It wasn't exactly a grand production.

"Excuse me." A voice pulls me from my thoughts, and I turn to a woman dressed in a blazer and a pencil skirt waving me down. "I think you dropped this," she says, holding a single sheet of paper out for me.

I take the paper from her and see my name in familiar bold letters at the top. "This is my résumé. The assistant said I could leave it at the front desk."

There it is again, that pitying look. "I found it on the floor by the recycling bin," she informs.

Her words strike like a razor blade to the heart. A half whimper, half groan escapes me, and I plaster on a smile to distract her from how hard I clutch my résumé.

"You know," she whispers, cautiously eyeing our surroundings. "The theater holds these auditions as a formality. Most ballerinas they've hired this season are ones who have major social media followings."

My mouth parts in shock. They're selecting dancers based on popularity? How is that ethical?

"You seem like a determined dancer, so I wanted to give you a heads-up," she says before rushing inside.

Her heads-up only manages to heighten the doomed feeling in my gut. My ninety-three followers are chump change. If being hired is based on popularity, they'll never consider me for the part. Despair clings to me as I toss my crumpled résumé in the trash and head to the train station, holding back a wave of tears I'll be sure to release during my shower tonight. It isn't until my phone rings that I shake off my depressing thoughts.

"I have a last-minute job for you." My uncle's voice filters through the speaker.

"Is it babysitting for your players' kids? They're cute, but one bit me, and I still have a scar on my finger."

Postgraduation, I was desperate for a job, but I had a rude awakening when I realized even a business degree couldn't score me a career in this market. Yay for college education!

So my uncle, who works for the NHL, extended a few offers for me to help out his hockey team during the regular season. Including babysitting, dog-sitting, and the one time I cooked for the team last year.

They never asked me to cook again.

"Not this time." He chuckles. "We need a dancer for our fund-raiser tonight. We had a last-minute dropout, and I thought you'd like a gig where you can actually do what you love."

My uncle has always been supportive of my ballet career. When I was younger, I used to dread looking in the crowd because of the lack of parents cheering me on, but he was always there.

"Thanks, but I'm not feeling very motivated—"

"It's a thousand bucks for a thirty-minute performance."

My throat dries, and my words catch. That's *three* zeroes for half an hour of my time? I'm discouraged, not stupid.

"I'll be there."

Currently, my only source of income is the ballet classes I teach near the university. I haven't cemented my career there either, because the sign-ups for my classes are embarrassingly low. Why have a perpetual soloist teach your kids when you can have experienced teachers who have booked numerous principal roles?

"I'll text you the address."

I locate the nearest Uber because the three-hour bus ride would not cut it tonight. Besides, the money I'll make would be enough to justify this one ride.

Note to self: One bad situation doesn't have to become a bad day.

HOURS LATER, I'M immersed in the backstage whispers and last-minute run-throughs, and I find myself shedding the weight of today's rejection along with my clothes. As soon as I slip into my leotard and my pointe shoes, there's a tingle that electrifies my body as I wait for my cue.

The first delicate notes of Ravel's *Boléro* hit my ears as I follow the other dancers onto the stage and find my position behind the second row. Silhouettes of the audience are visible under the bright lights gleaming off the polished wood stage, and just like that I'm absorbed into the one thing that never fails to help me escape. My thoughts disappear like mist when I glide in perfect formation with the other dancers, mirroring each step as I learned it only an hour ago.

I have a peculiar talent for replicating dances quickly, and that's probably the reason my uncle was so confident that I could fill in for the last-minute dropout. My focus is on the music, but my gaze wanders the audience for a glimpse of him. It might be the eight-year-old girl in me, but when I see my uncle to the left of the stage, close enough that the bright lights don't block him, I smile.

The group converges into a tableau, and as the finale approaches, we dive into grand jetés and lifts, the stage a mix of swirling tutus and poised ballerinas. The applause pulls me back to reality, and somewhere, somehow, I hope Aubrey Zimmerman knows that I won't give up easily.

When the curtains close, encouraging words and high fives fly around the group, giving me the same rush of excitement I'd felt at the age of eight, the first time I found ballet.

Up until then, my only focus was making sure the housework was completed and my younger brother, Sean, had everything he needed. I guess that feeling of responsibility comes with being mature for your age. At least, that's what every adult I encountered has had to say to me. Soon enough, you start realizing that's not a compliment. It's a curse.

But the one thing that would never be a curse? Ballet.

When I was younger, the trip to the convenience store by our house was the highlight of my Sundays, but it became the beginning of the rest of my life. The checkout counter was cluttered with magazines of famous faces and gossip wild enough to scandalize someone's grandmother, but on that particular day, only one stood out to me. Under the dust and fraying edges of the plastic cover, I saw a poster. *The* poster. Misty Copeland graced the cover of the newest production of *Swan Lake*, elegant and as beautiful as ever. I knew then that whoever she was and whatever she did, I wanted to be her.

The poster still hangs on my wall.

"Sage!" I turn to find my uncle climbing the steps backstage. "You keep dancing like that, and I'm sure they'll hire you full-time."

I shake my head. "I'm not stealing the poor girl's job, Uncle Marcus."

"I can pull a few strings," he offers, a glimmer of hope in his eyes, just like every other time he's tried to help me out. All my life, my uncle has felt obligated to care for my brother and me, but I've refused. We aren't his problem, and I never want him to see us as one.

"My auditions are going great. I'll secure that spot at NBT pretty soon," I lie.

His smile doesn't quite reach his eyes. "Never doubted you for a second." His phone vibrates before he silences it. "Get changed, and I'll have some food ready for you."

I give him a quick squeeze before darting backstage.

After changing my clothes for the fundraiser, I find a plate waiting for me at my uncle's table, filled with all my favorites. It isn't until I'm scarfing down seconds that I remember I need to call Sean.

My little brother is attending boarding school a few hours away. It's been a difficult adjustment, but I promised to call him every night. Excusing myself from the table, I try to find a quiet corner, but with the auction starting, it's impossible.

Outside, the rain brings a breeze to cool my skin in my black silk dress. It's the only nice dress I own, so I was sure to pack it when I headed over here tonight. No one needed to know it was also my prom dress. And my commencement dress.

The phone rings a few times before it's sent to voicemail. I can't help the prick of disappointment that pierces my heart. That's two days without a phone call, and both times it's been because of my crappy schedule. I text him instead.

Am I the worst sister ever? Promise, I'll call earlier tomorrow. I miss you, kid.

I stare up at the dark sky and try not to pity myself. That's when I notice a couple arguing in the corner. Their proximity suggests they're having an intimate conversation, but the guy backs away, his stance rigid and unwelcoming.

"I'm not interested," he says.

It's assertive, but not assertive enough to get the girl away from him. She is completely oblivious to his withdrawn attitude.

Definitely not a couple.

"You will be," she says, pure determination in her voice.

"Look—Lana, is it?" She must nod, because he continues. "You seem like a nice girl, but I don't know you. Showing up at my hotel and to my work events isn't helping your case."

She laughs. It's a pretty, soft one that most guys would probably love, but he only stands there like a statue. His dark suit suggests he works with the Toronto Thunder, but his height and physique would be wasted if he isn't an athlete.

"I can only play your games for so long," she purrs. This girl cannot take a hint.

"Does that game include showing up naked to ambush me in my hotel room?"

My eyes widen as I stifle a gasp, feeling tense as I eavesdrop on this embarrassing conversation.

However, Lana must not feel it, because she scoffs. "You're seriously turning me down?"

Yes! I catch the word before it slips past my lips, barely holding myself back from interfering. But when his head hangs, and his shoulders sag, my legs propel me forward.

Confrontation is clearly not his strong suit. Lucky for him, it's mine.

But the double doors screech open, and an employee dressed in black and wearing an earpiece steps outside.

"Eli, you're up in five," he says, waving him inside.

I halt, and *Eli* breathes a sigh of relief before slipping past the woman. His attention lands on my frozen figure, lingering for a split second, like he's realized I was eavesdropping the entire time, before he disappears inside. Lana watches his retreat with a fire in her eyes, and when her gaze lands on mine, I pivot and slip past the doors too.

The auction has started when I drop back into my seat just as my uncle excuses himself to head to the bathroom. I glance to my right and choke on my saliva.

Aiden Crawford is sitting at my table—or I'm sitting at his. Either way, I'm freaking out. Not for myself, but for Sean, because he is going to flip when I tell him about this. I don't pay too much attention to hockey, but from my uncle's praises of Aiden Crawford, and the jersey with his name that Sean wants for his birthday, I know he's a big deal.

"Are you okay?" His deep voice forces me to look at him again, only to see him holding out a glass of water. I nod a little too vigorously and drink the water to hide behind it.

"You're Sage, right? Marcus told us his niece was performing tonight. I'm Aiden."

I shake his outstretched hand, trying to clear my throat. "My brother's a huge fan."

"Yeah?" He smiles. "I can get—*shit!*"

My head rears, but when I look at Aiden, his eyes are fixed behind me. Following his gaze, I see Lana, the girl from outside, holding a bidding paddle and looking happier than she did a few minutes ago.

The auctioneer's voice snatches my attention to the stage. "Next up, folks, we have a date with Toronto Thunder's very own defenseman Elias Westbrook. Get those bidding paddles ready, and let's see who'll be the lucky winner!"

I'm shocked to see the guy from outside standing onstage, his jaw clenched and posture stiff. Safe to say, he didn't willingly sign up for this.

The auctioneer's voice slices through the hall, loud with excitement. "Let the bidding commence—who's ready for an unforgettable night with Elias?"

"Sage? How do you feel about doing me a favor?" Aiden suddenly says.

I pull my gaze from Elias to find Aiden's sheepish smile. What favor could I possibly do for Aiden Crawford? "Depends on what it is," I say warily.

"This is going to sound crazy, but I need you to outbid her." Aiden points at Lana, and my eyes widen. He hands me a paddle and types something into his phone before showing me. It's a sum. A large sum.

"M-me," I stutter, dumbfounded. Although, the request is reasonable considering what I witnessed outside.

Green eyes lock on mine. "Look, I promised Eli I'd have his back, and that girl cannot win a date. She—"

"Ambushed him in his hotel room?" I say, and he pauses. "I overheard them outside," I clarify.

His tense shoulders drop. "Good, so you know her winning wouldn't be good. I'll pay for it, but since I'm a part of the organization, I can't bid. Will you do it?" he asks again.

I fidget with the paddle, just as Lana shouts, "Two thousand!"

Did she say *two*? As in *thousands* of dollars? The amount Aiden typed is more understandable now. However, I'm not confident that my mouth could perform the motor function necessary to say that number out loud.

At another table, two older women whisper, paddles in hand like they're preparing for war. "Twenty-two hundred," someone else interjects.

A trickle of relief cools my panic as I turn to Aiden. "Someone else might outbid her. He seems pretty popular," I say, desperate for an out.

Aiden nods. "Hopefully, but if not, I will need you to bid."

"Twenty-five," a woman shouts, only for two equally eager women to raise the amount. My jaw drops with each increase, and my palms get sweaty when I realize I'll have to raise my paddle pretty soon.

The auctioneer repeats the number, eyes scanning the room for more.

"Twenty-eight." Lana's smooth voice carries an authority that has the overeager women backing off. *Uh-oh.*

"Wow! Twenty-eight hundred dollars, ladies and gentlemen. Can we top that?"

Elias stands there with an air of confidence, dark hair perfectly styled, and his muscular form cloaked in an expensive suit. It's no mystery why these women are throwing around two grand for one dinner with him.

Yet, I can't ignore the subtle tightness in his body as tension radiates off him in waves. He manages to stare ahead, doing his best not to engage with a very smug Lana.

"Going once . . ."

Aiden nudges my paddle, and I swallow, scrambling for an excuse. "I don't even know him," I whisper.

"Going twice . . ."

"Please?" Aiden shoots me a killer straight-teeth smile that has me chewing my lip in contemplation. Damn, he's good.

I sigh, knowing Sean would berate me for refusing to help his idol. My arm shoots up. "Five thousand!"

Elias Westbrook whips his head around to look at me. I force a wobbly smile as more people stare, but I can't seem to look away from the deep brown eyes that survey me with curiosity and a hint of recognition.

The auctioneer goes around the room three times before he smacks the gavel. "And sold to the beautiful woman in black!"

I won. Holy shit, I *won.*

THREE

ELIAS

SHE IS NOT someone's grandmother.

Aiden knocks into me as I make my way offstage. "I did good, huh?"

Good?

Her brown hair is pulled up into a bun, a loose curl framing her heart-shaped face and hazel eyes. She's darting glances around the room like she feels out of place—that makes two of us—as she pulls her full bottom lip between her teeth. My gaze drifts to the silky fabric of her black dress, held up by two thin straps and her perfect posture.

That's not something I've ever noticed before about a girl, but her upright position accentuates the length of her neck and makes her appear somehow graceful even as she sits.

Then her bright eyes catch mine, and I look away. I shouldn't be looking in the first place.

It's been four years, maybe five, since someone has caught my eye, and this perfectly prim-and-proper girl should not be the one to snatch my attention so easily. No one has challenged the rules I have for myself, not even in college, where I practically lived in a party house. But my mouth still feels dry.

"You couldn't find anyone else?"

Aiden scoffs. "If you want to complain, I can call your not-so-secret admirer over."

I shake my head, unwilling to look over to where Lana is probably stewing.

"You should thank her. She did you a favor," he reminds me.

With reluctance, I move to her table, my heart thumping. It's then that Marcus Smith-Beaumont slides into the chair beside her and hands her a slice of cake, and I freeze in place.

There is no way I managed to get a date with the one person who seems to know the man who despises my very being. I've been dodging him the entire event, and after the lecture Coach threw at me an hour ago, I know if Marcus Smith-Beaumont sees me, I'll be in for another one. With him, it won't be a gentle warning.

Pivoting, I head straight for the terrace, but I'm stopped by our goalie, Socket, who's just now coming off the stage after being auctioned after me. There's an elderly woman in the crowd who eyes him eagerly, and I assume that's his date when he waves and winks at her.

"Where are you off to, Westbrook?"

I clear my throat. "Getting a drink."

He raises a brow, but thankfully he doesn't question me, and I slip outside for some air. The server comes with a tray of drinks, and I opt for water. I need something to cool down whatever is happening to my insides.

I'm sipping on the ice water, forearms pressed against the balcony, when there's a tap on my shoulder. I turn to the same head of brown hair, the same heart-shaped face, the same hazel eyes that caught my attention earlier.

She smiles. "Hi, I'm Sage Beaumont."

Beaumont? Crap, is Marcus her *father*? I'm going to kill Aiden.

I'm staring at her outstretched hand like she has some sort of disease, but she keeps it there for an awkward amount of time, waiting for me to take it.

"You want to fist-bump instead?" she offers, curling her fingers. Like I'm five years old and haven't learned how to shake hands, though it probably seems that way from my guarded body language. I still haven't managed to turn fully toward her, my torso twisted awkwardly. I also think my words are caught somewhere in my throat.

My agent, Mason, must have followed me because he comes to my rescue before I can find my voice. He's watching Sage, calculating and assessing. "I'm Mason, and you are?"

Her smile evaporates when she looks between us. "Seriously? You need your assistant to talk to me?"

Mason steps forward. "His agent, actually."

Her scoff is one of disbelief. "Well then, Mason, can you tell your client I didn't do that for him," she says. "His friend asked, and my little brother happens to be a huge Crawford fan. So, you don't owe me anything, especially not a date, Elias."

Her words are sharp, but the way she says my full name is a dart landing a bull's-eye. No one calls me Elias, not my friends, not the fans, and definitely not someone who just met me.

"It's Eli."

She freezes, pivoting to look at me. "It talks! There's been a miracle," she exclaims. "Well, Mason, looks like you're out of a job."

Mason doesn't laugh, but I do. He shoots me an unimpressed look, then one at Sage, and turns to leave. I assume he's declared the threat neutralized because Sage doesn't seem like the type of woman to put me in a headline by tomorrow morning.

"Thank you," I finally say.

"No need. I didn't do it for you, remember?"

When she's going to walk away, I feel like an asshole. "But I still owe you a date." I'm not sure why I say it, and she must be thinking the same thing, because her brows knit in confusion.

She gave me a perfect out seconds ago, but I don't want her to think I'm an asshole—not only because I'm terrified of Marcus, but because she did something nice for me.

"No, thanks. I'm not really into hockey players anymore, and you just reminded me why." Her words are sweet, but the insult hits just the same.

"You've dated a hockey player?"

"Wish I hadn't," she mutters. "You're off the hook."

"But it's for charity." *Why am I pushing this?*

Her patience seems to be a frayed rope, but she relents. "Fine, you can put your number in my phone."

With her phone in my hand, I realize I'm in way over my head, but I add my number anyway.

"See you around, Elias." This time I don't correct her, and she disappears inside.

To escape the gnawing feeling in my gut, I pull out my phone to see it littered with texts from the group chat. Leaving college for the NHL was a huge change, but since Aiden and I signed with the Thunder back in November, we had time to finish all our coursework a month before the end of spring semester and left Dalton a few weeks ago, but it doesn't feel like it because of all the texts we get from our friends still at Dalton.

BUNNY PATROL

Dylan Donovan: Another girl in Eli's hotel room? I'm impressed.

Aiden Crawford: He's not happy about it.

Kian Ishida: No one's sneaking into Aiden's hotel room.

Dylan Donovan: Probably because they're terrified of Summer.

Kian Ishida: I don't mind this. Eli's barrage of fans found my account.

Dylan Donovan: Kian's never seen so many women in his DMs. I actually heard him giggling last night.

Aiden Crawford: Good. He can stop spending every free minute texting my girlfriend.

Kian Ishida: FYI Sunny was my friend before she was your girlfriend.

Dylan Donovan: Who votes in favor of bringing back Bunny Patrol 2.0?

Sebastian Hayes: Aye

Cole Carter: Aye

Aiden Crawford: Aye

Eli Westbrook: Aye

Kian Ishida: Now you answer?!

When Kian found out we had a group chat without him—Dylan's idea, and we called it Bunny Patrol 2.0—he moped, so we deleted it and promised never to make another.

Dylan and Kian are undrafted seniors, which means to avoid becoming free agents they're taking their time to finish their degrees by the end of the year. Neither has locked down where they're going to play hockey after—or if they're going to play at all. Sebastian and Cole are juniors, and aside from hockey and parties, they don't focus on anything else, which is the norm for NCAA hockey players.

The ice in my glass of water has melted in the time I've been out here, so as I'm heading back inside to orchestrate a getaway, my phone flashes with a text from my bank.

The monthly money wire has been successfully transferred into the respective account, and the name that flashes on the screen adds to the weight on my shoulders. It's not the money that bothers me, it's the reminder of the person who receives it that adds a drop of dread into my stomach. That dread darkens with guilt when I read the encouraging messages from my parents after last night's game. Another easy assist and nothing to be proud of, yet they cheer me on like I'd single-handedly won the Stanley Cup.

My parents have been great about not looking at the tabloids, so I don't worry about them seeing anything nefarious. When the very first defamatory headlines surfaced, they called me immediately, and I had to explain it was the media trying to sensationalize. That was an awkward phone call, but better than having them believe that I've hooked up with half of Toronto in the few weeks that I've been here.

When another text comes through, it's from Aiden, telling me it's time to bail. I don't waste another second and head straight for the doors.

FOUR

SAGE

"FIVE MINUTES." OUR stagehand's shrill voice catches my attention just as the lights power on one at a time. The glare forces me to squint as the bright lights attack my exhausted eyes and rebooting brain. The rest of the dancers trickle onto the stage for the first act.

Cursing under my breath, I take a deep inhale and redo the satin ribbons on my pointe shoes for a third time. The mundane task is second nature at this point, almost automatic, but today, my mind has been drifting off. Specifically, to the number that sits in my phone waiting for me to call it.

Elias Westbrook might be the first guy I haven't been able to break down in my head, and that fact is practically gnawing at me. So far, I've decided he's the slightly obsessive-compulsive type, the kind that keeps the house tidy and has a specific place for everything. Even for those little plastic bread tags that keep the loaves fresh. He probably has a strict schedule he never deviates from and eats the same thing every day. Like oatmeal.

But there's a look to him that tells me if I had known him at another point in his life, my assessment would be proven incorrect. That's where I hit a brick wall in my slightly psychotic hyper-analysis, and now there's a very curious part of me that wants to pry until I uncover all his secrets.

Maybe I have a proclivity for wanting to peel back the layers of people I find intriguing. It's partly due to the plethora of my own problems. Daddy issues? Mommy issues? Eldest daughter issues? Take your pick.

It's been two days since the fundraiser, and the rookie's been at the forefront of my brain. Even though I learned my lesson about athletes when I dated Owen Hart.

Owen and I met when I was a freshman and dated until my senior year. When I was studying at Seneca College in Toronto, he got called to play hockey for the developmental team of the Vancouver Vulture's. The last half of our underwhelming relationship was long distance.

Owen wanted me to follow him to Vancouver, but I would never move away from Sean. I chose to study at a cheap local college after paying for Sean's first year at York Prep. When my uncle found out I got into the University of Toronto, he offered to pay for both our educations. I couldn't let him pay for me. However, even my stubbornness wouldn't let me turn down his offer to help Sean. In turn, my uncle's help allowed me to stay in the dingy college dorms instead of scraping my last penny to afford off-campus housing.

That last year of my relationship with Owen was my breaking point, because with the long distance he became overbearing and controlling. He didn't like how much time I dedicated to ballet or to Sean. At the same time, Owen felt he was perfectly reasonable in his pursuit of hockey, despite his failure to get called up. He's the reason I didn't make friends in college during our on-and-off relationship. Even my roommate requested a dorm transfer after hearing us fight on the phone every night.

For some, the breakup would be fresh, considering it happened just a few months ago, but every cell in my body wants to move on. I wouldn't say I'm actively going through a breakup, but maybe a therapist would debunk that and tell me crying in my rusty shower every week isn't a coping strategy. But I'm not crying over *him*.

So, going on a date with someone who, quite frankly, is the hottest guy I've ever had in my phone sounds like a solid idea to me.

"Hustle, Beaumont," the director urges.

I snap out of my reverie, and with my pointe shoes on right, I fall into line with the rest of the dancers. As a soloist, I've taken on any and every role to remain an active ballerina. So, when my old ballet teacher invited me in for a guest spot as Titania in their company's annual *A Midsummer Night's Dream* showcase, I couldn't refuse. Today is the first day of the school shows that we use as practice performances before the big night. It's nothing fancy, and I don't get paid, but it helps keep me motivated.

Fixing my gaze ahead, I await my cue as two of the principal dancers acting as Hermia and Lysander complete their sequence, and that's when I see him.

Marcus Smith-Beaumont sits in the crowd, watching the performance with a tender smile, a prideful gleam in his eyes that makes me fight the burning sensation in my own.

The guest spot of Titania, the queen of the fairies, is ethereal and solely aided by the play's use of a love potion to entangle her in a spell where she falls in love with Bottom, a donkey-headed character. Our pas de deux is romantic, despite the donkey costume he's wearing that garners laughs from the audience. My chest heaves as we make our last moves in the ensemble dance and the act loops to its end, until the curtains close.

I watch the rest of the performance on the backstage monitor, itching to take off my uncomfortable outfit that somehow makes my headache worse. When one of the dancers offers me an ibuprofen, I take it. The final act finishes, so we all head back to the stage for our bows.

The director pops her head into my shared dressing room when we've finally changed out of our tight costumes. "Get some water, then it's time for notes."

By the time I've unwrapped my hair, wiped off some of my makeup, and peeled whatever's left of the gems on my face, I head down to where we get our performance notes.

A lack of musical phrasing, expressions, and coordination seems to be the theme for today's constructive criticism.

"Sage, I need you to pick an emotion and stick to it. Either hypnotized, infatuated, or playful, it's your call." She moves on quickly, and I make a mental correction for next time, already applying the note to what I missed in my performance.

As I shuffle out of the metal doors and into the warm afternoon air, I spot my uncle by his car at the end of the lot. When I reach him, he engulfs me in an enthusiastic hug. It's moments like this when I don't ponder an alternate universe where my entire family would be in the audience, cheering me on and waiting with flowers. The reality of their absence is so stark that even conjuring up a fake scenario can't distract me from it.

The most recent memory that's been trailing my thoughts every night before I try to sleep is from when I was fourteen. I took a not-so-legal dishwashing job at the local café to help cover my ballet lessons, and I stashed my earnings under my bed. Just when I had saved enough for a new pair of pointe shoes that wouldn't blister my toes on every plié and a leotard that actually fit my growing body, it all vanished, along with my parents. All that remained was a heavy burden of disappointment pressing down on my chest, and a dusty cardboard box.

"You did amazing. Best I've ever seen you," my uncle says.

"You say that every time."

He chuckles, shrugging innocently. "There was something different about you this time. It's like you had something to prove." His gaze practically lasers right through me.

I shift my focus to rubbing off some of the blue eyeshadow that stains my fingers. To escape the third degree about whether my life is falling apart, I pull out my phone and excuse myself. I don't know whether I'm prompted by recklessness or impulse, but I dial the number that's been taunting me all day.

The line rings a few times, and when it's finally answered, it's not the rookie's voice at all.

"Hi, can I speak to Elias?" I say awkwardly into the phone.

"Who is this?" the throaty voice asks, and somehow I feel like I recognize it. He sounds gruff and exhausted, as if he's been answering calls all day, and I've happened to catch him after a particularly bad one.

"Sage," I inform. "Elias gave me this number at the league's fundraiser."

There's a pause and some shuffling. "Auction Girl. Yeah, this is Mason, his agent."

I'm hit with a boatload of irritation. He put his *agent's* number in my phone? You've got to be kidding me. He practically insisted on going on a date, and then he crushed the smidge of hope I had for him.

"Can you give him the phone?" I mutter.

"Nope. He's training at the arena today. You're out of luck, kid."

The patronizing response grates against my ears.

"I can send him a text and I can coordinate a call if he wants to correspond."

"No, don't worry about it." When I hang up, there's a restless fire kindling somewhere under my ribs. I turn to my uncle, who's standing by his car. "Can I get a ride?"

It's obvious he finds this surprising, because I always insist on taking the bus. The less I rely on people, the less I'm let down.

"Sure, but I gotta stop by the arena first," he says quickly.

I smile. "That's what I was hoping for."

He drives to the music playing from some old radio station, and pretty soon I can see the blue and white of the arena illuminating the downtown core.

When he pulls into a spot in the underground staff parking, he turns to me. "You can stay here or come up with me."

"I'll come up. It'll be nice to see some of the staff again." And a certain hockey player.

We take the elevator up and head straight to my uncle's office. As he's studying a file, I pretend to look interested in some of the news articles he has framed on his walls. The Thunder's Stanley Cup wins, Sean's youth hockey league articles, and my first ballet review. My uncle turns to his computer, so I inch back toward the door.

"The bathroom is around the corner, right?"

He's not paying attention when he nods, so I slip out of his office and down the hall.

With determination fueling each step, I head toward the arena dressing room where the guys are changing after practice. The halls are deserted, and I don't encounter any security. I burst through the doors of the locker room. Not even the sight of naked guys, who startle at my sudden arrival, can throw me off.

Only a handful of the players are in here, and I recognize Socket, the goalie, gawking at me. I don't bother scanning the room further because it's not difficult to spot my quarry from the overgrown hair at the base of his neck and the unmistakably broad shoulders. He's too busy rifling through a gym bag to notice me.

"You." I'm pointing at Elias's naked back, but when he turns, I'm not prepared for his wet chest. Water droplets skid down his smooth skin, and in a sort of trance, I watch their descent. They disappear past his happy trail, soaking into the towel he has wrapped around his waist.

Somehow I manage to lift my gaze to a more appropriate destination, like his face, but it's equally distracting. Inky wet hair sticks to his forehead, neat brows curving gently above his eyes, and the narrow bridge of his nose, which is somehow perfect even though I know it's rare to play hockey unscathed.

Elias's gaze melts over me. He only looks away to glance over his shoulder at his half-naked teammates, all staring at the finger I have adamantly pointed at him.

The silence inches toward discomfort.

I finally find my voice again. "Do you make Mason do all your dirty work?"

Dark brows knit together. "What?"

Unbelievable. "Your agent? You put his number in my phone at the auction because you were too scared to just reject me like a decent human being."

There's a low sound of disapproval from his teammates, some of whom I've met from hanging out at the arena with my uncle or picking up the odd job here.

Seeing Elias's throat bob brings a cool sense of satisfaction to the fire that burned beneath my ribs earlier. The part of me that worried if he even remembered my name dissipates quickly when he awkwardly brings a hand to rub the back of his neck.

"Can we talk outside?" he says.

I nod, understanding that being half naked with an equally exposed audience isn't the best time for a confrontation. Though I have no qualms about it.

I head out, pacing the halls and hoping my uncle doesn't spot me.

When I'm taking a sip of water at the fountain, I hear his words. "You have every right to be angry, Sage."

I wipe my mouth and watch his approach. He's dressed in a dark blue Thunder T-shirt that stretches across his chest and biceps, easily snatching my attention and slowing my thoughts before I consciously reel them back.

"You remember my name?"

He stares blankly. "Don't be ridiculous. I'm sorry for giving you the wrong number. I was stressed that night, and as you know, I haven't had the best luck with women trying to come into my life."

When he pushes back the damp hair that was sticking to his forehead, I find myself mapping the contours of his face. His brown eyes, straight nose, and a bottom lip plumper than the top one blend together effortlessly. He's impossible not to stare at. It's a shame they make hockey players wear helmets that obstruct the fans' view of their faces. Maybe I should start a petition.

"And I'm always extra cautious. Giving out Mason's number is like second nature now."

Suddenly, I feel terrible for ripping into him for something that's a safety precaution. I don't follow hockey as closely as Sean, who knows everything about the players and their history, so this is past my area of expertise—which isn't much to begin with.

"I'm not going to stalk you," I finally say.

"I didn't think you were, but it's a habit." He digs his phone out of the pocket of his sweatpants. "Here. Put your number in and call yourself."

I'm already backing away. This is so embarrassing. Getting a guy to pity me, then bullying him into giving me his number, is a new low for me. "No need. I get it, I don't want to intrude."

"I want your number, and I want to take you on that date."

That's what he said last time.

"Are you sure this isn't a burner phone?"

He doesn't laugh as he hands me his phone. Snickering, I punch in my number and call my phone.

"Now, don't go handing that out to just anyone," I remark. "Unless they're seriously hot."

"I thought you weren't into hockey players."

"It seems I've made an exception."

He glances up from his phone with an easy smirk. "That makes two of us."

FIVE

ELIAS

THERE ARE A few weeks left before the hockey world falls into the frenzy of preparing for the Stanley Cup playoffs, a qualification no-body was expecting from the Toronto Thunder after the previous year's poor season. The pressure is on, because Mason's main selling point for me was my goal average at Dalton University. It was one of the highest in the NCAA, and it's no secret that the Thunder banked on my ability to execute that for them. However, with my current circumstances, none of that seems possible, and the eyes on me are a heavy, unrelenting weight.

To my surprise, even with the very real possibility of a trade looming over my head, my mind isn't on the road to the finals today. I'm thinking about the text I sent Sage earlier this week about our date. There's nothing good that can come out of taking her on a date, even if it's technically for charity, because if we're together, she's go-ing to be turned into another notch on my very public bedpost. How-ever, I'm staying true to my word and hope to avoid a repeat of the locker room confrontation. I arranged a date for us with Mason's help, and she agreed to meet today.

"You look nice," Aiden comments as he heads to the kitchen,

opening the refrigerator to grab a carton of orange juice. His gaze lingers on me as I slip on my shoes by the front door.

"I'm going out. Don't wait up."

"*Out?*" He chokes on his juice, slamming his fist into his chest.

"With Sage," I clarify. He grins with a knowing smile. I roll my eyes and leave before he starts gloating.

The drive to the restaurant is short, and when I head up, the host leads me inside to an empty room.

As my watch ticks thirty minutes past six and the server gives me a pitying look, I'm sure she isn't coming, but the ding of the elevator pulls my attention from my wrist.

Sage is wearing a simple lavender blouse and black jeans, whereas my button-down and dress pants scream try-hard. It's been a few years since I've been on a date, but surely, I'm not that much out of practice. There's a heavy contrast between the nervous energy thrumming off me and Sage's infectious confidence.

When she finally sees me, she beams, a soft, light smile that tells me this girl really doesn't hold grudges. It would be easy for her to rule me out and put me in a box with all her hockey stereotypes when I haven't done much to prove them wrong.

She scans the restaurant and the view of the city below us. I can't tell if she's impressed.

Do I want her to be impressed?

Her gaze falls to my clothes, then back to my face. "Where is everyone?"

"What?"

"The other diners," she says, tilting to the side to look behind a wall as if they're hiding from her. The revolving restaurant rotates three hundred sixty degrees every seventy-two minutes. It's the tallest freestanding structure in the world, and they have great food. It's impossible to get a last-minute reservation, but with Mason's help, we secured one.

"It's just us," I explain.

"Right, because you rented the place out." She laughs, but her smile quickly dissipates when she notices my blank expression. "Are you serious?"

I shrug. "Thought this would be more comfortable for both of us."

"Why? I doubt anyone cares that much." She looks at me critically.

This is never a fun topic to discuss. "I'm cautious. From the moment I went viral, I can't seem to catch a break."

There are a few rookies who met much the same fate, but none of them have defamatory articles written about them on slow news days. They're all in long-term relationships, so I became the ideal target.

I pull out her chair and move to sit across from her. The faint classical music playing in the restaurant serves as a buffer. When the server finally comes over, we both straighten, letting the attention fall on him.

"Oysters," he says, placing the plate between us.

When he's gone, it's quiet again, and for a second, I think this is how the entire evening will go. Then Sage slurps an oyster and drops the shell on her plate with a loud clunk. She stares at me intently. "Okay, don't ask me what my favorite color is or any of that crap. Tell me about your deepest, darkest secrets." She places her elbows on the table and rests her chin in her hands.

I'm stunned and find it difficult to answer. Or where to start. Sage stares at me for a long minute, patiently waiting.

Then she sighs. "Fine, I'll go first. My parents spent my childhood in some dark alley, using drugs I can't pronounce, and left me and my younger diabetic brother to fend for ourselves. They are currently on the run for their involvement in the sale of illegal narcotics, which means I haven't seen them in years. So, life is going pretty well, and I've gained extensive knowledge on type 1 diabetes and family law in case someone tries me. Your turn."

The torrent of information catches me off guard, but Sage spills it all with such ease that I can't help but envy her nonchalance in sharing the depths of her life.

I sip my water, processing that information. "You really don't hide anything, do you?"

"What's the point?"

"Privacy?"

She plays with the stem of an empty wineglass, surveying the secluded restaurant. "You don't get a lot of that?"

"I'm in the media at least once a week. I'm not allowed to have privacy."

She frowns, assessing me like she's trying to figure me out. Just then the server brings out the truffle risotto and lobster thermidor. Sage stares wide-eyed at the food.

"Wine?" the server asks.

I wave a hand to refuse just as Sage does the same. She watches me curiously.

"I don't drink," I explain.

"Me neither," she says. "Well, not before auditions or rehearsals, and I have both tomorrow."

"Auditions?"

She nods. "I'm a ballerina. That's why I was at the auction."

Suddenly, her posture being the thing I first noticed about her makes sense.

"How do you know Aiden Crawford?" she asks. "I know you're teammates, but he really went all out for you at the auction."

"He's like a brother. I've known him my whole life, and we went to Dalton together. Even lived together in the hockey house with a few of our other friends."

Sage's questions about hockey are limited, and I'm glad for it, but her personal anecdotes haven't ended, and I don't mind learning about her. When she talks about ballet, it's hard to miss the passion in her eyes, and it makes me curious.

"I want to be a principal dancer for the production of *Swan Lake*."

She leans forward, eyes twinkling. "Have you heard of Misty Cope-land? The first-ever African American woman to be promoted to principal dancer in American Ballet Theatre history? The first person to advocate for diversity in the industry?"

"She's your inspiration?"

"She's my everything. I want to do what she's done."

"But better," I add.

She snorts, looking at me like I have a few screws loose. "This is Misty Copeland we're talking about. If I can do half as good as her, I'll be happy."

I shake my head. "You won't get anywhere if you think like that. You need to know you can be better than the greatest. That's how you achieve even a fraction of their success."

She sits back, seemingly digesting my words and watching me with a look of curiosity, the type of look I haven't gotten from anyone in a while. A look that tells me she's seeing something in me that she hadn't before.

When the server comes with a dessert menu, I sit back to watch her order. Sage lists off the tiramisu and hazelnut éclair. Her deci-siveness is attractive, and that she doesn't shy away from food like I'd expect from a dancer makes me smile. Even athletes count calories or cut weight before a season, so it's refreshing to see someone who's not policing their meals.

"Are you judging me for getting dessert?"

A quizzical look settles on my expression. "Why would I judge you?"

She shrugs. "Some people do. You can't be a ballerina without the perfect body ingrained in your brain."

I can tell my earlier appraisal might be true, but it didn't come without struggle.

The dessert comes out only a few minutes later, and it's pretty fucking difficult looking at anything else but the girl who raves about every spoonful she puts in her mouth.

When her phone rings, she excuses herself, and I take the time to tip the servers before I wait for her by the elevator. She's smiling wide when she walks back toward me.

"Sorry, that was my brother," she says. "He's in boarding school a few hours away, and I didn't want to miss his call."

We walk out of the elevator and through the back entrance. When she steps onto the stairs, she's clutching the railing with a pained look.

"If I could strangle one person with the straps of these heels, it would be the designer." She limps a little.

Staring down at the tight straps of her black heels, I notice how they dig into her skin.

"Why do you wear them?" I ask.

"Because they're pretty."

"But they make your feet hurt."

"I'm a dancer. My feet always hurt."

"So, you want them to hurt more?"

She laughs. "You won't get it. It's like the time in high school when I spent hours gluing all these pretty gems around my eyes for *The Nutcracker*, and by the time I got onstage they had all fallen off. I cried for hours afterward, and my uncle had no idea why it was such a big deal."

"Marcus, right? He's your uncle?" Suddenly, it makes a lot of sense that he's not her father. As far as I know, Marcus doesn't have kids. But the new information doesn't relieve me in the slightest.

"Yup, the only normal-functioning adult in my life."

She's still smiling when her heel gets caught in a divot and she trips. I shoot out a hand and grasp her wrist, pulling her upright again.

"You'd think for a ballerina, I'd be more graceful on my feet, huh?" She exhales through a chuckle.

I look down at her feet. Before I can voice my concern about her raw skin, she bends down and frees her lilac-painted toes from the confines of the strappy heels. The moment her bare feet touch the concrete, she lets out a sigh of relief.

"What are you doing?"

"I can't walk in these."

As she attempts to continue our walk to my car, I gently wrap loose fingers around her wrist. "We're in an alley. You could step on a needle, for all you know."

"Lighten up. This is how humans were meant to walk." Sage twirls in her spot, and my gaze drops to her feet again. Then I step in front of her, blocking her path. She appears bewildered. "What's happening?"

"Get on. You're not walking barefoot in an alley."

Her confusion is palpable. "You want to carry me?"

"Yes. Now, get on."

I anticipate her refusal, but then her hand slides up my back, each movement sending tingles racing down my skin. She effortlessly hoists herself up, and my hands hook under her thighs as they squeeze around me. The light vanilla scent wafting off her is closer than ever.

Her arms tighten around my shoulders, and her laughter rings in my ear as I move. I'm smiling as I speed out of the alley, and she giggles with each stride. When we're finally at the car, there's a crowd along the main roads, so I open her door, and she climbs in as I quickly go around to the other side. Anywhere else, and I'd be free to walk around, but in Toronto, the fans are dialed into hockey, and they can spot any player roaming the city from a mile away.

"Where to?" Sage asks when I'm pulling onto the highway.

I glance over at her. "I'm dropping you at home. You live in Weston, right?"

"It's creepy that you know that," she says. "But it's nine thirty, Grandpa. Take me somewhere else."

I'm hesitant, but the way she deflated at the mention of going home sent unexpected disappointment through me. For some reason, I want this date to be good for her.

"Where?"

She instantly lights up and points to the expanse of water under the bridge. "There."

I look to where the evening sky darkens the water in the distance. "The lake?"

She nods.

It must be longing or nostalgia that colors her eyes and makes me take the next exit straight to where she pointed. I don't bother looking at her for a reaction because her excited squeal when I pull into the parking lot is enough.

Pine trees surround the area, and gravel crunches under the tires as I pull into a space. It's secluded at this time of day, but I still find myself scanning the area for rustling bushes that might hide photographers. Before I can park, Sage is out of the car and heading straight for the water.

I watch in shock but quickly snap out of my frozen state and run right after her. It's rare that the late spring temperature ever dips low enough to turn off air-conditioning, but the water is different. Today, the breeze is strong, and this girl is rolling up her jeans.

"Sage, the water's probably cold."

Her hair whips around her. She looks at me standing there, watching her, and shouts, "You coming, rookie?"

I remove my shoes and socks, with my head on a swivel to check for passersby.

But when I'm running toward the water, feeling the rough sand beneath my feet, I'm no longer thinking about the tabloids. I'm thinking about the laughter coming from the girl who just ran into Lake Ontario.

SIX

SAGE

THE WATER IS fucking cold.

The moment the bare skin of my ankles meets the icy lake, I can almost hear it sizzle. But I don't let it deter me from stepping further into the water to have it immediately soothe my sore feet. Elias comes in after me, but he stays a safe distance away at the bank.

As I move further into the tranquil lake with my jeans rolled up, my gaze fixes on the gentle ripples in the water stretching out before me. The air is filled with the rustle of leaves and the faint chirping of crickets. The sound of miniature crashing waves and the smell of fresh water calm me. The only light comes from the full moon right above us, and I can almost see my distorted reflection in the water.

"It's peaceful, isn't it?" I say after a beat.

He doesn't answer, but I know he's looking up at the moon too. Then the rhythmic splashing of water behind me echoes through the quiet surroundings. There's a spiky awareness on my skin when the warmth of Elias's arm brushes against mine.

"Why do I feel like this isn't your first time doing this?" he says. "Frankly, I'm surprised you aren't skinny-dipping."

I bite down a smile. "You think I'm wild?"

"We're standing in a Great Lake," he says matter-of-factly.

"It's kind of hot that you know your bodies of water." I gather my hair and fail to twist it into a bun. "And skinny-dipping requires nudity, and I don't think you're a 'second base on a first date' kind of guy."

He only shakes his head with a humored exhale.

"We can go all the way if you want. You first." I glance down, staring at the dark fabric of his pants.

"Do you come here a lot?" he asks, ignoring my suggestion.

I move my foot under the water, disturbing the smooth pebbles. "When I was a teenager, I'd be here every weekend. Just to escape."

"And today?" he asks.

I bend to scoop up a pebble and attempt to skip it across the water. It sinks immediately. "Sometimes when things aren't going my way, it's nice to drown out the noise. Literally."

He watches me for a long minute like my words mean something more to him. Before the gaze becomes uncomfortable, he looks away to stare at the sky.

"What's not going your way?" he prods.

"Well, right now, you refusing to skinny-dip," I say seriously, but when that stony look returns to his face, I laugh.

"Ballet," I admit. "I've been trying to secure an audition to become a principal dancer for the production of *Swan Lake*, but I haven't gotten the chance. They've opened auditions, yet they're cherry-picking ballerinas with strong social media followings to drive ticket sales. One of the directors quit a few months ago because she said it was unethical."

Elias listens quietly, not once interrupting me. It feels good to finally let out what's been on my mind without being told this is a dead-end career.

"So, what are you going to do?"

"Find a way to become an overnight internet sensation." I flash him a plastic smile.

"Trust me, it's not what it's cracked up to be." There's a faraway look in his eyes. I guess a stalker—even a nonviolent one like Lana— isn't something anyone wants to deal with.

This time there is something different about his closed-off exterior. Something vulnerable. I can't help but strike while the iron's hot. "What about you? Do you ever want to escape?"

"Doesn't everyone?"

Just when I think he's not going to give me a real response, he exhales and takes one of the rocks from my hand to skip it across the water. He manages to make the rock skip six times on his first try. Show-off.

"Ever since I've gotten to the NHL, it's like the media's discovered fresh meat and they want to utilize every scrap of it. As soon as they realized the fans enjoyed hearing about the newest rookie, they put my face under any headline that would get them views."

I give him a sympathetic smile. "Are the articles that bad?"

His eyes flicker with something new when he looks at me. "You haven't seen them?"

"Between work and auditions, gossip isn't on my radar."

He wears an appreciative smile before he turns to face the water again. I try to skip another rock. It plummets.

"When I first came to the league, they were praising me. So much that our social media team wanted to use me for every video." He pauses, playing with the asymmetrical rock before dropping it. "I haven't been performing like I expected myself to. Like everyone expected me to."

"I can't imagine it's easy to focus with all the media stuff."

We stare at the water glimmering under the moonlight. The waves distort the reflection.

"Do you want me to teach you how to skip rocks?"

From the flip in conversation and his shuttered eyes, I can see that topic isn't something he enjoys talking about. Especially not to some girl he doesn't know very well.

"Please."

"Okay. First, you want to feel the weight. It should be heavy enough for some momentum and light enough to skip." He takes my hand and drops a stone in my palm. "That one's perfect."

I nod, mimicking his actions and running my hands over the smooth surface. It fits perfectly in the curve of my hand. Elias bends to pick up another stone, turning it over in his hand to find one that meets his standards.

"Grip it like this." He places my fingers on the contours of the stone, and there's a buzzing sensation in my ears when he's close enough that I can smell his fresh cologne. "Start close to the water, then flick your wrist as you release."

I do as he says, focusing on the angle, and I let it fly. Just when I think I did it, it barely skips and sinks into the water. "I give up," I mutter.

"Nah, you're not a quitter."

I snort. "Not the first time a guy's told me that."

He stiffens, and I deadpan. Man, he's so easy to make uncomfortable. It's kind of my favorite thing.

"Try again, Sage," he says, a reprimand in his tone.

This time I flick it with a little help from him, and it skips. Once, twice, three times, and four before it sinks.

"It worked!" I jump, and in a moment of unrestrained excitement, I push him a little too hard. He tips over, completely caught off guard by the sudden push. He curses, and I almost yell, *Timber!* but he grabs my hand. I fall right on top of him in the shallow water.

He grunts when his ass hits the water with a splash, his wet arm slides around my waist and soaks the fabric of my lavender blouse. I'm crushed against his warm body, and the hardness of it does not surprise me at all. It only adds to the catalog of images of him I've stored in my brain. With my hands on his chest, I push back, still awkwardly on his lap.

"You grabbed me!" I splash him with water.

Even as I try to act angry because my jeans are completely soaked, I can't help the laugh that bursts out of me. He finally laughs too, and hearing that sound is almost as euphoric as the applause after a performance.

He wipes water from his face and gives me a narrow-eyed look. "Me? You're the one who pushed me."

I shrug, staring at his brown eyes that look up at me innocently. I decide not to make any remark about how wet we both are.

When the water starts to feel warm against my skin, I have the urge to float around untethered. Something I used to do in high school. But now, there's a split second where I want Elias to hold me tighter, to make me not feel so free—like there's something to anchor me. Something that *wants* to anchor me.

Instead, I let him help me up. "Come on, I have some extra clothes in my car," Elias says.

I wipe my wet palms on my shirt and follow him back to his car. He picks up his shoes and phone on the way back, and I shiver as I wait for him to unlock the trunk.

Elias holds out a towel, and I silently take it, drying off as he shuffles through a large bag. He hands me a T-shirt and shorts. Both are extra-large, but I can't complain. I don't want to sit in my soaked underwear the entire ride home.

Under the privacy of the white towel, I change into the baggy Toronto Thunder T-shirt and gray shorts. I roll the waistband three times to keep from flashing him. By the time I turn around, he's changed, and my wet clothes are in a bag, along with my heels.

He takes me home, and like a gentleman, he walks me right to my door. Not once does he mention the state of the run-down apartment or my scuffed door, which looks like rabid animals tried to gnaw their way inside.

"Thanks for the date. I had fun," I say.

Elias lingers at the door, and I'm secretly hoping he kisses me.

Because even though I've never kissed anyone on the first date, I'd make an exception for him.

But the kiss doesn't come, and Elias takes a step back. "Good night, Sage."

I smile at him, and he walks away, down the path and to where his car is parked.

And just like him, the smile disappears from my face.

SEVEN

ELIAS

AFTER OUR LAST game against Dallas, I've seen my physical therapist three times. Falling on my ass last night didn't help the ache in my body from a particularly brutal hit. Neither has it subsided when I wake up an hour before my alarm because the blinding sun pierces through my curtains.

I stare at my clock, only for the skipping stone on the nightstand to grab my attention. I forgot I kept it.

Suddenly, Sage's laugh sounds fresh in my ears, and the way she bursts with energy is so contagious that it was impossible not to feel it too. Carefree and happy. That's how I would have described her when I first met her, but after our date, I know that's not her reality. She's an open book and acts like nothing bothers her, but I know if I were to peel back the mask, it would show me something else. Something that would tell me her willingness to share the traumatic experiences of her life helps her hide a lot more. Like she's shielding it with a facade of honesty.

I rarely trust people easily, if at all. But Sage spoke about things differently. Her passion for ballet broke through any whisper of doubt I had about her. She wasn't on this date to get my number or snoop around my personal life. She was fulfilling her end of a deal she got roped into.

My thoughts scatter when I finally get up to shower and eat breakfast. There's an anxious flutter that squeezes my stomach before I even reach for my phone and see the notifications. It's not uncommon for me to receive a barrage of texts and tagged posts before a game, but this time it's different.

BUNNY PATROL

Kian Ishida: Eli has a girlfriend and I'm finding out from the INTERNET?

Dylan Donovan: We're coming to visit you soon, so you can't ignore us anymore.

Kian Ishida: They're gone for a few weeks and forget about us. Assholes.

In a panic, I click the link Kian sent and find another article from some gossip magazine about me. However, this time it's not alluding to a one-night stand or the new girl of the week. It labels the girl in the picture as my *girlfriend*. When I press the image, it's a picture of Sage and me when she had taken off her heels and handed them to me, jumping on my back as I carried her to my car. My lips almost twitch into a smile before I snap back to reality. This is bad.

It's only a matter of time before she's labeled as some gold digger, and people start to harass her on social media. When Brandy, our team photographer, was pictured with me, she had to disable her accounts because the messages were getting hateful. I can't imagine what Sage's will look like today. I know I have to warn her.

SAGE

Elias: Can we meet?

Sage: Am I dreaming? Cause I swear you were just a figment of
    my imagination.

Elias: Sage.

Sage: I can just picture you saying that. All growly like a little
    bear.

Elias: Little?

My phone instantly buzzes with a call. Sage's smooth voice comes
through when I answer. "Are you flirting with me, Westbrook?"

"Can we meet? I need to talk to you."

"Miss me already?" She laughs. There's music in the background
and some shuffling like she's moving things around. "Uh, sure. But
not for an hour. Can you meet me at U of T?"

"The university?"

"Yeah, I teach ballet at a studio on Brunswick. I can meet you at
the Bliss Café beside it."

Going to a college campus where we rocked their hockey team a
few months back, and then I got drafted to their national team, is
never a good option. But I caused this inconvenience in Sage's life,
so I can brave a visit.

When I pull into a parking stall, I realize my hat isn't doing much
to cover my face, so I pull my hoodie over it. Black sunglasses make
me look out of place, but it's better than being recognized as a hockey
player who can't keep his dick out of the media. It's humiliating
when you realize people aren't talking about how you play but rather
how much you play outside the rink. Spending my whole life working toward the league, I feel the burden of carrying a reputation that
demeans the sport and its players. Sometimes, there's no way forward
but through. It's the going through it part I can't quite stomach.

A flash of a pink fluttery skirt and curly brown hair dances across the large window of Elegance Ballet Studio. I lean against the hood of my car and lower my sunglasses. Sage smiles so brightly that the kids she's teaching replicate it. Studious faces follow her lead as she moves in cadence with the music. I can almost hear the classical notes through the window as I watch.

With hockey, it's easy to tell the difference between the players who work hard and those who eat and breathe hockey like it's a part of their soul. That's what I see when I watch Sage. Dancing is a part of her soul.

The class ends, and the kids exit to meet their parents outside as Sage turns to her phone to pause the music. When her gaze finds mine through the glass, she squints, pauses for a beat, then bursts into laughter. She doubles over like she's spotted a clown in the middle of the road.

I stand straighter, looking around to confirm she's laughing at me. Wiping away nonexistent tears, she places a hand on her stomach to catch her breath before she pulls out her phone and takes a picture of me. Ignoring her impolite greeting, I head inside the secluded café beside the studio and wait by one of the tables in the corner.

She's still beaming when she finds me. "Why are you dressed like a stalker?"

I glance down at my outfit. "I'm incognito."

"I'm pretty sure I saw a campus cop following you because you look suspicious as hell." She leans forward on the table and pulls off my sunglasses. The move is slow and deliberate and makes my heart thud harder. "That's better. Now, enlighten me about this secret meeting. Should we find a storage closet and get to it?"

I squeeze my eyes shut. Maybe I should have done this over the phone.

And have her ream you out for hiding behind your phone like a coward?

"Your picture is in the tabloids," I say bluntly.

She cocks her head, taking a long sip of the coffee I ordered her. Sage's hazel eyes widen like she's still processing the information.

"Oh shit. That's probably why my phone's been buzzing all morning."
She pulls it out, gawks at the screen before flipping it to me. Messages and follow requests fill her phone screen, and I wince.

I'm not even a full month into the league, and I can't go on one
date without it resulting in harassment. I feel terrible that my life
could somehow disrupt someone else's and I can't do anything about
it. I usually avoid thinking about how much worse it will get as the
years go on.

One of our captains a few seasons ago was caught by a fan leaving
the bar with a woman who wasn't his wife. The slandering he got was
deserved, but his pregnant wife didn't need to go through that publicly. The media has no remorse for how their viewers treat innocent
family members as long as they have their five minutes of airtime.

"For what it's worth, this is the first time they've written *girlfriend*
instead of *fling* or any other equally demeaning term."

"I've always been told I make a good girlfriend. There's just something wholesome about me."

I snort. "They haven't heard the shit that comes out of your
mouth, then."

She's surprised by the joke, and I try not to look offended. I don't
often let myself relax long enough to bring the carefree Eli out.

"Anyway, I wanted to be the one to let you know, so you're not
caught off guard if some dude with a camera starts following you."

"You can't be serious." She starts looking around the coffee shop
as if she'll see one of them here. "Since when did hockey players become a hot commodity?"

"Fuck if I know."

She gives me a long, assessing look. "I see it though. You're a
slept-on breed of insanely hot men. This would've happened sooner
or later."

I can't help it. "You think I'm hot?"

She takes an even longer sip of her coffee, and my smirk goes nowhere even though I know I shouldn't be acting like this. *Why am I flirting with her?*

"I think my exact words were *insanely hot*." Her gaze drops from my face to my arms and then back to her phone glowing on the table. "I mean, one picture with you, and I have thousands of follows. You might need an escape, rookie. I'll be happy to help."

"Why? So you can watch me skinny-dip in Lake Ontario?"

She bites her lip to keep from smiling. "Just trying to help you drown out the noise."

"Or drown me," I mutter.

Sage lights up with a smile, and I like it. Her gaze bounces around my face thoughtfully, before she straightens and her eyes widen.

"Oh my God, that's it!" She watches me so intensely I have no choice but to listen. "We don't have to escape anymore."

"What?"

"We should date. You and me."

My head rears. "Excuse me?"

She grimaces at my expression but continues. "*Fake* date. The last thing either of us needs is a real relationship. But if the media thinks you're in a committed relationship they'll leave you alone. And with you as my boyfriend, I can get the following I need on social media to get my dancing out there so the theater will notice me."

I try to form words, but every single one fails me. She wants us to *date*?

"Look." She unlocks her phone and opens the first article she's mentioned in. "They're not calling me a one-night stand. They think we're in a relationship, which means if we confirmed those rumors, they would probably get off your back. Your real fans wouldn't let that gossip fly if they knew you were committed. And I would get a chance to audition for NBT."

"I thought what the ballet theater is doing is unethical?"

She shrugs. "If you can't beat them, join them."

What she's saying isn't wrong, and I'm sure her presence in my life might help get the media to stop their scrutiny, but that doesn't mean I'd let her take the heat. Or that I want anyone—especially her—to have a chance to dig into my life.

"No."

My refusal only lights a new fire in her eyes. She looks out the windows of the café, and her fingers thrum against the wooden table. "What if I tell you it's for charity?"

"*Is* it for charity?"

She deflates. "No."

Watching her excitement crumble produces an uncomfortable twinge in my chest.

"All the media has ever done is lie about you. Don't you want to take back control?" she presses.

"By stooping to their level?"

Her brows pinch. "It's a clean break, and I promise I am nothing like Lana the stalker. If we're successful, you'll stay here and be the best rookie Toronto's ever seen, and I'll get to travel with Nova Ballet Theatre." She leans back in her chair. "Do you need me to throw in a test drive? A little glimpse of what it's like to date me?"

"You're not a car dealership, Sage. This is real life, and I don't date." My blank stare makes her smile fall into a frown.

"All the more reason for everyone to believe us," she contends.

"I don't lie either."

"Fine, I'll do the talking. You just have to stand there and look pretty."

"The answer is still no."

A storm brews on her face, and she stands. The screech of the chair breaks our back-and-forth. "I'm not one to be put off by rejection, but you could at least pretend to think about it."

I rub a hand over my face. "Trust me, it would never work. No one would believe this could be anything long-term."

She scoffs and steps back, looking offended. "You know what? Forget it. It's clear what you think of me."

My brows rise in surprise.

"No one would believe us being together because I'm me and you're you, right? You think because my life is such an imploding mess that I'm trying to sink my nails into the nearest famous athlete, and people would immediately sniff out that I'm some gold-digging washed-up ballerina."

Her harsh words leave me stunned. Pushing my chair back, I loosely touch her biceps to stop her. "That is not at all what I meant."

Her gaze flickers with something so vulnerable it leaves a hot, uncomfortable sensation to burrow inside my chest. Like fucking heartburn.

"I have to go." She yanks her arm from my grasp. "Good luck with life, Eli."

For some reason the nickname sounds all wrong when it comes from her. She walks out of the coffee shop, pink bow fluttering in her curly hair. I feel a deep, regretful storm in my gut, and just when I think to go after her, someone walks up to me.

"Eli Westbrook?" A tall guy, probably a student at the university, stares at me in disbelief and obnoxiously blocks my path. "Holy shit, man. I didn't think I'd ever see you here. Well, not after you guys beat us in the Frozen Four qualifiers."

It's then I realize I'd forgotten to put my hoodie and sunglasses back on in my hurry to stop Sage. Though even if she did hear me out, I don't think I could rectify the situation. She wants to put up a farce to help us both out, and I'd never be able to pull that off. It would be a disaster waiting to happen.

My lips form a tight smile, as my mind is still distracted by Sage's words that continue to loop in my head.

"Can you sign this?" He pulls off his Toronto Thunder hat. "You're who I want to be when I graduate."

There's a light spark in my chest when I turn to the bright-eyed kid, who doesn't look much older than a freshman. My smile is genuine when I take his hat, and he shuffles through his bag for a marker.

He chuckles to himself in disbelief as he hands me a black Sharpie. "You're an inspiration to all the guys in my frat. I mean a million-dollar contract without trying and unlimited girls, you are living the life. You got any tips?"

The words fall with a thump on my chest, and every muscle in my body contracts. The minuscule spark from earlier dies out and plunges me back into darkness. My smile dissolves into a flat one, and I sign the hat and hand it back to him.

"Nice meeting you," I mutter, heading straight inside my car and out of the parking lot.

EIGHT

SAGE

WHEN LIFE GIVES you lemons, it douses you in acidic juices that burn your skin too.

When I ruffled through my mailbox earlier, I expected to find flyers and coupons, but a white envelope stuck out in between the junk mail. I tore it open and found bold, red letters that read REJECTED.

The small ballet company I applied to a few weeks ago that exclusively performs for nursing homes seemed like a great opportunity. They are so old school the application required a mail-in audition tape. But the gig was stable, and I thought it might be nice to finally settle down. What a joke that was.

Inside my apartment, I toss the letter in the trash and head straight for the shower. To ease my impending meltdown, I light a lavender-scented candle in the bathroom. Shedding my clothes, I twist the handle only for it to clatter to the floor and land on my toe. I sit there, naked in the tub, clutching my foot with a quiet sob that I muffle with my hand.

My neighbors, Mr. and Mrs. Fielder, get grumpy when I disturb one of their afternoon naps with my crying sessions. According to them, women only cried when their husbands went off to war. Personally, I'd like to think they celebrated instead.

However, there's no cause to celebrate for me, because along with Elias boiling me down to an undatable mess, I have to face my very first rejection.

After a long, pitiful attempt at playing handyman, I turn the faucet only to the cold setting. I take the quickest shower of my life. Even in the freezing shower, and with my body in survival mode, flashes of Elias's disbelief from earlier play in front of my eyes. It was humiliating.

With my teeth chattering, I slip into jeans and a white top. In the kitchen, I empty the plastic bag of sugar-free cookies into a container. The moms would judge me if they found out I bought the cookies at a grocery store. But the oven in my apartment hasn't worked since I tried to cook a lasagna a few months back. I didn't tell my landlord because she would ask me to pay for it. So frozen dinners in the microwave are my go-to.

Today, Sean's school has a spring barbecue that's mandatory for parents and guardians. That means taking a train a few hours away to eat corn and pretend that everyone is not whispering about our family. The silver lining is that I get to see Sean after months, and although he understands I'm busy, I'd like to make up for the missed calls.

Scanning my Presto card at the station, I make it just in time for the afternoon train that takes me straight to York Prep School, the all-boys school in a quiet suburb, surrounded by houses with acres of land separating them from their neighbors, and women who keep their poodles in designer bags.

It's no secret that getting Sean accepted to York was difficult, but with some luck and a help from our uncle, he was admitted. He wasn't enthused about living at a boarding school, but his best friend keeps him sane.

Sean's best friend, Josh Sutherland, hails from a family of ranchers. He has a business tycoon for a dad and a motivational speaker who writes bestsellers like she's popping Tic Tacs for a mom. He's the sweetest kid I know and nothing like those snot-nosed boys who bullied Sean when he first started at York. Our family history is not a secret, and the parent board made sure the principal knew about the "delinquent" they allowed into the community. Sean never complained about any of the harassment, and I only found out because Josh punched his classmate for asking if Sean had an addiction too. Not a funny joke, and Josh made sure the kid knew that.

My sandals slap against the unstained pavement as I cross the short path, careful to watch for the self-driving cars that cruise by in an undetectable whisper.

Inspecting my Tupperware, I'm relieved I've kept the sugar-free cookies from crumbling on the shaky train ride. When I spot the fairy lights that run along the ivy-covered brick walls, they lead me straight to the picnic tables in the outdoor area, filled with homemade desserts and what looks like a vegan alternative for barbecue food.

The formality of greeting anyone at the crowded table has never been something I had to worry about, so I slip past them to the bowl of strawberry refresher. It isn't long before I feel the weight of a gaze on my skin, but I focus on eyeing the area for Sean or Josh.

But with my luck recently, it's not Sean that finds me, it's my miserable past.

My ex-boyfriend is waving at me.

Owen Hart weaves through a swarm of judgmental parents and their equally irritating children and beams brightly at me. I spot his brother sitting on the bench, giving me a tight smile before focusing back on his phone. He was a part of the group of kids who bullied Sean four years ago when he first started at York Prep. But when the parents were called in, Owen showed up with his parents and apologized profusely for his brother's actions. He offered to drive me home that day, and we had been together ever since. Well, until a few months ago.

He's staring as though I'll disappear if he looks away. I couldn't even if I wanted to. I'm stuck in place like an immovable boulder. There is a part of me that wishes we could have stayed together, because it would make my life much easier. He was the only stable thing in my life I could cling to, but ultimately, that's what broke us.

I assumed he'd been drafted to a team somewhere out of the country, so I wouldn't see him today.

This is not what I had in mind.

"Sage." He pulls me in for a hug that leaves an itchy feeling under my skin.

"Owen. What are you doing here?"

It's obvious what he's doing here, but I'm not one for inventive small talk.

"You didn't hear the news?"

"What news?" I've been strategically staying away from the news after Elias mentioned there may be a man with a camera who will start following me. Though I'm sure they would get bored rather quickly.

"I got called up."

No.

"I'm the new right-winger for the Toronto Thunder." His words project like rocks aimed at my head, and I try not to flinch. "Your uncle was the one who called me about it."

I'm going to be sick.

He touches my shoulder. "Hey, you okay?"

My face feels hot from my hairline down to my neck, and I find it hard to look at him. "That's great."

"Yeah? Because I was hoping we could talk."

My tight-lipped smile masks my grimace. "About what?"

"Us."

Can one word trigger a tsunami in your stomach? The *us* tumbles into the dark pit, burning in the acidity.

"Sage!" To my relief, it's my brother Sean, like the little angel he is. "I've been looking all over for you. The new vice principal wants to meet you." He nods over to where the teachers are gathered by the snack table. The save is much needed, and judging from the look of urgency on Sean's face, he knows it. He doesn't bother acknowledging my ex-boyfriend, but that doesn't stop Owen from moving forward to greet him.

"Shit, you're getting tall, kid."

Sean cuts him a dangerous look, and my gaze bounces between the two of them. Sean has no idea why we broke up, but he does know I couldn't stand Owen by the end of our relationship. "If you're trying to get back with my sister, you have a few hockey players to go through first."

Owen chuckles. "I'm sure I do. But I think it might be worth it." His longing gaze freaks me out.

Sean pushes between us. "She's dating someone."

My head whips to him so fast it stings on the side of my neck. *What the hell?*

"Ever heard of Eli Westbrook?"

Oh, hell no.

Did I call him an angel? I meant the devil.

Owen harrumphs. "Yeah, right." But when my complacent gaze meets his, he balks. "He's serious?"

I don't say anything because frankly, I can't. My mind is planning ways I can get back at Sean for this. But a smaller, pettier part of me is basking in the way Owen's face is turning an ugly shade of red.

"I have to go," I mutter, pulling a smug Sean with me. I move toward an empty area where parents aren't around to hear me yell at this reckless fifteen-year-old.

"Do you need medical attention?"

His smile seeps from his lips. "No?"

"Because you have to be having a stroke to tell my ex that I'm dating a professional hockey player!"

"Oh . . . that."

"Yes, *that*. What the hell, Sean?"

He sheepishly scratches the back of his head. "But you are."

"Who told you that?"

"I saw it on TMZ."

I sigh loudly, wanting to pull my hair out. "What have I told you about gossip?"

"That it's what people who have nothing going for them do to feel better about their boring lives?"

"Exactly, so why are you looking at that stuff?" I ask. "And how? You have restricted internet access."

He shrugs. "Loopholes."

Crossing my arms, I give my most parental stare, and he shrinks under it.

"I'm sorry, okay! He was staring at you all weird, and you looked uncomfortable." He sighs. "Besides, it wasn't a lie. I saw the photo."

Who knew a charity auction could complicate my life to this extent? Or that being rejected by a hockey player could backfire so terribly? "It was one date for a charity event. I doubt we'll ever talk again."

"Well, I don't even know Eli personally, and I like him better than that Douchetron 5000."

My serious demeanor cracks when I erupt into laughter. Parents stare, but we don't acknowledge them.

"Come on, take me to your vice principal."

He walks me to the snack table, and I wear my best responsible guardian face.

"Ms. Beaumont, I've heard lots about you," the vice principal says.

"Good things, I hope." When he gives me a sympathetic nod, I assume he's been privy to the information about our family. "If you're reading Sean's file, I can explain the fights and behavioral issues—"

"The past is the past. I want to move forward as I transition into this role. We have not had any issues with Sean. He's a smart and talented young man, and I suppose we have you to thank for that."

His words melt my anxiety and prevent my overcompensating word vomit. "It's all him. He's a good kid."

Sean looks pleased with the praise, and I chuckle when he grins. The vice principal informs me about the changes in curriculum since he's taking over, and I focus on the words rather than the shadow of a dozen gazes sticking to my back. I feel a claustrophobic tightness in my lungs, and when I look at Sean, he's glaring at them. One of the moms stares so vigilantly you'd think we were going to rob the place of their vegan hot dogs.

"Wanna get out of here?" I ask Sean as soon as the vice principal excuses himself to greet another parent. There's a flush of relief on his face, and I'm going to spend money on an Uber I can't afford, just to hang out with him for a few more hours. Somewhere that doesn't have him second-guessing himself.

"Are you suggesting we sneak out?"

"It's called an Irish goodbye. Besides, if they have a problem, they can take it up with your guardian."

"You are my guardian."

"Exactly." I shrug as if I'm being spontaneous, but I'm already eyeing the sign-out board by the exit. I'm responsible for him, and I'd rather not make the school wonder where he took off to.

When I drape an arm over his shoulder, I realize that at fifteen he's already taller than me. Pretty soon, I'll start looking even less like a respectable adult and more like his little sister.

Sean beams and tells me a story about something that is definitely against school rules. But I make sure not to treat him like a kid, because I want him to know we can still be siblings, even if I have to fill the parental role.

"So, tell me about this date," he says as soon as we're inside the Uber. I'm transported back to that night, and the reminder puts a smile on my face. Sean's teasing expression is replaced with one of pure shock. Curiosity lights his eyes, so I tell him about my date.

Well, most of it.

NINE

ELIAS

REGRET IS A heavy feeling. It snatched away the sleep I would've gotten on our flight back home and left me exhausted by the time Aiden and I got to our apartment last night. We ordered takeout because even cooking can't help me out of this funk. I spent the night tossing and turning, staring at the red glare for the time on my alarm clock. Each minute dragged by, and I found myself dwelling on the reason for my haunting regret.

It's the look on Sage's face after she assumed I thought she wasn't good enough for me. If my mouth had been on my side, I would have been able to tell her that our relationship wouldn't be believable because I've never been in one. I've only ever had casual hookups, and the last one was over four years ago.

The icing on the cake is that even a week after our date, the rumors are still alive. They've only gotten worse, and I've had to stop myself from checking how many people are leaving comments on Sage's posts, ripping into her life and asking about my addition to it, because I know I'll do something stupid like reply with frustration. But Mason would kill me if I interacted with the noise; it's like fighting fire with fire.

When my alarm clock blares, I'm up and ready to go in minutes. The morning is quiet as Aiden and I move on autopilot through the kitchen. My best friend is well rested, and he must see my dark under-eye circles, because he offers to drive. But I don't let him. So Aiden takes our gear bags and loads them in the trunk of my Bronco. I can't bring myself to make any conversation on our way to the arena. It's evident he's noticed the tension thrumming off me earlier in the kitchen, but he doesn't ask. The thing about our friendship is that we don't push each other to talk. We open up when we're ready. That's how it's always been.

I've tried calling Sage to apologize, but the calls go straight to voicemail. I've made it clear that I regret saying anything that hurt her. But the message is received loud and clear, and the silence makes me feel even shittier. The last thing I want to be is the type of guy who fills up voicemails and harasses a woman for ignoring him. If she wanted to talk to me, she would.

"I think I fucked up," I blurt.

Aiden turns to look at me, but I stay focused on the road. "Fucked up how?"

"I hurt someone."

He exhales a long breath, still watching me. Probably suspicious about this topic of conversation.

"Did you apologize?"

"She didn't want to hear it." The *she* slips out before I can stop it, but I know he already knows this is about a girl. Sometimes, he's a mind reader.

"Have you tried sending her flowers? I know the perfect ones."

I glance over at him. "Flowers won't fix this, and I don't even know if fixing it is worth anything. I probably won't see her again."

"She's the GM's niece. You will see her again," he says knowingly.

A mix of a scoff and laugh escapes me. Fucking mind reader, all right. Before I can decide if flowers or an apology blimp will do, the car's console rings with a phone call.

"Why aren't you here yet?" Mason's high-pitched voice tells me he's freaking out. "Marcus wants to talk to you, and the press conference is in thirty minutes. You better pray there's no traffic on a Monday morning."

The mention of our general manager has me on edge, and Aiden glances at me.

"He wants to talk to me?" I ask.

"Urgently."

I swallow. "What's the press conference for?"

Mason sighs loudly. "Refusing three postgame interviews means you're making it up today. It's mandatory."

I hang up, cursing as I pull onto the busy highway. Mason is lucky we're friends and he's a killer agent, or I'd have fired him a long time ago for being a pain in my ass.

At the arena, we head up to where the press conferences are held and where Marcus Smith-Beaumont's office is located.

Aiden heads to where his agent stands by the conference room door, next to a very on-edge Mason, who motions for me to head into our GM's office and taps on his watch face.

I knock and the door creaks open. "You wanted to see me?"

The GM motions to the seat in front of him. There's a stack of papers he's flipping through on the wooden desk. His suit jacket hangs on a coatrack, and his sleeves are rolled up. Marcus clasps his hands in front of him.

"I've seen it before, you know. Plenty of times." He's simmering under his calm exterior. "Rich Ivy League kid who gets into the pros without lifting a finger."

Despite having heard the description countless times, it bothers me when he says it with a tone bordering on disgust.

"I'm sure you've seen my stats. I'm not here on a favor, sir."

He lets my words rest between us before leaning back in his chair.

"Your stats have nothing to do with whether you deserve to be here or not. I look at every player's development throughout the season, and in just the short time you've been here, you haven't shown any."

When I open my mouth to say something, to either defend myself or promise that I've been trying my best to improve and get back to the Eli who could outscore every other NCAA player, he holds up a finger to stop me.

"I didn't call you in here to have a debate on your ability to perform. The proof is clear, and there hasn't been any improvement since you've been here." His gaze doesn't cut away as he speaks his next words. "I've talked to the board, and they've agreed to give you the rest of the regular season to show there's hope for improvement."

He looks less than pleased with their ultimatum. I have a feeling he's eager to sign the papers for a trade, but the organization must still see something in me. The ultimatum is no surprise. I hoped I could postpone this talk, but with how poorly I've been playing, this was inevitable. With my head hanging, and my gaze on the floor, I nod. I'm unable to come up with any words without my voice cracking.

When he stands and heads to the door, I follow.

"Eli," he says, stopping me. Instead of the look of sympathy that I mistakenly hoped for, Marcus gives me a once-over. "I've heard the weather in Russia can be brutal. I'd suggest asking your parents to buy you a coat."

He shuts the door behind me. The insult alluding to a European league move annoys me more than anything.

"Eli!" Mason hisses.

He's down the hall, still waiting by the conference doors when he sees me. He stops his pacing and waves me over. Aiden shakes his head beside him. I'm sure he's caught on that whatever Marcus said wasn't good.

"Crawford, you wanna join?" asks Mason. He starts rolling non-existent lint from my suit jacket. This isn't a formal event, but we're expected to show up in suits before a game.

"Hell no."

I mouth *Asshole*, and Aiden flips me off and heads around the corner to the locker room.

Mason stops lint rolling. "Heads up, they are loaded with questions, so use 'no comment' sparingly."

"Sparingly?"

"Don't use it."

Head high, I prepare to be watched by every camera and eye in the room, and I step toward the mic. Marcus's words weigh heavily, and even as I try to shake them out of my head, it's impossible to focus on anything else.

Cameras click and reporters shuffle through their notes, and the chatter begins.

"Eli, what adjustments are you making to improve your goal-scoring opportunities in future games?"

"You have always been a high scorer through college, and at world juniors. How do you stay motivated when you haven't scored once in your career in the NHL?"

"Are your off-ice activities distracting you from achieving success as we head into the postseason?"

I tug at the collar of my shirt as I repeat the same answer for each question. "I'm keeping my head down and trying not to let the noise distract me. I'm improving my game every day to put an end to this scoring drought."

That may not be working for me yet, but with the ultimatum dangling over my head, I have no choice. I've caught my dream in my hands, and in only a few weeks, I could lose it forever. A high-pitched sound, like a pressure cooker on the brink of whistling, fills my head.

My heartbeat quickens when a woman in a blue dress pipes up with the question I've been dreading, and one they've all been waiting for. "Do you have anything to say about the recent reports made about you in the popular media? Would you like to clear up any speculation about your off-ice activities with the girl of the week?"

Girl of the week.

A stupid, naive part of me thought I wouldn't be asked about that, but the media always wins. The words of that freshman at U of T ring in my brain, and I clench my jaw. Their invasion of privacy has been taking over my life. This is the last time I want to hear about any of this shit or to be referred to as a playboy who's sitting on a big pile of money and women, not providing anything to my team.

I grit my teeth. "The media's job is to spin stories, and I don't have the leisure to pay attention to every headline."

"But your fans are paying attention," she counters, unrelenting. "You know how to choose the girls, clearly." That gets a chuckle from the room. I haven't been reading about it, so their laughter puts me on edge. "Is it true Ms. Beaumont's parents were charged for drug possession, and are currently trying to avoid imprisonment?"

My head snaps up so quickly that I feel a pull in my neck.

Mason says something, but I can't hear him. Anger grips my throat, and my chest constricts at her words.

How the fuck do they know that?

Everything in me turns protective. My hands tighten into fists, and I have half a mind to flip over this mic and storm out of here.

I'm not sure if I'm exhausted by the contact intrusion, Marcus's ultimatum from earlier, or the image of Sage's hurt face that flashes in my mind, but the words spill out of me.

"She's my girlfriend," I blurt. "And I won't entertain any disrespect toward her. So, that's all the questions I'll answer about my personal life."

Camera shutters pause before they go off with a cacophony of more questions.

Fuck.

TEN

SAGE

TORONTO THUNDER'S ROOKIE IS OFF THE MARKET! CHECK OUT THE ARTICLE BELOW TO FIND OUT MORE.

Six thousand followers in twenty-four hours. After the news broke that Elias Westbrook is turning a new leaf with a serious relationship, my phone blew up with so many notifications it got hot enough that I had to turn it off.

I'm exhausted from an audition where every time I'd so much as plié, my foot would cramp. The director of the ballet company noticed my wince and immediately wrote me off. At least I think she did, because when I was done, she yelled, "Next!" and I was swept offstage like dust by a broomstick.

Once I got on the bus and put in my earphones, I fell asleep. The noisy rumbling of the engine and my head bumping against the glass window jerked me awake. That's when I checked my phone.

It wasn't until I watched the full interview that my stomach dropped.

She's my girlfriend.

I hate everything about it. The way he looks so hot in that stupid charcoal gray suit. The way his hair is so perfectly done, even though

I know it's naturally wavy like that. The way his face shadows with protectiveness when an interviewer brings up my name. I know he's just irritated that it has gotten this far when the last thing he wants is to be attached to me.

He could have told them that we're not dating. But he didn't, and I don't know what's worse.

The judgmental knife he left in my sternum is still there, reminding me that everything about my idea was a mistake. Like I'm some bimbo who goes around offering fake, no-strings-attached relationships to rich athletes.

He's a famous hockey player, while I only had about ninety followers before meeting him. My few awards and competition prizes mean nothing compared to his achievements in high school and college. I can't even bag a role in a production without using someone else. It's pathetic. My streak of ballet rejections hardly makes me appealing as a girlfriend either.

I never should have asked him in the first place, and I never should have expected him to say yes. But now, with his impulsive response all over the news, I bet he's waiting for his slipup to die out, just like my career.

I can't bother to switch on my phone to read anything else about my fifteen minutes of fame. I can't even bring myself to leverage the limelight to my advantage. It would just feel plain wrong, knowing he's already turned me down.

It isn't until Sean video-calls me on my laptop that I have to process the damage that interview has done. Elias Westbrook is officially on my shit list.

"Eli Westbrook is your *boyfriend*? I thought you said it was one date," he practically shrieks in his high-pitched voice that's becoming deeper as the days go on. I never thought my little brother going through puberty would bring tears to my eyes.

"It's complicated."

He appears skeptical. "Need me to set him straight?"

I chuckle. "I think I can handle him."

His eyes are wide like he can't believe I'm confirming what he's heard. "Does Uncle Marcus know?"

Falling back against the couch, I sigh. "I bet he does now." There's a part of me that hopes he hasn't seen the news, but it's probably impossible since he's the general manager of the damn team.

"Some of the articles say you're getting married."

My burst of laughter hurts my stomach, and it takes several seconds for me to recover. Elias was right. They write anything to get views. "False. Stop reading the articles."

"I'm not! Some other guys were trying to tell me about it, but I wanted to hear from you." Sean runs a hand through his hair. "Are you happy, Sage?"

Sean's round hazel eyes watch me closely like he's preparing to detect a lie. Sometimes he looks so much like my mom that it trips me out. The curly brown hair, the long, straight nose, and his light brown skin. He's every bit as Moroccan as my mother. Both of us got our hazel eyes and height from our dad. Sometimes I think I got his attitude too.

Now, the look Sean's giving me is reminiscent of the one he gave me as kids. Whenever our parents would be off on a bender, I had to make up an excuse to tell Sean. I hated hiding things from him—especially because he just wanted to know where our parents were, and he had every right to know. So, when it comes to real things that affect both of us, Sean always gets the truth from me. I'd never treat him the way our parents treated us.

One of my last memories of my parents, my mom, who had been sober longer than I'd ever seen her before, looked me dead in the eyes and said, "It's a curse being a part of this family. You'll try your whole life to fix each other, but we're not fixers, Sage. We burn things to the ground, and we'll never be good enough to even sweep up the ashes. Don't ever think you're worth more than what you came from."

Then she walked out after the paramedics to follow my dad to the hospital.

When you're stuck in a house like that, the only thing you wish is for time to speed up—to live the life where you're no longer tormented by the decisions of the adults who were supposed to protect you. I have that, and I'm holding on to it with both hands, even if it's nothing like I imagined. I'd happily continue working double shifts just so Sean wouldn't have to struggle the way I did.

Constantly working and being on the move with auditions keeps those creeping thoughts at bay—the ones that tell me to slow down and that running won't make my past disappear. But I can't listen, because those thoughts bring the sick feeling of knowing that, no matter how terribly I've been treated and no matter how long I haven't had contact with my parents, if they showed up at my front door today, I'd let them in. Just to pretend I had their love. I want to be loved unconditionally and not for what I can do for someone.

But this time, it's not about our parents, it's about my miserable love life, and I don't need to tell my little brother about that. "I'm always happy, bud."

From the way his lips thin, he knows I'm lying, and this time he pushes. "I mean, like for real. The 'in love' kind of happy."

"What would you know about that?" I quirk a brow, and he shrugs sheepishly. "I'm not in love, but I'm happy. I have ballet and you."

"And Eli."

Elias is so far removed from my real life that everything in the media feels like a fever dream. I've even stared at the picture of us from our date a thousand times, still unconvinced that it's me. The happy, smiling girl who let him carry her like she felt safe enough to let go of control—she doesn't feel like me.

"Yeah, him too."

After Sean fills me in on school, I let him off the call only to have a Hugger notification snatch my attention. The bright orange logo of the dating app makes me cringe, and I swirl back to last night's reckless activities.

When Elias said we'd never work, I came home and downloaded every dating app possible. It may have been fueled by a bitter, resentful part of me, but at the time it seemed like a great idea. After looking at a total of sixty guys and losing hope with each swipe, one caught my attention, and I messaged him to continue my string of bad decisions.

However, the bad decision is looking extremely attractive right now. Derek's message asks if I'm available for a date tonight, and I'm surprised that I'm considering it. The chunk of self-confidence that escaped me after Elias's refusal almost fuses itself back in place.

Because the only logical thing to do when an irritatingly attractive man rejects you is to find another one.

ELEVEN

ELIAS

Bunny Patrol

> **Kian Ishida:** WTF was that interview?
>
> **Aiden Crawford:** One minute he's sulking in the car, the next he's declaring his love on a live broadcast.
>
> **Dylan Donovan:** Who is this girl? I've never seen Eli so worked up.
>
> **Kian Ishida:** Never? Did you forget the time we accidentally broke his precious Staub pans trying to play ping pong?
>
> **Sebastian Hayes:** He confiscated our phones for a week like we were teenagers.
>
> **Cole Carter:** He even refused to make me breakfast. I was living on beans.
>
> **Sebastian Hayes:** We know.

Our afternoon game ended in a loss, and yet another game without a goal from me. No surprise there. In the highlight clips I watched before bed, Marcus Smith-Beaumont shook his head when I missed. My assists are no longer enough to keep me afloat. It's like a fucking curse, and now I feel desperate to break it. Desperate enough to put myself in a relationship on national television with a girl who doesn't even want to talk to me.

At least, that's what I'm telling myself, because nothing can justify the reaction I had in front of those reporters. It was so visceral, I couldn't just sit there and let them speculate about a girl who doesn't deserve anything negative said about her. After I left the conference hall, Mason just stared at me, speechless, until I had to head into the locker room before the game.

I didn't bother reliving my words for Aiden. He found out on his own after the game, and laughed at me like a fucking clown. He even replayed the audio from the clip on the Bluetooth.

Today, as I head out of my morning physical therapy session, everyone knows about it, hence the stream of texts and pictures of the guys laughing while watching the interview.

As I hop into my car, Coach Kilner's encouraging text is the first thing I see. Well, encouraging only if you know the inner workings of our college hockey coach.

You didn't play like shit yesterday. Get that damn goal already.

I'm sure he saw the interview or one of the guys showed it to him, and this is his way of bringing my focus back to the game. Or at least trying to show me that that is what matters.

An incoming call rings in the car. I answer it and turn up the volume. "I try to stay away from tabloids, Eli, you know I do. But when my son declares his relationship status on live television, I'm bound to hear about it."

I curse under my breath, pinching the bridge of my nose.

"Hey, no cursing. Your father and I want to know what's going on with you."

"Sorry, I wasn't thinking straight. It's nothing serious."

My dad barks out a laugh. "If it wasn't, it sure as hell is now. That girl will be waiting on a wedding ring with that kind of declaration, son."

Either a ring or her fists. It depends on how much I just screwed up. "Trust me, it's really not like that."

"However it is, we want to meet her. You better bring her home during your offseason."

"After game seven," adds my dad. "We want to see that cup in your hands."

My dad isn't a hockey fanatic, but he likes to pretend he is for my sake.

I chuckle weakly. "That's the plan." Once they've caught me up on their day and I don't spill about the ultimatum, I hang up and look at my texts to see that Sage hasn't messaged. I'm sure she's seen the interview.

Dropping my phone in the console, I pull out of my parking spot. But as I merge onto the highway, I realize Weston isn't far from here. Before I know it, I take the exit toward Sage's apartment. I need to see her.

Brick-covered buildings line the entire block. Squinting, I stare out my car window to read the numbers. It was dark when I dropped her home after our date, but I still remember which door is hers. I step on the brakes, jerking in my seat when I realize what I'm doing.

There's nothing creepier than showing up to a girl's apartment when she hasn't answered your calls. Yet here I am, making a fool out of myself for the second time this week. I'm mentally scolding myself for thinking this was a good idea.

As I'm reluctantly peeling away from the curb to drive home, something pulls my gaze to the golden numbers on the door at the corner of the complex. The fourteen gleams like a polished ring, and I grip the steering wheel to force myself to drive away.

Either the stress is melting my brain, or I took some brutal hits in yesterday's game, because I'm out of my car and jogging toward her door. There's a light drizzle of rain as I head toward the number calling my name.

The short black fence, with absolutely zero security, screeches open with a flick of my hand. The concrete path that leads to her apartment is covered with yellow, overgrown grass and weeds that stick out of the cracks. I read the welcome mat laid out in front of her door. COME BACK WITH TACOS.

My smile disintegrates quickly when a drop of water lands on my head, making me look up to where the porch ceiling leaks a rusty brown liquid. I wipe it away and move to the side before I force myself to stop delaying. I knock and wait with a tapping foot, just as a series of rusty brown water drops trickle onto my face. Stepping to the side again, I bring up the hem of my shirt to dry my face.

"That's one way to assure I won't slam the door in your face," Sage says.

Pulling my shirt back down, I see her eyeing where I just covered my torso. Sage stands there in heels and a black dress that reminds me of the one she wore to the auction. A curly tendril of hair frames her face, and her hazel eyes shine brighter with dark eyeliner accenting her almond-shaped eyes.

I clear my throat. "I've never had a door slammed in my face."

"I'd happily be your first." She swings it closed, but the move is slow. It only takes my hand against the door to stop her from closing it.

She sighs, opening it wide again. "Are you going to say something, or are you here to rob me?" She hikes a thumb behind her. "I don't have much, but I'm sure my candle collection can get you a few bucks."

"I'm not here to rob you."

"You sure? Because you just showed up at my apartment without an invitation." Sage crosses her arms. "I know you think I'm your girlfriend, but this is a lot even for me."

With her eyes on me, it's hard to come up with words. The ones I rehearsed for days don't make sense anymore. "What I said at the conference—"

"Was a mistake," she interrupts. "You were right. We don't know each other. I wasn't thinking when I suggested pretending to date. It was a mindless idea. One that should never have been said out loud. Now, if you will excuse me, I have somewhere to be."

She turns to grab her purse from the coffee table in what I assume must be the living room. I'm not sure because the kitchen and the couch are all in the same place, which would be normal if there wasn't a rack with all her clothes there too.

When she puts her purse onto her shoulder, she doesn't look at me as she comes outside. I move back to give her space to lock the door. Sage jiggles the doorknob a few times and manhandles the door to get it to shut securely.

"Can I at least apologize?"

She sighs. "I heard your voicemail, Eli. No need to drag this out. Don't worry about announcing I'm your girlfriend to the world. It's only a matter of time before they pin you with the next girl of the week."

I wince, knowing she watched the interview and heard what they said about her.

Then she drops her keys into her purse and descends the short steps.

"Where are you going? I'll give you a ride," I offer.

She walks past me, but I follow her anyway, watching as she side-steps the cracks on the pavement and the muddy pockets of puddles left over from the earlier downpour.

"You can't possibly walk in those shoes."

"They're fine, and I'm taking the train. That's what us gold diggers like to use."

The jab finds my sternum. "Let me drive you."

"I don't take rides from strangers."

"I've seen you use Uber."

"Fine, I don't take rides from *assholes*," she shoots back.

I wince, and if I'm not mistaken, she does too, but I deserve it.

"Sorry," I say. We're already way past my car, but she halts on the sidewalk. "I'm sorry for making you feel less than or like I didn't want to be attached to you. That was never my intention, and questioning your character is not why I refused your offer."

She gives me nothing, but I know if I don't explain now, I'll only make this worse.

"I know firsthand how the media and the fans act. The comments you got these last few days? Those are mild compared to the stuff Brandy, our team photographer, got on her social media when she was seen with me. The stuff they were saying about her isn't even worth repeating, but I'd never want you to go through that. I never wanted to hurt you."

There's a beat where she's silent and all I hear is the rain and the buzz of the streetlights.

"Well, you did hurt me," she whispers.

"I know." My voice is heavy with regret. "And I'm sorry. Being impulsive has never benefitted me, so I avoid it at all costs. I couldn't throw caution to the wind and say yes to you."

Caution to the wind? I rub my face in my hands and then look to see that she's still giving me her back. With a few strides, I stand in front of her.

"Hear me out, Sage." When she steps to the side, probably to head to the Weston train station, I stop her with a touch to her arm but drop my hand just as quickly.

"I'm late, Eli."

Eli. "We can talk in my car on the way there."

"You don't even know where I'm going." I watch her defenses crumble, but not fully.

"Then tell me. I'll take you." Doing something for her might just be for my own ego, but I need to know she doesn't hate my guts for invading her privacy.

She gazes down the sidewalk before looking at me. Hazel on brown. "So you show up at my apartment unannounced, and now you're forcing me to get into your car?" she deadpans.

"You've been in my car before."

"That's because of the auction. You could still be a part-time body parts collector." She eyes me skeptically. "Your actions are proving that theory."

My nervous laugh doesn't help dampen the allegations. "Just tell me where you're going, and I'll drop you off. You can take a picture of my license and send it to a friend if you want."

She laughs, and as good as it feels to hear that, I don't feel at ease yet. "I have no friends, remember?"

"Is that a yes?"

"Yes, you can give me a ride." She pulls out her phone. "I'm headed to the Pint."

"Downtown?" My curiosity isn't concealed well, and when she nods, it only makes me wonder why she's going to a bar. But I don't ask because there's only so much I can push.

Inside my quiet car, my mouth feels dry as I try to come up with words.

Sage's ringing phone cuts off my thoughts, and she answers. From the bits of conversation I catch, I know she's talking to her brother about a mix-up at the pharmacy with his medication. The next twenty minutes of our car ride are spent with her calling multiple people. I drive slower, but I can't delay our arrival any longer.

Sage hangs up just before I turn in to the roundabout at the front entrance. She's ready to hop out, but on instinct I lock the doors.

She whips her head around to me. "This is creepy on so many levels."

"I think we should talk about what I said at the press conference."

Sage checks the time on her phone. "It's fine. Just forget about it."

"What if I don't want to?"

She searches my face like she's trying to believe that I just said those words.

"My date is waiting for me, Eli."

"What?"

Everything halts. There's a mess in my brain, and her words make it so much worse. I had just announced Sage as my girlfriend, and she's going into this bar to meet another guy?

"I'm meeting someone here for a date, and you're making me late," she clarifies.

My mouth feels numb. As she reaches for the handle again, I finally unlock the car doors, the collective *click* resonating. She casts a fleeting glance in my direction, a trace of what I interpret as pity in her eyes.

"But people think you're my girlfriend. Won't this be . . . improper?" I protest.

She shakes her head, as though hoping my words might make more sense that way. I feel like I've bared my soul, but she reacts as if I've thrown sand at her.

"You said yourself that the possibility of *us* is unbelievable," she says sharply. "And 'improper' happens to be my middle name. Goodbye, Eli."

There it is again. The damn *Eli* and not Elias. She's started calling me the nickname when I screwed up, and now she's sticking to it. I don't even know why I care; nobody calls me Elias.

Sage climbs out before I can say anything else. Watching her retreat into the bar, I'm restless. As I sit in the driver's seat, still staring at the door, I'm hoping she'll run right back to my car. Minutes drag as my gaze remains fixed on the black-framed doors where the Pint's logo—a foaming beer mug—is etched into the glass.

When someone behind me honks, it jerks me back to reality.

My fake girlfriend just went on a date.

I'm about to drive off to head home like I know I should and reevaluate my life choices. Instead, I pull into an empty spot and park. Then, before I can second-guess myself, I exit the car and head inside the Pint.

TWELVE

SAGE

I'M HAVING A good time. I'm having a good time. I'm having a good time.

Damn it. This whole "speaking it into existence" crap isn't working, and it's screwing me over right now. In the nine minutes I've been here, Derek has proven to be a real person, not a catfish, but unfortunately, that's where the positives end. He took the liberty of ordering my drink, opting for a fruity blue margarita with a tiny umbrella. Presumptuous.

He talks about how he almost made it to the NBA until an ACL tear thwarted those solid aspirations. He's currently playing for his local YMCA as a benchwarmer. No judgment here though, because as far as ballet goes, I'm a benchwarmer too. But keeping my interest focused on his what-if rambles is close to impossible. When he attempts to place his hand on my thigh, I instinctively recoil.

At some point during the nine minutes, I mentioned ballet. Derek seized the opportunity to duck under the table to stare at my feet—visibly beat up from yesterday's rehearsals—for an uncomfortably long moment.

I've never wanted anything more than to have retractable body parts.

Somehow, I picked a date with the most touch-starved man in the downtown core.

As I take a tiny sip of my overly sweet drink, I pat my lips to keep the blue tint from clinging to them.

"You have beautiful lips," Derek says.

I hold back from shuddering. "Thank you."

I hate myself for saying it. But cursing his entire bloodline wouldn't play well for me, especially because this man looks like he'd follow me home and hide in the untrimmed hedges by my apartment.

Self-preservation is a lesson every girl should learn before she ventures out of the house. However, I learned about it by getting into situations no young girl should ever endure. Self-taught self-preservation is a true badge of honor.

Attempting to drown out his voice, I scan the crowded bar, only to find Elias's words creeping back into my mind. The Pint is a popular establishment, particularly on game days. Basketball and hockey games are broadcast on various TV screens, with the matchup between Vancouver and Los Angeles garnering the most attention from patrons. This confirms Elias's concerns about someone recognizing me.

"Another margarita?"

My head whips back to Derek, who's standing now. My first one is pretty much untouched. "No, thanks. I'll just take some water."

"Okay, I'll order us some appetizers too," he says, flashing me a crooked smile.

When he takes off, I deflate back into my seat, regretting my every decision. Angry Sage is not to be trusted, and vengeful Sage is apparently even worse.

Before Elias showed up at my door, I was arguing with myself in the bathroom mirror about whether to read every intrusive comment left about me on my profile or just leave the house and forget it. Seeing Elias reminded me of the shitstorm he dropped me into.

It's something I could weather, but he rejected me, goddamn it. He can't decide on a random Monday on live television that he wants to try out my "unbelievable" plan after all.

So, when he stood there, with rain drizzled across his tight gray shirt and that wounded puppy dog look on his face, it solidified my decision. I needed to distract myself with another man, or this one and his unsurprisingly perfect abs would stick to my brain like taffy.

Derek is back in a record amount of time. "So, ballet. How's that going?"

He sits and drags his chair forward so his abdomen presses against the wooden table. The space between us is no longer a comfortable bubble, and instead his knees press against mine, and his face is only inches away.

I push my chair back to make up for the lack of space. "I got two rejections in one week, so not great," I say, not bothering to impress him with a lie.

My first rejection was for that small theater that performs for nursing homes, and the second rejection was for a short summer stint with a ballet school. Nothing too disappointing, but just the cherry on top of an already miserable week. However, my daily refresh of the Nova Ballet Theatre website showed they haven't updated the casting for the dual role of Princess Odette and Odile, which means they haven't decided on anyone. That's all the motivation I need to keep going until I find a way to wiggle into an audition. But I have seen the new casting for Prince Siegfried, played by Adam Culver, and Rothbart, played by Jason Levy.

The company opened their auditions for international soloists, so they're currently traveling the globe to find their swan queen after securing most of the cast. Since this is Zimmerman's first production of *Swan Lake*, he is looking for nothing short of perfection.

"I'm sure that won't be the case for long. There's something about you that screams dancer. Probably your legs."

I laugh, tucking my legs under my chair because he's eyeing them like he's assessing them for the potential to sell on the black market.

He smirks, leaning closer, and I hate this. His overpowering scent, and the manly musk mixed in, wafts around us like a dark cloud. My throat runs dry from the uncomfortable gaze, so I reach for my water and take a long drink. Then just as I place the glass back on the table, his calloused hand engulfs mine, and I watch in horror as he brings it toward his mouth to kiss it.

"You—"

"I'd suggest you take your hands off my girlfriend."

That voice creeps up my back and crawls into my ears like fire ants.

Derek looks up, his gaze fixed on the man behind me, his expression awestruck. I don't have to look to know what he's seeing. Tight T-shirt, impressively hard chest, face that is the definition of perfection. I'd have to dig up my dictionary to confirm there is a picture of him next to the word.

I take a deep breath before I turn to the stone-jawed man who just walked into a very crowded bar to announce—again—that I'm his girlfriend. Elias is wearing workout clothes, and he still looks better than anyone else I've encountered today. It's unfair.

There's no doubt he's a catch in this disappointing litter of male specimens, and I'm not clueless about the women *and* men admiring him right now.

"G-girlfriend?" Derek stutters, his lips still frozen midway to my hand.

My forehead creases so deeply, a headache blooms in my temples.

"I am not his girlfriend," I say through clenched teeth. Derek continues to stare behind me, wide-eyed. I know he's recognized Elias in the point five seconds that he's taken to come stand by my side.

Annoyed, I snap my fingers to get Derek to refocus on me. "What were you saying?"

He swallows, still staring at Elias as he shakily kisses my hand. "You have beautiful hands."

The compliment is on par for him, but I giggle, smiling shyly and fluttering my lashes like a showgirl. More to annoy the man who declared me as his girlfriend.

The air is awkward when I turn to the rookie hovering over me like a fly. "Sir, you must be mistaken."

His jaw twitches. "It was never a mistake, Sage."

What the hell? This pretentious rich hockey player thinks he can walk into my date and expect me to fall at his feet now that he's decided I'm his girlfriend?

Ridiculous.

It takes a lot for me not to dignify that with an answer. When I turn, expecting to find a still-awestruck Derek, he stands and carelessly drops my hand on the table.

Great, I just lost my date to a hockey player.

"Eli Westbrook, right? I saw your interview—" He pauses, his gaze bouncing back and forth. "Wait. This is *your* Sage?"

I drop my head in my hands in defeat. "I'm not *his* anything," I mutter.

Derek's not listening to me as he looks at Elias apologetically. "I'm sorry, man, I had no idea." He looks back at me. "You do know Hugger is a dating app, right?"

I shoot him a glare, but it's like he's finally seeing us. He's not the only one, because I start to feel the touch of invasive gazes on the back of my neck, and the whisper of Elias's last name circulating through the bar.

I expect Elias to walk out, since he's famously not one for attention, but he stands beside me, unperturbed.

Derek watches us dubiously before his eyes spark with renewed interest. I reach for my water to help my pounding head.

"Unless this is like your kink. Weird, but I won't tell anyone." He does a zipper motion on his lips.

"Yeah, this is our thing," Elias says, putting his arm on the back of my chair. "She makes me jealous, and I punish her for it at home."

I choke on my water and have to hit my chest to find my breath again. Heat electrifies my spine, and I try not to dwell on his words, because I'm convinced he couldn't have said them. Confused beyond belief and fed up with this back-and-forth, I stand, pushing back my chair to grab Elias's arm. I pull him straight down the hall and outside through the back exit, where the breeze is blowing now that the sun has disappeared below the horizon.

He looks pleased that we're out here alone. The shock factor of his statement was executed perfectly. "I don't know why you thought coming in was a good idea but—"

"I want to do it."

I blink. "Do what?"

He takes a step closer to me, lowering his voice. "I'll be your fake boyfriend."

In all the scenarios that could have resulted from tonight, this is one I did not anticipate. I really overshot with this one.

I cock my head to the left, then to the right, assessing him. "If I recall correctly, just a week ago you told me that could never happen. If you're doing this because you pity me, you can count me out. This was supposed to be mutually beneficial."

"It will be—it is. This morning, they gave me a brief for questions I have to answer for an upcoming conference, and they all have to do with hockey. Not a single personal question."

Impatience taps my foot. "Okay?"

"Haven't you read the articles?" he presses.

There's no part of me that cares about what random people on the internet have to say about me. You don't get through thirteen years of ballet without developing thick skin and a filter to block out useless opinions.

"No. I don't read that stuff."

His lips quirk, and he watches me with a sort of wonder. "Well, I was wrong. They believed the girlfriend thing and mostly respected my wishes to keep us private."

Us.

"And now you want to date me?" I ask slowly.

He nods.

A renewed confidence fills me. "So what you're saying is, I was right all along."

"Yes, Sage, you were right."

"Wait." I pull out my phone. "Can you say that again? I'll make it my voicemail. And alarm. And ringtone."

He holds my hand to stop me. "Will you be my fake girlfriend?"

I tap my chin in contemplation. "I don't know, Elias. There is a great candidate right inside the bar." I can't show him all my cards.

"Better than me?"

"Believe it or not, they do exist."

His face is serious. "What do you want me to do?"

I'm surprised at his response. He's just given me a world of opportunities, and I can't contain my wicked smile. "Beg."

"Excuse me?"

"I want you to beg. Extra points if you get on your knees."

He raises a brow. "Is this fueling some fantasy of yours?"

"My fantasies are a lot more graphic than that, Elias."

Bemused, he shakes his head, then shifts to lower himself to his knees. Before he can really start begging on his knees, my arms shoot out to stop his descent, checking around us to see if anyone's watching. I burst into laughter, smacking his arm as I try to catch my breath. "Oh my God. You totally called my bluff."

He blinks in confusion, and that serious look doesn't drop from his face. He stands, and even when I'm wearing heels, he's so much taller than me.

"So, you'll do it?" he asks with a smidge of hope resting between his eyebrows.

"Yes."

His smile is bright, and I can't help but return it. "Your uncle is going to hate me."

"If it makes you feel any better, he already does."

My uncle is hard on his players because he wants them to be the best. That's what happens when the team hasn't won a Stanley Cup in years. People get frustrated.

When Elias extends his hand, I take it, walking behind him but feeling the burn in my feet with each step. Damn Derek and his foot fetish. Somehow, he cursed my feet.

"What's wrong?"

I shrug. "I had rehearsals yesterday. My feet are punishing me for wearing these heels now."

Elias stops walking and stands in front of me with his back turned. I stare at the dark T-shirt stretched across his back. "Come on."

I balk. "You want to carry me?"

"We both know it's not the first time."

Biting back a smile, I contemplate whether to do it, but when he crouches, I don't hesitate. My dress is long enough that it flows around me and doesn't give anyone a free show. Then, as he lifts me up, I feel an instant relief of pressure on my soles.

He walks back into the bar instead of around the complex like I half expected, and straight across to the front exit, where all eyes are on us.

That girl from the picture, who was laughing when he carried her through the streets of downtown, pries herself out again. Here, I feel safe, and I don't suppress my laughter.

When we're out of the bar and heading to his car, he turns to where I rest my chin on his shoulder. "Is this how we're always going to end our night?"

"Me pressed against you?" I hold him a little tighter. "God, I hope so."

He chuckles. "There she is."

THIRTEEN

ELIAS

THIS IS THE first week since I was eighteen that I haven't had my recurring nightmare.

It starts with both my parents looming over my bed with a look of horror painted across their faces. My mom's crying, and my dad is shaking his head in disappointment. A searing pain pounds against my skull as light flickers in through the window. Then, I'm transported back to a dirty house where a woman is screaming in the kitchen, and a man cracks his beer bottle against the countertop. It's that sight that jerks me back to consciousness.

The frequency of those nightmares fluctuates depending on whether or not I'm stressed. In college, they were rare, but since joining the league, they're relentless. I anticipated one last night, but it never came. There's only been one change, and it should be stressing me out because I hate lying.

But there hasn't been much logic involved when it comes to my decision-making skills lately. The only pushback I received about my dating life was from Aiden.

"This whole fake relationship thing is not you, Eli," he'd said.

"You haven't lied a day in your life, but now you're doing it just to get the media off your back?"

I told him I cared what the fans thought, but he wasn't convinced.

"And you think this is better? Forget the media. You haven't been in a relationship in years, and the first one you're in is fake. I hope you know what you're doing. But know if you ever feel yourself getting to that place again, I'm here for you. We all are."

That place is when I found out my biological father was blackmailing my parents. I didn't let that ruin my life, and I won't let this get to me either. I know what I'm doing.

So Sage and I decided to meet to iron out the details to avoid someone unraveling our plan as quickly as Aiden did. But she's pushed that coffee date three times. Today, as I head home from the gym, she texts me the same excuse.

Rain check? Another ballet emergency.

I'm not sure what kinds of emergencies occur in ballet, but they can't be serious enough to delay our meeting by a week. Especially since our game against Chicago is on Saturday, and I'm hoping we can talk before I leave for the weekend.

"Wanna order takeout?"

I glance up from my phone as Aiden enters the living room, towel drying his wet hair.

Deciding not to dwell on Sage's message, I toss my phone on the couch. "Nah, I'm in the mood to cook today."

He nods appreciatively, sinking into the couch and powering on the game console. It's the usual time for the guys at Dalton to join in, so they play together. "What are you making?"

"Tacos."

In the kitchen, I begin by tossing the ground beef into the pan, waiting for the sizzle before adding spices. I dice and sauté the vegetables in another pan before warming the tortillas. Cooking is my meditation—the rhythmic chopping and blend of movements always ground me.

When I was living with my parents, I'd cook every night to impress them. They were always receptive, and that's what made me the designated cook in our off-campus house. Making food for the guys let us have a meal together, and I think it brought us even closer.

Aiden pauses his game to help assemble our plates in the kitchen. But as he offers me a drink, I decide to have my dinner elsewhere tonight. "Do you mind if I take the extras with me?"

His chews his food. "Where are you headed?"

"I have to check on something."

Aiden chuckles as he takes his plate back into the living room. "Tell her I said hi."

I pack the food and head straight to Weston. I don't bother texting Sage because I know her response. *Ballet emergency.* But if I'm right, she's home.

Arriving in Weston, I park in front of Sage's apartment and notice the gate is wide open. There is no security in this place. I knock, and I'm assessing the rusty hinges of the damaged door when it's yanked open.

Sage gasps, her tiger face mask shifting. She turns away, then back to me, then away again. "You are not supposed to see me like this."

"Like what?"

"This!" She points to her face mask. Her hair is pulled into a bun, and she's wearing an old oversize Sidney Crosby T-shirt and nothing else. Her toned legs are shiny like she just lathered them with lotion, and her toes are freshly painted pink with those foam separators still between them. "Maybe you can leave and come back in five minutes. That way we can both forget about this."

"Sage, you look comfortable. Why would that bother me?"

She sighs when I don't move, then notices the paper bag I'm holding. "Takeout?"

"Dinner," I answer. "I'm assuming you haven't eaten?"

"Are you forcing me to have dinner with you? You could've just asked, you know."

"I would have, but you've been avoiding me."

She winces, sheepishly gesturing for me to enter. With a hip slam to close the door, she secures it with four bolts and double-checks each one.

The water-stained popcorn ceiling and flaking paint on the walls catch my eye first. Then the rough gray carpet, reminiscent of the ones I've seen in public schools. The chipped cupboard doors in the kitchen dangle from their hinges. Though spotless, it's completely run-down.

"It's self-care night, and I wasn't expecting company," she explains hurriedly. She moves a pink basket filled with nail polish and colorful bottles to the side table, nearly knocking over the nearby clothing rack. Her laptop plays a movie at low volume on the coffee table, beside which sits a framed picture: her and, I assume, her brother, beaming at one of her ballet recitals.

There's a mildly concerning collection of candles on one side table. Three different ones are lit, crackling softly in a mix of scents. Vanilla, lavender, and another I can't quite pinpoint.

Sage peels off her face mask and tosses it in the basket. She gestures for me to sit on the couch, and dusts off nonexistent debris. It takes me a second to realize she's nervous, which throws me off, because I've never seen her like this.

"Do you want one?" Sage pulls out a container of silicone-like patches and puts one under each of her eyes. Her hopeful expression lifts the clear eye patches that have tiny gold stars inside them.

I only give her a look but can't help smiling.

"You're smiling! You so do." She uses the tweezers to remove two more. "Okay, I might freak out. Nobody has ever wanted to do this with me. I don't have many—or any—girlfriends, and Sean is not into all this stuff, so I'm warning you."

That sparks my curiosity. "Not even any of your ex-boyfriends?"

"The last one wouldn't touch me with a ten-foot pole if he saw me like this."

"Why not?"

She avoids my gaze and busies herself with putting the patches under my eyes. I can smell her vanilla-scented lotion when she's this close. It momentarily distracts me from my lingering question.

But then she answers, "He saw me as a wind-up ballerina, ready to perform whenever he twisted the key."

Protectiveness makes my body grow rigid.

Sage holds up a green tool. "Do you want a facial roller? It's fun to use."

I'm still reeling from the anecdote about her ex when I notice her excitement. It's damn near contagious. She's never done this with anyone before, so I give in. The cold stone feels nice against my skin when I try it, but the way she holds back a laugh tells me I must look ridiculous.

She whips out her phone and comes next to me to snap a picture. I can confirm—I look ridiculous. She laughs at me, but I don't think I mind it.

"Are you going to tell me why you're avoiding me?" I finally ask.

"About that." She pauses the movie that was playing on her laptop. "I think we're way in over our heads about this whole fake relationship."

"You're backing out?"

"No!" she exclaims. "Well, not entirely. I just mean we have no idea what to expect. There aren't any rules to this stuff, so how do we know if we're doing it right?"

This is the only thing going right for me, and now she's second-guessing, maybe even backing out, before we've even started. "Is that what you need? Rules?" I ask.

She shrugs, watching me like I'll have all the answers.

"We'll set some terms and conditions, then," I declare. "But we're having dinner first."

"Fine with me." Sage gets two plates with napkins as I arrange the tacos. She sits cross-legged on the couch to face me.

When Sage takes a bite, her eyes widen. "Did you make this?"

I can't seem to pry my gaze from her mouth when I nod.

"You could have just cooked for me, and I would have agreed to date you." She wipes her mouth with a napkin and chews like she's tasted heaven.

"You like it?"

She hums in appreciation, and something warms my chest. We eat in comfortable silence, forgetting the rules for a few minutes. When she takes my empty plate to the sink, I follow her, drying the dishes after she washes them, like this is our practiced nightly routine.

"Okay, so what's the first rule?" Sage asks.

"We can start with who is allowed to know that this is fake. Aiden and a few of my friends back home already know, so if you have anyone you trust, you don't have to lie to them."

She only nods, and when we're finally settled on her couch again, she pulls out her phone and types **fake-dating for dummies** into her Notes app. Her shoulders are still tight, but she's stopped anxiously chewing on her lip. "That's easy. I don't have any friends."

I've never heard someone say something so sad with that much confidence. She's said it before, but I've always thought she was joking. "None?"

"None. And no, I'm not a loser, I just never had the time to make friends in college and I didn't keep in touch with anyone from high school." She says it casually.

I don't get it. My friends are what made my college experience worthwhile. Other than my parents' house, the hockey house was home for me.

"What about your brother?"

"No way. He said I look genuinely happy with you, and I couldn't tell him it's not real. I don't even know what I'll say if he finds out from someone else."

"Is that it? You're afraid that people will figure out we're pretending?"

"Yes," she says, dropping her head in her hands. "I may have read some of the stuff people are saying, and you were right. There's no way I'm good enough to be dating you."

I bark out a laugh, and it makes her lift her head from her hands to look at me.

"Remind me to never be vulnerable with you again," she mutters.

"I'm sorry, I'm not laughing at you. People will talk, and like I've said before, I don't share that thought. You're talented and beautiful. Frankly, they should be wondering what you see in me."

Flustered, Sage shuffles to sit beside me so she's not facing me anymore. The side of her arm touches mine, and I ignore the spark of connection.

"Okay, first, let's outline what we want from this. Like Build-A-Bear but for a fake relationship. Build-A-Boyfriend!" She pats herself on the back for coming up with that.

"Do I get to Build-A-Girlfriend too?"

"Nope, I come well equipped."

"And I don't?"

Sage stares at me blankly, like I'm missing something.

"What?"

She appears reluctant to continue. "When reading my comments during that one moment of weakness, I came across some about you too. They said you haven't been in a relationship, like, ever. Or if you were, it was never made public."

"I haven't."

She hides her surprise. "Exactly. So, I'll turn you into the perfect boyfriend. I'm basically doing your future girlfriend a favor."

"Is this the charity part of our relationship?"

Her smile surfaces. "I won't make you do anything you don't want to do, Elias."

"I doubt there's something I wouldn't want to do with you." The

words spill out easily, and I don't mean for them to sound so sugges-
tive, but her eyes widen.

I clear my throat. "So what does this perfect boyfriend look like?"

"You," she blurts, then sits straighter. "I mean, someone who's
loyal and kind. The type of person who's not rude to waiters and
admits when he's wrong. And he should care about me."

"So . . . the bare minimum."

She scoffs. "Trust me, most of what I'm saying is a reach for a lot
of guys."

It's hard to keep the pitiful look off my face. "What else is on this
unattainable list?"

"He should be tall. Taller than me, at least." Then her gaze skims
upward to my biceps, where my dark green full sleeve molds around
my arms. "And strong. Definitely strong."

Then she types another bullet point: **social media**.

"Since you already hard-launched our relationship on live
television"—she gives me a sidelong glance—"we can just post a picture of us this week and go from there."

I let her fill the screen with her own rules, hoping it makes her
feel at ease with all this.

"Flowers, chocolates, expensive gifts. We don't need to do all
that," she says. "People know you have money. And this is fake, so
you don't need to spend anything on me."

"Flowers aren't going to break the bank."

"I don't even like flowers."

I've learned from my mother that if a woman—anyone for that
matter—says they don't like flowers, it's probably because they've
never received any. Or they're deathly allergic.

"None? You don't have a favorite flower?"

She shakes her head, continuing to type the ridiculous rule. It
doesn't make sense to me, and not because I haven't been in a serious
relationship before, but because she seems uncomfortable with the
prospect of someone doing something so simple for her.

I take the phone from her this time and type **dates**. "We'll need to be seen out in Toronto a few times for this to look believable."

She quirks a brow. "When's the last time you went on a date?"

"Last week. With you," I say matter-of-factly.

Sage's laugh is delicate. It reminds me of the first time I heard it when we were at the lake, and it almost makes me smile, but then I realize she's laughing at me.

"That was not a date. It was practically an auction-ordered hangout."

An auction-ordered hangout? That was the first date I've been on in years, and she's boiled it down to *hanging out*?

I relax my jaw. "Then we'll have to have one that counts."

"Sure, but nothing over the top like last week. I'd be happy with falafel from a food truck and going to that old theater that plays *Dirty Dancing* once a month."

"*Dirty Dancing*?"

"It's my comfort movie. I watch it every year for my birthday too, with a McCain chocolate cake I share with Sean." She points to her screen. "I'm watching it right now." Her screen is paused on a couple swimming in a lake. Then she turns to me again. "So, what else?"

"We'll have to attend the pre-playoffs dinner hosted by the Thunder's owners. And you should probably come to one of my games next week."

The prospect doesn't seem to make her nervous, which is a win.

"I have a small performance coming up next Thursday, so I can come any day after that."

"Then it's settled. I come to your performance, you'll come to my game."

She freezes. "What—no. You don't have to come to my performance. It's really small."

I quirk a brow at her reaction. "Are you telling me *no*?"

"It's not the ideal night out. Don't feel obligated because I'm going to your game."

"I'll decide how I spend my Thursday night, Sage," I say. "Anything else for our list?"

Sage sighs, then taps her chin in contemplation. "You already know about my family and my failing career. I don't have any crazy exes to worry about. I think."

"You *think* you don't have crazy exes?"

Her expressive eyes shutter. "I'm sure."

"I'm surprised we've hit something you're not willing to share."

She gnaws at her lip and stares at me through her dark lashes. "Let's just say he recently reappeared in my life."

"Is he bothering you?"

"No," she says quickly. "He won't interfere with us. You don't need to worry."

"That's not why I asked. If he's bothering you, I'll take care of it."

Sage fans her face. "That was hot. Keep up the whole protective boyfriend thing."

I don't pry further because she's back to joking. But there's a part of me that wants to know her for more than who she says she is. To see what's under all those jokes.

"Should we practice kissing?"

Sage's deflection works because I choke on my words and have a coughing fit. "No. There's no need for any PDA," I croak.

"At all? Do you need me to get tested or something? Because standing beside each other like a pair of cousins isn't going to make this believable."

"It has nothing to do with you."

She cocks her head. "You expect me to believe that?"

"No PDA," I affirm, and it gets her to stop trying to read me like a newspaper.

"Fine, but no other girls, then," she says. "I'm not jealous, I just mean you should keep it hidden, at least where the media is concerned."

"There won't be any other girls." There haven't been in a long time.

"None?" Her brows raise in surprise. "Don't stop doing what you do on my account."

I realize why she's lax about me seeing other women. And I hate it. Sage believing that shit strikes hotter than the rumors themselves. "You believe them?"

"I wouldn't say I *believe* them," she starts. "There are just a lot of headlines, and you don't exactly date. But I know what it can be like in your world. It's normal."

"Not for me."

She raises her hands in surrender. "Okay, jeez. I was giving you an out."

"I don't need one. Do you?"

"If I want to have sex with someone, I'll let you know, warden."

I squeeze my eyes shut. "If you're inclined to *date* someone, then let me know and we can end this. I don't need to know about your sex life."

She's smirking now. "Why? Does it make you uncomfortable? If it helps, it's just me and one very reliable battery-powered friend."

Talking about her vibrator that is likely in one of those boxes she has all her stuff in is not how I imagined my night going. It feels awfully hard to swallow right now.

"We forgot one," she says. "No falling in love."

I freeze. That one was not on my radar.

Sage sees my stricken expression and bursts into laughter. "Your face!" She wheezes as she hits my arm. "Don't worry, you'll be running for the hills by the end of this."

My laugh is brittle and not at all believable.

"So, it's settled. When your season ends and I get word on my NBT audition, we'll end this. No strings."

"No strings." I shake her hand. And just like that, I have a fake girlfriend.

"Before you go . . ." She trails off, tapping on her phone until mine pings beside me. The picture is blurry, but it's clear who's in it.

Sage is on my back, arms looped around my shoulders, and I'm carrying her heels as we head out of the Pint. "That's for you to post later," she says.

"When did you take this?"

"I didn't. Someone tagged me in it."

"You want me to caption it *'best part of my day'*?" I read her text, trying to hold back a laugh. "A bit presumptuous, don't you think?"

"Drop the no-kissing rule, and it'll be true."

I'm rendered speechless, but Sage just grins at my discomfort.

"Don't forget to tag me, Elias."

FOURTEEN

SAGE

MANLY FIREFIGHTERS SURROUNDED by smoke have always carried a certain appeal. But that appeal quickly dies when I realize the smoke is coming out of my apartment, and the firemen are soaking my belongings with a hose.

After teaching my last class of the day, and successfully posting my first dancing video on my page, I took a bus across town to audition for a last-minute role. I got an email that the National Ballet was having open auditions. I'm hoping my routine this evening met their standards. With the nasty feeling of anticipation, I was set on taking a hot shower before getting ready for my first real date with Elias. He's supposed to pick me up in an hour.

But of course, life had other plans.

I stand frozen on the sidewalk, because with one step toward the scratched door, I'll be forced to live in the reality of what's happening in front of me. A part of me wishes I could brush off the scene and turn to another apartment that isn't clogged with smoke and large men in yellow uniforms. Some are even dressed in those navy T-shirts that tightly stretch across the expanse of their chests. This situation would be ideal in any other scenario.

A man standing by my front door turns to me when I finally approach. "Miss Beaumont?"

I nod, staring wide-eyed at my ash-filled apartment, still hoping this is all some big joke and they're actually strippers giving me an early birthday present. "What happened?"

The man pulls off his yellow helmet and gives me a look like he pities me but also wants to scold me. A fatherly look, I suppose, not that I would know. "Do you recall lighting this?"

He holds up a broken glass cylinder, blackened wax crusted on the sides. My magnolia candle from this morning sits on the palm of his gloved hand, and I wince.

So much for self-care.

"I swear, I remember blowing it out. This has never happened before."

He nods, dropping the candle in a pile of my burnt things. My comforter, a table lamp, and some clothes. The fire must have spread quickly because my tiny living room, doubling as my bedroom with the Murphy bed, is crisped. My kitchen took the brunt of the destruction.

"That's always the case. But even if candles seem harmless, a lit one can be deadly. You need to be careful. This could have been much worse."

Emotion clogs my throat as my eyes start to water, and not because of the smoke.

Another firefighter enters with a clipboard. "I'd suggest sleeping somewhere else, ma'am. The smoky smell bakes itself into the walls."

Mulling over his words, I assess my options. If I call my uncle, he'll have another reason why my living alone was never a good idea. He's been hoping I'd move in with him since the bank seized my parents' house, but I've always refused. I'm not his burden.

I don't have a friend or enough money for a motel. That dark cloud of smoke that contains my apartment shadows me, and I try not to sob in front of the hot firefighters.

Debris crunches under my feet, and I notice my laptop is also burnt to a crisp. If I had insurance, this might be less devastating, but right now panic clutches my chest. My breathing comes out shallow and the smoke feels like tar on my lungs.

The firefighters finish soaking what's left of my things and gather their equipment. I lean against a corner of the countertop that's untouched by the fire and rack my brain for where to stay tonight. So far the bushes outside are looking pretty comfy.

Desperate, I turn to the retreating firefighters. "Do you have a spare bed at the station?"

They give each other a look and chuckle at my imposition. "If you need resources—"

"Sage?" My front door flies open, and all six feet four inches of Elias Westbrook come rushing in. Of course, he arrived early, before I could ask to reschedule our date. He's wearing a black flannel over a white tee and simple jeans, and his hair is disheveled as if he ran. Somehow, he looks hotter than the fire that burned my belongings to soot.

He stops short of cupping my face. "Are you okay? Are you hurt?"

Elias scans my body for . . . burns? I don't know. But he looks more worried than I've ever seen him, and it takes me a minute to realize he's worried about *me*. A foreign tingle burrowing beneath my skin makes me stand straighter.

"Looks like you won't be needing those resources," says the fireman. "We'll see ourselves out. And please put out your candles before leaving a room."

My gaze follows their retreat, but my mind is still stuck on Elias. The look on his face. The way my heart skipped when I saw him.

"A candle did all this?" Elias takes inventory of all my stuff. Which isn't much, because it's all been reduced to ashes.

"It's not that bad. There's still a dry spot over there." I point to a space that wouldn't even house the rats that run around here at night.

"Sage, you're not staying here."

"I can't exactly splurge on a motel right now, and the coffee table is sturdy enough."

He glowers. "Do you have a spare bag?"

"It's drowning." I gesture to the soaked bag, suppressing my emotions for when I'm alone. "I can leave my clothes out to dry. No biggie. And I have all my ballet stuff in this bag." I lift the bag I take to class. As long as my expensive ballet attire is untouched, I can ward off a full breakdown. I move to stand by the door to see him out, but he frowns.

Elias Westbrook is angry.

"If you think I'd let you stay here, you must think I'm a pretty shitty person."

I know he wouldn't, and that's the problem. A moment ago, I had no options but to sleep somewhere outside. Knowing that Elias is not only worried but cares enough to insist I not sleep here makes the tingling sensation in my chest move to my gut.

"I don't think you're a shitty person. You're kind of the opposite," I say.

The smell of smoke and the distant sound of closing fire truck doors fill the air around us.

"You're not staying here," he repeats.

Maybe I'm being stubborn, but I need to be alone. That's how it's always been. "All my clothes are soaked or burnt, and I don't think a cheap motel will feel any better than this."

"You're coming with me. You can wear my clothes, and I'll put yours in the wash."

We stare at each other for so long, it borders on discomfort. He's already helping me with ballet and randomly bringing me dinner. I can't take more. I won't be a burden.

My lip lifts in an attempt to break free of this stalemate. "You just want to see me in one of your T-shirts, don't you?" I joke, dropping my gaze to the melted self-care basket. *Screw you, magnolia.* The longer I avoid his irritated look, the more I recognize my burnt things on the debris-filled floor.

"I want to be sure you won't pass out from smoke inhalation."

"There are windows. You're overreacting."

He releases a gruff breath and comes to stand just inches from me.

"You know what I think, Sage?" He's close enough that I have to strain my neck to look at him. "I think you talk a lot of shit, but when someone offers to take care of you, you hide behind your jokes to avoid asking for help."

I swallow.

"So, I'm not asking. Gather what's left of your things, and get your ass in my car or I'll carry you there."

Whoa. My whiplashed brain leaves me no choice but to quickly pick up my wet duffel and some toiletries. I can't ignore the knot of uncertainty that finally untangles in my stomach.

Elias watches me from the threshold, leaning against the door-frame with his arms crossed and a stern look on his face. Sweet Elias is nowhere to be seen, but that might be my fault.

He takes the bag from my hold and shuts my apartment door behind us. Then he slips his hand into mine as we head to his car.

SMOKE NO LONGER lingers on my skin. Instead, I'm sniffing Elias's body wash. I'd pay good money to have it injected into my veins.

We didn't talk much on the drive to his place, nor when he sat me at the dining table and I devoured a bowl of creamy rigatoni pasta. After my shower, I changed into his large sweats and a T-shirt.

In the living room, Elias, Aiden, and a stunning girl with long brown hair and eyes to match turn to look at me. Their conversation halts, and I stand there awkwardly.

"Didn't mean to interrupt," I say quietly.

"You're not," the girl says. She stands and engulfs me in a hug. "I heard what happened. I'm so sorry. That must be devastating."

"It's not too bad. I didn't have much stuff anyway." I play it down, but I'm screwed. Crashing with Elias isn't permanent, and soon I'll need a place to stay. Nothing is as cheap as my rent-controlled apartment, and I know my teaching salary won't cover much.

When Elias comes to stand beside me, his arm brushes against mine, and a static charge shoots to my fingertips. "This is Summer, Aiden's girlfriend," he informs.

"Totally meant to introduce myself. But it's like I already know you with how much the Thunder fan base talks about you," Summer says.

"Oh God, I can't imagine what they're saying about me now."

"Don't worry. Aside from the few trolls, it's all good things. And the guys are constantly talking about you. You're basically a celebrity at the hockey house."

Elias calls the house they lived in during college the hockey house, so she's referring to their friends.

"They'll be ecstatic to meet you when they come to visit soon," Aiden says. Then he glances at the time on his phone, wrapping his arm around Summer to pull her with him. "We're going to head to bed, but make yourself at home, Sage. You can stay as long as you need."

"Thank you," I say, watching their retreat. I'm hyper-aware it's just Elias and me now.

"You can take my room," he simply says.

I'm about to refuse and suggest that I take the couch, but I don't get a chance to because he walks past me and across the hall to the main bathroom. I stand there, deciding to wait, but when I hear the shower turn on, I head back to his room.

It takes everything in me not to snoop, but when I'm going to switch off the bedside lamp, I notice a smooth flat stone sitting on his dresser. Like the one from our date. When the hall washroom door creaks open, I drop the stone and turn off the lights before slipping under the comforter.

That's the moment I realize how shitty my mattress at the apartment was. In the dark of his room, I close my eyes as I feel the exhaustion hit.

Hours later, I'm still wrestling with my mind, wide awake.

The heavy awareness of Elias sleeping just a few feet away is what I'm choosing to blame my sleepless state on tonight. Not the insomnia I've had for most of my life.

The occasional sound of cars passing or an ambulance siren wailing and washing the walls in red accompanies my restless mind. Then a loud noise from inside the apartment jolts me upright. Thinking it's Elias, because Aiden and Summer are asleep on the opposite side of the hall, I tiptoe out of the room, in need of some conversation that takes place outside of my head. A sharp intake of breath and a grunt from the living room make me turn toward it and that's when I see him.

The quick rise and fall of Elias's chest and the twitching of his arms look exactly like someone having a bad dream. No. Not a bad dream. A nightmare.

His body is bent awkwardly, and his legs stretch past the length of the couch. The six-foot-four defenseman has never looked more uncomfortable. Yet, he's sleeping here because I'm hoarding his room like a homeless troll.

Elias jerks, and the moon illuminates the light sheen of sweat on his forehead.

When Sean was little, he used to have night terrors. My parents were never home, so I'd check on him periodically through the night. Hello, insomnia.

But what I learned was never to wake someone in the middle of a night terror. I know why Sean had nightmares; you don't come from a family like ours and grow up to be normal. But Elias seems so secure. Like he has it all figured out and sticks to his made-up life plan like it would kill him if he deviated from it. I stare at him for so long it might seem like I'm trying to read his mind, but I can't even do that when he's awake and talking, much less when he's asleep.

What chaos is trapped in that beautiful head of his?

Quietly, I kneel by the couch and slip my hand into his shaking one. To my surprise, he grasps it like a life raft. His breathing and pulse level out, and his exhausted body deflates.

My focus remains on his hand, which doesn't release mine, and I let him keep it, trying not to think about the smile that touches my lips. Drawing tiny patterns on his skin with my thumb relaxes me, and I debate whether I should just sleep on the floor next to him, but I don't ponder for long because his even breaths halt, and brown eyes are on me.

When he sees our intertwined hands, he sits up and releases me so quickly, it leaves a cold sensation in my palm and in my chest. He looks worried, I must look hurt, yet we both try our best to school our expressions.

"I can't sleep," I blurt, not wanting him to feel embarrassed.

"Is it my bed?" he asks in a raspy, sleep-laced voice that tightens my abdomen. His tone is rough, as if he's irritated that his bed is the reason for my lack of sleep. Like it's become his number one enemy at this moment.

"No, your bed is perfect." *And it smells like you too.* "I just have this super fun thing called insomnia."

"How?" He appears quizzical. "You're like the chirpiest person I know."

"I'm going to take that as a compliment, for your sake." He winces but I don't let him apologize. "I developed it when I was a teenager, and it shows up occasionally." *Like every night for the past year.*

When Elias stands, he gestures for me to follow him. I feel like an inmate who failed to escape the prison and is being taken back by the warden. A warden I kind of want to sleep with.

"I never realized how much light comes through those curtains," he says, standing by his bedroom window, glaring at the streetlamps and city lights.

"Don't worry, I'm always like this. Light or no light, I still wouldn't be able to sleep."

He stops for a beat, then heads for the door. "Call me if you need anything."

Anything? My body is on high alert, and I know if he leaves I'll lie here and stare at the ceiling thinking about him. When he's passing the threshold, the words tumble out of me.

"Elias," I say. He turns, and I swallow. "Will you sleep with me?"

He blinks several times.

"Sage . . ." Elias starts.

"Just for tonight!" I rush out. "That couch can't be comfortable. You're kind of huge."

"It's not that bad."

"Please?" I stare up at him. "I think I'll be able to fall asleep if there's someone beside me. To put my mind at ease, you know." I'm lying. That's never worked. Sometimes Sean would come into my room after a nightmare, and I still couldn't get a wink of sleep.

"I'm not sure that's a good idea."

I walk right up to him. The thin T-shirt probably isn't helping my case. "Why not? You're hot and all, but I can keep it in my pants for one night, rookie." I allow my finger to trail down his hard abs in a teasing move. I poke him. "Unless you don't think you can."

A strangled noise leaves him, and a spark of satisfaction rolls through me. I watch him for an answer, his chest rising and falling evenly like he's weighing out the pros and cons.

Then his tense shoulders drop. "To help you sleep."

The ground shakes, or rather, I do. His response leaves me blinking until I regain enough composure to come up with a nonchalant reply. "Yeah, yeah. Now come on, I have classes to teach in the morning."

Elias Westbrook is following me to bed!

Elias removes his shirt. His corded back muscles flex with the movement, and his broad shoulders fall on an exhale. Lusting over your fake boyfriend should come with an advisory notice. Not that I would heed it anyway.

My internet sleuthing revealed the video that got people talking about the rookie, and I don't blame them. He's as sweet and attractive in the video as he is in real life. There isn't much else needed past that point. After that, I fell into a rabbit hole of watching his Frozen Four goals and interviews. Now, this private strip show is curated for every dirty thought in my mind. I snap out of my hallucination when he glances at me, and I dive under the covers.

"Night," I say, my voice muffled under the comforter.

"Good night, Sage."

With one click of the lamp, we're bathed in darkness. In the quiet of the room with the heat of his body in the king-size bed, I realize this might be my stupidest idea yet. Sleeping with my fake boyfriend, and pretending I'm not as susceptible to catching fire as a match to a flame, isn't very bright.

Minutes pass, and I've reverted to counting sheep, but they start looking a lot like a bunch of shirtless Eliases, and I'm hot all over again. I flip onto my side, then curl up in the fetal position, then turn on my back once again to stare at the ceiling.

"You good?" There's that raspy voice again. Pure torture for my overactive brain.

"Mm-hmm." I clear my throat. "Counting sheep."

It must be an acceptable answer because he doesn't say anything else. I, on the other hand, have found a way to twirl horizontally to try to discover the perfect spot.

"Come here." Elias's deep voice cuts through the silent room and startles me.

"Are you talking to me?" I whisper.

"No, I'm talking to the other person in bed with us," he deadpans. "I said, come here, Sage."

The demand hits me like a jolt between the legs. There are so many other contexts in which I could imagine him saying that, but right now I can only think of one, and it's better left unsaid. I don't even have a comeback for his sarcasm.

My eyes have adjusted to the darkness and find him looking right at me. "Where?"

"Here." He lifts his arm, like it's the most natural thing. "You're tossing and turning, and you said it would ease your mind if someone's sleeping beside you, right?"

Did I say that? Sage from a few minutes ago was a complete idiot. I scoot closer, leaving plenty of space for the Holy Spirit. But as I'm frozen in place, he pulls me against him. I squeak, and I have a split moment of insanity where I want to press my ass into him. I don't. *Obviously.*

"Better?" he whispers right by my ear.

No. He's warm and cozy and safe. "Yup."

His thumb absently strokes my stomach, and it might as well burn through my shirt. There's something very alive under these sheets, and I'm terrified he'll feel the pulse if he moves just a few inches lower.

The weight of his arm, the clean smell of his soap, and the even beat of his heart against my back feel all too soothing. A second ago, there was no way I would fall asleep, but after lying in his arms like this, it's scary to admit my made-up remedy might work.

"You always smell like vanilla." I can feel his voice in my hair. It makes me shiver.

I give an awkward chuckle, unsure what exactly is happening between us right now. Is this an invitation? Is *vanilla* a code word? Should I take off my clothes?

His contented sigh is all I hear, like somehow my lotion has put a spell on him.

"Are you asleep?" I ask.

There's a long pause before he shifts to fit me into the curve of his body. "Trying to."

"Oh."

He sighs, and I don't particularly like it. "What's on your mind?"

I'd do anything to make this less awkward, but Elias seems

completely okay as we are. "Nothing. You should sleep. Just because I'm an insomniac doesn't mean you have to be too."

"I'm awake." My long silence pushes him to continue. "I don't get them every night."

My ears perk like an excited dog. "The nightmares?"

"They used to be rare, but once I got to the league they've gotten worse. They come back when I'm stressed."

Cuddling and revealing his deepest darkest secrets is so unlike Elias, I have the urge to turn and make sure it's not a very warm robot. "Have you talked to someone? Sean used to get them, and his child psychologist really helped."

"No. I never want my parents to know and feel guilty about anything."

I try not to say something that might offend him, but I can't hold back. "That's not really fair to you. All that extra stress on your body can't be helping hockey either."

Instead of pulling away like I expected, he buries his head in my hair. "Guess not."

Judging by his tone, I'm assuming the conversation is over, but even as my eyes start to close, I ask, "Does it help you too? Having someone here, I mean."

"I wouldn't know. This is a first for me," he replies.

"You've never just slept with someone?"

"Never. But I'm beginning to think you'll always be the exception."

FIFTEEN

ELIAS

I'VE BURNED THREE pancakes in the span of ten minutes.

Scraping the pan clean, I toss the charred ones into the compost and restart the batter.

Cooking usually relaxes me, but today it fails because I've been on edge since last night.

I can still feel Sage's cold feet resting on my calves. She only fidgeted under my hold for a few minutes before falling asleep. I'm not sure how long it usually takes or if I helped, but I'm glad she got some rest. The number of classes and auditions she does requires sleep. But the trade-off with last night's arrangement is that *I* couldn't sleep. Not when I felt her *everywhere*.

With her body cocooned against mine and our conversation replaying in my head, I didn't realize how much time passed. It soon turned to morning, and the light from the shitty curtains sliced through the room. I ordered blackout curtains as soon as I slipped out of bed.

I'm plating the first decent pancake when Sage ambles into the kitchen. It's still early so I'm surprised to see her because neither

Aiden nor Summer is awake. Aiden and I have to head out in an hour because we have a game in Tampa tonight.

Sage looks a little lost, and she freezes when she spots me. Her eyes drift down my torso. I should have thrown on a shirt, but I didn't want to wake her by opening the squeaky closet door.

She rubs her eye, and the collar of my shirt slips off one shoulder, showing the smooth skin that's there. She looks both rested and disheveled, and I have to turn away, just in time to save another pancake from burning.

"Sit. I'll bring you a plate," I say.

"Don't treat me like a guest, Elias," she scolds.

Then the sound of cupboards opening is the only noise in the kitchen besides my thumping heart. I try my best not to stare when she shuffles on tiptoes to find the right cupboard.

Aiden and I put the dishes pretty high because it's just us living here, but seeing Sage struggle to reach them, I realize that might need to change. I let her try on her own until she lifts her leg to climb onto the counter. I lower the heat of the stove to move behind her.

She stumbles into my chest. I reach an arm around her to grab a stack of plates.

"I could have reached them," she mutters, sounding breathless.

"I think you mean *thank you*."

She twists and her gaze catches mine, holding it for a beat. "Thank you, Elias."

I nod, knowing her words have less to do with the plate and a lot to do with last night. I break our eye contact and focus on plating her food.

"Are my pancakes smiling?" she asks, amused. I hadn't realized I'd done it, but I'm so used to making them for the guys at Dalton, it's autopilot. Kian would suggest something lewd, and I always indulged him by arranging the chocolate chips.

She's beaming as I follow her to the table and take a seat across from her. Before I can reach for the maple syrup to pour it on my pancakes, she snatches it. "I'll do it."

She flips the bottle to draw a swirl, but her aim runs askew, and the syrup coats my thumb.

Sage's eyes widen as she assesses my blank expression, waiting for a reaction, but I don't give her one. I only stare right at her.

"What? Want me to lick it off?" There's a teasing lilt to her voice that sends a lance of heat straight to my groin. She looks at my throat and watches my Adam's apple bob with amusement, giving away my thoughts.

Then in a moment of what can only be caused by my lack of sleep, I lift my hand and hold it between us on the table. My thumb is inches away from where her lips are parted in shock, and the silent challenge dangles between us. The room is so quiet you can hear the water dripping from the faucet in the kitchen.

She leans forward, and bluff or not, the only thing I know for sure in that moment is I'm truly fucked. Sage takes my thumb in her mouth and seals her lips around it. She hums when her hot tongue touches the syrup and licks it clean before she takes me deeper.

Our eyes lock.

Her pink lips form an O around my thumb, causing all the blood in my body to rush south. My jaw is set tightly to keep a groan from escaping my throat.

Then door hinges creak down the hall, and Sage pulls back, releasing me with a *pop* just as Aiden and Summer step into the dining room. I drop my hand back to the dining table.

Aiden wordlessly heads to the kitchen, probably to make Summer chai as she slips into the chair beside Sage and exclaims, "Pancakes!"

Summer is particularly interested in getting close to my fake girlfriend. But even as Sage has a full-blown conversation with Summer at the dining table, I can see the way her neck is flushed and how a deeper color flares onto her chest.

I can barely move with how hard I am. For the entirety of break-fast, she doesn't look at me, not even once, and I can't seem to take my eyes off her.

Sage 1, Elias 0.

THE THREE-HOUR FLIGHT didn't go as expected, because I spent the handful of hours fantasizing about maple syrup and a certain pair of lips. The image is bad for my brain, and it doesn't help that soon I'll be in a hotel room with some time to kill before the game. Though I'm trying my best not to imagine those lips sucking something else.

It doesn't help when Socket, our goalie, who's been on the team for five years, and Owen Hart, our newest right-winger, who are sit-ting in the section next to Aiden and me, continue to talk about the women they've been with while in Toronto. But their conversation doesn't interest me at all because, unlike Socket, Owen still talks about women like he's in college. Hearing him go on about things he does with girls doesn't sit right with me.

"Mind keeping it down? We don't want to hear about that shit," I say, interrupting Owen's useless conversation. That grabs his atten-tion, and Socket winces when he looks at me.

Owen nods, but the smirk on his face is a knowing one, and from the looks of it I'm missing something. Before I can ask him what he finds so funny, Aiden pulls my attention back to the tablet we're us-ing to help me figure out a better play for my lagging goal. This time he's identified a play where he can assist, and allow me to let go and break out of the box I've built around myself.

It's still before noon when we land in Tampa. Our game isn't for another few hours, so we head to our respective hotels. This time I don't need to worry about naked women waiting in my room and instead fall straight into bed. It's a foreign feeling not being stressed about what people might be saying about me next, and I owe that to Sage.

My room service order follows shortly after, and when I've eaten my pregame meal, I'm checking my gear bag before the bus is set to pick us up.

When we arrive at the Amalie Arena, I'm already in my gear, eager to hit the ice for our pregame skate. Finally on the rink, I knock over the mountain of pucks stacked against the boards and send them sliding across the ice for our warm-up. We glide toward the nets, focusing on our shots and passes, feeling the familiar rhythm of our routine. The sound of blades cutting through the ice fills the air, and with each shot of mine surpassing Socket stationed in front of the net, I'm ready.

Right as the game starts, my mind drifts to the girl who's been on my mind all day. I wonder whether she'll watch tonight's game with Summer at the apartment, or if she's busy.

"Tonight's your chance." Coach Wilson comes up behind me, his gaze on his clipboard.

He's right. Tampa is the worst-performing team in the Eastern Conference, and I should be able to use that to my advantage tonight. The ultimatum dangling over my head adds to the pressure of today's game, and I lock in to finally prove everyone wrong. Mostly to shove the goal in Marcus's smug face.

"I know," I say, slipping past him to skate to the centerline for the national anthem. When the whistle blows, we're in full swing. It isn't long before I'm taking shots at the net.

In the second period, my wrist shot flies past the goalie's glove, and my heart stops as I watch the puck whiz past him in slow motion. The noise of the crowd fades to a muffled static in my ears. Then it pings off the crossbar, landing on the opposite side of me, and connects to the stick of Tampa's defender. The tension in my body returns, and the guys bump into me in a silent show of support for the miss.

Blood pounds in my ears and ignites a fire under my skin for the rest of the game. It shoots me forward for each shot to the net, but I only end up assisting every single goal scored tonight, including the tiebreaker from Aiden, which gains a chorus of boos from the crowd when the buzzer goes off, and we win 4–3.

"That was sick!" Socket shouts, bumping into me in the locker room.

I'm fresh out of my postgame shower and still replaying all the shots I missed. Assisting goals for my teammates is all a part of the sport, but I'm tired of it. I can imagine the organization crossing each game off the calendar, waiting until Marcus can sign the papers for my trade and get rid of me for good.

"We're celebrating tonight. My friend's family owns a bar in the city," says Socket.

Aiden glances at me, and I shake my head, not at all up for being surrounded by my drunk teammates.

"I'm still sore from the last game. I'll see you guys tomorrow."

"Me too," Aiden says, packing his bag.

When Socket groans and mutters something about us being the most boring rookies, he turns to the rest of our team to convince them to come out.

"You don't have to stay back because of me."

Aiden glances at me. "When have I ever wanted to celebrate something without you?"

"You scored the game-winning goal, man. That's worth a celebration."

He only shrugs, and I can't help but feel bad for dragging him down too. But I can't fake it right now, so I let myself believe he's not in the mood to go out either.

SIXTEEN

ELIAS

"ARE YOU ONLY calling me because you don't want to seem like a loser all alone in your hotel room?" Sage asks.

The minute she answers, I know I made the right choice by calling her. Just the sound of her voice eases the disappointment of tonight's game.

"Has no one ever taught you that words can be hurtful?" I feign offense.

"Didn't really have the best role models growing up, so no," she shoots back, and I almost apologize, but she's quick to speak again. "I saw your assist, and your shots on goal percentage. You killed it tonight, whether you want to believe it or not."

"Hardly impressive. I still don't—"

"Have a goal, yeah, yeah, we know," she interrupts. "If I ask you to do something, will you do it?"

Yes. "Depends."

"I want you to go out."

I chuckle. "You know you can hang up if you hate talking to me that much."

"One, I love talking no matter who it is. Two, you need to leave your pathetic reverie and go out with the team. Even Aiden hasn't celebrated his overtime goal because you want to be chained to your mattress."

"How do you know that?"

"Summer was just on the phone with him, and I assumed his reluctance to go out was because of a certain grumpy rookie."

Even though she's taking a dig at me, it puts a smile on my face that Sage has Summer to talk to because she's mentioned not having friends.

"So you don't want to talk to me?"

"No—well, technically yes. I want you to go out with the team and celebrate."

I don't answer.

"Elias." She huffs. "You have this twisted idea that keeping your expectations low and not being excited about good things in your life will save you from disappointment, but you're wrong. Good things need to be celebrated, because bad things will find a way to be acknowledged regardless."

I sit up on the bed. "It was a few assists. It's not impressive in the slightest."

"It was to me. It was to your teammates, and it was to your fans," she urges. "Now, go out with your team and celebrate the win. Paparazzi be damned!"

"What if they spin a story? I don't want anyone to question whether I'm faithful to you."

"Let them. I'll be more than happy to remind everyone that you're in a happy committed relationship with the love of your life."

"Love of my life, eh?"

There's a pause. "Give or take."

"Okay." I give in. "But I'm only going for a few minutes."

"An hour."

"Thirty minutes."

"Forty-five," she counters.

I chuckle, shaking my head at her dedication to the cause. "Fine."

"Really?"

The excitement is clear in her voice, and it's sweet that she cares about whether I'm stuck in my hotel room or out with friends.

"When are you going to learn that I'm incapable of saying no to you?"

THE BAR THE guys chose is much classier than I expected. The rooftop bar is covered in ambient lighting that provides a cozy feel. From the looks of it, the staff has reserved the entire rooftop to accommodate us, so we can relax without having our every move caught on camera.

Aiden was in his room exactly like Sage said, and when I asked if he wanted to join the guys, he was up and ready to go in minutes. I'm guessing his girlfriend told him to get out of his room too. Although neither of us plan to drink, the easy conversation that flows between the guys makes this outing worthwhile.

I hate to admit it, but I am having a good time getting to know the players off the ice. Some of them, I've looked up to for years.

"What made you come out tonight?" a tipsy Socket asks.

"Sage."

He likes my answer, because he pats my back like a proud father. "That girl is good for you. I mean, just look at everything you did today."

His happy words confuse me. "What do you mean? I tried to get one so many times, with everyone's help, and I still choked, exactly like you said all rookies do."

"You still played a hell of a game. You didn't score, but none of your plays looked amateur. One of the reasons we won today was because of your assists. Celebrate that."

I clink my nonalcoholic beer with his bottle, and he takes a swig before walking off to sing along to the song playing over the speakers. Sitting back in my chair, we're all laughing when a few others join the off-key chorus. And even as I'm sitting there having a good time, my phone feels heavy in my pocket, so I pull it out and send a text.

SAGE

> **Elias:** How much longer before I can bail?
>
> **Sage:** You're ridiculous.
>
> **Elias:** I'm serious.
>
> **Sage:** You're having fun, I know it. Stop texting me and socialize.
>
> **Elias:** Fine, but at least tell me you're having fun too.

Texting her turns into my own personal torture because she sends me a picture. Summer's in the background with a face mask, and Sage beams brightly. She has a towel on her head and those eye patches with tiny gold stars under her eyes. I'm assuming it's a self-care night because she's got a foot up on the couch with the foam separators and a bottle of nail polish, and she's wearing only a white T-shirt. She looks stunning, and I have half a mind to ditch the team plane and take a red-eye back home just to watch her do something as mundane as painting her toes.

> **Elias:** Jesus. I'm in public, Beaumont.
>
> **Sage:** Huh? I'm just wearing a baggy T-shirt.
>
> **Elias:** And you wear the hell out of my T-shirts.

The text bubbles pop up twice before finally disappearing. I'm still stuck in our texts, staring at the picture of her for an unhealthy amount of time. When I scroll, I notice the one she sent the other day for me to post with the generic caption. Instead of using the picture she sent of us leaving the Pint from a few weeks ago, I find another one that makes me smile. I open the app and post the picture. Shoving my phone back in my pocket, I turn my attention back to the guys and try to focus on something other than her for once.

SEVENTEEN

SAGE

WHEN PERFORMANCE DAY rolls around, the preshow jitters are running rampant.

Elias got in early this morning, and I only knew that because my insomnia was in full force. The latest video I posted online was liked by all types of accounts, two of them being the NHL and Toronto Thunder page. But the one that had my hands clammy was a like from the official NBT page after multiple people tagged them in the comments. I've made it clear that my goal is to dance for the company, and now that I know they're aware of my existence, I'm terrified.

But my thoughts are divided between the possibility of fulfilling my dream and the picture Elias posted last night.

Yesterday, Summer and I were having a self-care night and watching a Turkish drama she insisted I would love. She was right, because I was glued to the TV by the second episode. It was something I'd never done with someone else before, and it felt nice. Relaxing, even.

When I told her about my performance next week, she was willing to delay her flight back to Dalton to attend. Obviously, I didn't let her do that, but the thought swelled my heart.

Then, as she was showing me embarrassing videos of their friends in college, she gasped. Elias had posted the picture of him and me with the star-infused under-eye masks, the one I took the first night he came over. Our heads are right next to each other, and he's staring at me while I'm smiling. He captioned it **the best part of my day**.

I had a physical reaction to seeing those six words under a picture of us posted by his own volition. Not even because they led to my followers ascending into the five-digit category, but because I felt hot, my hands got sweaty, and I had to continuously remind myself that it was fake. Summer's teasing didn't help the heat burning my cheeks.

This morning, Elias was sound asleep, so I slipped out to head straight to the studio for a quick practice session. Now, the organized chaos backstage in the auditorium of Rosedale High School gets my adrenaline pumping.

I sent the address to my uncle, and I hesitated, then deleted the same text I was about to send Elias. He's exhausted from his away game, that much was clear from him sleeping in, and I'm sure he only said he'd attend to be nice. He's doing more than enough by posting me.

My dress feels tight, and I hope it's tight because of my nerves and not because I've gone up a size. I push the automatic thought away. I don't think like that anymore. But it only took a few bad ballet directors during my teenage years to make those thoughts run constant. It's been hard keeping them out, but I try. I don't give myself food restrictions or focus on a certain size.

I wear my clothes, my clothes don't wear me.

When there's a knock on my dressing room door—which doubles as the janitor's storage closet—I finish sticking a final gem on the corner of my eye and open the door. I'm expecting to see our stage manager or the dancer I'm sharing the small room with, but it's Elias.

My breath whooshes out of me, and I stare at him, completely stunned. He's in dark jeans and a black T-shirt under a thin midnight blue jacket. The cotton fabric of the shirt underneath stretches across his chest, and I secretly wish it would spontaneously tear off. His body crowds the threshold, and he holds a bouquet of pink and white peonies.

"You're here," I say breathlessly. His eyes roam the green costume and the delicate chiffon with silver embroidery. I'm wearing a jewel-encrusted crown and a moonstone necklace to emulate Titania, the fairy queen.

He clears his throat. "I said I would be."

I eye the flowers. "Are those for me?"

Elias doesn't answer. Instead, his gaze soaks into me, burning a path in a slow perusal of every inch of my skin. My heart thumps wildly against my rib cage.

"Elias."

His gaze flicks to mine, and he quickly hands me the flowers. I assess the pretty bouquet, smelling the sweetness with a hint of citrus.

I shoot him a pointed glance. "What happened to the no-flowers rule?"

"I didn't like it."

I scoff. "That's not fair. What about the rules *I* don't like?"

"Why?" He takes a step closer. "You think you'll need a good luck kiss?"

A hot flush ignites a chaotic fire beneath my skin. I swallow, letting my gaze fall to his lips. "Wouldn't be the end of the world."

The silence breeds anticipation in my thumping heart.

"Might be," he whispers before he moves to the vanity lighting the room. "So, what's your pregame ritual?"

He fiddles with my makeup and notepad. "I usually make notations of the choreography and run through each position in my head. But it always feels like I miss a few anyway."

He nods, quietly taking in the tiny space. A knock sounds, and my stage manager pops his head in. "We're on in five, Sage."

When the door closes, the air feels tight again. I worry I'll be too short of breath to perform if he stays here a second longer. But when he enters my bubble, I let him.

Elias leans forward, and everything else ceases to exist. The noise of the dancers in the hallways, the dragging of props by the stage crew, and the PA system announcing the time till curtain up. At this moment, it's only him and me. And the cardiac event I'm having.

But instead of claiming my lips like I hope, he kisses my forehead. "Good luck," he whispers, then walks out before I can comprehend any of it.

My mind is in a whirlwind when I make it to the side stage and wait for my cue. But the second I hear the first notes, I focus only on dancing.

The blinding stage lights flush me in white and make the sparkling fabric in my dress shimmer as I move into my first position. This time when I glance out into the crowd, I see my uncle right up front, smiling as always. But the face that sends a dart to my chest is Elias's. His gaze sticks to me like magnets to steel, and I feel a static charge envelop me.

When my act is complete, I watch the rest of the show from the side stage, and I'm still high from my performance when my old teacher, Madame Laurent, taps my shoulder.

"Sage, I've seen your clips online. My students absolutely love you," she gushes.

After a performance, it's hard to reel in my emotions, so my eyes water when I hug her tight. Amy Laurent has been a constant in my life from the age of eleven to eighteen, so she's seen me grow through all the big phases of my life.

"How have you been?"

Her sweet query makes me smile because I remember her as the strict ballet teacher who always pushed me to the limit. "Auditioning. I'm waiting to secure an audition for *Swan Lake*."

"Your goals haven't changed, but you have," she says thoughtfully.

"And the moment they see you dance, you'll be in. I'm sure of it."
Then she cocks her head. "Is the hockey player in the front row your
boyfriend? I'd like to meet him after the show."

I nod, and I'm hoping she doesn't see what just a mention of him
does to my face.

Shortly after, we assemble back onstage for our final bow and
performance notes from our directors. When I head to the main
lobby of the school, I spot my uncle.

"You killed it. Amy was ecstatic to have you perform the guest
role," he says.

For the longest time, I thought Madame Laurent and my uncle
would make a great couple. He was in a relationship a few years back,
so I never said anything. But now is perfect.

"She's single, you know."

"I see your teenage dream of us getting together hasn't gone away."

Uncle Marcus broke up with his fiancée a few years ago. He never
talks about it, and I never ask, but I've always had a feeling it was
because of us. I doubt that any woman would be okay with her partner neglecting her for the children of his drug-addicted half brother.

"Never."

He gives me a stony look. "Come on, I'll drop you at home."

It's then I realize he has no clue about my disastrous apartment
fire or that I'm living with his rookie. "I'm going to stay a bit." I try
to ignore the conversation we should be having.

He's impassive. "It's hard to miss a six-foot-four hockey player in
the crowd, Sage."

My face feels hot. "I meant to tell you."

"Before or after he announced it in an interview on live television?"

I wince.

"I know you're an adult, and you can make your own decisions.
But just let me be a part of some of them, yeah? Even if I'm not particularly enthused about this one."

"He's a good guy, Uncle Marcus. You haven't even given him a chance."

"Trust me, I've given him a chance."

As if on cue, Elias comes up behind me, sliding his arm around my waist like any regular boyfriend. That doesn't stop my breath from hitching though.

"Eli," my uncle acknowledges.

"Marcus," Elias returns.

"Text me when you're home, Sage," my uncle says before he walks out the doors.

Elias watches my uncle's descent with a grimace. "You two need to figure something out," I say, turning to him fully. "So, what did you think?"

"About?"

I knock a playful hand to his chest. "Everything. Rate me."

Elias finally looks at me, and his slow perusal makes me regret asking.

"The outfit, a solid ten. The makeup, another ten. But the performance . . ." He trails off.

When I'm going to smack his arm, he captures my wrist and pulls me right to him.

Elias removes a paper from his pocket. It's the notes from my dressing room with my dance sequence. "An eleven. You were amazing. I googled all the moves, and you hit every single point."

I'm unsure what to make of this. "Why would you do that?"

He must understand what I mean, because his brown eyes hold mine. "Because you second-guess yourself and think you're doing terribly onstage when you're not. Just in case you forgot, I wanted to be the one to remind you."

His words cause physical reactions in my body. But he mistakes my shiver from his compliment for being cold and slips off his jacket to slide it over my shoulders.

I pinch the jacket tighter around me, and when I reach into the pockets there's a familiar pack of shiny gems. "What's this?"

"Your extra glue and crystals."

It's the pack I left at home. "Why did you bring them?"

"You told me that one time they came off before you even got onstage and how upset you were. I didn't want that happening again."

A foreign feeling grips my heart, and to escape it, I engulf him in a tight hug. My hands barely make it around his shoulders, but Elias easily lifts me off my toes, and I melt into his arms.

Back on my feet, I keep smiling. "A hug like that and I might forget this is fak—"

He cuts off my words when he seals his lips to mine.

The kiss is gentle and tentative, like he's surprised to feel my mouth on his, ready and reciprocating without even a hint of delay. My fists tighten in his shirt, wanting him closer despite the sweltering summer breeze. He tilts my head to deepen the kiss, and my nerves jumble into a tangle of colorful Christmas lights. He fists the back of my hair, and the sting accompanies the hot lust igniting my core. My mind works overtime to make sense of the possessive touch, the action like a dusty puzzle piece you find on the floor to finally complete the picture.

Elias Westbrook likes to be in control.

If my own wasn't so erratic, I'd be shocked to find his heartbeat hammering under my palm. The sigh that leaves me is of pure pleasure and satisfaction, but his answering moan is tortured. The quick, teasing sweep of his tongue leaves a tingle in my mouth that begs for more.

When he pulls back, I'm disoriented. Like I've gotten off a roller coaster and have to lean against something to get my bearings straight. But if I leaned against Elias, I'm sure I'd rip my clothes off and ask him to take me in the school bathroom or something equally as stupid.

There's a flash of white that brings me back to earth. A teenager stands in the crowd of families and shamelessly points his phone at us.

My gaze slips back to Elias's blank expression, and for a second, I think I imagined the kiss. But the smudge of shiny lip gloss on his mouth tells me it was real. I want to cover him with glossy lip-shaped marks and claim him like an animal.

"You must be the boyfriend."

Amy Laurent's voice makes me stiffen, and I push away from Elias. He shakes my former teacher's hand, and nods proudly. "Yes, ma'am."

"I've been teaching Sage forever, and I've never seen her this free when she dances. It's nice to see, and I'm hoping it's partly thanks to you."

"It's all her. She's a whole new person on that stage." Elias pulls me into his side, and she watches us with a wide smile that has to hurt her cheeks.

"Come on, we need a group picture," Madame Laurent says.

The dancers bring in their partners, and parents, as they crowd around us.

When the dancers are shuffling to take a picture, I can't hold back. I clutch the fabric of his shirt and yank. "What happened to no PDA?" I whisper when he leans down.

I can see his Adam's apple bob before he answers. "It felt necessary at that moment."

"So, it wasn't fake?" My heart thumps wildly.

"No."

"No?"

"You were a second away from blurting that this is fake, with people all around us. Filming us with their phones. I've seen articles about this being a PR stunt and didn't want to add fuel to that fire."

I deflate. He was trying to shut me up, but even as my hope withers, my mind latches on to the last part of his sentence. "You're still reading those?"

He shrugs.

Even with my lips still tingling from that kiss, I'm irritated that Elias still lets headlines get to him. He doesn't deserve it, and I want to be the one to show him that.

Elias takes a seat on the bench beside Madame Laurent, then he loops an arm around my midsection to pull me into his lap. I stiffen.

His lips brush against my ear. "Relax."

My wobbly smile barely holds, then the flash goes off, and I realize Elias didn't look at the camera at all. His eyes are on me.

EIGHTEEN

SAGE

THE EVENING LIGHT bathes the studio in a soft glow, illuminating the wooden floors of the room as I guide my students through a series of movements. "Arms lifted, extend your lines, and remember, soft movements."

Today's class is a coed class for ages six to nine years. We're practicing the basics to give them a solid foundation. They mirror my movements, and I let them practice on their own for a few beats. Nina, one of the older students, flutters around the class to help others. The eight-year-old girl reminds me so much of myself that I harbor a soft spot for her.

There have been times that I've caught her walking home alone, so I'd accompany her. Based on how she shuts down when I ask about her parents, I know that things aren't great for her at home. So far I'm here to step in if need be, but I know more than anyone what it's like to have shitty parents. Ballet is a solace for me, and I'd never muddy her experience by overstepping.

My phone vibrates on the edge of the studio's mirrored barre. My attention moves away from Nina to peek at the screen. There's a voicemail from the National Ballet, which I auditioned for last week.

The riot that ensues in my chest is nothing like the soothing piano notes that fill the room.

"And arabesque, extend those lines," I encourage, even as a sliver of anticipation seeps in. Not wanting to wait any longer, I grab my phone to play the voicemail.

"This is Sonya, speaking from the National Ballet of Canada, and we're calling regarding your recent audition. Unfortunately, you have not been selected at this time. Our fall auditions . . ."

Rejection causes an ugly knot to form in my throat and a black inky liquid to pool in the acid of my stomach. I take a steadying breath, masking the disappointment that threatens to spill over.

For the next forty minutes of class, the voicemail sits on my chest like an anchor, and breathing around it feels impossible. But I manage to finish the class without any of the kids seeing me break down into a blubbering mess. I'll take that as a win. My only win of the day.

When I enter Elias's apartment, I hear the TV in the living room, and it eases the lonely feeling a smidge. The guys were out of town for an away game, so I spent the last two days living on the lunches Elias put in the fridge for me, and teaching a few extra shifts because suddenly, I can't stand being alone. I know I shouldn't get absorbed into his life because I haven't had this before, but now that they're back, it doesn't feel like something is missing.

A part of me wanted to go back to my apartment, but my landlady said it won't be ready anytime soon because of the delayed insurance approval. I'm sure if they knew I foolishly left a lit candle unattended, they'd deny her faster than the fire that ate my clothes. Thank God for renter's insurance.

I smile when I walk past the guys, trying to appear jovial but faltering when Elias catches my eye. In the kitchen, I'm hoping he's baked something that will suppress the feeling in my chest. A sigh of relief escapes me when I find a batch of blueberry muffins on a tray.

I've only taken a bite when Elias steps into the kitchen.

"How was class?" He goes to the fridge to pull out a water bottle that he unscrews and hands to me.

His question hits me right in the solar plexus, and I try not to let the dam break. But when he's near, that heavy load that's weighing me down begs to empty itself onto his strong shoulders. Everything about him screams comfort.

"Good," I say instead, taking a sip of the water.

With one stride, he closes the space between us and lifts my chin. The touch causes a devastating flutter to take place in my stomach. "I think I've earned the right to filter past the lies."

I swallow the lump in my throat. "I got another rejection."

"Come here." The hand rubbing my back deflates the weight that's been sitting on my shoulders this entire week as I fall into his chest. For once in my life, I feel like I'm allowed to cry outside the shower and in front of someone who won't crumble if I do.

"I thought this was the one," I say into the fabric of his T-shirt. "I guess I'm not as good as I thought."

"Not true." Elias pulls back to cup my face. "You're amazing. I'm not just saying that because I think it, but because I've seen how people react to seeing you onstage. The little kids in the audience light up when they watch you." His brown eyes bore into mine so intensely, my breath hitches. "They have pictures of you and write letters to you. You're an inspiration, Sage."

"You think?"

"I know."

My gaze lands on the pink roses by the kitchen sink. "Whose flowers are those?"

"Yours."

There's a warmth in my chest that doesn't ease. It gets worse when my eyes drop to his lips without thinking. I look up just as quickly, but Eli catches the move, the tension between us crackling to a restless heat. The idea of kissing him for real implodes my mind, and I become desperate to feel his lips on mine.

Everything in me wants to test my dwindling self-control. He smells so good I have the urge to tear his shirt from the collar down to the hem and smell his skin to determine the exact mix of fragrance. But I can't forget those damn rules.

But then he pulls away, as always. And my chest deflates, as always.

"We're here!" a deep voice shouts.

Two huge guys, just about as tall as Aiden and Elias, stand in the foyer with suitcases. In between them, Summer beams brightly at me. Her gaze settles on Elias and me, like she's interpreting our proximity to mean something.

"Miss me?" she asks, pulling me into a hug.

I've never had the kind of friendships that feel like family. But I've never really had a family to compare them to anyway. But with Summer, I have the overwhelming need to tell her everything and expel my inner thoughts without judgment. To let her in. To not be lonely.

When she pulls back, I can still feel the warmth of her hug. I peek at the two guys who could easily be Hollister models standing behind her. Summer must see the curiosity in my gaze because she waves them over.

"That's Kian and Dylan. Eli's probably told you all about them."

"I've heard some stories," I say.

"Dirty ones, I hope," Dylan interjects with a wink that I'm sure only a guy who looks like him can pull off.

"This is Sage. My girlfriend," Elias says as he comes to stand next to me.

The words sound like a threat, but his friends know about our ruse. Summer holds back a laugh at my expression before she slips away to help Aiden with the luggage. He doesn't let her, so she just follows him down the hall.

"Right, the *fake* girlfriend," Dylan emphasizes.

Kian is grinning, staring at me with a sort of bright-eyed wonder.

He's wearing a T-shirt and shorts that expose his tattoos. Black and red ink designs cover his thighs and arms.

Then the guys move in for a hug, and they smell so good, I get a head rush when they're surrounding me. It's like drowning in a sea of beautiful men.

"Why are you here?" Elias's abrupt question makes them pull back.

"For the playoffs kickoff party. We've been texting about it for weeks," says Dylan.

"I even asked for your opinion on my outfits, but you never replied," adds Kian, looking miffed by his friend's lack of response.

Elias grows more confused. "How did you get invited?"

As far as I know, the pre-playoffs dinner is for the team and some of the retired veterans, so plus-ones are limited. Especially because it's more of a superstition than a party. Elias told me the one time they didn't have one, the Toronto Thunder were sacked in the first round.

"Summer's dad. Lukas Preston? He loves me, man. Where have you been?" Kian says.

"Clearly, on another fucking planet." Elias turns to me. "Lukas Preston likes nobody but his wife and daughters."

"And now Kian," I add. I've heard about the rough time Aiden has had trying to get Summer's hockey Hall of Fame father to like him. So this is an unexpected development.

"Anyway, he said I could come, and I brought Dylan as my plus-one."

"Translation: He annoyed Summer's dad enough to score two guest passes," says Dylan.

I chuckle as Kian just shrugs, beaming with pride for securing the invites.

When we move to sit in the living room, Elias hands Dylan a water bottle. Dylan frowns. "No beer?"

"You think you should be drinking this early?"

There's something in the air that grows awkward with the question. I feel like I shouldn't be here. Though it doesn't seem like either of them care.

"Don't tell me you're going to be on my case about this too," Dylan mutters.

"Yeah, I am. You can't let yourself go during the offseason."

"What part of letting myself go does this count as?" Dylan lifts up his shirt to show off his abs. Washboard abs. I try not to gawk and instead stare at my hands like a scandalized nun.

The universe must finally be doing me a favor, because Summer walks in with Aiden, cutting the tension in the room. Kian moves to the spot between Dylan and me.

"It's so nice to finally meet you, Sage. Eli cannot stop talking about you," he says with a mischievous smirk.

"I find that hard to believe." My words draw curiosity from the guys. But I'm saved from any questions when Aiden cuts in.

"How did you guys get the time off from your classes?" he asks.

Kian looks over at Dylan, who doesn't appear to want to enlighten anyone with a response, so Kian answers. "The semester is almost over and we only took one class. Fall semester is going to be rough, though."

When the guys start talking about hockey, I kind of zone out, but this comforting chaos isn't something I've ever had. Where no one is fighting, and it's just a group of friends having an easy conversation. Elias looks happy when he's with them. It's the most carefree that I've seen him. Even the way he laughs is open and unrestricted.

When Kian starts to complain that he's starving and Aiden asks what everyone wants to eat, we settle on pizza. I'm the first to head to the door when it arrives, letting everyone catch up. But when I'm carrying it into the kitchen to get plates, Elias is already behind me. The soft brush of his torso against my back as he opens the cupboard lights an awareness on my skin. He grabs the plates even though they're in reach now that everything is moved down one shelf.

When he steps back, I awkwardly fidget with my hair tie. The post-wash curls make it almost impossible to achieve a neat bun.

"Need help?" A lazy hint of humor touches Elias's words when he sees my struggle.

"It's not funny," I say.

A lopsided smile stretches across his face. "Turn around. I'll do it."

My arms are tired after the fifth try, so I give up and hand him the hair tie. I'm sure he has no idea what he's doing, and that much is confirmed when he yanks my hair.

"The hair pulling is really working for me, but your friends are in the next room."

"Shut up, Sage."

Elias concentrates, and I watch his expression through the reflection in the microwave. His mouth twists with every loop and tug, and then finally he reveals a satisfied smile.

He looks so damn proud of himself, I let the knotted mess be, even though I know it's going to hurt tomorrow. "You're a natural."

"You're beautiful," he says suddenly, playing with a curl that's slipped out of my bun.

"Are you drunk?" My gaze slips over to the can on the counter to check if it's open.

His lips tip into a devilish smirk. "I don't drink."

Goose bumps riddle my skin, and his eyes are hooded in a way that tells me his thoughts might actually match mine for once. Minutes transpire, thick and syrupy, as I watch him.

"You guys better not be eating the pizza by yourself," Kian shouts, and we both flinch away from the string that tightens between us. I help Elias take everything to the living room, praying the faint blush on my cheeks blends in with the natural flush from the heat.

"What should we watch?"

Summer brightens mid sip of her chai. "I have an idea."

"No," everyone says in unison, and she slumps back into Aiden's arms. He whispers something to her, and she nods, a little happier now.

When I suggest a horror movie, everyone agrees, but Summer warns that she'll fall asleep halfway through. Apparently, she only has an attention span for her Turkish dramas.

I must be suffering from the same problem because by the time I'm jostled awake, Elias is gently placing me in his bed. Then, when I think he's going to go back to the living room, he lifts the comforter and gets in beside me. We've been sleeping together most nights since I tricked him into bed with me, and we keep our distance. But this time, I don't miss the arm on my waist that pulls me tight against his body or the kiss he plants in my hair.

"Elias?"

I'm sure he thought I was asleep because he takes a minute before he responds. "Yeah?"

"Why do you buy me flowers?"

He answers after a beat. "Because I like seeing you light up, even if you say you don't like flowers."

Every time I see a touch of pink or a bright yellow in a vase, something akin to longing blooms in my chest. Something that shouldn't be there.

"Wouldn't want us breaking any other rules," I say, half joking. But there's one I'd love to break. Especially right now as he wraps me in the cloak of his warmth. There's something about this connection. A transfer of something created in our own bodies that we're willing to share. It's small, minuscule even, but it sets my heart alight. I steal the warmth of Elias like it's mine to have, and he gives it to me like that's true.

"We won't."

When Elias slips his arm off of me, I barely refrain from pulling him right back. The response feels like a heavy rejection, and when he flips onto his side to face away from me, I know I won't get any sleep tonight.

NINETEEN

ELIAS

IT'S A FUCKING zoo trying to get out of the apartment to go to the event. The guys and Summer head out before me, because I was waiting for Sage to get off work. She left early in the morning so I didn't get a chance to talk to her about the party tonight or arrange to pick her up after my practice.

Now, she's been in the bathroom for an hour, and I'm impatiently pacing my bedroom. I don't try to rush her because she's been apologizing since she barreled through that door.

"I'm so sorry. The line at the pharmacy was extra long today, and my payment for Sean's meds didn't go through, so it was a whole thing. I feel terrible for making you late."

Sage never tells me about her financial problems, but it slipped from her so quickly that I'm sure she didn't realize. Everything the insurance won't cover she pays out of pocket, and I know her ballet classes don't pay much. I doubt she has anything left for herself by the end of it.

She would never ask me, but I'm desperate to help her out. Just a little.

"Do you know where Summer put the purse she said I could

borrow?" Sage asks from inside the bathroom. Summer left Sage one of her dresses, and a purse to match.

"Got it right here."

I've been holding the bedazzled thing in my hand for the last hour or longer, but I don't know because I stopped staring at my watch every minute. I move to sit on the bed so as not to sweat in my suit from all the pacing.

Then the door opens, and heels click on the hardwood floor. "If you hate it, just tell me."

I look up from the floor to find white heels, long brown legs, and the light blue dress hugging every curve. The contrast is striking against her glowing skin. As my gaze slides up, I find the fabric draped off her shoulders, leaving her neck and shoulders exposed. I wonder how good she'd smell if I buried my face there. The thought has me ripping my gaze away so quickly, my pulse jumps.

"You hate it."

I swallow the thickness in my throat to have the courage to finally look at her face, and it's the killer. I might have blacked out for a minute there. Her dark hair is waved, so it frames her face along with the earrings that shine almost as bright as her eyes. There's a brush of pink across her brown skin, and she pulls her glossy lip between her teeth as she waits for my response.

It's going to be a long fucking night.

"I definitely don't hate it."

She steps forward, and I can tell my response isn't enough. Fuck, if she knew what I wanted to say, we would never leave this room. I stand, just because I know seeing her tower over me in those heels won't be good for my imagination. But my step away from her has her studying me. Her hazel eyes narrow, and a smirk lifts her lips.

I can't remember the last time I felt this way. Desperate, needy, fucking *insane*. There's too much I want to say, and too much I want to do. With Sage's gaze lifted up to mine, it feels like a challenge.

Like I need to wipe that smirk right off her face, and give her a better use for those perfect lips.

"Don't be scared, Elias. I don't bite," she teases.

I step into her orbit and lean forward to nip her earlobe. "I do."

Suddenly the teasing note that tinged the air around us turns molten. My gaze settles on her lips for so long that she shifts uncomfortably.

"You look beautiful. Unreal."

She blinks, long lashes and a dark swipe of color over her eyes making the hazel pop. "Oh," she squeaks. "In that case you look pretty unreal too."

I raise a brow. "So, you're only complimenting me because I complimented you?"

"You know you're hot, Elias. People beg you on a daily basis to take your shirt off."

And now I can't stop fucking smiling.

I don't know if it's her intoxicating scent or that we're finally alone in the apartment, but I tilt my head and say, "Is that what you want to hear, Sage? How hot I think you look in this dress and how much better it would look sliding off your body?"

Her eyes bulge and her lips part, as if her retort gets stuck in her throat, but she recovers quickly.

"Who knew after breaking you out of your shell you'd become such a flirt?" Her words are nonchalant, but the heat that puts a deeper tint on her chest and neck gives her away.

"I guess it just takes the right woman to come along."

"And I'm the right woman?"

"The perfect one."

BOUNCING MY LEG only makes my anxiety worse. Any minute now one of the coaches or managers is going to come up to me and realize what an utter failure I've been to the team since my arrival. It feels like my stats are printed on my forehead with the way everyone is staring at me. It might all be my anxiety talking, but there is no use trying to convince my brain that everything is okay.

I had attributed the appreciative glances I received on my way inside the venue to having Sage as my date. I mean, the girl is stunning, and her curly styled hair, hazel eyes, and glowing complexion make me look like a plain cardboard cutout in comparison.

And the girl wonders why I buy her fucking flowers. I'd empty an entire flower shop just so she could decide on her favorite.

Tonight, I'm happy to have the attention away from the reality of me as a player. Coach can give me props on my assists and gameplay all day, but as long as that goal isn't in the net, I'll always be behind the rest of the team. Marcus Smith-Beaumont's expectations of me are proven right every single day, and this relationship is my only hope to get on track.

A warm touch melts into my palm, and Sage's small hand with her pearly manicured nails—that she swore she didn't want, when I insisted—intertwine with mine on the table.

My leg stops shaking because the concern pinching her brows throws me off. Concern for *me*.

"Drinks!" Kian and Dylan barrel toward us, putting four shots of some type of colorful alcohol in front of us.

Summer reaches for one, but Aiden puts a hand over hers. "What's in it?"

"It's basically juice, stop being a hard-ass," says Dylan.

Sage chuckles beside me, looking at my two best friends who act like clowns whenever they're together.

"I'll take one," Sage says, surprising me.

"Me too," says Summer.

Aiden slashes me a look from across the table, clearly giving up on monitoring how much our friends are going to drink tonight. Just like that the four shots lift off the table, clinking together before they are knocked back.

"Amaretto and tequila?" Summer splutters.

"That's evil," coughs Sage, gulping down the water I hand her as I'm laughing at her sour expression. When I look to the bar I spot Socket and Owen taking a bottle from the open bar and slipping through the balcony doors. Then my gaze catches on Marcus watching me from across the room, his face giving away nothing but still managing to drop an icicle of dread into my stomach.

A warm pressure on my hand pulls me from Marcus's look to the quiet reassurance in Sage's eyes. I feel the need to apologize again or to say something to fill the silence, but she beats me to it.

"We can sneak out the back. I'll say I'm developing a fever." She looks around cautiously, then whispers, "I'll even pretend to faint by the door."

Fuck, I want to kiss her.

"I'll be fine. It just feels like everyone's staring at me. Like they're silently judging me for being the guy who's going to get traded any day now."

Sage shakes her head. "I've known hockey people a long time. Trust me, the hotshot executives are only thinking about themselves. If anything, they see you as a dollar sign, and they aren't thinking about anything past that."

"That's comforting," I say dryly.

"Yeah, well, that's why you need to play for yourself. Not because you're afraid of what they're going to think, but because this is your dream, and you want to make it last." Sage pats my hand. "Now, will you finally go back to being your talkative, extroverted self?"

I chuckle. "I talk to you more than to anyone else I know."

"Jeez, your throat must be tired from carrying that heavy load, huh?" It doesn't take much to realize she's making jokes for my sake. I don't feel it anymore, but my body language must still be tense because she doesn't stop giving me those small squeezes to my hand.

Suddenly, she feels too far away. I like our little bubble. It's the first time in two hours that I'm relaxed and not being held to some impossible standard. I grab the base of her chair and pull her close until her knees knock into mine.

"Was that supposed to be a dirty joke?"

She gasps. "I didn't realize! I swear I'm on my best behavior tonight. Very conservative."

"There is nothing conservative about the way you look in that dress right now."

She fidgets nervously when she looks down at her outfit, her voice sounding slightly panicked. "Then give me your suit jacket or something, I'll cover up."

"Are you kidding?" I say. "If I could put you on a damn pedestal and show you off all night, I would."

Her laugh is warm and bubbly, like champagne. "I'm sure I can find a pedestal somewhere."

When I bring up her arm to kiss the inside of her wrist, she blushes, eyes shying away to focus on the people joining the dance floor with some sort of longing. This girl is a dancer at heart, and just hearing the slow beat of the music, I can tell she wants to be there.

I don't dance, but she definitely does.

"Come on, they're playing our song."

"We don't have a song."

"We do now."

With our hands already intertwined, we walk to the dance floor, listening to the smooth beat that transitions into a slow dance. As much as I'm trying to avoid the spotlight tonight, not letting this girl's light shine would be a stupid thing for anyone to do, let alone her boyfriend.

"Fade Into You" by Mazzy Star plays on the speakers, and it does something to me when I watch the way Sage lets me guide her hands to my shoulders. She rests her head against my chest.

"You don't seem like the dancing type."

"I'm not. But you are," I say, pressing a kiss in her hair that I don't think she feels. Or I hope she doesn't.

Because it's fucking confusing when she looks at me with eyes that don't seem like they're faking anything. Or when she says things that feel so real, I want to believe them. But there's a hard line that disappears in those feelings, which I need to uncover as a reminder to myself that this is all fake. It's selfish of me to want her in the way that I do. Especially when a relationship is the last thing she wants.

Sage sways in my arms, and I feel myself wanting to somehow hold her closer. Everything about her feels like it's mine. Mine to hold, mine to touch, and mine to admire.

I'm so fucked.

When she pulls back, she catches my gaze, and whatever she sees makes the long column of her throat twitch. "You shouldn't look at me like that, you know," Sage says.

"Like what?"

"Like I'm yours to look at."

"What if I want to?"

She pauses. "Then you can do a lot more than just look, West-brook."

My throat grows dry. I'm lost in her vanilla scent and the feel of her silky dress under my palm when someone taps my shoulder. I can hear his voice before he even speaks.

Mason clears his throat. "This is sweet, but you need to do your rounds."

Sage pulls away from me first when she hears my agent's voice. "Rounds?"

"There are cameras outside that Eli conveniently snuck past when you two arrived." He shoots me a scathing look. "Sage, will you please escort your boyfriend to the carpet for some pictures? It's great press for both of you."

Sage extends her hand to mine, and I slip it into hers without a second thought. I'm beginning to think I could do anything if she's beside me.

At the front entrance, cameras flash when we stand where Mason directs us on the short carpet. It's no surprise because these parties have gotten bigger through the years. Our captain and a few other players have been dating famous singers for a while, so our team garners a lot of media attention.

My skin itches to get this over with because the questions they throw my way are still too personal. It was better for a while, and I'm assuming not scoring a goal has got to do with the shift.

I'm overthinking when Sage turns to me and whispers, "Go any lower and you might be able to reach under my dress. That'll give them something to talk about."

I snap my hand back to her waist, careful not to let it drop again after groping her in public. She lets out a short chuckle when she sees my panicked expression.

"Never said I minded, rookie," she says, this time into my neck. It's the smooth lull of her voice that flows through me like a gentle stream. One that makes me stop worrying and focus on the girl on my arm. Sage is perfection draped in silk. My tongue feels heavy in my mouth when I look at her, and there's an ardent flame that brushes all the way up my spine.

It feels impossible to ignore it.

We pose for a few cameras, and I'm hoping we're done, but Mason gives me a look that tells me we have to stop at each marker along the carpet.

My grip on Sage must tighten because her hand covers mine on her waist, and she meets my eyes and grounds me. It makes me more restless, not because she doesn't calm me but because having her near me, smiling like that, only makes the rattle in my chest more excessive. My eyes must betray my thoughts because Sage's gaze turns longing, and her eyes search for something. The cameras love it. I know they expect a kiss, but I won't—I *can't*. Not for them.

Suddenly, Sage blinks away that look like she had momentarily gotten distracted. If it wasn't for the shouting men, I might have forgotten too. Reaching the end eases some of the tightness in my chest, but when Sage turns to me, it all comes crawling back.

"Sorry about that," she whispers softly. "I got caught up in the moment."

In a reckless move, fueled by the heat of her gaze and her fucking dress, I take her hand and pull her off the carpet. Event workers move past us, and I can see our team in the foyer of the hotel. But I don't take us there. I pull Sage through the first door I see. Luckily, it's a storage room with a single countertop, stools, and signage.

It must be the click of the door when I close it that snaps something in my brain because I turn to Sage, and the haze in my mind implodes my every logical thought.

"What are you—"

I cut her off when I pull her toward me, and grip the backs of her thighs to lift her on the counter so she's nearly eye level. Her squeak of surprise coincides with my anguished groan. I rest my palms on her knees to pull her legs apart so I can step right into the heat of her. She welcomes me instantly, and now that I'm this close, I wonder how I ever kept my distance. Something is taking over my body and burning my self-control to ashes. It's either the nerves of being here messing with my motor function, or it's because she smells so damn good. Her nervous swallow is audible, and the Sage from a few seconds ago has evaporated, just like my patience.

"I don't want to kiss you," I rasp, running my nose along the column of her throat, feeling her warm skin.

"I know the rules," she mutters.

The drop in her expression makes me groan. "I *can't* kiss you."

Her breath is more of a gasp when she speaks this time. "It's just a kiss, Elias."

The way my name drips off her tongue makes me grip her chin and have her lips brush against mine. It would be so easy like this, so perfect. In one move, I'd be kissing her, letting her consume every part of me that's been aching for her.

"It's never going to be just a kiss for me. Once I do this, Sage, I won't be able to stop."

Her gaze flickers between my eyes and lips. "Then let me go," she whispers.

"I can't do that either."

She's so close, watching me like she has no idea what I'll do or say next. She's caught off guard, and I love the way her body heats me up and cools me down all at once. It's a dichotomy I can't quite wrap my head around.

A question swims in her eyes, but it's not the same one she voices. "What can you do?"

She's giving me an out, but the question only tackles me off the high. She's vulnerable, and she's wrapped around me like all the times I've dreamed about this. I've got this beautiful girl who brightens every room she walks into, and I can't kiss her. It's fucking embarrassing.

"Nothing, this is too much already, I shouldn't have touched you like that. I don't know what I was thinking." I step away entirely, dispelling the haze.

Sage is vulnerable. We're *both* vulnerable. But she has no place to stay, works herself to exhaustion to have a shot at NBT, and trusts me to let her fulfill those dreams without any obstacles. The shit I went through in high school made me strict on my rules. But if I let go now, I'd never forgive myself for letting us both fall deeper into something that isn't real. Something that has a clear expiration date. Because at the end of all this she's going to leave, and I'll still be here, stuck in the allure of her.

Sage pulls me from my thoughts. "Why can't you touch me?"

The question is an ice pick to the chest, and there's a fire in her words that won't be snuffed out until I give her an answer.

"Because I'm celibate."

TWENTY

SAGE

CELIBATE. ELIAS WESTBROOK is *celibate.*

Oh.

My.

God.

After he dropped that bomb on me, I couldn't breathe, let alone give any type of coherent response. So when he helped me off the counter and to my feet, I simply followed him back inside the venue.

The revelation has me slamming down drinks like a sailor coming off a monthlong expedition. I swear there's a laugh track playing somewhere. There's a part of me that blames Kian and Dylan for getting me started with that one disgusting shot, but I know the real reason. The alcohol was supposed to dim the sad swampy feeling in my stomach, but instead it makes me want to sulk. I don't like to drink, and I don't like to think about why. With parents that are addicts, it's difficult to think of alcohol as separate from them. However, when every nerve ending in my body is begging for Elias, none of that comes to mind. So, the alcohol doesn't sting as much as it would have otherwise. Especially when my fake boyfriend, who I've been having dirty dreams about while he sleeps next to me, just told me he's celibate. Anyone would drink to that.

Just when I think I could find myself getting lost in Elias, that big bold *Do Not Cross!* sign comes between us like the cockblock it is.

His celibacy is a literal cockblock, but I have to respect his decision. He's been nothing but respectful with me. Except in that tiny room where he handled me exactly like I wanted him to: rough and desperate.

I shouldn't have touched you like that.

The words could easily wound anyone's ego, especially when his lips were close enough to taste. But we have rules, and now I'm extra adamant about sticking to them because I'd be causing myself unnecessary disappointment if I strayed. No PDA, no sex, no getting attached. The last one is for my own benefit.

As I'm about to down another shot, someone snatches it from my hand. It's Summer, who takes it instead, wiping her chin before beaming at me. "Now we're even."

"You were counting?"

"Nope." She hiccups. "But Eli was, and he said I should probably cut you off."

My gaze slides to where Elias and Aiden are having a conversation, but I must look for too long because he catches me watching and those brown eyes make me feel sick.

Because I'm celibate.

I want to scream and grab his beautiful face and crush his lips to mine. But I've realized I'm the only one who's been blurring the lines, and Elias sees them clearly for what they are. I'm not a romantic in the slightest, but lately, I can't help the way my heart flutters when he presses a small kiss to my wrist or brushes my hair from my face like he hates that it obstructs his view.

Don't get me started on how many meals he cooks for me. Whoever said the way to a man's heart is through his stomach is right on the money. Except in this scenario, Elias cooks and I eat. Instead of plaque from high cholesterol, the only thing clogging my heart is confusion.

"The team booked some rooms in the hotel nearby. Are you and Elias staying?"

"He's allergic to me." I snap my mouth shut as soon as I say it, but Summer laughs.

The alcohol is making me bitter.

"You're one hell of an allergy to have, then, 'cause he hasn't been able to take his eyes off you all night."

I snort. "Probably making sure I'm not telling a dirty joke to an executive."

"Probably not."

There's something about Summer and that feeling of warmth I get when she's near that makes me want to spill all my feelings and have her braid my hair or something.

She takes my hand in hers, face serious. "Look, I haven't seen Eli with anyone as long as I've known him." She glances to where he sits, before leaning in. "And from what I know, letting someone in is not his top priority. But with you, he's different. I've never seen him so . . . relaxed."

I shake my head. "We've both gotten pretty good at pretending."

Summer sighs but doesn't say anything else as she orders two margaritas.

"I thought you were here to cut me off?"

"I don't always do as I'm told." She winks, slides over my drink as soon as it arrives, and watches me with excitement when I drink the fruity thing for her sake.

"Wanna dance?" I ask her, and she holds out her hand. I take it, avoiding the burning gaze that follows me to the dance floor. Kian and Dylan easily find us in the crowd, pulling us into their circle as the music and the buzz from the alcohol make me feel weightless. When I spot a glimpse of Owen in the crowd, dread pools in my stomach. I duck to avoid him, but the universe must be on my side because Socket pulls him outside.

"Your boring boyfriend didn't want to dance?" Kian asks, leaning down right by my ear so I can hear him.

I stand upright. "I didn't ask him."

He laughs and nods like he's proud of me. Elias thinks I'm *too much*. I must be stewing in self-pity, because Kian takes my hand and twirls me right toward Dylan, who easily slips his hand into mine. His movements are fluid and relaxed, matching the tempo perfectly. Dylan Donovan can dance. I see it in the way his body is loose and swaying to the music like it's his second nature. Just like how I am with ballet.

"Are you a dancer?" I ask him.

He shrugs. "Sometimes."

Dylan's cagey response makes my eyes narrow, but then he pulls me into him. "What are you doing?" I ask.

"Making your boyfriend realize he's an idiot for not dancing with you."

I glance over my shoulder, watching Elias, who sits at the table now, eyes zeroing in on both of us. It's a heated look aimed right at Dylan, who appears totally unaffected. I ignore him too, because if he cared that much, he should be the one over here. Not the one rejecting me twice in a night.

"He doesn't care."

He gives me a look like he thinks I'm stupid. "Yeah, 'cause that's definitely the look of a man who *doesn't care*." Dylan spins me and dips me in his arms, and I adjust to his tempo, laughing as he dances like a natural. *Sometimes*, my ass.

The heated glare on my back gets hotter. Elias has gotten on his feet, and Dylan lets me go immediately. By the time Elias reaches me, Dylan's disappeared, and I'm standing there like a fish out of water.

"If you want to dance, ask me next time."

I look down at our feet. White heels and pointy brown dress shoes. "I doubt there'll be a next time," I say, though my words are slurred. The alcohol is still thrumming in my bloodstream. Summer really should have cut me off.

His expression flattens, and I immediately feel bad. I'm not a mean person, but the lingering hurt from his earlier words make the darkness lurking behind my ribs visible. I want to apologize, but I can't. Not when it's true.

"Ready to go?"

Summer bumps into Elias, holding up a strict finger. "Stop being a killjoy. We're still dancing." She pulls me into her, and I bite back a laugh. Elias looks to Aiden, who just shrugs.

TWENTY-ONE

ELIAS

"YOUR GIRLFRIEND DOESN'T like you very much," Summer says.

When Aiden went to his hotel room because I insisted on bringing the girls, I didn't think it would be like this. The four of them—the girls, Dylan, and Kian—danced until there was barely anybody left. The DJ wanted to go home too.

Somehow, we left and dropped Sage off to the room first, and now I'm walking Summer to hers.

I know, I'm a coward.

But in my defense, Sage didn't want to be alone with me either, and I'd much rather have her sleep off her drunkenness than have her say something that makes me question everything. I told her that I'm celibate, and I think that calls for some space.

"She's not my girlfriend. It's fake," I remind her, though telling drunk Summer anything logical never registers.

"Shh! You're going to blow your whole cover." She looks around the empty hallway. "Are you sleeping in her room?"

"What—no." I specifically requested two rooms, but I would have slept in the lobby if I had to.

Coward.

She halts in the middle of the hallway. "You don't think someone might think that's suspicious? You can't trust the concierge, you know that firsthand," she says. "Do you seriously not know the first rule of fake relationships?"

Though she does have a point, I raise a skeptical brow. "And you do?"

"Have you seen my bookshelf?" she says matter-of-factly. "After handing me off to that annoying guy I call my boyfriend, go to her room. Trust me."

"I don't think that's appropriate."

"Good. It should be very *in*appropriate." Summer shoots me a terrible wink.

I try to ignore her suggestion because that's exactly what I shouldn't want.

Aiden opens the door before I can knock. "It's two in the morning. It took you this long to get them off the dance floor?" He's scanning Summer from head to toe, as if I'd ever let anything happen to her.

"Your girlfriend isn't a very agreeable drunk."

"Hey! Yours isn't either," Summer shoots back before falling into Aiden's open arms.

Aiden smiles down at her. "You're so drunk, babe."

"I'm as sober as ever. I'll blow on something to prove it."

And that's my cue to leave.

"Think about what I said!" Summer whispers loudly before the door closes, and I make my way down the hall. Despite my not wanting them to, her words circle my thoughts like a noose.

Going to Sage's room at this hour is a bad idea.

But what if she's so drunk she needs someone to take care of her?

Jesus, am I seriously considering advice from a plastered Summer? There would never be a situation where going to Sage's room would be beneficial for either of us. Especially because I haven't been able to get the image of her sitting on that counter out of my head.

It's been four years and I've never felt like this. The desperate, aching need to feel her sweat-damp body slide against mine. The thought feels dangerous. But the look on her face after I told her I'm celibate pops the lustful bubble.

Somehow, I come to stand right in front of her room, and when my fist hits the door, I know I've already lost whatever self-control I may have relied on.

A few minutes pass before an irritated Sage answers. "What?"

She's still dressed, heels on, her purse over her shoulder and everything. She looks half asleep and ready to drop at any given moment.

"Just checking in on you. Why aren't you in bed?"

"It's embarrassing." She stares at the ground. "I tripped and was lying on the floor until you knocked."

Immediately, I'm scanning every inch of her. "Are you okay? Did you hurt yourself?"

"Peachy."

She doesn't look peachy. Her knee is scratched, and her feet are red from her heels. "Can I help?"

"Isn't that treading a bit close to the real boyfriend category?" She points a finger at me. "No mixing them up. You're off-limits."

Off-limits. Fuck me.

"Sage, just let me help."

"But I'm peachy. See." She attempts to balance on one leg. The show of soberness doesn't hold up when she twists and falls into me with a yelp.

"I'm coming inside."

"I wish."

Walking across the room, mostly with my support, she sighs when I sit her on the bed and kneel to undo her heels. When I unintentionally squeeze her instep, she moans and falls back on the bed. So, naturally, I do it again, eliciting the same reaction. "Feels good?"

"So good."

I chuckle, placing both her shoes aside and massaging her feet because I know she's in pain. It might also have to do with the appreciative noises she makes with each press.

"You're a god."

"You've never had a foot massage?"

"Never."

"That's criminal."

"You know what else is criminal?"

"Hmm?"

"A man has never made me come."

I almost choke on my tongue. "Sage."

You'd think I'd be used to her bluntness by now, but it gets me every time.

"Sorry, I almost forgot that you're . . ." She hiccups. "But it's true. I can't even make myself come when I'm with a guy. It's like I shut down when I'm expected to perform. Ironic, I know."

We're treading dangerous waters, and I know with everything in me that I don't want to explore this topic of conversation. Especially not with what I said earlier, and definitely not when she's drunk.

I clench my teeth to stop myself from replying, but what she's saying is blasphemy. I can't imagine that not one dude has pleasured her for her enjoyment. Or their own enjoyment.

"Never?" I ask despite myself.

"Nope. It's just too hard, and I'm too much. Too difficult."

"Who told you that?"

She snorts. "Every guy ever. You included."

"I've never said you were difficult, Sage. You're definitely not easy, but I like that about you."

"You don't act like it. I'm certain you think I'm a witch who trapped you in my imploding mess of a life."

"Hey." I pull her by her arms so she's sitting upright. "You didn't trap me. I wanted to do this."

"Then why can't you look at me. It's like you can't stand the sight of me."

I laugh. A genuine hearty laugh.

She frowns. "Wow. No need to rub it in."

"At the risk of saying too much, I don't want to look at you too long because I like it too much."

She tilts her head, and I know she's trying to decipher my words. But her drunk brain is hindering her from doing so, and I'm hoping it makes her forget them too.

I'm still kneeling before her, watching her hazel eyes blink rapidly as if she's trying to see through a fog. I press a gentle hand to her leg. "And if I'm being honest, any guy who's skipped out on giving you an orgasm is an idiot. You're better off without them."

"Some have tried. It just doesn't work like that for me."

"Then they're doing it wrong."

"It could just be me."

"It's not."

"Eli—"

"They're wrong." I level our gazes. "If it were me, I'd worship your pussy until you came at just the sound of my voice asking you to."

She falls back on the bed, mumbling something. When I clear my throat, standing to take a step away from her, my body feels hot, and I'm sure if she were to touch me, I'd burn her.

"What were you planning to sleep in?"

"Nothing."

Jesus. The dress she's wearing now is all she has, and from the looks of it, it's uncomfortable as hell, because Sage pulls and itches at it like it's suffocating her.

Giving up, I take off my suit jacket and unbutton my dress shirt. I pull it off and don't acknowledge the way she stares at my shirtless torso.

"Here." I place the shirt on her lap.

Wordlessly, she grabs it, brings it to her face, and inhales. When she breathes out she looks so content, I have to hold back a laugh. I'd just taken it out of the wash, so it probably smells like the fabric softener I use, and I suppose a bit like me too. But the way she takes her time with it tells me she really likes the scent. When she unzips the side of her dress, I turn to face the wall to give her some privacy.

"Nothing you haven't seen before," she mutters.

True, but I have a feeling that if seeing her toned legs makes me lose focus, the rest of her could do irreparable damage. After I spend a few moments listening to my heartbeat and the quiet noise of silk fabric, the comforter rustles and I turn to find her buried beneath it.

"You didn't take your makeup off."

She groans. "I'll suffer the consequences."

Growing up with a skin care–focused mom, I know that sleeping with makeup on is a nightmare for the skin. Though Sage's skin is flawless, so I can't really tell when she's wearing makeup or not. But today the shimmer on her eyelids and the smoky outer corners make that obvious.

"What do you use to take it off?" I know nothing about makeup, but I think I could manage taking it off.

"Micellar water, but it's in the bathroom, and I'm not getting up. That's a problem for future Sage."

Shaking my head, I slide open the bathroom door and sort through her toiletries to look for whatever the hell micellar water looks like. After examining each label, I find the clear liquid in a pink bottle, grab a face towel, and sit on the edge of the bed.

"Sit up for me."

She grumbles a refusal, so I have to lift her higher onto a pillow to have better access to her face. Dabbing some of the water onto the cloth, I wipe away the glitter first, then use more of the water to get her whole face. My thumb brushes against her smooth skin, and her eyes just barely flutter open.

She watches me as I continue taking all her makeup off. "This is above and beyond for fake boyfriend duties," she whispers, words slurred from exhaustion and alcohol.

Once her face is clean and her moisturizer is on, we still don't move. A hint of watermelon scent lingers on my hands and soaks into her brown skin. My neck aches from our awkward position, but I can't find it in me to move or care when she looks at me like she's mapping an entire constellation with her eyes.

"No, this is just Elias and Sage."

"Unfiltered?"

I chuckle. "Yeah. Unfiltered."

TWENTY-TWO

SAGE

THERE'S NOTHING MORE embarrassing than running through the streets of downtown Toronto in a leotard. It's a Monday, so my schedule is packed, and the hangover from the weekend's festivities did not help. It's easy to pretend under the ruse of alcohol that I forgot about all the stupid things I may have said or the things Elias did that made my hands clammy. I've pretended like the night went the way it looked on social media when I posted about it.

The music in my headphones accompanies my sprint to the pharmacy, but the stares on the way there prevent me from getting lost in my playlist.

I forgot. *Again.*

Many things go into being a good older sister, and continuously forgetting to call your little brother or not making sure his medication is paid for before it runs out are not among them. Spotting the green cross, I'm almost to the pharmacy. A woman in a white coat stands behind the glass, reaching to flip the open sign to closed, but I barrel past the door, pushing her in the process.

"Sorry," I say when I finally catch my breath. "I need to pay my invoice."

She fixes her crooked glasses, giving me a look that is not nearly as friendly as the first time I met her. She recognizes me—or rather recognizes my tardiness.

"Ms. Beaumont," she practically tuts. "Late payment again, I presume."

I feign a smile, taking out my wallet as she leads me to the front counter. "Sorry, I just needed a little more time. The deductible is more than I expected."

Instead of helping me herself, she waves over a technician whose smile I've become accustomed to from the many times I've had to come here. I'm lucky enough that the pharmacist doesn't need to deal with me, otherwise her judgmental looks would risk me getting banned from the pharmacy.

"Sage, I'm glad you could make it," says the technician. She taps at the keyboard, pulling up Sean's profile. Her eyes widen.

"What's wrong?" I ask, leaning over the counter to look at the screen.

She hums, her lips pressing together as she clicks a few more times. "Looks like you had an unpaid invoice from last month."

"I can pay for it now," I rush out.

"And the new brand Sean is using has increased in price."

My throat feels dry at her words. An increase? I can barely afford the current one while the deductible hasn't been met.

"As for his deductible—"

"I swear I can pay for it. Just give me a few more days, and I'll have my paycheck."

"Ms. Beaumont—"

"Please, you know I'm good for it. His supply ran out, and I would never be this negligent, but you have to trust me."

She puts a hand over my frantic one and looks at me levelly. I think she's about to refuse, and I know I'm about to cry or threaten to rob this pharmacy. Jail be damned.

"Ms. Beaumont, it's already paid for. Actually, it's paid in full.

Sean's deductible is settled, and the remainder that insurance doesn't cover is also paid for."

I blink several times as if that will help me hear better. "What does that mean?"

She smiles, pushing back her glasses. "It means that his prescription will be renewed and sent to him as needed. No more dealing with us."

"How?"

She turns back to her screen and after a few more clicks angles the monitor my way. "Paid in full by Elias Westbrook."

No.

ELIAS

THE MOMENT THE front door slams and a heavy purse drops behind me on the kitchen counter, I realize it's not one of the guys or Summer.

"How could you?" Sage's voice is charged with emotion.

I peek over my shoulder to find Sage in her ballet outfit, staring at me with a fire behind her eyes that I've only ever seen once before—when she stormed into the guys' changing room to lash out at me for giving her Mason's number.

For some perverse reason, I enjoy it when Sage lets me see her whole range of emotions. It makes me feel like I scored the winning lottery ticket.

My sauce for the alfredo pasta we're having tonight bubbles.

"Try this." In one quick move, I stir it and bring the spoon over to Sage, slipping it between her parted lips.

She can't react quickly enough, and when the flavor hits her tongue, she gives an involuntary sound of appreciation, and her stomach makes an approving rumble. When her eyes open again, she's disoriented, but then she returns to her previous expression.

When her gaze slips to the bouquet of pink and blue carnations, Sage glares at the flowers. Okay, not her favorite.

Dropping the spoon in the sink, I turn back to the stove and lower the heat, only to hear a frustrated exhale before she slams the cupboard. Sage pours herself water and gulps it down.

I assess her stiff posture and turn to give her my full attention, leaning against the counter to look at her. "Is there something you want to talk about?"

She scoffs, turning dramatically, her curls bouncing off her shoulders.

"I don't know. Is there?" She narrows her eyes and stares at me like my face alone is driving her crazy. She lets out a frustrated breath. "If I knew you were insane, I wouldn't have offered to fake date you."

"I believe your exact words were *insanely hot*." I can't help when my lips curve into a smirk, and her tight expression is only amusing me more. Ever since the night of the party there's been a thick haze floating around us.

"Don't play innocent. How could you pay for Sean's medication without telling me?"

Oh. I should have known that was coming. "I didn't think it was a big deal."

She looks at me with big angry eyes. "It is to me! He's my brother."

"And you're my girlfriend. I don't see the problem." I hold her gaze. This is a speech I might've practiced in my head a few times because Sage is allergic to help. "You've set up your life to never have to rely on anyone, but when you've come to a point where you need to, you're angry about it. Why can't you let me do this one thing for you?"

She pinches the bridge of her nose. "Because people rely on me. What do you think will happen if I'm relying on someone else? It would all fall apart, Elias."

I know what she's saying is all from experience, but I hate that she forces herself to deal with it all alone. I care about her, and it's not only because of our arrangement.

"It doesn't have to," I say.

"I can't rely on something that isn't even real." She runs a hand through her hair. "You can't make promises you can't keep. I've had enough of that in my life, and I won't let you do it too."

"*God*, Sage, it's like you want to live in this place where you don't even have a second to breathe, just because you think you have to carry it all alone."

"That's all I know!" she exclaims. "It's not easy to let it go and let someone like you in."

"What does that mean?"

"Nothing."

I don't let her off the hook. Instead, I take a step toward her and wait for an answer.

She catches my gaze and sighs. "You have your shit figured out, Elias. Soon enough, you're going to realize my life is exactly as everyone says it is: a disaster. It's a facade because I ruin things. I ruin people."

"You haven't ruined anyone."

"Sean's been late on his meds a million times because of me. Not to mention he was getting bullied at school for months before I found out. My parents? They never wanted to be home because I reminded them of everything they wanted to escape. It all pushed them to just up and leave."

"None of that is your fault. Sean is a strong, capable kid. And don't you dare put your parents' choices on yourself. They are not yours to carry."

Sage drops her gaze. "It's not just that. It's like no matter what I do, no matter how much I try, I'll always be scraping by. I'm a goddamn mess."

"You're my mess."

Sage snorts. "Was that supposed to be romantic?"

"It's supposed to be me telling you that I'm here, and all of this—all of *you*—is safe with me."

She registers the words like I've spoken a foreign language. Slow and confused.

"But you're right." I step back. "I shouldn't have done it behind your back."

She meets my gaze. "I'm paying you back—"

"Don't," I interrupt. "I get where you're coming from, but what I did wasn't for any other reason than wanting to help out. So, no, you're not going to pay me back."

She doesn't like that answer. "Just—don't do it again."

"I can't promise you that. But next time I want to do something for you, I'll tell you first."

"I think you mean *ask*."

I don't, but I'll let her think that for now. "You know, you can say *thank you* and move on, right?"

She huffs, silently simmering by the sink. "Thank you."

I don't expect her to be okay with this immediately, but I don't want her to think it's a bigger deal than it is.

Taking the boiling pot off the stove, I move to the sink to drain the pasta into a colander. Sage doesn't move.

When I move back to the sink to wash the pot, my phone rings and our heads snap to where it lies on a kitchen towel by the stove. "Do you mind getting that?" I ask, showing her my wet hands.

She nods once and brings it over. "It's your mom."

"Answer it."

Her eyes widen. "She's video calling you. What if she realizes we're lying and I'm some gold digger—"

"Answer the phone, Sage."

"Hi," she says when she finally answers, waving at the phone screen.

My mom is silent for a long time, and Sage's gaze bounces from mine to the phone. She's nervous. It's cute.

"Ian! Come quick, it's Eli's girlfriend," my mom shouts. Sage is smiling when she twists to show me the screen too. "Oh, Sage, we've been begging our secretive boy to let us meet you. You're just as gorgeous as you are in your dancing videos."

Then my dad pops into the screen, beaming brightly. "We made all our friends at the country club follow your account. You have some big fans here in Connecticut."

Sage chuckles. "Thank you, that means a lot."

"Is he treating you well?" my mom asks. "What's your number? I'll call—"

"Mom," I scold.

She deflates. "Right, sorry. Apparently, I can be overbearing when I'm excited."

"Don't be rude, Elias." Sage shoots me a narrowed glance. "I'd love to catch up with you whenever you want to call."

My mom beams in victory when she gets exactly what she wanted. "Are those carnations? Those are my favorite flowers."

Sage appears stunned, and when she turns back to the camera, she bites the inside of her cheek. "Elias wants me to have a favorite flower, so he buys me a new bouquet every week."

"That is so romantic!" My mom practically swoons, and wears a satisfied smile. "Will you be coming home with Eli in his offseason? We'd love to meet you in person."

Sage stutters. This thing between us will be over by then, and I can tell she's not going to lie to my mom or give her any false hope. Jane Westbrook has that effect on people.

"Mom, we'll call you later. Sage just got back from teaching, and she's exhausted. Right, baby?"

The word slips past my lips, and I freeze. And so does Sage. Her head snaps to mine, and her eyes are wide like I cursed in front of my mother.

There's a palpable awkward tension before my mom clears her throat. "Okay, send me her number, then, Eli."

I wipe my soapy hands and take the phone from Sage when they hang up.

"They seem really nice," she says, backing away to where she left her purse. "Which one of them did you take after? I couldn't tell."

The question throws me off. I face the sink again and continue rinsing the dishes. "Neither," I say. My response is curt.

Maybe too curt because she doesn't say anything after that. The next thing I hear is her walking out of the kitchen and the door to our—*my* room closing.

TWENTY-THREE

SAGE

WALKING PAST BUS stands with your fake boyfriend's face on them is an odd reality.

I spent the entirety of the bumpy ride back home from work on the phone with Jane Westbrook. Elias's mother is as sweet as they come, and it's no wonder Elias is such a gentleman.

Since his parents are retired, they spend most of their time on vacation, and she told me on their most recent one they attended the ballet in Paris. Apparently, I've had an influence on them.

On my way down the block to the apartment, my phone vibrates again, but this time it's a video call from Sean. When I answer it, I point the camera to the large posters of Elias on the bus stand, and Sean's favorite, number twenty-two, on another poster beside it.

"I wish I was there," he says when I flip the camera back to myself.

"Want me to sneak you out?" I joke.

"You're a terrible influence." He laughs. "But I actually called to ask you something."

"What's up? Is it to get you a signed jersey?"

"Oh, yeah, thanks for sending that, by the way. They're sick. Josh was stoked to get one too." He moves to his closet to show me his brand-new Toronto Thunder jersey, with the back signed by the entire team. "I got it in the mail a few days ago."

Elias had to have sent them to him. Of course he did.

"So, back to why I called. One of my friends invited us to hang out at his place during our midsemester reading break. He's got this new console that hasn't even come out yet."

When Sean first started school, he was an outcast. He didn't fit in with the rich kids, and the teachers didn't approve of him being there. But after a few years, I'm glad he's made some solid friends.

"That sounds fun. But remember the rules. I'll need your friends' names, their parents' numbers, and the address."

"I'll text it all," he assures. "Oh, and you need to confirm with the school that his mom can sign us out."

"Okay." I shuffle through my purse for my key. "And do you remember the phone rule?"

"I have you and Uncle Marcus on speed dial, and I'll call you every day."

I smile. Our uncle would love to know that he's on our speed dial. "Good, I'll call their parents and confirm with your school before you go. Call me every night, Sean. If you miss one, I'll show up there. With a bat."

His laugh is brittle. "So . . . you really don't mind?"

"Why would I? I guess hanging out with your older sister gets a bit old, huh?" My apartment is still damaged from the fire, and I'd never make Elias house more Beaumonts under his roof. One is more than enough.

Sean doesn't answer.

"What's wrong?"

"It's on the twenty-eighth," he informs. "It's the day I was supposed to head out so we could celebrate your birthday."

I halt on the sidewalk and mutter an apology when someone bumps into me. My heart twists into an uncomfortable ball that squeezes so tight I think it's going to pop.

"I'm sorry. I don't even know why I asked. I can cancel. We were just—"

"No." I fight through the stinging behind my eyes. "Don't cancel. We'll celebrate after your semester is over. You should spend time with your friends."

He sees right through my act. "Sage, it's really not a big deal. We always celebrate your birthday. I shouldn't have even said yes to them."

Talking is difficult when it feels like there's a knife jabbed into your throat. "Sean, I don't mind. I have that big showcase coming up, and I'm so busy it would have been hard to make time around that."

"You're sure?"

I nod tightly. "We'll celebrate another time. I have to go, but I'll call you later!"

Ending the call, I finally let my face fall into a frown. The last time I was alone on my birthday, Sean wasn't born yet, and my parents left me home alone to go do God knows what. I hated my birthdays for the longest time, until Sean and I finally left that house and made them special again. But I don't think he ever realized how important those days were for me, because I made sure on his birthday he would never experience the loneliness that I felt. There's a deep pit in my stomach that feels a lot like betrayal, but I can't blame Sean for wanting to hang out with his friends. If I was a teenager I'd want to do the same thing. And if he's happy, I'm happy too.

When I open the door to the apartment, I head straight past everyone laughing in the dining room. Elias's friends are great people, and I love hearing their crazy stories. But today, their laughter stings. I've never had the luxury of friends, and now it's hitting a lot harder than usual. I wave when they spot me, and find the nearest door to lock myself behind. It happens to be the main bathroom, and once I'm inside, I regret not sulking in Elias's room instead.

My tears are a broken faucet, and they fall harder when all the rejections weigh on me.

Rap. Rap. Rap. "Sage?"

Shit. My heart takes a leap when Elias's voice comes after the knock. I stare at my tear-soaked face in the bathroom mirror. Taking a deep breath, I try to compose myself.

"Just a second!"

There's shuffling on the other side of the door, and just when my heartbeats calm, his deep voice filters through the door again. "Can you open the door for me?"

I'm a hot mess, and all his friends are here. He's going to think I'm crazy. "I can't," I say, my voice not doing a good job of concealing my emotions this time.

"I know, but I want you to."

With a sudden sweep of confidence, I open the door to see Elias's softening gaze. His eyes dart around my blotchy face and before I know it, he's stepping inside and locking the bathroom door behind us. His hands cup my face as his thumb runs a smooth touch along my jawline.

"Why are you crying?" His words are laced with concern.

My gaze drops to the floor. "It's stupid."

"Not to me."

Without any forewarning his large hands frame my waist, and he hoists me onto the counter. Shocked, I sit there as he goes over to the sink to grab a small towel from the shelf, soaking it under the faucet.

Elias steps between my legs, taking up all the space. "Can I?"

I'm not sure what he's asking permission for, but I'd do anything not to be the loser crying in his bathroom. So I nod, and when he presses the wet towel to my face, the warmth of it seeps into my skin and descends to strangle my heart. He gently wipes my tears, one hand around the nape of my neck as he focuses intently on the mascara stains under my eyes.

"You don't have to tell me. But whenever you want to talk, I'll listen."

This time it's the gentle words that break the dam, rather than the weight of rejection. Tears spill down my face, and I can't help the wobble of my lips. But Elias doesn't leave, he stays. He stays and wipes my skin with a warm wet towel, and places a gentle hand on my neck.

I sniffle. "I don't want to bore you."

"You couldn't if you tried."

"I don't think I can talk right now," I finally admit.

"Then I will."

My gaze snaps to him in pure shock. Elias offering information is a rarity. Not even when I spilled all my family history on our first date did he share anything. The man is a vault.

"Remember when you talked to my parents on the phone, and you asked who I took after?"

I nod.

"I'm adopted. The Westbrooks took me in when I was a kid, so that's why I don't look like them. I look exactly like my biological father. We even have the same name. That's why everyone calls me Eli. I'm not exactly a fan of my full name."

I wince, knowing I've adamantly called him that since the first day we met. He must see that I'm about to apologize for that because he cuts me off.

"I like it when you say it."

I suppress an idiotic smile. "You're giving me a lot of your firsts, Elias. Careful, or I might think you like me for real."

"I do like you, Sage."

My heart sings a happy tune when our eyes lock, and it makes me want to drop the weight from my shoulders. "My birthday is a week away," I start. "Yet every year I get older, I'm always stuck in the same place. It feels like I'm always running but never getting anywhere."

He listens intently.

"And I hate crying like this, but I wasn't allowed to feel back then, so now when I have an emotion, I don't suppress it. I could say my head hurts, and my mom would say she has chronic migraines. I would cry about my shitty ballet teachers, and she'd tell me she's cried so much in her life that she's run out of tears. She made it a competition, and sometimes it felt better to just lose.

"One of the reasons I joined ballet was to escape my house a few times a week. It was rough being around my parents when they fought, and it got worse when Sean was born. I felt powerless. Like I was too much, yet never enough. I could barely keep up with school and home life, but I knew if I let ballet go, I'd fall into the pit that they dug for me, and I'd never get us out. Lately it's been feeling like I'm still there."

Elias drops his hands to either side of me on the counter. "Sean is in a great school, and probably headed to an even better college. You've won awards, done so many showcases, and now you're going to secure an audition for one of the most prestigious theaters in the world. You're far from stuck."

His words soak into me like warm oil.

"Your parents left you with a massive responsibility, yet you continue to blame yourself for them abandoning you and your brother. They decided drugs were more important than their children, and they left a fucking kid to take care of a kid." He exhales harshly. "You persevered through all of it and came out as this strong, capable, beautiful woman. There is nothing about you that says you're weak. That word doesn't even belong in the same sentence when describing you."

I take a hiccup of air, gulping it down like I've just resurfaced from the ocean. "Wow. You're kind of good at this pep talk stuff."

My whole life, I've been the one taking the lead. As exhausting as it is, there has never been a moment where I could turn that part of me off. It's always felt like it's me against the world, and it may be, but even the illusion of someone carrying the weight for me is enough to loosen the age-old knot in my stomach.

He rubs his thumb against my cheek. "It's pretty damn easy when I'm talking about you."

I smile and so does he, and when there's a knock at the bathroom door, he shoots me a look that asks if I'm okay, and I nod. So we head back out. Hand in hand.

SUMMER AND I retire to the balcony after dinner to watch the colorful skies slip away into darkness. The guys were complaining about having to head back to Dalton tomorrow morning, and I can't help but miss all of them.

"You okay?" she asks, leaning against the black metal railing.

"Yeah. Elias kind of has a way with words."

She nods. "He'll always make sure the people he loves are cared for."

This time, I don't correct her. For once, I'd like to be included in that category, even if I know it's not true.

"Sum," Aiden calls her. "Remind Dylan why your dad does not like him."

Summer glances back at me with an amused expression, then follows Aiden back inside.

I sit on the ground to watch the quiet sunset. This is a view I've never seen from my apartment. The most I could see was abandoned shopping carts and overgrown bushes.

"Saved you a cupcake," Kian says when he steps onto the balcony.

He lowers to sit on the ground beside me, holding out a pink-frosted cupcake. I crack a half smile and take it from him. The silence isn't uncomfortable. I'm not sure what it is, but his presence is oddly comforting.

He looks at me with a soft smile. "You know, sometimes it takes time to realize there are people in the world who want to help you without wanting anything in return."

I have a feeling he also noticed something was wrong when I came out of the bathroom with puffy eyes. Nobody brought it up and

I was grateful for it, but I'm pretty sure it was because Elias gave them a silent warning.

"Sometimes it isn't so easy," I whisper.

Kian turns to the dark sky. "I don't know if that's true. I think people show you who they are pretty quickly. It's up to you to decide if you want to trust them."

He's right about that. Elias showed the kind of guy he is immediately. I didn't need to think long about wanting him to be my fake boyfriend.

I take a bite of the cupcake. "Philosopher Kian tonight?"

"You don't know? I'm like an advice wizard to these guys. They can't do anything without my help."

"For some reason, I actually believe that."

He bumps his shoulder against mine. "I think we're going to be great friends, Sage."

"Is it because I'm the only one who won't rag on you?"

"Pretty much." He gives me a sideways look. "Don't go changing that."

"I won't."

We sit like that for a while. The only conversation is the one happening inside, and I can't help but bask in the quiet understanding that settles between Kian and me. It's the kind of quiet that makes you feel heard. Something I never experienced before I met Elias.

Note to self: Let the light in.

TWENTY-FOUR

SAGE

CRYING ON MY birthday is my own little tradition. Except this year it's less existential and more about feeling like a loser. The clock on the wall of the ballet studio glows red; it's been three hours since I came in here. Everything I have is going into perfecting my pieces for the roles of Odette and Odile, just in case I get an invite to audition for NBT. The rest of the time I filmed content for my page and posted it to share with my followers. It's already 4:00 p.m., which means I've worked away more than half the day.

Being alone on my birthday feels like torture. Though it's not like I had special plans. I have no friends in Toronto, Sean is at his friend's house, and even my fake boyfriend is busy watching game tapes with his team. I'm officially pathetic.

The glass door of the studio chimes, and my students slowly trickle inside. I didn't bother taking the day off when I didn't have any plans, but this is my only class of the day. The interest in our beginner program has been overwhelming, and when the studio emailed me about taking on additional classes, I agreed. It turns out that some of my followers live in Toronto and looked me up online. I don't mind because with my days packed, I can actually keep my bank account afloat.

When the time ticks to four thirty, I play the music on the speakers and instruct the class to show me what they remember from our last session. I walk around the room, correcting and praising each one of my students.

"Miss Beaumont, I can't do the extensions," one of them says.

"I used to struggle with this too, Jamie. Let's focus on some exercises that can support your movements."

I show him the use of développés and battements to emphasize control and alignment throughout every movement. When he tries again, I encourage him to repeat the form to get the best extensions possible. He nods happily, and I head to the front of the class.

With a few more practice rounds, we near the end of the class, and I teach them some ballet terminology. The French is mangled on their tongues, but soon they're pronouncing it correctly.

They repeat after me, but I pause mid-word when the door to the studio jingles and Elias walks inside. I can't take my eyes off him. He's wearing a blue Thunder T-shirt and jeans, hair tousled from the wind.

It's the gasp from one of my students that draws my attention back to them. "It's Eli Westbrook!" one of the girls announces.

The mix of ballet and hockey fans in this class never fails to amuse me. The kids stand and run up to him. Elias is so tall they barely come up to his abdomen. He looks to me with an alarmed expression, hands up in surrender when they start spewing questions at him.

"Did you drink a lot of milk to get that tall?"

"Are you dating our teacher?"

"How much money do you make?"

"All right. Leave him alone, guys." I disperse them by standing in front of Elias like a shield. "Your parents are waiting outside."

They groan in unison, but head out to their parents, eyes still on Elias. That's when I spot Nina, quietly packing her things, and not partaking in the kids' thorough interrogation of Elias.

I stop her before she can head out to where a beat-up pickup truck honks obnoxiously. "Hey, you've been quiet today. Everything okay?"

Watery eyes meet mine. "I'm fine. My mom signed me up for another ballet competition this week. The prize is a lot of money, and I don't want to disappoint her."

"You'll do great no matter the outcome. And if you ever need help, I'm here." I pull out one of the studio's business cards, and write my personal number on there too. "That's my number in case you need it."

Her eyes flicker with an emotion I haven't seen from her. Something like hope. But it disappears when the horn blares again and she rushes out of the studio.

When the room clears, it's just Elias and me.

His gaze hits my legs first, and slowly drags up my outfit to meet my face. The sweaty, blotchy one that should never be looked at, much less by a man who oozes sex appeal on any given day. The perusal has goose bumps riddling my skin, making me fight a violent shiver.

"I wanted to see you."

Is it weird that my heart skips a beat? "You did?"

"Don't sound so surprised, Sage. This is what boyfriends do." I want to make a quip about him not knowing that, but my sunken mood wouldn't let me fully enjoy one of his stony stares. He moves past me to look at the pictures I have pinned to a corkboard. They're Polaroids from when I first started here, along with a few from the showcases I've done with my students.

"When was this?" He's staring at a picture of me at my first performance.

"I was eight. It's from my school talent show. My uncle made so many copies of it, I had to find somewhere to put it." I move to my small desk to clean up the papers and put away the speakers. "What are you doing here? I was going to take the bus home because your practice was supposed to run late."

He doesn't answer for a long moment, but when I turn to look at him, he's putting something in his pocket. "Maybe I want a private dance," he says.

The question makes my face redden. It's so intimate here, I can't imagine having all his attention on me as I dance. There is no way he doesn't notice the bout of heat that blooms on my chest because he stares for a whole minute—or an hour, I really can't be sure—then looks away without mentioning it. Another drop in the bucket for his charitable efforts, I presume.

"Gotta pay extra for that, rookie," I manage to choke out.

"Would a date work?"

"A date?" An embarrassingly giddy rush of excitement zips through me, and I pause to wonder if he knows it's my birthday. But I didn't tell him the date. "Shit. Did I forget about something we're invited to?"

"No. I want to take you somewhere. We can stop by the apartment for you to change or we can go out as you are. You look perfect either way."

The casual compliment hits my chest like he loaded it into a slingshot. I glance down at my leotard and the sheer wrap skirt, then back up at Elias, who watches me expectantly, seemingly unaware of the effect of his words.

"I brought a change of clothes." My clothing selection is limited, but I have a simple pair of jeans and a pretty top to change into after my class.

When he nods, I go to the back room and change out of my tight leotard. When I return, he smiles. "Beautiful."

I fidget with the fabric of my blouse. "You like the color?"

"Sage happens to be my favorite."

When he reaches for my hand, I link mine with his. I've had worse birthdays.

AS WE ARRIVE at an abandoned farm area, I wonder whether he's going to ditch me in the woods. Elias backs up the truck—Aiden's truck—where there's a white billboard-looking screen behind us. He hops out before circling around to open my door.

There's a sliver of orange cast by the evening sun that still glows on the horizon. There are trees surrounding the overgrown grass area and not another car in sight. I follow Elias to the back, where he opens the tailgate, and I spot a blown-up air mattress.

My brows raise. "You know, there are better places to see me in my birthday suit."

Elias blinks in confusion then looks at the truck bed, scratching his head as if he's just now realizing what I'm thinking. "Trust me, you'll like it."

"To be fair, I'm pretty sure I'd like anything you do to me."

There's that unimpressed look again. "Shut up, Sage."

I comply, only because his large hands bracket my waist and hoist me up. Elias hops in behind me, and that's when I notice the chocolate cake. Before I can ask any questions or make another joke, bright light blinds me from the projector directly in front of us. What the hell?

When "Be My Baby" by the Ronettes plays, I freeze. I'd know that intro anywhere. I look at the white screen that's lit up with my favorite movie.

The title card for *Dirty Dancing* pops up, and I realize we're at one of the old drive-in theaters located on the outskirts of the city. I turn back to the once creepy air mattress, and now I want to cry. Elias sits there smiling, with a candle in the cake in front of him.

"Who is that for?" The words wobble off my lips, betraying my mask of indifference.

"I heard it's someone's birthday."

"How did you even know?"

"I have my ways." I pin him with a skeptical look, and his blank expression cracks with a smile. "Sean texted me," he admits. "Now, come here."

The command slithers right between my legs, and tries to pull my pants down. *Relax, Sage.* I bounce on the air mattress and wait as he lights the candle on the cake.

"I always let Sean do this part for me," I say. My brother and I have spent almost every birthday together since he was born, and this one hurts a little.

"What do you mean?"

"Sean blows out my birthday candles."

Elias's gaze is pitying, and I raise a brow at him. "So, you have one day out of the year to celebrate yourself, and you still manage to make it about someone else?" He pauses briefly. "Which is sweet, by the way, but that doesn't mean it's your day."

"That's how it's always been."

"You mean you taking care of everyone but yourself? Yeah, I know."

He's right; I do things for someone I love, but not for myself. I try to squash the thought. It's a terrifying revelation to think you don't love yourself the way you love others.

The candle illuminates his face. "This time, make a wish for you."

If genies were real, I'd think Elias might be one. He's made my birthday special. He made sure Sean got his medications. He is single-handedly making sure I have a fighting chance at starring in my dream ballet production. With everything I've ever wanted within my reach, I close my eyes and make the only wish I can think of.

I wish Elias makes his first career goal.

Pulling out the candle, he cuts a slice, and I take the first bite. It tastes like the cake I buy every year. The memories start flooding in. "A McCain chocolate cake? You're spoiling me," I say through a mouthful.

"You deserve it, but it's not McCain."

"It's not?" He could've fooled me, it tastes identical, actually maybe even better. "You didn't have to buy me an actual birthday cake."

"I didn't. I made it."

I almost choke on the huge chunk of chocolate cake and icing in my mouth. Not attractive at all. I take my time swallowing to comprehend what he's saying. "You baked me a birthday cake?"

He nods like it's no big deal. "I got you a McCain cake too, but it's at home. I thought you and Sean might want to keep that tradition between the two of you."

At *home*. How did I end up fake dating the most thoughtful man on the planet? My eyes sting, but I don't want to close them. I want to keep looking at the man who baked me a birthday cake.

He even thought to include my brother. Sean wished me a happy birthday this morning, but it didn't feel the same. I would never tell him, but I sobbed for a good ten minutes after our phone call. "It's weird seeing him get older, but I understand why he wanted to go to his friend's. I mean, I didn't want to hang out with adults at his age."

"You're allowed to feel hurt, Sage."

I shake my head. "He didn't mean to hurt me. I don't blame him."

"You don't have to. He's a teenager; of course he wants to hang out with his friends. But it's okay to feel sad when the one person you've always had by your side is growing up. It doesn't make either of you bad people."

A harsh burn envelops my heart. "If he turns out to be anything like you, I'll know I succeeded."

I hesitate for a second before wrapping him in a tight hug. He does the same, holding me close enough that his lips skim the crown of my head, leaving a brief kiss in my hair.

The glow from the movie lights his face, and his eyes sparkle. Breaking the intense eye contact, I finish off my cake and lick my plate clean like an animal.

He chuckles, taking the plate from me. "Promise me one thing."

I gaze up at him.

"Don't check your email until midnight."

I'm surprised by his request, and I stare down at my phone like an addict being told their next hit is getting revoked. I constantly check my emails for new auditions and the not-so-fun rejections. The moment NBT emails me, if they ever do, I want to be ready.

"Your email will still be there tomorrow. And Sean has both of our numbers. I know you already called them, but I called his friend's parents to introduce myself too."

My heart flutters, and I can only credit it to his featherlight words. "But—"

"And in case that doesn't satisfy you, I got their neighbors' contact information."

"Eli—"

"Both neighbors. On each side."

I can't help the laugh that bubbles out of me. I put my phone in his hand and close his fingers around it. "I was going to say that I'll leave the ringer on, but I won't check until tomorrow. Midnight is only a few hours away."

"You're sure?"

"I'm sure."

He takes the opportunity to pull me in, allowing me to lean on him like my personal pillow. Elias fusses over the fuzzy pink blanket, ensuring it covers my legs, and situates his own pillow behind him. The movie plays, and although this is one of my favorite birthday traditions, there's a part of me that wants to sit and talk to Elias instead. To hear his voice and the low vibration of his chest when he speaks. To let the overflow of serotonin wash over me anytime he focuses on me.

With a light brush of his lips against my ear, he whispers, "Happy birthday, Sage."

"Thank you, Elias."

The smell of chocolate lingers in the air as the glow of the drive-in movie projector washes us in bright light. A gentle breeze sweeps past the truck bed, and I snuggle closer to him, forgetting just for one night that this isn't real. Because I know how long I'll have this, and it's not nearly long enough. But tonight, I want to spend my birthday in the arms of a thoughtful hockey player and not worry about a damn thing.

TWENTY-FIVE

ELIAS

INSTEAD OF HEADING back home like I had planned, when Sage fell asleep in my arms halfway through the movie, I didn't wake her up. She doesn't often sleep this well. So we stayed here all night.

Wisps of curly brown hair shine like gold-infused thread in the morning light. The breeze isn't cool anymore because time must be crawling toward noon for the temperature to be this warm. Our blanket is long forgotten as Sage lies on top of me, her legs tangled with mine and one hand splayed over my chest. It's pure fucking bliss.

But also pure torture. Because her hand is like a brand on my chest, and as if the nerves in my body know she's near, they send a jolt straight to my dick. My morning wood isn't concealed well, but I'm trying my hardest not to have it be the first thing to greet her. I look at her to refocus on the pretty features of her face, and not her perfect body clinging to mine.

To distract myself, I pull out my phone to take a picture of a sleeping Sage and post it. I've noticed how hard she's been working by posting every week and replying to her comments. So, if one post from me helps relieve the pressure, I'd do it without her having to ask.

As I swipe a loose strand from over her eye, she blinks. Her hand slides up my chest, and I hold it. Instinctively, I kiss the inside of her wrist and feel the flutter of her pulse against my lips. She likes it when I do that. The simple, affectionate touch makes her whole face light up, and although she tries to hide it, I see her shy smile.

"Did I wake you?" My voice is raspy from sleep.

"No, but I can go back to sleep if you want to continue watching me like a creep."

I chuckle. Only Sage can be disoriented from sleep and still have a quip ready.

"I checked on your brother. His friend's mom said she'll tell him to call when he's up."

"What made you like this?" she asks. "So caring and sweet. Was it your mom?"

The question makes me smile. "Yeah, she is probably a big reason, but I think ever since I was adopted, I've liked caring for people." It made me the overprotective father figure in our friend group, and the guys like to rag on me about it.

"How old were you?"

"Four."

She sits with that for a minute, and it feels weird to talk about this, but with her, I want to. I want her to ask me anything just so I can continue to hear her voice.

"Do you talk to your biological parents at all?" When she looks at me, she must see something tense in my face, because she pushes up to sit. "Sorry. Don't answer that, I'm sure that's an annoying question."

"No, I want to tell you."

A tsunami of emotions surges across her face as she waits for me to continue.

"I don't know them, but I'm in contact with my dad because I send him money."

Perfect brows furrow. "Why?"

"So he doesn't try to blackmail my parents for a quick check. Again," I reveal bitterly.

Sage twists her body to face me and give me space, but I want to touch her. It's so much easier to talk about this when I can feel her in my arms as a tangible, stable thing.

"I was eighteen when we won the world juniors, and I knew that was the high I wanted to chase for the rest of my life. Except that night we celebrated, and it got out of hand. The visiting team crashed our party, and everything changed."

Recalling it after so many years feels like removing a sharp object that's been stuck in my skin, but Sage draws soothing patterns across my palm that urge me to continue.

"The party was happening in a few of the adjoining rooms, and we were all drinking. For us, a championship, alcohol, and a few girls made it feel like we were on top of the world." I give a wry laugh at how naive we were. "We weren't letting in just anyone, only people from our school, because our coaches would be pissed if they found out we were drinking, but there was this one girl that I happened to hit it off with."

I recall that night clearly. There is no way I could ever forget.

"She stayed for a while, and soon enough we were in my room, and we ended up sleeping together. I fell asleep thinking she was right beside me, but the next thing I knew, I woke up to see both my parents at the edge of my bed. They were staring down at me with looks of disappointment that still haunt me to this day."

I take a deep breath and go on. "Turns out the girl only snuck into the party so she could target me. She had pictures of me drinking, and later, when I went to sleep, she took more pictures, ones that made it look like I had taken drugs. And she sent them to my parents."

"Why would she do that?" Sage asks in horror.

"Apparently, my biological father found out my adoptive parents are rich. He was struggling, and he found an equally desperate college student who was willing to do anything to pay her loans. So, he blackmailed my parents with the threat of releasing those pictures.

If that happened, I'd be banished from hockey in seconds. My acceptance to Dalton would be revoked, and my dream to play in the NHL would be just that. A dream."

"Did your parents believe him?"

"When they came around they heard what I had to say and decided they trusted me. And the girl who took the pictures came clean a few days after the whole thing. I told them I did have alcohol, but I'd never touched any type of substance. That's all they needed to get one of the best lawyers on the case."

"Is that why you don't drink now?"

I nod.

"And it's why you haven't . . . ?" Sage trails off, but I know what she's thinking.

"I haven't been with anyone since," I confirm. "I don't know if it's because I'm paranoid or because I can't get the memory of my parents' disappointment out of my head, but it's easier this way."

Sage nods quietly, staring at me in a way that feels like she's holding my heart in her palms. "And your father? Why isn't he in jail?"

"We settled. If the whole thing went to court, the media would have followed it and he'd get what he wanted. My parents believed that he would be out of our lives after they paid him."

"But you're still paying him?"

"He threatened me after the fact, and I never wanted my parents to regret letting me into their life. So, I never told them, and I've been paying him for years."

Sage's lips part in shock. "But he tried to extort you, to ruin your career and blackmail you. How could you give someone like that a dime?"

I understand where her outrage is coming from. I feel it myself, but I've lived with it for so long, it doesn't matter to me anymore. "I needed him gone. The disappointment on my parents' faces that day was enough to solidify that decision."

"And your parents still don't know?"

I shake my head.

She gives me a sympathetic look. "Are you ever going to stop?"

"One time the money transfer was delayed, and the second he didn't see the money, he asked how much I really cared about my new NHL career."

"That's blackmail. It's—"

I shake my head. "It's not. The arrangement was my idea, and it's working for me. Nothing will change that."

Sage sits up straighter to level our gazes.

"But it's *not* working for you. You can barely let yourself relax around people. What that girl did to you because of him . . . you won't let anyone in, Elias. Not even me." Her voice cracks.

I pull her onto my lap, holding her face in my hands as ragged breaths puff past her lips.

"I feel more myself around you than anyone else. You make me feel like I don't need to hold back, and—*fuck*, Sage, you have no idea how much I want to let go when I'm with you."

"Then why don't you?" Her hands move to my shoulders. "You carry so much weight on your shoulders, Elias." Her gaze settles on mine with a sort of heavy determination. "I want you to give some of it to me."

Her words do the opposite of what she intends, and I feel gutted. This girl who carries everyone's pain and problems is earnestly asking me to give her more. To give her my problems because she would rather carry them than see me crumple under the weight. Sage is beautiful and strong, a ray of light in a field of darkness.

"I don't want to know you like everyone else. I want the real you," she says.

I glide my thumb along her smooth cheek. "Then that's what I'll give you, but be patient with me, yeah?"

Sage brings up my hand and kisses the inside of my wrist. The warmth of her lips singes my skin. "Always."

TWENTY-SIX

ELIAS

WE'RE ONE GAME away from the playoffs, which means I'm one bad game away from being traded. The constant reminder at practice has been causing the kind of stress that leads to my recurring nightmares. Each time I've jolted awake, Sage has been there, holding my hand and reminding me it's just a dream. She eases the constant feeling that if I go to sleep, I'll wake to someone's disappointment.

Since I told her about my biological dad, I feel lighter. There's something new in our interactions, like we both feel more at ease. The line between us should be cemented, but the moments we share in the darkness of my room only make me want to step over it. We don't talk about the nights, but the memory is alive in the way my gaze latches on to her when she's near.

I've never been more tempted to break this vow. But despite wanting to touch Sage the way I've dreamed of, I know it'll just complicate our relationship. The only thing helping me separate my feelings from our fake relationship is my celibacy. It's been difficult for me to trust anyone since what my biological dad did, and trusting Sage enough to break my celibacy only for her to leave would make it harder for both of us. The last thing I want for Sage is to throw my feelings at her when she hasn't even gotten a chance to live out her dream. I would never hold her back. I *can't*.

For our pregame warm-up, Coach went easy on us and set us up in the weight room for calisthenics. I'd much rather have been on the ice, practicing before the game to ensure I can rid myself of this goalless curse. Some days, I think it'll never end, but then I provide an assist, and it feels a step closer to the real thing. Now, back in the locker room, I feel myself crawling back into those negative thoughts.

"It's called choking."

I pause taping my hockey stick to find Socket standing in front of me. "What?"

"The thing that happens to you at the goal line. I see it in rookies all the time. They come right up to my face, so determined, ready to bag a goal, and then they freeze. I can see the doubt creeping in. And poof, the opportunity slips from right under their nose."

"I know what choking is," I mutter.

"Of course you do. I just mean you don't have to be stuck there. But you're letting yourself sit in that box of doubt, and no one can play hockey like that."

Socket's been a goalie on the Thunder for a few years, so he has experience.

"How do you suggest I get out of the box?"

"Break it. That moment of doubt needs to be shattered. You know you *can* do it, and now you *have* to. Don't think, and you won't choke."

Don't think. I mull over the advice in my head, mumbling a *thank-you* when he turns to his stall. His words are wise for someone who drank beer out of a skate because of a dare.

I let my music resume, but there's a shift in the air that makes me look to the doors of the locker room. Marcus and our right-winger, Owen Hart, walk inside. They're laughing together, something I've never done with our GM.

"Afternoon," Marcus says, waving a hand. "Since it's the last game of the regular season, I won't say much. I'll save the speech for the playoffs next week, which for some of you might be a faraway dream." I try to ignore the way he meets my eyes. "But it's here, and if you kill it out there tonight, the rest will be a breeze."

His cutting words don't fester deep today because I played well at our last game. Even if I haven't scored, the executives had to notice my improvement. This can't be it for me.

Coach walks into the dressing room. "Don't embarrass me out there. But after these past few games, I've seen what you can do. And I need all your RSVPs for the dinner, or the wife won't be happy if we have leftovers."

He shouts the reminder again to the guys that trickle in late.

Coach decided last night that he wants to boost team morale because two of our defensemen got into a heated argument on the ice during our last game. Their gloves came off, and they spit out their mouth guards before we broke them apart. The media blamed our organization for promoting poor sportsmanship. Now, the executives have hammered down on Coach Wilson to ease the tension.

When the music in my ears pauses, I check my phone to find a text from Sage.

Sage: A jersey with your name on it? A bit presumptuous, don't you think?

I can't help the smile her words bring to my face. Our team manager got me a jersey in her size, and I left it on the bed this morning. This is the first game she's attending, and as my girlfriend, she'll be expected to wear my jersey. But that's not the only reason I want her to wear it.

Elias: Were you planning on wearing someone else's?
Sage: What if I did?

Elias: Wear it and find out.

Sage: Don't tease me, Elias. Do you really want me to wear it? Isn't that cheesy? You already have plenty of fangirls.

Elias: You're the only one that matters.

"Isn't it awkward?" Socket's voice pulls my attention away from the appearing and disappearing bubbles on my screen. When they stop and Sage doesn't reply, I toss my phone back on the bench.

I pull out an earphone. "What?"

"Owen being here?"

"Why would it? I've met plenty of guys I've matched up against in the past."

"No, I mean because he dated your girlfriend."

My head snaps to attention. "What?"

A burning sensation sears through my veins.

"Uh, never mind." Socket turns to focus on the pull-up bar like it's a complex machine.

"What do you mean they dated?"

"If Sage didn't say anything I'm sure it's for a good reason. She probably doesn't even know he got traded here," he deflects.

I'm trying to think back to whether she told me this, but the only thing she said was that a boyfriend had reappeared in her life. Suddenly, it's starting to make sense.

"When did they date?"

He sighs. "He said they dated for a few years. I think they broke up a couple months ago. But that's all I know." He raises both hands in surrender.

The information doesn't ease the burn in my chest. I want to call or text Sage to find out more. But if she wanted to tell me about her ex, she would—the girl's an open book.

Owen continues talking to Marcus before he walks to his stall a few benches down. The pat on the back and the smile he got from

Marcus make me envious. I've been here for longer and haven't gotten a simple hello in return, but Sage's ex seems to be our GM's best friend.

"Westbrook," Owen acknowledges when he walks by.

Now, this interaction feels tense. "Hart."

"I have a good feeling about today's game," Aiden says, finally showing up after spending the night at Summer's parents' house.

"Why?"

"It's your girl's first game. No better motivator."

I roll my eyes and toss the cloth tape at him.

"Is Sean coming? That kid used to hang around here all the time when I first started," says Socket as he ties his skates.

"No, he's in school a few hours away."

"York Prep, right?"

Our heads whip to Owen, who smiles innocently. The question starts a dangerous bubbling in my veins. Aiden glances at me with a look of confusion.

"My brother's in the same year as Sean."

It's impossible for me to not glare at him.

Socket's laugh cuts the tension. "Man, I would have never survived at a boarding school. They would have kicked me out as soon as I started playing hockey in the halls."

His comment gets a laugh from a few of the guys around us and starts a conversation about reckless things they've done in school.

Suddenly, even as the conversation moves on, I can't sit here any longer. That feeling propels me to walk through the double doors, ignoring Aiden's call for me, and straight down to where Marcus is retreating into his office.

"Marcus, do you have a second?"

He folds his arms and exhales loudly, but he nods, and I follow him to his office. I might be making things worse, but I need to make an effort to cement my position here.

"Wanted to see me for a final farewell?" Marcus says.

I ignore the pointed jab. "I came here to assure you that I won't let this opportunity slip away easily. I know tonight's the final day before the organization's decision about me, but I won't give you the chance to sign those trade papers."

If looks could kill, no one would survive the one he's giving me.

"And how are you going to do that? Because you haven't been stepping up to where we need you. You're a good player, we can see that, but if that doesn't translate to goals, we have no use for you. Assists are great until there isn't anyone to assist."

"But I'm—"

"And whatever damage control you're trying to do with my niece won't help your case." His glare turns lethal. "I trust Sage to make her own decision, but if your reputation interferes with her life, I won't stand for it. You hurt her, and I'll make sure your career never recovers."

The threat should make me cower, but I can't help but feel relieved that even though Sage doesn't think so, she has people who have her back. Me included.

"I'd never let my public image affect her. She's with me because we care about each other, and she knows I'd do anything for her. It's the reason she's staying with me."

"Staying with you?"

Fuck. From his deadly glare, I'm assuming Sage didn't tell him she's living with me. First Owen, now this. The girl couldn't make it any clearer how temporary I am in her life.

He scoffs. "So, in the midst of your career dangling by a thread, you think you can focus on a relationship? You can barely focus on your game. This isn't the NCAA, where you can get away with your parents signing a check."

His constant reminders of my family's wealth, dissolving my skill into a mere favor, tighten my fist. I have to clench my jaw to keep from saying something that might get me kicked out before I can even play the last game I have to prove myself.

"I don't think you have what it takes to be great, Eli." Then he goes in for the kill. "And frankly, I don't think you're good enough for Sage either."

TWENTY-SEVEN

SAGE

HOCKEY FANS ARE obnoxious and loud, and I can't wait to be one of them.

The Scotiabank Arena is bustling with blue and white as I follow the long line through security. After my bag is checked, I make my way to the suite that the team keeps for the players' families. I've sat here a few times with my uncle. But this time, walking in to find a close-knit group of hockey wives and girlfriends makes me feel like a fraud. Before I consciously make the decision, I start back down to the lower sections where the team has a few reserved seats. Since it's our last regular-season game, it's not packed, so those seats are often empty.

"We need to talk." My uncle's voice cuts through the chaos of the arena, and I wipe the somber look from my face. I'm surprised to find that he isn't his usual happy self tonight, but I have an inkling of what this is about.

Marcus Smith-Beaumont has been there for Sean and me since we were kids. All my good childhood memories include him. All the ones without him have to do with my absent parents and police ransacking our house when my dad got into illegal narcotics.

When you grow up around chaos, the happy moments are like life rafts. But when I turned eighteen those life rafts no longer felt safe. I worked hard and saved enough money to never lose my brother to the system and show that I could provide a stable life for him. Luckily, I was an adult, which meant I could take on Sean as my dependent. However, when my uncle found out what happened with our parents he offered to adopt him, and I felt threatened. Threatened that another adult in my life was going to take something away from me.

Seeing this, Uncle Marcus immediately took back his offer and assured me that he knew how important it was that I become Sean's guardian. Since then, he's been the only adult figure in our life. He's never overstepped, but that doesn't prevent him from playing up the uncle card.

"About what?"

He narrows his eyes. "Don't be a smart-ass. When were you going to tell me you're living with Westbrook?"

Oh crap. "I've been kind of busy . . ."

"I asked you to keep me in the loop."

"You weren't going to approve."

Uncle Marcus crosses his arms. "Since when does my approval dictate how you live? You're dating the kid I made a mistake drafting to this team. And as much as I'd like for you to continue being happy, it won't save him from being traded."

I scoff. "He doesn't need me to save him. He'll prove himself, you'll see."

He pins me with his best parental stare. "You couldn't have chosen anyone else?"

"Like who? Owen?"

Uncle Marcus always liked Owen and never understood why we broke up, because I didn't tell him. To be fair, Owen was the ideal hockey-playing Canadian boy. Any general manager uncle's dream.

His jaw tenses. "You know what? Maybe just stay away from hockey guys entirely."

I snort. "You're getting better at this fatherly advice thing. You should get married and have kids so you won't have to practice on me anymore."

"Maybe they won't slash my tires."

I wince. That incident was in the same era as the guardianship debacle. It was before I had the conversation with him like a real adult. I found out Uncle Marcus had gone to a family lawyer to discuss Sean's adoption, and in a fit of teenage anger, I used my pocketknife to slash one tire. His use of the plural is an exaggeration.

"You sitting in the box?"

I shake my head. "Rinkside."

"Have fun, but don't expect to see anything meaningful from your player."

I roll my eyes. "He's *your* player, and don't be rude."

He grimaces and disappears down the hall where the rest of the men in fancy suits follow him. Those are the executives that are watching every player tonight. I'm sure they have a lot riding on the guys tonight, but I know no one feels as much pressure as Elias does right now.

By the time I find my section, the game has already started. I thought my outfit was cute, but I didn't take into account that it would be cold at a hockey game. It doesn't matter though, because I feel good. For years, I've worried about not looking good enough. Too big, too tall, too skinny, too *everything*. Now, after years of hard work, I've poured love into my body. The reason I get to do what I love.

So, when I get looks from other fans for my overdressed appearance, I don't pull down my skirt or fidget with my jersey. If I did, I'd probably pull out some threads, because I've worn this skirt so many times it should be in the trash. But I'm a reuse, reduce, recycle type of girl. Sue me.

Right against the glass, I can see everyone clearly. I've never been inclined to watch sports on my own, but because of Sean and my uncle, and now Elias, I hold a soft spot for hockey.

I'd say it's a little uncomfortable to sit at a game where a girl holds up a sign asking my boyfriend to *puck* her. *Fake* boyfriend, but I'm still jealous. I know it and the girl's about to know it too. Maybe when my fist meets her face—

"Sage!" Summer's voice hits me and I turn to see her approaching. She's not wearing a jersey; she's got on a jacket with Aiden's number on it. "I was looking all over for you. You didn't want to sit in the box?"

I look back at the women in the family box, having drinks and cheering on their partners. "Sean said it would be a disservice to hockey if I didn't sit rinkside."

"Smart kid." Summer takes the empty seat beside me and offers me some popcorn. "These have always been my favorite seats. That's why my dad reserves them for most games."

"Do you come to all of Aiden's games?"

"It was easier when he was at Dalton, but I still try to attend most of them. It's nice to know someone's there for you, you know?"

There's no better feeling than looking into a crowd of strangers to find one that puts a smile on your face.

My smile slips when a familiar body bangs against the glass. Owen winks at me, his grin toothy and wide.

"You know him?" Summer whispers, giving the guy a once-over.

I stuff my face with a handful of popcorn to avoid answering her, but she gasps. Clearly she's a genius. "That explains it."

"Explains what?"

She points to number eighty-eight, Elias, who's staring at Owen with an eviscerating look, one that does not make them seem like they are on the same team.

"Elias doesn't know I dated Owen." I say it to Summer, but it's more of a reassurance for myself.

"Not to point out the obvious, but that's a man who knows more than you think."

I swallow, watching the hostile interaction between Elias and Owen. Even when Aiden approaches, Elias ignores whatever his friend says, and skates to shoot a practice shot in the net. It flies right by Socket with a precision that makes the fans behind me cheer.

Fidgeting with my hands, I feel an odd sensation in my gut.

"You okay?" Summer places a hand on my bouncing leg.

"I should have told him." I chew my lip.

Summer laughs and shakes her head. "I know Eli doesn't share a lot of his feelings, but trust me, being mad at you would never be one of them."

"How do you know that?"

"Because he likes you."

I choke on her words, or maybe a lonesome kernel from my handful of popcorn. Summer hands me her drink, and I swallow some of it.

There are a lot of questions in my head, but all of them go unanswered because Summer is already up and yelling at the refs as the game continues.

Elias does not like me. If he did, he would have at least kissed me by now. The only time he's said he likes me was when I was a blubbering mess in his bathroom. He practically had to say it then.

For the rest of the game, I'm stewing in my thoughts, but I'm pulled right out when there's a breakaway. The arena echoes with the crowd's roar, and Elias surges forward, hungry for what he knows is his. I'm stiff with anticipation, willing him to succeed. He seems different, a new purpose behind his blades as he sprints forward.

The puck is glued to his stick, then he releases a wrist shot that cuts through the air, and time suspends just as the horns blare.

He scored. Elias scored his first career goal.

The crowd behind me goes ballistic. My heart pounds, and my scream is so loud I know my throat is going to be sore tomorrow. We bang against the plexiglass and watch as Elias does a short lap around the side of the rink. When he sees Summer and me waving at him, he cracks a smile. He bumps against the glass, putting his gloved hand right where mine meets the plexi, and even with the barrier I feel the warmth of his touch.

When he's skating away, his teammates pile on top of him. My eyes blur with tears, especially when the Jumbotron shows the executive suite where my uncle fails to celebrate, but I know he's happy.

In the remaining two periods, Elias manages to score two more times with an assist from Aiden and a surprising one from Owen. The hat trick sends the crowd into a frenzy, and I'm celebrating with anyone and everyone, knocking over bags of popcorn and tripping out of my seat. Summer and I are hugging each other by the end of it, and I can feel the energy of the crowd vibrating through me.

Elias has worked so hard. I've seen him beating himself up over not having the goal and how the media treats him. But now it all feels worth it. It's a middle finger to everyone who doubted him.

While the arena slowly empties, Summer pulls me down a narrow hall toward the dressing rooms. She hasn't let go of my arm, and it makes me smile. The security guards greet us, and we easily move through to wait for the guys. My earlier anxiety practically disappears as I hear the way everyone talks about Elias. It's a little late, but I couldn't be happier that he's finally getting the recognition he deserves.

When Elias finally appears in the hall, I can't help but jump. This is huge, and even if he's not wearing a smile, I'll wear one for him.

"You did it!"

He pulls the strap of his bag higher on his shoulder, and he surveys the jersey I'm wearing. But even though there's a flicker of something behind his eyes, he only gives me a tight smile in response. It pricks at my chest that he's not happy, so I tiptoe to wrap my arms around his neck and pull him in for a hug. He stumbles, not touching me at all, but I don't let it deter the strength of my grip.

"I'm proud of you," I whisper into his neck, squeezing him tightly.

Then with a deep, rumbling sigh, he slides his arms around my waist and lifts me off my feet. "Thank you," he says softly and puts me down way too soon.

Socket pops out of the locker room and slaps a hand on Elias's back. "Drinks on you. That was one hell of a first goal."

"Well worth the wait," says Aiden, grinning wide as he ruffles a hand through Elias's overgrown hair.

Elias shrugs Aiden off, fixing his hair, as if it could look any better.

"I'd say you had your good luck charm," Summer says, bumping me with her shoulder.

Elias's expression is blank. "Send me the bill. I'm going to head home."

Socket steps in front of him. "You're not getting off the hook that easily. It's your first goal, and you know the rules."

"He's right, Eli. You gotta pay your dues. We all did." Aiden turns to the group of guys gathered in the hallway. "Drinks at our place. Everyone's invited."

My gaze darts to Elias, who appears resigned and nods. The guys holler and pat him on the back as they pile into their cars to follow us to the apartment. Aiden and Summer head to the car, and Elias finally moves when the hallway clears out.

I can't handle the sudden silent treatment. I won't stand here and let him get away with this sulky act of misery. Especially not on the biggest night of his rookie career.

When he opens the passenger-side door for me, I start to say something, but with both his friends in the car I remain silent.

There's a sinking feeling in my stomach when he shuts my door. As we pull out of the parking lot, Elias stops to sign a few autographs out his window first.

"Sign my forehead!"

"Can you say hi to my son? He loves you."

Elias happily obliges all their requests, making small talk that he had to have learned in media training. Though he's got a reputation for being the quiet golden boy, so I assume everyone knows how he is. But he handles it all with aplomb.

A few of them say hi to Summer and me. One young girl lights up when she notices I'm in the car. "Your performance in last year's *Giselle* was beautiful!"

I'm so shocked, it takes me a full beat to process what she's said. Elias turns to me, gauging my reaction. He wears a faint, proud smile.

I have never been praised for a performance months after it's taken place. I've always assumed it's because I'm not a memorable ballerina. But being recognized here, outside a hockey arena in downtown Toronto, for my performance in a small showcase I did last winter, plants a happy hum in my heart. I thank the girl who doesn't realize the impact her words have on me, especially when I've been down about not getting an audition for *Swan Lake*.

Summer excitedly squeezes my shoulder from behind me.

When the window whirs shut, the smile on my face goes nowhere. We drive to the apartment, and the quiet settles back in. I'm reminded of the seemingly simmering man in the seat beside me. But I'm a determined woman, so I won't let Elias get away with his solemn attitude.

TWENTY-EIGHT

SAGE

LAUGHTER FOLLOWS ME back to the open glass doors of the balcony, where all the guys are seated. Once we made it home, we ordered food and alcohol, so everyone ate and talked until they moved outside for drinks. The balcony is large enough that everyone who could make it sits comfortably on the outdoor couches and chairs.

I slip past some of the guys to place the platter of snacks and fruit on the glass table. When I start to collect the empty beer bottles, Aiden stops me.

"I got it," he says, and takes the bottles from me.

Summer gives me a gentle smile when I stand there like a deer in headlights.

"Yeah, join us. We can all help ourselves if we need something," says Socket.

The guys welcome me, and I stand there for a minute realizing there's not any seat available. Even the chairs from inside are out here and taken.

"Here, you can take my seat." I turn to find Owen standing.

The smile he gives me crawls under my skin.

"She'll sit with me." Elias's command is low but holds a heavy authority. When I turn to him, finally meeting his eyes, he doesn't look needy or desperate. He made a simple statement, but he said it like he's so sure of me, I'd be an idiot not to move.

Owen continues to stare at me as if he expects me to sit in the chair he's offered, but I grab a plate of snacks and head to Elias. He doesn't move over, only leans back and taps his thigh.

The unspoken command is so authoritative I feel a tremor move through my body when I obey. But I won't show him how his order affects me, or how it sends an electric feeling twirling between my legs.

Clutching my plate tightly, my hand trembles as I settle onto Elias's lap. He's warm, and comfortable, momentarily distracting me from the torment. His palm flattens against my abdomen, and he draws me back so I'm flush against him.

My unruly hair is in his face, but he makes no move to brush it away. Elias chimes in to the conversation every now and then. I finish off the few pretzels and fruit on my plate, and when I start to get up to take it inside, he stops me. "Stay. I'll take it in later."

With his arm on my stomach and his hand on my leg, I'm trapped. I'm hyper-aware of the patterns he draws on my thigh and every stroke of his fingertips. When his hand moves past the hem of my skirt, it ignites a wildfire beneath the surface, but I'd never tell him to stop.

With nowhere to go, and the cool breeze on my skin, I burrow deeper into Elias. As the guys discuss tonight's game, I let myself focus on the man beneath me. When he shifts, my head falls in the crook of his neck, lulled by the gentle hand that smooths my hair. It's like hypnosis, and I find myself drifting off even as I fight sleep.

This is new because I've never had to fight to stay awake.

Only when I feel the telltale dampness of drool around my mouth, accompanied by the faint scrape of chairs against the balcony floor, do I open my eyes again. I lift my head from Elias's chest and find Elias watching me. His gaze maps my face, and it must be the haze from my sleep that makes me want to burrow further into him. To have him watch me with the kind of hunger I have to be dreaming up.

Then I hear his name called, and I jerk back. *Shit.* I fell asleep on him.

"I'm so sorry! Why didn't you wake me up?" I whisper and wipe at his shirt, although there's nothing there. I just need to do something with my fidgeting hands. I can no longer feel the breeze, only the hot ache between my legs when he looks at me like that. Like in this moment nothing else exists but him and me.

"Why would I do that?"

I narrow my eyes. "Oh my God, did I snore? Is that why you're being so nice to me? Because I embarrassed you in front of your teammates?"

"Not really." His lip tips upward like he's lying to me. "Besides, with you moving around in my lap I couldn't have gotten up even if I wanted to."

Oh. *Oh.*

Elias brushes my hair from my face, like he didn't just admit to me giving him a hard-on. I have to keep my mouth shut to not say anything. *He's celibate, Sage.*

"Eli," Socket shouts for him by the sliding doors.

There's a split second where he doesn't move at all. Like he wants to say something but gently shifts me off his lap, and we stand. He takes my plate with him when we head inside, where his teammates converse in the entryway.

"Thanks for having us," Socket slurs, engulfing Elias in a hug. "You're the man! The MVP! The best rookie . . ."

I take the plate from Elias and head for the kitchen as Socket continues to praise him.

"Sage," a soft voice whispers.

I curse under my breath before turning away from the sink to find Owen walking straight to me. He hugs me, and he's so heavy it's hard to even push him. Alarm bells ring in my head. My ex-boyfriend is an emotional drunk.

"Owen," I croak.

"Sorry, I forgot you have a shiny new boyfriend." He pulls away. "Do you hate me?"

I sigh. "I don't hate you, Owen. We just grew apart."

"But I'm back now. We can grow together. Something real."

Real. The one word shoots a sharp sting up my spine. It sounds foreign.

"You used to dance for me. Remember that?" he continues. That's an exaggeration because the only time he's seen me dance was the one time I practiced in front of him. He never came to any of my showcases. "Dance for me one last time," he says. His brown eyes are bloodshot when they widen. "I want to see—"

Then my view of Owen is completely obstructed because Elias stands between us. The only thing I can see is his crisp white T-shirt, clinging tightly to his back.

"You're drunk, Hart," his deep voice rumbles. "Go home."

A nervous swallow catches in my throat. He's about to protest, but Aiden walks into the kitchen with Summer. She glares at Owen like she'd gouge his eyes out if I asked her to.

Owen audibly swallows and drags his feet out of the kitchen.

There's a quiet buzz in the air that stays there even when we follow him out. Elias hasn't looked at me, and the realization makes my hands clammy.

"We're going to walk everyone out," Summer says suddenly. She pulls a confused Aiden with her. "And maybe go out for dessert. So, we'll be gone for a while."

She emphasizes the last part with a pointed look aimed at me. Then the door clicks shut, and it's just Elias and me.

I turn away from the door to finally talk to him, but he's already retreating to the living room. I glare at his back in irritation and follow hot on his heels. When he stops in front of the couch, I start to say something, but words fail me when Elias pivots, standing mere inches away.

"Who are you here for, Sage?" he asks suddenly.

The question throws me, and his towering frame doesn't help bring me back on track either. "Y-you," I stutter.

His hand moves to the hem of my jersey, crumpling the fabric. "Whose name is on your back?"

Heat zips up my spine. "Yours."

Elias runs his thumb along my bottom lip. "And whose name were you screaming in those stands?"

The warmth of his touch makes me shiver. I swallow. "Yours."

"No one else's?"

I raise a brow. "Why would there be anyone else?"

He drops his hand. "Because your ex-boyfriend might think differently."

His words are a blast of cold air. Summer was right.

"You know about that?" I ask sheepishly.

"Yeah, I know about that." He scoffs. "And you claim to be an open book."

I'm too stunned to speak, and he walks away from me to face the opposite wall. Like he can't stand looking at me.

"I *am* an open book. Owen's just my ex. I would've told you if it was important."

Elias doesn't turn. "He's on my team, Sage. I found out in the locker room before the game that you were together for *years*. That's pretty fucking important."

"Why does it matter?" I let out a frustrated sigh. "It's not like you're offering up information about your exes."

"Because she's not going to show up to your showcase as one of the ballerinas."

"Fine. I should have told you, and I'm sorry I didn't. But he doesn't mean anything to me."

Elias glances over his shoulder, looking doubtful.

"I'm serious. We only stayed together that long because it was comfortable. It was nothing more than familiarity."

"He knows things about you that I don't," he says quietly.

I snort. "Like what? My GPA in freshman year and my middle name? None of that is important. He only knows the old Sage. He doesn't know me anymore."

He's still facing away from me, and then I notice his hands balled into fists.

For a second, I think my eyes are playing tricks on me, but then it hits me like a fucking truck. "Are you *jealous*?"

"No." Elias turns to exit the living room. I block his path.

"Oh my God, you so are!" I can't keep the grin off my face. "Quick! I think he's coming back. Kiss me like you own me."

His stony expression only eggs me on. I stop him by the couch with both hands on his firm pecs, halting his retreat completely. His gaze falls to my hands on him, and even though it burns, I don't remove them.

"Come on, channel those caveman emotions." I'm smirking when I tiptoe to whisper in his ear. "Ask me whose name I'd like to scream. I promise you it's not Ow—"

Elias cuts me off when he grips my hair to tug me back. The sting only lasts a second because he seals his lips to mine.

The kiss steals everything from me.

To stop the shaking in my hands, I sink them into his hair. I don't waste time slipping my tongue into his mouth, feeling his own slide against mine. I know he's a good kisser, but right now there's no restraint, and he proves it as he gives me more.

I have half a mind to check if there are cameras here, but it's just us. He's kissing me for *real*, and I let him taste me however he wants. My lungs burn and I desperately need to breathe, but I need this more. I need *him* more.

When he presses his hips to mine, letting me feel the hardness, I moan. He caresses my mouth with every sweep of his tongue, electrifying every dormant nerve in my body before he pulls back. I make a noise of protest, but then his palm glides over my cheek, and I lean into his touch, unable to resist the heat of his gaze thawing something reckless within me. As the pad of his thumb gently frees my lip from between my teeth, I whimper. I actually fucking *whimper*.

"Sage," he rasps like it's a warning, and I swear I lose every brain cell in my head. This time, I lunge at him and press my mouth to his so suddenly, he loses his balance. Elias snakes an arm around my waist and falls backward on the couch, with me on top of him.

Then, when I think I broke him, and he's about to toss me off his lap, Elias drags my mouth right back. He kisses me with a kind of fervor that sends me into a dizzying spiral.

I swallow his grunts into my mouth. Every ounce of pressure from his lips descends to my core. My hips move of their own accord, and I shift so his jean-clad thigh is positioned between my legs, exactly where I want all of him. He studies the new position, and the warmth of his stare ignites my longing. I think he might say something to stop me, but instead he pushes his thigh upward, pressing it right against my throbbing core.

I'm nothing but need, flushed and wet from the crackling sensation of his touch. Testing the waters, unable to hold back any longer, I roll my hips, desperate for the friction. His gaze slides down my body with a fascination that nudges me to the edge.

It's depraved, sinful, dirty, and yet I can't stop. My hands rest on his shoulder, and I'm sure my nails are digging into him. A moan escapes me when he flexes his thigh, and I see the obvious bulge in his jeans. I reach behind me to rest a hand on his knee, lean back, and shamelessly rub myself on him like a cat in heat.

When his hands land on my thighs, I think I might pass out.

"Are you going to come on my thigh, Sage?"

Yeah, definitely going to pass out.

I become a whimpering, moaning mess when his fingers press into my soft flesh where my skirt has ridden all the way up. It's been so long, I'm practically a hair trigger at this point, and I'm not ashamed. With his jaw clenched, he watches me grind against his thigh to apply a touch of pressure against my clit.

"Let me see you."

I don't hesitate. I pull my panties to the side so he has the perfect view. Another roll of my hips brings a moan to escape me.

Hearing it, he groans so loud, he muffles the rest of it with his hand. Elias's gaze slides down to where my panties meet his jeans. "Touch yourself."

I'm beginning to think Elias Westbrook could tell me to bark and I would.

Shamelessly, my fingers slip to my core, and I rub my clit as he watches. If I wasn't so lost in my own haze, I'd swear he shivered.

Arousal coats my fingers when I slip them inside, and I wish they were his. The thought would make me fall over if it weren't for Elias's heavy hands resting on my thighs.

"Oh God," I cry at the fire of ecstasy that whips through me, desperate for release.

His grip becomes tighter, and he squeezes his eyes shut like he's in pain before leveling our gazes again. "Tell me what you're thinking about, Sage."

"You," I say immediately. I try to stop there to keep myself from saying something stupid, but my mouth doesn't get the memo. "Y-your fingers. Your tongue on my—"

Elias cuts me off with his lips. He devours every inch of my mouth, exploring it with his hot tongue. I practically come apart from that pressure alone.

I moan into the kiss, sliding one of my hands into his hair. Elias curses.

That's when his thigh jerks, causing blinding friction against my clit. I yelp when my fingers hit the perfect spot, and buckle under the pressure. I burst into my release and slump forward onto his shoulder as my orgasm racks through me.

We stay like that for minutes that feel like hours. I don't look up because I'm embarrassed for riding his thigh like a fucking horse, and now that the high is wearing away, I might say something equally stupid. But Elias makes that decision for me, because he stands and lifts me in his arms.

I instinctively lock my hands around his neck. "What are you doing?"

"Taking you to bed."

The devil between my legs clenches in anticipation, and I hope Elias doesn't feel the way my heartbeat soars into overdrive. As we enter his room, he places me on the bed and strides over to the window to draw the blackout curtains shut. Wrapped in darkness, my eyes gradually adjust, revealing him as he gently lifts the comforter over me. *What the hell?*

He sits on the bed beside me, noticing my bewildered expression, and plants a tender kiss on my forehead. "I'll sleep on the couch," he murmurs, and stands to leave.

Oh. I desperately want him to stay, but I know there is only one way I should end the night. And it's not with Elias pressed against me.

"And, Sage?" He pauses at the door. "Don't ever again say you're too difficult."

TWENTY-NINE

ELIAS

IT'S BEEN TWELVE hours since I let myself do something reckless. Or four years if I'm really counting. When she sat in my lap despite Owen insisting he take her seat, I felt the possessive need to have her, and remind her that she's mine. She told me he meant nothing to her, and I believe that. But the image of Owen looking at her in the kind of way that I probably do sent a wildfire raging in my chest. At that moment the word *fake* hadn't popped into my head once. The only thing I saw was her smooth brown skin and strong thighs wrapping around me, and the heat of her core pressing into my leg. The roll of her hips against me made me desperate to know how she'd look completely naked and taking all of me.

"*Fuck.*" I brace one hand against the tiled wall. My fist wrapping around myself in the shower isn't nearly as satisfying now that I've seen the way her lips part on an orgasm.

Last night, I simply shut the door to my room with her in it and slept on the couch. I was determined to sleep away the painful erection rather than taking care of it myself. Trying to relieve the pressure would only make the thoughts running through my mind worse.

I had rules for myself. I *have* rules for myself.

Ever since my biological father sent that girl to me all those years ago, trusting myself to let go with someone else is impossible. It's not that I haven't tried. During freshman year, I partied with the guys. I quickly realized that getting drunk and stumbling into a random room in a frat house wasn't going to help. It wouldn't take away the heavy disappointment that still sits on my chest from when my parents saw me that morning four years ago.

With Sage, alcohol doesn't flow through my veins, but it sure as hell feels like it.

It's a special kind of torture knowing she's right across the hall. I opted to use the main bathroom this morning instead of the en suite where all my things are. There's a part of me that knows if I see her sleepy face and messy hair, or hear her call my name, I won't be able to leave the room until I hear the sounds she made last night again.

A flash of her pulling those barely there panties to the side and showing me exactly what I wanted—no, what I *needed*—drives my hand to pump my length. I imagine those mischievous eyes watching me through wet lashes, letting the water from the shower slide down her body, and soak the thin white tank tops she usually wears to bed.

Her soft hands crawl up my sides, and she licks her lips. *Let go, Elias*, she whispers. *Give it all to me.*

Then she takes all of me, plump lips and hot mouth suctioning around me as her cheeks hollow. It's only seconds before I'm throwing my head back and pouring into her throat. The orgasm violently racks my body. But even as I catch my breath, I still feel unsatisfied. My brain conjures up an image of her kissing a path up my wet torso until I'm desperate to pin her against the tiles and slip into her to hear her moan my name.

No.

I blink back to reality. If I go there, I won't be able to look her in the eyes again.

When I'm rinsed off and out of the shower, I find Aiden sitting in the living room watching a game. Summer left for Dalton early this morning, so that's why he's awake. The pillow and blanket from when I slept on the couch are placed in the corner.

He eyes me like he knows a little too much. "You used the main shower?"

I shrug, stepping into the living room. "Making sure the pipes don't rust."

I step around the couch to watch the game. It's New Jersey, the team we'll be up against tomorrow.

"You good?" he finally asks.

Suffering. "Great, why?"

He only shrugs, chuckles, and then heads back to his room. I roll my eyes.

When heat burns the back of my neck, I know Sage is awake. She heads straight for the kitchen, not seeing me in the living room. The coffee machine starts, and I follow her, like a fucking puppy. It's impossible to keep her at arm's length despite knowing that I should.

Sage leans into the refrigerator, and those tiny sleep shorts ride up her ass. Pure torture. I look at the ceiling.

When she gasps, I drop my gaze back to where Sage holds a yogurt cup to her chest. "You scared me! What were you looking at?" She looks to the ceiling too.

I clear my throat. "Nothing."

Standing there awkwardly only makes the reminder of last night louder, so I pivot to the sink. "Coach Wilson is hosting a team-building get-together since we're in the playoffs." I scratch the back of my neck, and she listens patiently. "And we're invited."

She doesn't meet my eyes when she perches on a stool and dips a spoon into her strawberry yogurt. "Cool. I'll probably order takeout, no need to worry about me." Her sweet smile confuses me. She finishes off her yogurt, licking the spoon like—*never mind.* I process her words.

"Why would you do that?"

"A girl's gotta eat, and I don't want to risk burning your kitchen down."

"Sage. *We* are invited, not just me and Aiden. As in, I want you to come with me as my girlfriend."

The scraping of the spoon against the cup stops. When she meets my eyes, there's a smudge of yogurt on the corner of her mouth. "Me?"

"Wasn't aware I had another girlfriend."

Her chuckle is brittle. Something possesses me to wipe the side of her mouth with my thumb. She inhales sharply, and I bring my thumb to my mouth and lick it clean. "So you'll come?" I ask nonchalantly.

Her eyes stay focused on my mouth. "Sure. I'll just get off work early."

"I'll pay you for what you miss."

Her brows pinch, annoyance written in the line between them. "I'm not an escort, Elias. I don't need your money."

I lean forward. "I know. But you're probably going to need a dress, so I'll pay for whatever you need."

When I start to pull out my card, she stands. "You can't be serious."

Dropping the card on the marble slab, I look up to meet her eyes again.

She crosses her arms. "I'm already living in your apartment, and now you want to buy me clothes? I'm a lot of things, but a freeloader isn't one of them."

"You're also my girlfriend, and I would never let you pay for a dress you need to wear to go out with me."

"That's not fair. This is fake. Those rules don't apply."

I cock my head. "I don't recall that being a stipulation when we started this."

Full lips press into a straight line, but when her shoulders drop, I know she's given in. And this victory feels better than any goal I've made.

She begins to protest.

"You're not paying me back," I say before she can even suggest it. "I'll send you the details. I'll be gone for a few days, so text me if you need anything."

The *anything* makes her gaze snap to mine, and now I know we're both thinking about last night. Pretty hard not to when I can still feel the phantom movements of her hips grinding on my leg.

But she looks embarrassed when her eyes dart away. "About last night—"

"Heat of the moment," I finish for her. "You don't have to explain anything. We can just forget about it."

Sage nods slowly. The atmosphere feels scalding until she clears her throat. "It's Hakima, by the way."

"Huh?" I'm confused, but the switch in conversation is a welcome savior.

"My middle name, I never told you. It's my mom's name. It means 'wise,' just like Sage."

I recall our conversation from last night before . . . everything. "Hakima? That's beautiful."

She shrugs. "I guess my mom gave me one good part of her."

"Every part of you is good, Sage."

She smiles but it feels all wrong as she slides off the stool. "I should go. I have a class of very studious eight-year-olds to teach in an hour."

"Right. I'll see you in a few days, then."

We awkwardly linger in the kitchen before dispersing.

THIRTY

SAGE

SCREAMING ON THE bus is a very appropriate reaction to finding out I've secured an invite to audition for the principal role in *Swan Lake*. But the old man sitting next to me did not agree.

It's been a week since I've thought about anything other than Elias's tortured expression when I sat on his lap. But today, only the NBT invite occupies my brain.

As soon as my following pivoted from hockey fans leaving inappropriate comments to supportive ballerinas and ballet moms, recognition from other popular dancers started pouring in.

This audition guarantees that I'll be judged by Zimmerman, and that bitter part of me is desperate to stick the landing. I want to prove to him that this *nobody* has come a long way from that day he laughed at me outside my first audition.

I haven't told anyone, not my brother and not Elias, because there's a part of me that doesn't want anyone else tied up in my hopes. Rejections are tough, but I've been through so many, I'm sure I can weather that storm again. But if either of them sees me lose the one thing I've strived for since I turned eight, it'll only embarrass me.

The kicker though? My feelings for my fake boyfriend don't feel fake at all. I'm on the verge of making my lifelong dream a reality, and my mind wants to focus on the way he flexed his muscular thigh between my legs.

Not only that, the dress I'm supposed to wear tonight, gifted by him, is so beautiful I can't believe it's mine.

When I get to the empty apartment, I head to Elias's room to stare at the ruby red fabric hanging in the closet. Despite my refusal, he was right about me having to buy a dress. I couldn't reuse the black one I've been wearing everywhere. But that's not the part of the conversation that's been a pin in my side.

Elias only mentioned my desperate act of rubbing myself over his thigh because he wants to forget it. Like it was a lapse in judgment, a stupid mistake by a horny girl lost in the haze of her lust. Well, maybe that description is a little accurate, but I was not lost or being stupid. I was as aware as ever that the hard plane of his thigh was perfect against my throbbing core, and, if I recall correctly, that hazy lust caused him to flex his too. We're both equally guilty. But why do I feel like the one that's been sentenced to prison?

I'm dressed and waiting for Elias to pick me up, since he's getting changed at the arena after practice. He's been stressed these past few games, so I've been laying low. They swept round one, so the team has been training hard to keep their streak. However, Elias said Coach Wilson isn't pleased with everyone's performance and thinks the team-building get-together is necessary since they only managed to score in overtime or with power plays.

I'm peeling the liner off one of Elias's homemade carrot muffins, waiting for his text when the front door opens. Footsteps echo against the floorboards before I see him. Dark hair is tousled just enough that a single strand curls against his forehead, even as he sifts his hand through it. The black suit hugs his frame, accentuating his athletic build and confident posture. His black shoes reflect the kitchen lights, each stride leading him toward me as my mouth falls agape. I almost choke on the muffin when I see him close up.

If I died right now, I wouldn't even be mad if this was my last sight.

"You look beautiful," he says, snapping me out of my trance.

"Definitely the dress," I say, shyly sliding off the stool.

"Definitely you."

THE GET-TOGETHER IS intimate, and nothing like the party we attended a few weeks ago. Only the starting lineup and some of the players from the second line are here. This time, we're at Coach Wilson's house. The French-style home is located in the suburbs not too far from Sean's school. Inside, we pass the grand foyer and a set of sweeping staircases to the dining room, where a crystal chandelier decorates the space. The house is massive, and I have to remind myself to keep my jaw from hanging.

The dinner is filled with questions and introductions, most of which make me feel like an imposter. Elias notices when I retreat into myself because he puts his hand over mine under the table. A touch just for me. It slows my thoughts until Coach's wife leads us outside to gather around the table that sits on a stone-paved patio.

The other guys on the team mingle as they sit with their girlfriends and wives, some of them having brought their children, who play together in the courtyard, while others have gone home with sleeping babies in their arms.

This whole thing was to boost team morale, and I think Coach Wilson's idea is working. I kind of wish Summer was here, because she would make being surrounded by all of this a little easier. But she's at Dalton, and Aiden is practicing on her parent's indoor ice rink with her dad between games.

So tonight, it's just Elias and me.

Socket helps start a fire, and everyone takes a seat around it when the cool breeze dips the temperature. But Elias doesn't let go of my hand. Instead, he pulls me right in his lap when he sits down. I try to appear comfortable, but ever since the last time I sat on his thigh, there's no telling what I'll do. But knowing my uncle is across from us has me on my best behavior.

Elias pulls my legs across his lap, and I try my hardest not to sink into his touch.

"How did you two meet? I know Marcus sure as hell didn't introduce you," Coach Wilson asks.

I cut a glance to my uncle, who is staring into his glass of water.

"We met at the auction." Elias places his hand over mine on the table. He's been extra touchy today, and I can't make sense of it.

"I go to the bathroom for two seconds, and he's made a move on my niece. Classy." My uncle's rough voice makes Elias stiffen.

A few of the players surrounding the table turn to look at us.

"Actually, I was the one who bid on him," I interject.

Coach Wilson laughs. My uncle grimaces. I'm sick of him treating Elias like he's not good enough for me. If anything, I'm the one who isn't good enough for him.

"But I still had to convince her to come on a second date," Elias adds.

Hearing the topic of conversation, Owen turns too. "I had to ask her out for an entire year before she agreed," he chimes in.

The easy atmosphere plummets to hell.

"And we were on and off for years," he says from his place a few seats down, slurring his words. "But loneliness seemed to always bring us back to each other."

I'm willing the skies to open up and strike me down.

Owen continues, "But I'd do it all over again if she would—"

"I'd be careful with how you finish that sentence." Elias's threat is low and rough. His deep voice makes this entire interaction even more unbearable.

Owen laughs. "Relax, Eli, you know I'd never overstep."

I look up at Elias, staring ahead, watching Owen with a danger-ous glint in his eyes. *Uh-oh.*

We've been over this, and Elias knows there is nothing between Owen and me. But I don't expect him to become best buds with my ex. Suddenly, I can't stand being here.

"It's getting late. Will you take me home?" I ask.

This time emotion flickers in Elias's brown eyes, but he blinks it away. "You want to leave?"

I nod. We say a quick bye to everyone, and we're off. In the car he doesn't touch me. No hand on my thigh, and no conversation. The music is loud yet deafeningly silent. The walk to the apartment is even quieter.

I'm itching to talk but seal my lips together to not be the first to speak. Inside, he shuts the front door behind us and there's a hot tingle that races up my spine. The click of my heels against the hard-wood matches the thudding of my heart as I head to his room.

"Was he telling the truth?" Elias's deep voice startles me. "You went back to him whenever you felt lonely?" He says the words calmly, but there's a frustrated lilt to his question. One that seemed to have been simmering the whole ride here.

"He was drunk," I deflect. I remove my heels and head straight to his room and into the bathroom.

The closed door doesn't stop him from walking right into the bathroom with me. On any normal night, this bathroom is big enough for a small party, but today it feels cramped and sweltering. I drop my earrings on the counter and reluctantly meet his eyes in the reflection of the mirror.

"It was a long time ago. I didn't have friends," I say. "Feeling lonely was inevitable."

Elias steps closer. "Do you feel lonely now?" His warm breath falls on my neck, and a quiet shiver rustles through me.

"I don't know," I whisper, clutching the edge of the countertop.

"That's not an answer, Sage."

I huff. "Why does it matter? Are you still jealous of him or something?"

"Does it look like I'm fucking jealous?" he says. "I don't care about him. I care about you."

There's a hunger in his gaze that could devour me in minutes, and I know with everything in me that I should walk away. Not because I don't want this to happen. I want it badly, even desperately. But I know if we go on, any boundaries I'm still holding on to will be crushed. Any that he doesn't already control.

When he dips his head to the crook of my neck, my breath catches. Elias runs his nose along the side of my neck, where my pulse goes wild. My fingers might break through the marble countertop, but then his hands come to bracket mine. Caging me in.

His lips brush against my ear this time. "I'd never let you feel lonely."

Oh *God*. His words. The heat thrumming off his body. My rattling heart. It all blends to send me into a mindless stupor. Like a butter knife to my softened heart. All my jokes have abandoned me, because the moment the possibility of Elias feels real, I can't joke.

He drops a whisper of a kiss on my shoulder, and I can't help but turn to look at him. Brown eyes flicker to my throat when I swallow.

Being near him is like an itch I can't scratch, or a sneeze that never comes. We've been this close before, but I've never seen his gaze like this. Hungry. Longing. *Molten.*

I'm playing with fire, but I'm not someone who's afraid to get burned. And damn do I want Elias Westbrook to burn me.

I push my hips into his and he groans. A deep, guttural groan. "Then show me," I say.

That's all it takes, because in the next moment, Elias seals his lips to mine.

The kiss isn't soft and sweet, it's demanding and rough, like the frustration that lined his words seconds ago. Like he's proving something to me. Or to himself.

Warm lips find their way down my neck and to the column of my throat, where my pulse quickens. He nips the skin lightly, leaving a sting before his tongue soothes over it. I slide my hands down the front of his dress shirt. I feel too hot to be in this suffocating dress. My chest heaves, and he brings his lips down until he's kissing the swell of my breasts. The move nukes any thought of self-control, and I push my body into his to feel his hard length pressing into my navel, just inches away from where I want him.

He hesitates but I'm impatient. I pull away to face the mirror again. "Unzip me. *Please*," I plead.

Elias's gaze appears conflicted as it crackles with lust and he presses his hips to my ass. "Tell me to stop," he rasps.

"I don't want to."

He groans louder this time. "Don't say that." He nips my neck, and I arch into him. "Jesus. You're killing me, Sage."

"Then do something about it."

It's brave. Maybe too brave, because Elias freezes. We stay like this for so long I have no idea what he's thinking. But then he sighs, and removes his hands from the counter.

I quickly step away, and a flicker of insecurity flashes across his features. "I'm sorry. You're celibate, I shouldn't have said that."

He shakes his head. "It's not your fault if I wanted to."

My face blanches.

Elias closes the space between us to cup my face, steadying my spinning thoughts. "It's hard for me to go there after everything, and I don't want to put that on you," he says.

"I don't mind," I say way too quickly.

There's a smile on his lips like he finds my eagerness amusing. "You're perfect. And if there's anybody I'd break my vow for, it's you."

"I would never ask you to do that." I drop my head and notice my dress is indecently bunched around my waist and my nipples are hard. My body is doing all the asking apparently.

He exhales a heavy breath and averts his darkened gaze. "I know, and that's sweet. But the more you talk, the more I want to bend you over this sink and taste exactly how wet you are."

I open my mouth to suggest he do exactly that, but snap it shut. *He's celibate, Sage.*

I run a hand through my hair, and my dress rides up in the process. I shove it back down, sheepishly watching him from beneath my lashes. "I want you, Elias. But I don't know what you want me to do," I say. "I can't—"

"Say that again."

I'm thrown off by the sudden demand as Elias takes a tentative step closer. Like the thread he's desperately hanging on to just needs one good tug and it would snap.

"What?"

"Say it again, Sage," he says with a trace of impatience.

I swallow. "I want you, Elias."

His throat rumbles with an appreciative sound. Elias grips my waist and pushes me back into the edge of the counter until it digs into my spine. I don't register the sting of pain because he drags his tongue up the side of my neck to my ear.

"Again," he rasps.

I inhale a tattered breath when he picks me up and deposits me on the countertop. The cold marble touches the sizzling skin of my thighs, making me dig my nails into his shoulders and whisper, "I want you."

An audible snap can be heard in the stuffy bathroom.

I've never seen Elias drunk, but I assume this version of him is how it would be. The version that drinks me in like smooth liquor. But just as I think he's going to rip off my dress and take me on this counter, Elias's kiss lingers on my forehead for so long it's almost as if he's counting. Or admonishing himself.

He's shaking his head when I look up at him. "What's wrong?"

His breathing evens out. He tucks my hair behind my ear and helps me off the counter.

"You should get some sleep, Sage. I'm going to shower." Elias doesn't meet my eyes when he slips out of the perfectly good bathroom and heads to the one in the hall. A harsh truth spits in my face as I watch his retreat.

Elias Westbrook is the most gentle man I've ever known, but if he wanted to, he could tear my heart to pieces.

THIRTY-ONE

SAGE

WHAT DOES IT mean when your celibate fake boyfriend kisses you like he'd die if he didn't? There's no manual that can give me an answer, and Google isn't proving as smart as it claims to be. I feel like I've been defeated in a game nobody told me I was playing. Elias's celibacy has tossed me into a downward spiral almost as complicated as our fake relationship. I recall things I've said or done when he's been close, and I shiver in horror. He probably laughs about all the times I've humiliated myself in front of him.

When I step out of the shower, I change into fresh clothes. The fabric of my sundress is flimsy and resembles cheap tissue, but it's the only thing I own that's not currently in the wash. Elias took my pile of dirty laundry this morning and ran a cycle. *God*, the man is pure evil.

When I'm running a comb through my tangled hair, I hear a hushed curse from the kitchen and rush down the hall, only to find Elias shaking out his hand.

"Are you okay?" I take his hand to inspect the burn, ignoring the current that shoots up my fingertips.

"It's just a burn," Elias says.

I lead him to the sink and hold his finger under the cold water. "Baking again?"

"Trying something new," he says. "Do you like scones?"

"Never had one, but I'm sure anything you make, I'll love."

He's still watching me when he turns off the tap and dries his hand on a kitchen towel.

My wet hair drips down my back, and every drop jerks me with the heavy awareness of my sizzling skin.

"You showered?" he asks.

A drop of water hits my neck, and I try not to flinch. "Mm-hmm."

He cocks his head. "You seem a little on edge this morning. Are you feeling okay?"

Another drop. This time it slides down the side of my neck and trails down my collarbone. "Never been better."

His gaze catches on the slow-moving droplets, and my body is electrified. The problem is, water and electricity don't mix well. I quiver as something dark swims in his brown eyes.

"Take a picture, Elias. It'll keep you occupied on your flight."

"You think I'd need a picture to remember how you look right now?"

The silence is long and uncomfortable. I glance at the stove to read the time, realizing it's only noon and he leaves in a few hours. The past few minutes already feel torturous—I'm not sure I can survive *hours*.

He steps right into my orbit, reaching for my dress. "What are you trying to accomplish here, Sage?"

The question makes me hot. Elias's hand is big and strong and veiny, and I wouldn't say a damn word if he yanked off my dress.

I tilt my head. "I'm trying to survive the heat."

His eyes narrow. "The apartment has AC."

Maybe I should have been more specific. I meant I needed to survive *his* heat.

"I run hot."

"I've had your ice-cold feet on me almost every night."

He's goading me, but I refuse to fall into the trap. "Whatever it is you're trying to make me say, it won't work. I don't have ulterior motives. Unlike you, I say what I want instead of talking in riddles."

"What's that supposed to mean?"

I straighten, trying to appear taller even though he's towering. "That you claim to be the most honest guy on the planet, but you can't for one second admit you're lying to yourself. And that's probably the worst type of dishonesty there is."

There's a storm brewing on his face. "I'm not lying to anyone."

I snort, rather unattractively. "Keep telling yourself that. But you've been celibate for so long because you're punishing yourself for something you did years ago. You think this eases your conscience, but you're only hurting yourself."

I didn't know until this very second that it bothered me. Realistically, I'm not his girlfriend and I have no right to question his reasons, but damn does it feel like a punch in the face when he knows nearly everything about me. Sex life included.

This all feels too risky now. My feelings. His. Whatever they are. It would be enough to throw me in a white-walled room with no windows and a straitjacket. Riding his thigh the other night, then begging for him last night only brings the heat of embarrassment back to my face.

Suddenly my confidence evaporates, and I turn to get the hell out of his vicinity. Elias pushes forward, backing me right up against the fridge and causing a magnet to fall to the floor. A picture of all the guys at this year's Frozen Four falls by my feet.

His calloused hands skim the bare skin of my thighs, then he slides upward, lifting the thin fabric of my dress. Even if I wanted to say something, I wouldn't.

"I don't lie," he rasps. "And I'm not being dishonest."

My voice comes out as a whisper. "Your nose is growing, Elias."

He chuckles, the warm breath hitting my skin like the lash of a belt. "You wanna hear a lie, Sage?" His wandering hand moves to my hip bone, right to the string of my thong.

I trap a whimper, unwilling to embarrass myself any more than I already have.

"Seeing you walk around in this fucking dress doesn't make me want to tear it off."

I swallow.

"Your lips haven't been stuck in my mind since I tasted them the first time."

My breaths are shallow.

"And I didn't jerk off to the thought of you last night."

Holy shit.

Talking to him is like playing with the red and blue wires on a bomb and not knowing which one is going to knock you on your ass and burn every inch of your skin.

"Satisfied?" he asks.

"Never," I say.

He snaps the string of my thong, and I squeak. The sting on my skin feels like he's spanked me. "What if I think you're the one who's lying?" Elias says.

I'm at the mercy of his hands, but I feign offense. "I'm not."

"No? So, you're not frustrated because I didn't fuck you last night?"

My throat feels heavy.

"Come on, Sage. I thought you were an open book," he goads.

I narrow my eyes. "You don't know me."

"Maybe." His hand leaves the tingling skin of my bare thigh and clasps my wrist, and he runs his thumb over my thundering pulse. "But your body is saying something different."

"My body says a lot of things, but I don't suppose you'd know how to read it." I'm hoping my words slash at that cocky look on his face.

"You think because I haven't touched you, I don't know what will make you come?"

Reading between the lines is pretty damn easy when his eyes flash with a look that says, *My thigh can get you off in under thirty seconds.*

As annoying as the smirk is, he's beautiful, and so is the hand that snakes under my dress to toy with the scrap of fabric between my ass cheeks. Then he pulls it, and the tightness almost makes me keel forward, but I lock my knees.

"Careful, Eli, that's a lot of sex talk for your vow of celibacy."

He tuts. He actually fucking tuts at me. "I'm not afraid to talk about sex, Sage, but I think you're nervous just thinking about it."

My thoughts scatter. Like rats running out of an alley at the sound of footsteps.

My laugh is unconvincing. It's cut short when the oven timer sounds and slices through our stare-down. Elias backs away, and so do I.

I spend the next two hours sewing my pointe shoes to perfection, giving him only a small nod when he tells me he'll be back in a few days.

THE FINAL SHOWCASE of *A Midsummer Night's Dream* makes me feel like a celebrity. It even makes me forget about the earlier call from my landlord. My apartment is clean and should be ready for me to move in again. But thinking about that makes the pit in my stomach grow deeper than an abyss.

Amy Laurent, my former teacher, thanks me profusely when she spots me backstage. I don't understand why at first, but apparently my post about tonight's show with links to the tickets helped sell out the house.

Electric energy buzzes backstage as act two begins and the

curtains draw open. You'd think performing the same dance would feel mundane, but it only makes me feel excited. Every time I perform my solo as Titania the fairy queen, I know I've gotten better.

The dreamy notes of the nocturne by Mendelssohn play when I'm onstage, and I don't think. I don't let myself get lost in my head.

This time, I don't search the crowd, because my uncle is away with the team, but he did make sure to hound me for the link to the live performance. When the curtains close, I'm off the stage and talking with the families up front. A woman taps my shoulder.

"My son is a huge hockey fan," she begins. "And ever since we saw you at the Thunder games, my daughter has been ecstatic. She's obsessed with all your performances."

She points to her daughter, who's wearing a tiara atop her head, her curly hair fashioned into a bun. The young girl hugs me and hands me a handwritten letter. It's just like Elias said about being an inspiration to them. It makes me wish he was here to see it.

After a long bus ride, I finally return to the empty apartment. The urge to call Elias gnaws at me, but I know his hockey game is in full swing. So I settle in front of the TV to watch him play. Away games are the worst, and they leave me feeling a pang of loneliness. Especially tonight, with the exhilaration of my performance still coursing through my veins, I would kill to share this moment with Elias, to witness the sparkle in his eyes whenever I talk about ballet.

As the game enters its third period, I search for Elias amid the chaos of players darting back and forth. A surge of relief floods through me at the sight of him coming off the bench, but it's short-lived because the commentators recount a brutal hit against him in the first period.

As the replay flickers across the screen, my heart seizes, captured by the bone-chilling moment of Elias's body colliding with the unforgiving boards. The sheer intensity of the impact sends shivers down my spine, as if I can feel the reverberations echoing through my bones. The subsequent fight that erupted after the hit only adds to my distress, with Aiden retaliating against the player who targeted Elias.

It's a given with a contact sport like hockey, but I can't help the pang of helplessness.

As the end of the game draws near, a tentative sense of relief settles over me. But just as I begin to breathe a little easier, my worst fears materialize in front of my eyes. Elias goes hurtling into the boards again, his skates fully leaving the ice in a terrifying display of momentum. Time freezes when he crashes back to the ice and lies motionless. The stadium is engulfed in a deafening silence, and so are the commentators.

My heart hammers against my ribs like a trapped bird. I desperately strain to catch any glimpse of movement, any flicker of reassurance that Elias is okay. But then, I see his discarded helmet and the mouth guard he spit out.

I can't tear my eyes away, even as every instinct screams for me not to look. The medical team rushes onto the ice. Then the camera abruptly cuts away. The announcer's voice finally breaks through the scene, delivering the devastating news that Elias won't be returning for the rest of the game.

The remote slips from my trembling fingers and clatters to the floor.

THIRTY-TWO

ELIAS

THE HIT PLAYS over and over on a loop in my mind, each replay dredging up a fresh wave of regret. I should have known better than to get cocky.

My first goal of the evening had ignited a hunger for revenge in our opponents, and when Pittsburgh's right-winger came charging at me, I had no choice but to brace for impact.

After that, I was flying past the defense again, but as I was chasing the high of a potential goal, the second hit truly knocked the wind out of my body.

"You're not concussed, but the bruising on your body is concerning," our team doctor says as he flashes a light in my eyes after a baseline test. "We'll keep an eye on it. You'll need to rest and take ibuprofen for pain."

Only one question hangs in the air. "Am I clear to play Friday?"

It's our second game of round two playoffs, and the thought of missing it fills me with despair. There was a split second after the hit that fear rampaged through me. Fear that my career was slipping from my fingers again.

"No, Eli, you can't play with bruised ribs and a near concussion.

You're out for the round, and I'll reevaluate you for round three," says Dr. Harris before stepping out.

My shoulders slump, weighed down by disappointment. I exhale a long sigh that causes a sharp pain to radiate from my bruised ribs.

Outside the dressing room, I can hear the muffled voices of Coach Wilson and Dr. Harris in conversation. When the doors finally swing open, Coach is there, wearing a somber expression.

The beginnings of a headache pound on my skull like a relentless drum. I place a bag of ice on my head.

"It's not the news we were hoping for, but your health comes first," he says. "You played a good game tonight, Eli. Let's make sure it stays that way so this isn't the last time we see you in the playoffs."

A reluctant acceptance blankets me at his words.

"We'll arrange for a driver to take you back to the hotel. Rest up, and we'll head home tomorrow morning." Coach's voice is tinged with sympathy.

I exit the room, burdened by the bitter aftertaste of failure that lingers. The ache of missing not only tonight's game but the next one gnaws uncomfortably at my core.

When I arrive at the hotel, I don't linger. I zip up my suitcase, summon an Uber, and make a beeline for the airport. Instead of texting Coach, I shoot Aiden a message to let him know I'm leaving. Coach would never sanction my decision to fly after taking a hit like that, but being home is all I can think about. Because Sage will be there, and she's the only one that can make this situation slightly bearable.

My first thought after being slammed into the boards wasn't whether I broke any bones or if my vision would return. I thought of Sage.

That night when I crushed my lips against hers and drank her in like water on dying grass, her response matched my intensity. Hearing the sound of her soft moan of pleasure slipping from her lips and down my throat etched itself deep into my mind.

Her enthusiasm is not good for my imagination. Sage is my

undoing, and I'm not sure I'd know how to handle all of her. I knew I fucked up when my tongue swiped across hers, and the spark of electricity made it nearly impossible to stop. It was like I could hear the clink of metal armor falling off her body and to my feet, and something in my chest clicked into place. But the realization of what she wanted and what I shouldn't give her hit me hard.

The flight from the Pittsburgh airport is short. I try to sleep, but with the uncomfortable seat I got at the last minute, dead center between two other people, and the ice on my head, I can't relax. When I land, I pull up my hoodie and take an Uber back to my apartment.

Our doorman sees me approach, and when he tries to rush over to help, I stop him. My limp is bad, but I don't want to call more attention to myself. Shooting him a smile, I hobble into the elevator and slump against the mirrored wall on my way up.

My body screams in agony, yet a part of me wants to move faster. My jingling keys fall from my hand to the floor. I reach down to get them with a series of grunts, and when I'm about to insert the key, the door flies open to reveal a misty-eyed Sage.

She stands there, eyes sweeping over me from head to toe. Her curly hair frames her face, and her fingers grip the doorframe tight enough that they whiten. The weight of her gaze practically emanates from her expression, enveloping me as if I can feel it physically.

Sage reaches for my arm and lets me shift my weight to step inside. I put just enough weight on her, but she'd be crushed if I leaned on her the way I need to right now. Once we enter my room, she retreats a step, leaving me to stand alone. She looks either terrified or nervous, but she doesn't say anything to tell me which one it is.

"I'm okay," I reassure her, hoping that's what she's looking for.

The smallest breath of relief pitches her tense shoulders down. "I saw the hit, Elias. Both of them." She doesn't meet my eyes. "It was terrifying to see you like that."

Her words catch me off guard, and a warmth spreads over the pain in my ribs.

"You were worried about me?" I can't suppress the smile that tugs at my lips.

"Comes with the job description." Her deflection is lined with bitter humor. She fidgets with her hands and doesn't look at me. I don't like it.

"Is it a self-care night?" I ask.

"It's Wednesday, I don't usually . . ." Her voice trails off, her gaze shifting over my bruised and battered body with a blend of pity and concern. "Yeah, it's a self-care night."

She helps me to the bathroom, using all her strength to aid my limping form. Then she twists on the faucet to fill the bath with water and sifts through the cupboards.

"You'll need to soak in a hot bath first. I have Epsom salts," she informs me, pouring the lavender-scented salt into the steaming water.

"Take it with me."

She freezes.

"I saw your performance. Probably one of your best, so I'm sure you need one too."

She stares at me wide-eyed. "You watched it?"

"Wouldn't have missed it," I say, "but next time, send me the link so I don't have to ask your uncle." I take a step closer until we're mere inches apart. Her breath hitches when the backs of her thighs meet the edge of the bathtub, and I resist the urge to wince as I lean in. "Will you join me?"

The long column of her throat moves before she looks at the water and then back at me. "But you're . . . you know."

"It's not a bad word, Sage."

She sighs. "I know. But I don't want to make you uncomfortable."

I run my thumb along her jawline and meet her eyes. "I'm in pain, Sage. Make it better."

She barely nods, her body betraying her reluctance as she steps closer, drawn in by an invisible force.

As I shed my clothes and sink into the hot water, every ache in my body seems to melt under the heat. Meanwhile, Sage lingers by the tub, her demeanor cautious as she stares at my reddened skin. It's ironic—the girl who straddled my lap with abandon is uncertain about something as simple as sharing a bath.

"Need me to close my eyes?" I tease. But I spot a flicker of unease in her gaze that makes me stop. "What's wrong?"

"It's just I know my body looks different and my muscles are more defined," she starts. "But I love my body, and I told myself a long time ago that I will never let anyone dictate how I feel about it." She breathes heavily, and I can't understand why she has to say this. "I've worked really hard, and I've fought through a lot of self-image issues. You don't become a ballerina without every instructor from the age of eight telling you that you can stand to lose a few pounds. Or that beauty is pain, and starving yourself is a part of that pain."

Her words hit me like a semitruck. "You think I'm like them? Those sick people who prey on people's self-esteem because they have no clue that healthy bodies look different?"

Sage blinks rapidly. I want to reach out and comfort her, but I know that my words are what she needs.

"Jesus, Sage. From the moment I saw you, I couldn't look away. And it had nothing to do with your body or face. It was just you. Your energy, your determination, your strength. That's all that I could see. It was blinding."

"You can't mean that."

"Come in here, and I'll show you how much I mean it."

A surge of victory ensues when she strips off the long T-shirt—one of mine—and then her panties before dipping her foot into the steaming bath. I bite my fist to keep from groaning out loud at the sight of her. She tries to maintain distance as she sits between my legs.

Alarms go off in my head. Too close. Too much. Too good.

To distract myself, I run a loofah over her back. When I feel her under my palm, and smell her sweet scent, I can't help it. Making sure she's taken care of doesn't have to mean I'm compromising my rules. I want to show her that she's not too much. That she deserves to be taken care of.

With a hand on the bare skin of her waist, I pull her against me, and leave light kisses where her neck meets her shoulders.

"You did so good tonight," I whisper.

She shivers, turning her head in the other direction.

I tidy her twisted bun, knowing she won't want to get her hair wet. There's no stopping the way I feel right now, because even with the worst pain I've ever felt in my body, I recognize how good she feels this close to me.

"We c-can't," she stutters.

"Can't what, Sage?" I whisper against the shell of her ear. "I can't touch you like this?"

I trace a slow finger down her spine. My rules were muddied the moment I felt her lips on mine. But I never wanted Sage to feel like she had to perform some impossible role just because I was breaking a rule for her. I want her to know that if I touch her, it's because I want to. Because right now, she needs it and I want to give it to her.

She whimpers. "What are you doing, Elias? You're celibate."

"*I'm* celibate," I whisper. "But you still deserve to feel good. I can do that. Let me make you feel good, baby."

She grips the side of the tub so tightly her knuckles turn white, but she doesn't move.

I'm sure she feels my heart hammering against her back too. "Let me take care of you."

Her breath hitches as if those words have never been spoken to her. "I don't need to be taken care of."

Minutes pass without another word, and her declaration lingers in the air. It's as if it's a practiced sentence. Like she actually believes that shit.

"You know, the ones who say that usually need it the most." I'm careful when I brush a strand of hair behind her ear, delicate and gentle, just like she needs. "If you think that's the truth, I'm going to show you it's not."

After a long silence, she whispers, "I don't expect you to prove anything to me."

"I don't need you to," I say.

No one has ever taken care of Sage Beaumont, and I have the inclination to be the first.

My fingers find her smooth thigh under the water, and slip to her core to feel her arousal. She's squirms under my touch, desperate for a release. Shaking with nerves and anticipation. "Tell me what you like, Sage."

"You," she says on a gasp.

Fuck. I insert two fingers, unable to wait any longer. She moans so loud, I have to clench my jaw to keep from doing the same. This is about her. "Ride them."

She moves faster, then her uncertain gaze finds mine. "I don't want to hurt you."

"The only thing that would hurt me is not seeing you come. Take what you need, Sage."

She doesn't hesitate this time. Sage rides my fingers, her moans echoing as she reaches her climax, her head resting in the crook of my neck. She curses, and squeezes her eyes shut when she comes on my hand. Beautiful.

My body aches from the effort of restraint. "Turn around," I grunt against her temple.

She turns, straddling me, mindful of the bruises starting to purple my skin.

I brush my palm against her cheek, and she leans into the touch. "No more jokes?" I ask.

She smiles weakly, her hazel eyes hot with desire. "Now you know how to shut me up."

"I never want to shut you up. You're the only person I ever want to talk to."

With a hand at the nape of her neck, I draw her lips to mine, kissing her until I moan with pleasure. I could never get tired of feeling her yield to me, relinquishing control and allowing me to hold her completely.

"Can I touch you?" she asks. "You should get to feel good too. I'll do whatever you want me to."

Jesus. Her words are like a honey trap. The sincerity on her face only makes my shaking head want to nod. If I feel her fist wrapped around me, I'll never recover. Never be able to placate the part of me that doesn't want to let her go. And that's the last thing she needs.

I know I'm testing the bounds of my self-control, but I can handle it. I can handle this. To make her happy even if I'm fucking miserable.

"Making you feel good makes me feel good."

She doesn't seem convinced. "I want you to come with me."

Having this woman tell me what she wants might be my favorite thing.

"How's this?" I bring her attention to where I wrap my hand around my erection. She watches my rhythmic movements through the soapy water, and her throat bobs.

"Is that—do you have piercings?" She barely contains her shock. The shiny metal piercing gleams under the soapy water. Her hands rest on my thighs, and the touch makes me shudder. I got the piercings in college, so no girl has ever seen them. Now, with Sage toying with my self-control, I hold back from asking her to touch them with her tongue.

"Long story." Sage doesn't need to know the reckless shit the guys and I did at Dalton.

She regards me with a smirk. "It's cute. Unexpected, but cute."

I groan loudly. "Don't call me cute when you're staring at my cock."

She laughs at my plight. So I pull her to my lips and kiss her. Tasting every inch of her mouth, and desperately wanting more. It would be so easy like this. To have her how I've imagined.

"Stand up," I command softly against her lips.

When she pulls back, her eyes are wide. She doesn't question me, allowing me to guide her to my mouth as she stands. I hold her right where I need her, feeling her shaking before my lips seal around her clit. Her hands find my hair, clutching it so tightly it stings my scalp. With my fingers and tongue working in tandem, Sage doesn't last long, panting my name along with a cascade of pleas until she shatters in ecstasy.

She slips down my body, and I catch her in my arms before she falls on my aching thighs.

Sage rests her head on my chest. "That had to have broken some rule. Does celibacy come with a manual?"

I bark out a laugh. "I'll let you know." We take turns soaping each other up and then rinsing off. When we're dry, I limp into bed.

She helps me under the covers and brings me an ice pack from the kitchen. "Call me if you need anything."

I catch her wrist. "I need something."

"What?"

"You."

She rolls her eyes. "Elias, you're injured. And we already . . . I don't want to make it worse."

"Then sleep here and make it better. Sleep with me."

She wears a wry smile. "You're just setting yourself up at this point."

"You know what I mean. Come here."

And she does. There's a stabbing in my abdomen when she lays her head on my chest, but nothing is worse than the dull ache in my chest when she's not there.

Sage is unusually silent as we try to sleep. I'm used to her random questions and fidgeting to find a comfortable position. "You're awfully quiet. Did I break you?"

Her amused breath falls on my chest. "Yeah, your magical tongue and fingers deserve a reward."

"Your pussy was the reward."

Her eyes bulge. "Who the hell are you, and what have you done with Elias?"

"I think we know what happened to him."

Then Sage is quiet again, running her hands over my abdomen and up my chest. There's a nagging feeling that makes me restless. I tap a finger on her temple. "What's on your mind?"

"My landlord called."

My pulse quickens, and words fail me. I'm relieved that she doesn't look up, for fear she might see the dread etched on my face. Having her here has felt like this is how it's meant to be, and the possibility of her leaving never even crossed my mind. There's a rough ball in my throat that doesn't allow me to speak.

"She said the insurance finally got back to her, and she's called the cleaners. The apartment should be ready for me by Monday."

"Monday," I repeat numbly.

She brushes her palm over a bruise, focusing her attention on that. "I have an early class, so I'll leave my key on the kitchen counter."

"Don't go."

I shift to get a better look at her face, but the movement sends a searing pain through my ribs. Sage studies my expression, as if she's uncertain she heard me correctly.

"Your studio is nearby, and all your auditions are downtown. Besides, if you have to come to my games or attend an event with me, it's better if you're here. It doesn't make sense for you to move back."

"I can't stay here forever, Elias."

But I want you to. "I'll help you find an apartment when it's time."

"You will?"

"I'd do anything for you, Sage." And if I let her leave now, I won't survive it. Not after having her ignite something within me that makes me want to let go and only hold on to her.

THIRTY-THREE

ELIAS

THE HIGHLIGHTS OF my days consist of baking and waiting for Sage to get home. And the occasional text from Sean when he asks me where I'm at in my recovery. Occasionally, he tells me to take care of his sister because she needs it. I always listen. However, today's text is him being the epitome of a little brother.

> **Sean:** My sister might be a little grumpy today. Just a heads-up.
>
> **Elias:** What'd you do?
>
> **Sean:** Tanked my physics exam. It's not my fault your team was playing when I should have been studying.
>
> **Elias:** I think that's quite literally your fault, buddy.
>
> **Sean:** My friend's having a party next weekend. You think she'll let me go?
>
> **Elias:** That's a hard no.
>
> **Sean:** Can you convince her? She's never been mad at you.
>
> **Elias:** Never is a stretch, but I'll put in a good word if you ace all your other exams. Deal?
>
> **Sean:** Deal.

I turn back to the highlights from the last Thunder game. Despite our team killing it in the playoffs, I can't wipe away the melancholy draped over my excitement. They lost the game where I was hit but went on to win game six. The Eastern Conference finals against Boston were a breeze, but most of those wins are credited to their goalie and defensive line being injured. It's a stroke of luck no one saw coming, and now that we're in the Stanley Cup Finals against Vancouver, everyone's on the edge of their seats, especially me. I've been checking in every day to find out whether Dr. Harris has approved me for practice, let alone to play a full game, and I've been at home for longer than I've ever had to be. It would be torture if not for Sage.

I expected my days to be filled with us in bed, but with her NBT audition in two weeks, that's all she can think about. On game days, I start my morning with a short walk, then come home to a bath Sage runs for me and a book from Summer's collection. Sage usually gets home just in time for dinner, likely because I make something different every day and because I let her put whatever face mask she wants on my face. Today is one of those days, and I'm in the kitchen, baking lasagna while watching each minute tick by on the oven's digital clock.

"They had fresh baked rolls at the supermarket," Sage announces, her voice mingling with the creak of the door and the jingle of her keys. She smiles brightly when she spots me, but the exhaustion on her face is evident. Her curly hair has flyaways framing her face, and the faint bags under her eyes reveal she hasn't been sleeping well.

Sage walks past me to put the bread rolls on the counter, but before she can slip away, I pull her in by her waist. In seconds, she melts into me, and I practically have to hold her up. When she allows herself to relax with me, it ushers my brain into euphoria.

Sage doesn't allow people in as easily as she pretends. She hides her guarded heart beneath a cloak of openness that not many have the privilege to pull back. It's when I saw her break down over her rejections and Sean's absence at her birthday that I realized Sage just wants to be taken care of without asking for it. To be known without reopening old wounds that have barely healed after all these years. There's an unsnappable string that tethers me to her, and the more I ignore it, the tighter it becomes. I would take all her problems, but she doesn't need to take mine—not when she's just managed to get a shot at her dream. I'd never hold her back.

"I think your lasagna is burning." Sage's voice is muffled by the fabric of my shirt. I jerk back to turn off the oven before I blacken the layer of cheese on top.

"Got a scent for fires?" I tap her nose.

"Oh yeah, I'm practically a smoke alarm now."

Sage moves to the cupboard to grab plates to set the table like every night. "Aiden's out with Summer. It's just us tonight," I say.

"Right, she texted me earlier." She removes a set of plates. "By the way, I officially got out of my lease for my apartment. I can stay here for a few more weeks, if you still want that."

"Of course I want that, Sage. I would never let you go back there."

"It wasn't that bad. That place is the only reason I could afford ballet. And the rats only chewed my laptop wire sometimes."

I chuckle, and pull her toward me, taking the plates from her grip to set them on the counter. Her gaze bounces between my lips and my eyes, and I can't help but smirk. We haven't talked about our time in the bathtub or where I stand with my celibacy, so she's hesitant when we get this close. The only reason I hold back is because of that vow and the pressure it would put on her if I broke it. It would be so damn easy to hike her up on the counter and feel the warmth of her on me, but I know Sage, and I know how much this one thing could complicate everything. I won't be another person that takes from her. Because I know if I have her in the way that I want, there's no going back for me.

Our rules are good. We're both clear about when this is ending, and we'll both have what we started this for: her with her spot in NBT, and me with my place in the Thunder secured.

But right now, as we teeter a fine line, Sage's hands fist my shirt, and quick heartbeats thud against mine. I hold back from kissing her because I know if we start, I won't be able to stop until the lasagna's gone ice cold.

"How was your day?" I say instead.

Sage's expression drops. "Good. Except for the fact that my fouet-tés feel off even though I've done them a million times. And my jump is heavy and sluggish. Oh, and don't get me started on Sean's grade for his physics exam."

She pinches the bridge of her nose. Of course, on top of all that she's thinking about her brother too.

"Sean is a smart kid. I'm sure he'll ace his other exams." *He better.* "You need to focus on yourself. You're exhausted, get some rest and I'm sure you'll be perfect for audition day." To alleviate the stress from her features, I massage her temples and watch her relax with each circular motion.

"Sometimes I think you do too much for me."

"Nothing is too much when it comes to you."

Our gazes lock, and this time I don't have the strength to ignore the magnetic pull. She hums into my mouth like she missed the feel-ing. I did too, and I show her exactly that when I deepen the kiss. We've been straying from the touches that lead to more to not aggra-vate my sore muscles, and although it's been torture, everything from that first night in my bathtub is still fresh enough to keep me com-pany all day.

Suddenly, Sage jerks back. I watch her through hazy vision, still feeling the ghost of her lips on mine.

"How's your headache? And did you take the Epsom salt bath I drew for you this morning?"

And she thinks *I* do too much for her. "I'm great, and so was the bath. Just waiting for Dr. Harris to clear me to play."

"Good." She thinks for a minute. "Okay, you can kiss me again."

"Thank you," I say with a smile against her lips.

The rest of our evening is spent watching the second game of the finals with panda face masks and Sage in my lap lulled into sleep by the sound of the reporters and my hands playing with her hair. It's chaotic, yet she appears peaceful. At this moment, I'm sure that even this damn injury is worth it if this is how I get to spend my nights. Even if it's just for now.

THIRTY-FOUR

SAGE

IS PROJECTILE VOMITING on the director of Nova Ballet Theatre considered unprofessional? I hope not, because my stomach twists into a knot when I get to center stage and see three very prominent faces of ballet in the auditorium seats with their eyes on me.

These last few weeks have been more taxing than the time I danced in *The Nutcracker* for four straight shows. Elias has been recovering from his injuries and watching games from home with a grumpy frown. However, when I come home to more baked goods and he persuades me to try them, the smile on his face is the widest I've seen in weeks. It didn't last, though, because after Thunder beat Boston in the Eastern Conference Finals they lost three out of five games, which means if they lose tomorrow, it's all over. Since Elias has been given approval to train today, he'll likely get to play, so the pressure is on. He said I'd make a great nurse because I was very strict about helping him heal. I refused whenever he tried to lure me into his hypnotic embrace with one of his tantalizing touches. That gave Elias time to study game tapes while I rehearsed for my audition.

I've made sure everything was perfect: my pointe shoes, my outfit, my hair—which Elias helped me put rhinestones in—and most of all my performance. The piece of both the White and Black Swan that I prepared tirelessly is imprinted in my brain, and not even the anxiety leaking into the pit in my stomach can offset that.

The judges occupy the three center seats in the auditorium. Aubrey Zimmerman, the artistic director of NBT; Sarah Chang, the renowned prima ballerina; and Adrien Kane, the esteemed choreographer. I did extensive research on all three of them, though I'm well aware of their influence on the ballet community.

A flicker of recognition ignites in Aubrey Zimmerman's gaze, a fleeting acknowledgment, but it's enough to make me feel on top of the fucking world. He has to remember me from the first open audition I showed up to, and I'm hoping he's eating his words right now.

When the music starts, I forget about all the rejections that piled into my email, and I let Tchaikovsky take over my body. A surge of adrenaline courses through my veins, drowning out the pounding of my heart and the relentless chatter of doubt in my mind. The soft notes guide my movements with the same resilience and determination I've held on to with both hands—because the moment I let it go, I know this will all be over for me.

Every extra work shift, every fight with my parents, and every hour I've poured into providing for Sean—they're all woven into the fabric of each plié. But now I'm done letting the weight of my past dictate my future. This is my opportunity to show exactly that.

As I glide across the stage, I catch glimpses of the judges' faces— Zimmerman's piercing gaze is fixed on me, Chang's expression is inscrutable, and Kane's keen eyes betray a hint of awe.

For a fleeting moment, doubt threatens to engulf me, but I push it aside, refusing to let it derail me. When the music switches into the faster tempo, signaling the arrival of the black swan, I abandon every reservation in my body and fuel her darkness.

And then, just as the final notes of the music echo through the auditorium, I execute the pièce de résistance—a grand jeté that seems to silence everything. In that fleeting moment of weightlessness, I feel an overwhelming sense of euphoria, and a sort of peace with this role. Whether I secure it or not, I know I gave this my everything.

With a lightness I've never felt before, I step into my final rotation. When I look up, all three judges are standing. They don't say anything. My chest heaves, and my breaths are ragged as I try to find my voice. The nerves kick in, and the anxiety falls right back into my body.

"S-should I go again?" I ask with a shaky voice.

Zimmerman shakes his head. "We've seen enough."

My heart drops to the hardwood floor.

"It's yours." The words come from Adrien Kane, and I'm sure that I'm dreaming.

"Sorry?" My voice is squeaky.

Kane leans forward. "Ms. Beaumont, we haven't seen an emotion-driven audition like this in ages. You are exactly what we picture for the principal role. You are our swan queen."

I can't feel my fingers. I can't feel any part of my body aside from my heart beating out of my chest. I'm fairly certain I'm having a medical emergency.

"We won't announce it for a few weeks, but you'll be hearing from us," says a scrutinizing Zimmerman.

As the assistants usher me off the stage, I can barely move. But instead of letting me cry in the nearest bathroom, Zimmerman catches me in the hallway.

"Tell that nobody that she knows exactly how to make me eat my words." He smiles before walking out of the glass doors and to a car, exactly like he did all those months ago.

Vindication tastes so damn sweet, I'm not sure I'll ever get enough of it.

My first thought as I'm inside the bathroom changing, and sobbing, and gulping for air on the stall floor, is to call Elias. That scares me because I've only ever wanted to share good news with Sean. But this time there's one more person who reminds me of how much he believes in me, and I want him to know it was worth it.

The silence between each bout of rings feels like hours, but finally he picks up. "Sage? Is everything okay?"

His voice grounds me, and takes me back to everything I have done to get here. Everything *we* have done. It takes me back to the other night. Allowing Elias to see every inch of me without a sliver of doubt skating between us was scary and vulnerable and so open that I couldn't imagine I'd feel this way. It's what I've wanted, and now that I have it, it terrifies me.

"Elias," I manage to say through a broken sob.

There's muffled commotion in the background before a door bangs and it's silent again. "Where are you? I'll come get you." He sounds out of breath, and when I check the time, I know he's still at practice.

"N-no, I'm fine," I say. "I just wanted to call to tell you I finished my audition."

"Yeah?" He blows out a breath. "I'm so proud of you, Sage." The smile in his voice makes me cry. "Don't cry, baby. I know you killed it, and the decision will tell you exactly that."

"I got the part, Elias."

"What?"

I'm not sure if he didn't hear me, because the voices in the background resume, so I wait till I can control my shaky voice and speak louder. I'm wiping tears when I say it again. "I got the part. I'm going to be the principal ballerina for *Swan Lake*."

He repeats my words loudly, and all I hear next is a surge of excitement that reverberates through the phone, and Elias's voice, now almost drowned in the uproar, exclaims, "Hell yeah! Of course you did, baby. Didn't doubt it for a second."

"Let's fucking go!" I hear Aiden's voice through the phone, and I hiccup a laugh. I lean against the bathroom wall and stare at my reddened face and puffy eyes in the mirror. The guys are probably running on adrenaline before their game tomorrow, so their excitement is intense.

"You're the first person I called," I admit.

Elias responds with a booming laugh. "From the look on Marcus's face, I can tell."

My uncle's voice comes through the receiver. "I'm so damn proud of you, kid."

Whooping and hollering escalate around Elias.

"I love you." My words spill out so fast I don't bother stopping them because they have never been more true. There's a long pause, and I have to check if he hung up.

But then I hear Elias. "She says she loves you."

My confusion morphs into realization. He thought I was talking to my uncle.

I consider correcting him, but before I can, Elias's voice returns, filled with pride. "You hear that? You've got a whole cheering squad here. Are you happy, Sage?"

His question makes the beam of light in my chest even brighter. "So happy," I say, a little watery and broken. "I can't believe it. I didn't think it would actually happen."

"No? You always seemed pretty confident." He chuckles.

I'm smiling like an idiot now. "It's called faking it."

Then there's a tense pause that chokes the line, and the word *fake* sits heavily in the silence between us.

"I guess we're both pretty good at that, huh?" he says softly.

My brain refuses to come up with a response.

I love him. I'm bursting with so many emotions right now, I'm not sure how to say it in a way where he'll know that I mean it. I need Elias to believe that I want him for real. Not the famous hockey player, but the boy who cooks for me and doesn't complain when we do my self-care routines. Elias has been hurt before, and I never want him to feel that again.

"Congrats, Sage," he says, and the somberness in his voice feels wrong. Then his name is called and he's quiet for a moment. "I've gotta go, but you should celebrate, okay? There's no one who deserves it more."

And then the line drops, and somehow I keep my heart from doing the same. Because just like I secured the role, I'm going to secure the boy too.

IT'S LATE WHEN the guys come home. I can hear their hushed voices down the hall, and when Elias steps into his room, my stomach squeezes tightly and so do my eyes.

Suddenly, all the confidence I built up this afternoon evaporates into thin air. Elias heads to the bathroom, and while he's in there I'm clutching my pillow, hoping to fall asleep before he comes back. Before I blurt out *I love you* again and freak him out.

Everything we did—this entire fake relationship—was for the sake of our dreams, and now that we have them, we're seconds from puffing away like dust on a windowsill.

The bathroom door opens again, and I can't remember if I ever learned how to speak. Even in the dark I know he's only in his boxers.

But instead of heading to his side of the bed, Elias sits beside me, by the curve of my body. The mattress dips under his weight, but I keep my eyes closed. Then, I feel his lips press against my forehead, his fingers threading through my hair, and his thumb moving back and forth in a soothing motion.

"Sage," he whispers. "You have insomnia, I know you're awake."

My whole face flushes, and I'm grateful the lights are off. I pretend to sound groggy when I open my eyes. "I was trying to sleep."

"Is that why you were breathing so hard?"

"Maybe I was having a really good dream."

"Yeah? Who was in it?"

"Same guy who's always in my dreams. He's got these big hands, and he runs them all over—*ah!*" Elias's finger jabs at my waist. "Did you just *poke* me?"

He chuckles. His hands on my waist create a tingling sensation. "Why dream if you can have the real thing?"

We sink into a silence that I can't help but break.

"Can I have the real thing?" I whisper.

He breaks eye contact, but his hands are still under my palms. I can't let him leave without giving me an answer, but I don't have it in me to repeat myself.

"Did you tell Sean you got the part?"

The redirect shatters my hope. This time when I try to silently urge his gaze to mine, it doesn't work. "I did. He wants to celebrate when he finally comes to visit."

Elias looks at our hands. "So, that's it, huh? You'll be busy with rehearsing and then traveling with NBT?"

The pit in my stomach deepens to an abyss. "Yeah, rehearsals start soon, and after the first month, we're booked for shows in different cities. I'll probably have to look for a place."

A muscle in his jaw jumps. "And have you? Been looking, I mean."

"Not yet."

Because it's true. I can't look at those dingy one-bedroom apartments and imagine being there all alone. Staying here with Elias and having his friends visit has corrupted my mind. Somehow, I've made the terrible discovery that I like having friends, and I can't go back to living in an empty place.

"But I've seen a few places available for rent by the theater."

"That's good."

Is it? There are so many things left unspoken that I can't hold back anymore. I sit up on the bed and turn on the bedside lamp. "What are we doing, Elias?"

He blinks, adjusting to the light before his gaze roams my face. "What do you mean?"

I stare up at the ceiling and then look at him again. "I mean that I need to know what this is. Because this—*us*—is coming to an end, and I can't bear it if I don't even know what's real."

Four beats of silence pass. I know because I count every single one of them.

"You want to know what's real, Sage?" he says. "What's real is what I told you in that hotel room. That I can't look at you sometimes because I like it too much. And I don't want to stand next to you and touch you like you're mine when that's never been the truth."

The knot in my throat feels like barbed wire.

"This is temporary. You're going to leave, live out your dream, and become the star that you deserve to be. And I'll be here, because we both know this was never going to work beyond what we agreed on."

"But things are different now. You know they are." I hold back the emotion in my throat.

"Sage." My name is broken on his lips. "I won't let myself need you more than everyone else already does."

"But I want you to need me," I say.

Elias's expression softens. "Because that's all you've ever known. You care about everyone else so much that you don't realize you're depleting yourself in the process."

His words peel the makeshift patchwork over my past like paint off an old wall.

"I will never be the one to wear you down or keep you from what you deserve. You might not see it now, but a few weeks, a month, a year from now you will, and it would pain me to watch that disappointment take over. I know what that's like, and I can't watch you go through that because of me."

I hate every word. Only because they slam against my ribcage harder than my heart.

When his palm brushes my face in a coaxing touch, I pull away from the confusing feeling.

"So, this is it? We're not going to try?" The last word cracks in two. "You're okay with leaving us like this?"

Elias's exhale is long and heavy. "That's not fair, Sage. We both made those rules."

"I don't care about the rules!" I exclaim.

His brows raise at my outburst, and words seem to stick to his throat.

"Because I'm sitting here trying to tell you that I love you."

It's like every atom in the air settles, and Elias pulls back like I've pushed him. There's a ticking time bomb that sits in my chest when our gazes lock, and he freezes.

"I'm in love with you, Elias. And I'm pretty sure I have been for a while now," I admit. "So, what are you going to do about it?"

THIRTY-FIVE

ELIAS

"I SHOULD GO."

Those are the words that came out of my mouth. Those are the words that made Sage's head rear back in shock. And those are the words that make me want to bang my head against the wall.

She told me she loved me, and I choked.

Suddenly, Socket's words of wisdom about breaking the box come back to me. But the sound of his voice is a distant memory, because I've officially discovered hell on earth. You'd think living in the hockey house for so many years, I'd have witnessed it long ago. But this, *this* is torture.

When I left Sage in my bed after saying those words, I couldn't stay in the apartment. I drove to Socket's house. He was more than happy to have me, so I slept on his couch. The sleep was terrible, and my nightmares ran rampant. When I woke up sweating, I hoped to find Sage's soothing touch, but I was alone, and regretted my every decision.

The look on Sage's face last night has stuck to my mind like a leech. Trying to detach from the mess I made has proved useless.

And now, I have to face the media.

"They say behind every great man is an even greater woman. Do you think you owe any of your success this playoff season to a very popular ballerina?"

As they ask their questions, a feeling that's somewhere between heartburn and death roars in my chest.

I was too cowardly to say anything, because the emotion in her words had pulled all mine out of my head. The reason I've been single for so long doesn't feel so important anymore. I've realized that my determination not to let my biological father interfere with my family has made me suffer alone for so many years. I've been avoiding new relationships to protect myself from being exploited, but being with Sage has never felt like I was compromising my rules.

Her plea to try ripped me up, because as much as I may be ready to forget the rules and say yes, I can't.

She doesn't need to have her heart split in two because I'm too greedy to let her go. I've seen the way she is with Sean when he's in school; she berates herself for missing his call after a long day of rehearsals and teaching. It gets her down, despite him reminding her that it's okay. It makes her question whether she's a good sister.

If she ever questioned herself with me, it would destroy me.

I could be selfish, and *fuck*, I want to be. But I could never take from her. I'd happily give her every part of me, if I could be confident that it wouldn't hurt her to leave. But I know Sage, and I know she gives her all to the people she cares about. She'll try her hardest to give her all to me, when she should be focused on her career—the reason we started this whole thing. And I won't be the one to make her forget it.

I clear my throat. "Her devotion to her career inspired me to do more with mine. She's my anchor, and I owe her for more than just my improvement on the ice."

"As hockey fanatics we all have our superstitions, so the fans want to know if she'll be joining us for game six," another reporter asks.

Fuck if I know. I might have screwed up everything last night. She was spilling her heart out, and I couldn't even speak.

"I'm sure she'll be supporting the team just like she has every step of the way."

I doubt she'll be here tonight. I've been trying to avoid thinking about that. I'm not supposed to have any distractions right now, but when there's a bullet-size hole in my chest, it's inescapable.

The questions don't change course, but when Aiden walks into the locker room, the reporters are quick to head over to him next. Based on the look he gives me, he's only talking to them for me.

When he's done his round of press, he comes to me.

"Here to check on me?" I mutter.

"Fuck, no." Aiden appears frustrated. "I told you to tell me if you started feeling bad again. But you didn't, and now look at you."

"I feel fine," I lie.

"Yeah? So, last night when you left the apartment, that was you feeling fine?"

I scratch the back of my neck.

"You can tell me, man. I'm here," he urges.

"It's this thing with Sage—I can't fake it anymore." I drop my head in my hands. "But a relationship isn't a possibility with us, it never was."

"You love her?"

I stare at him. "Of course I fucking do."

"Then tell her that," he urges. "Sage looks at you the same way you look at her. As your roommate it's uncomfortable as hell, but as your best friend it makes me happy for you. You haven't allowed yourself to be with someone the way you've been with her, ever, especially after what happened at worlds."

There's a rusty knife that stays lodged in my sternum. "Because when you let people in, you let them see all your vulnerabilities. She doesn't need to see all of mine."

"Did she tell you that?" he probes. "Because I'm pretty sure you know that she'd say you're an idiot for thinking she doesn't want all of you. What's really stopping you?"

I groan. "She's leaving. After she finishes the performances here, she'll have to go on a tour with the company, and she'll be gone for a year or more."

"You know, I used to think you were the smarter one between the two of us." He releases a sardonic breath. "We grew up together, Eli, so I know how your weird brain makes you think you're not worth it, but I'm telling you, you are. And I'm sure if you had the balls to ask her, she'd say the same thing."

"I don't want to be the one to make her choose between me or her dream."

He laughs this time. "Who said she has to choose? Long distance exists for a reason. I'm living proof of that."

Summer and Aiden have created a schedule that works for them. Those two have never been more in love, and even when she's not visiting, he's happy because they both get to do what they love and still have each other.

"She won't just be a few hours away. She'll be across the world for months at a time. If this year is any indication of how busy the season gets, I won't have the luxury to go see her whenever I want."

Aiden stands abruptly. "When you realize that one day you'll get the chance to wake up and have your whole world right beside you, a few months or years is nothing. The distance might test your relationship—and trust me, it fucking does—but it doesn't define your outcome. That's up to you to decide. So, considering you're in love with the girl, you should probably tell her before she thinks you're not."

When he steps away, there isn't enough oxygen in the room. I barrel through the open doors and into the hall, wiping my face with a towel and mulling over Aiden's words.

I spot Marcus Smith-Beaumont walking down the hall right toward me. He doesn't speak, only tilts his head toward his office before disappearing inside. I follow, wiping the sweat beading my forehead.

"I don't like you, Elias."

Yeah, no shit. "That's why you called me in here? To tell me that?"

He sits on a corner of his wooden desk. "I'm not one to mix personal and professional business, but when my niece asks to stay with me for the first time in years, I need to know what's going on."

My gaze snaps from the floor back to him. "She did?"

"I assume it's worse than I thought if you don't know."

My exhalation is loud. Marcus Smith-Beaumont is the last person I want to admit to that I've done something idiotic. "She was vulnerable with me, and I choked. I disappointed her. I couldn't say what she needed me to because I don't know if I'm good enough for her."

Marcus pinches the bridge of his nose like I'm a nuisance. This is going as well as I expected.

"So, out of everything I said to you, that's what you listen to?" He mutters something to himself. "I've seen my niece through many phases, and she's never been the way she is with you."

I don't know if that helps the pain or makes it worse.

"Sage feels the need to perform. I've seen her do it with her parents and her ex. But when she's with you, she becomes the Sage I saw before her childhood was ripped away from her." He looks at me dead on. "I don't know you, Eli, despite thinking that I did. I'm taking a second look because of what Sage has brought out in you. This is the first time you seem like you know what you're doing. On and off the ice."

"Because it's easy with her." My mouth doesn't get the memo to stop speaking, because I continue. "But I know she'd be a lot happier without having me as a burden."

"You sure? Because that girl cares about you almost as much as she cares about Sean and me. I don't see a reason for you to think that you're bad for her, unless you don't care about her."

"Of course I care. I care more about her than about hockey." I shut my trap immediately. This is the fucking general manager, and telling him hockey isn't my priority might be the dumbest thing I've done all season.

"Don't ever repeat that to anyone, but I'm glad to hear it. You take care of her, Eli."

"It's not like that with us. She's leaving and I'll be here. It . . . it was never supposed to be like this."

"Plans change when you least expect them to." He finally motions for me to sit, and I do. "A few years back, I thought I had a beautiful fiancée, a house, and a career people dream about, but then those kids needed someone. I took a hiatus, and the woman I thought was going to be my wife said things about those kids I can never forgive. Not everything works out as planned, but as long as the people I love are with me, I don't care about the rest."

"You gave it all up for them?"

"It's not giving anything up when you know what you're gaining is much more valuable. I only made sure they knew they were my priority, even if they decided to go another route." He taps the desk with his fingertips. "So, I won't interfere, because you two have some things to figure out. But if you hurt her, Eli, I'll find a way to hurt you much worse. And if you hurt yourself in the process—well, I won't go easy on you then either."

The weight of a decision sits on my shoulders like a bag of rocks.

And now, with the biggest game of my career about to begin, I can't stop thinking about everything I should have said to Sage.

THIRTY-SIX

ELIAS

THERE ISN'T A single player in blue without a broken something. Broken stick, broken teeth, broken bones, and now we're seconds away from a broken dream. There's no words of encouragement, no optimism, and definitely no smiles.

"We're fucked," mutters Owen.

Though most of the shit he says is nothing I relate to, this sentiment is spot-on. Because we're losing, and even though I've scored two of the five goals on the board, it doesn't feel like an achievement. Aiden's still on the ice and he was the reason we got our fifth goal, but Vancouver pulled through. So now we're truly fucked.

Coach nods for me to head out as another player ends his shift. I'm set on pushing us into overtime. I glide past Aiden to make sure we're on the same page. Years of playing together have honed our ability to synchronize.

We're quick to execute the gameplay. Aiden receives the puck, then pivots and charges up the ice with a burst of speed that catches everyone off guard. With a lightning-fast fake-out, he leaves one defender sprawling, then another. The crowd roars as he gains the offensive zone. I'm trailing, ready for the precise pass that cuts through the chaos. I spot a gap between the goalie's pads and send the puck flying into the net.

The arena erupts in a deafening roar as the buzzer lights flash. The score evens and a sliver of hope lights behind Coach Wilson's eyes.

But the moment the clock starts again, Vancouver comes back harder, vengeful even. They fly past our defense, and our guys are too slow to catch the movement. Then when I think the game may still be salvageable by Socket's quick saves, Vancouver's captain gets control of the puck. Aiden tries to slow him down, but their captain reaches the net and sends a blistering wrist shot past Socket's gloved hand, crushing the dwindling hope left in the arena, when the horn blares.

Vancouver wins. Toronto loses.

I don't even register the horn or the celebration from one side of the arena. The green and blue confetti falls on the ice, and the announcers congratulate the Stanley Cup winners.

Aiden skates past me, holding his helmet in his hands as he heads straight for the locker room. The rest of the guys follow, heads hanging in defeat and sorrow clouding over them. I feel it too. Loss embeds itself beneath my skin and crawls out as dark failure.

Coach knocks a hand on my helmet, doing the same to the rest of the guys. It's a silent stabilizing touch, a reminder that at least we didn't play like shit.

As I'm moving off the ice, stick raised and listening to the crowd's cheers and boos swallowing the arena, one thought sits at the front of my brain. In a split second, everything we've trained for and got injured for has slipped out of our grasp and into someone else's. Something we wanted so bad is no longer ours, because of a few careless mistakes.

In the chaos in my mind, one person, one girl—*my girl*—appears in the center of my thoughts. I imagine she'd wear an encouraging smile and an expression that would make the ache in my chest turn into something entirely different.

But after last night, I know that image will be a reality only in my mind.

I head straight down the tunnel and to the locker room. The depressing feeling of loss drips from everyone, and then Coach enters, followed by Marcus Smith-Beaumont.

"In the darkness of defeat, winners find lessons that lead them to future victories," Marcus starts. "Each and every one of you played with heart and grit, and this win was not handed over easily. But now, it's time to recharge and reflect."

Coach steps forward. "Onwards and upwards."

"Onwards and upwards," the locker room repeats before the haste to leave the arena begins. There is nothing worse than being surrounded by the winning team after a loss like this.

By the time I'm done cleaning out my stall, Aiden's already showered and ready to head out. He silently pats my back before he walks out of the double doors. Summer and her dad are waiting for him, no doubt going to do their best to cheer him up.

With a few quiet goodbyes, I head down the tunnel, finding the silence of the walk looming like a dark cloud.

But then there's a coil around my heart that tightens when I catch a glimpse of pink. Like a guiding star in the night sky, Sage glows against the blue walls of the corridor.

I stop dead in my tracks.

"I wasn't going to come," she starts. "But I couldn't miss it. I didn't think you'd want me here anyway."

My chest tightens when I see her ripping her heart open for me. Like a ray of sunlight, Sage cuts through the dark clouds distorting my vision. I realize that no matter what, I'd spend my entire life trying to be good enough for her.

She sniffles. "But I told you I loved you last night, and I meant it. And maybe you were right—I do neglect myself sometimes, but with you, I've never had to. I'm done letting go of what I want, Elias. So, either you'll have to tell me to leave, or—"

With three quick strides, I cut her off by pulling her right to my chest. Sage stiffens but quickly recovers and wraps her arms around me. "Don't leave," I say.

The rest of the team walks down the hall to exit, but neither of us moves, and no one interrupts us.

She melts further into my hold. "Are you okay?"

"Now I am."

Sage pulls away, and her lips lift in a sad, confused smile. She seems to hold back from what she wants to ask. There's a talk we should be having, but of course right now my girl is thinking about how I feel.

"If it helps, you looked totally puckable out there," she jokes. Even now Sage tries to use humor to disguise the sadness that swims below the surface of her hazel eyes.

I put that emotion there, and now I want to eviscerate it.

She's the only person who could pull a smile out of me at a time like this. "You really have no filter," I say.

"You want me to?"

"Nah, Elias and Sage unfiltered. That's how I like it, remember?" Taking her wrist, I press a light kiss on her pulse. The faint blush that falls against the brown of her cheeks is instant, and she watches me carefully, like she's trying to read my thoughts.

"Are you sure you're okay? Or at least you will be, right? I mean, I can't imagine how you must feel, so if you need some space, I've already asked my uncle to stay at his place."

"Sage?"

"Hmm?"

"Shut up." And then I kiss her. Desperate and urgent and exactly how I wished I had last night. She melts into me, hesitating before she lets go and completely surrenders to the all-consuming kiss. Her soft moan gets trapped in my mouth when she parts her lips and I slide my tongue over hers. We fuse in a burst of electricity.

Sage pulls back for a breath, and I rest my forehead against hers, unable to contain my grin when she chews on her bottom lip.

"I think you're sleep deprived. Did you sleep at all last night?" she asks.

"If I'm not sleeping next to you, I'm not sleeping at all."

She blinks like she's holding back tears.

"But I did forget to tell you something last night," I say.

"What?"

"I love you." I let the words hang in the sliver of space between us. "I've known from the first time you laughed at me. The first time you made one of your dirty jokes. The first time you slept in my arms. I've known it all along, and I'm sorry for letting you think I needed time to realize it."

With my palm cupping her cheek, I press a light kiss to her forehead.

She blinks at my chest, still not meeting my eyes. "Real or fake?"

Fuck. The question chafes my heart, and I hold back a groan as I level my gaze with hers, knowing that I want her to never have to ask that question again.

"Real. So fucking real."

The tears slip from her eyes, and I wipe them away.

"Don't cry, baby," I murmur softly.

With a tattered, broken breath, she says, "I've waited so long for this to be real. To hear those words from you. But hearing them now feels like I'm making it all up in my head."

"You're not making it up." This is the last time I'll let her cry because of this, because of me. "I love you. And I should have told you last night, but I think we both know you have a knack for leaving me speechless."

She lets out a watery laugh, then meets my eyes. "But I snore."

"Music to my ears."

"I have really cold feet."

"I run hot."

"I'm a people pleaser."

"Then let me be the one to please you." I watch her shock turn into realization. "I want you to be mine. If anyone in this world deserves someone who's there for them, it's you. There's nothing I wouldn't do to make you believe you're worth every bit of worry and care."

She blinks away her tears.

"Do you want me, Sage?"

That does it. She lunges at me with her arms around my neck. She's practically hanging off me. Even through my hoodie, I can feel her touch warm my skin. I lift her and she hooks her legs around my waist.

Sage buries her head into the crook of my neck. "I've always wanted you, Elias. Just been waiting for you to catch up."

"I'm sorry it took so long."

"As long as I get to end up in your arms like this, it's worth it. *You* are worth it."

I pull back before she can kiss me. "So, it's not because of my magical hands?"

Sage bursts into laughter. "Oh no, I've tainted you."

"Let's go home and you can taint me some more."

Her eyes widen before she nods obediently. Just before I'm going to let her back on her feet, a flash of white hits us and we turn to the team photographer, Brandy, giving us a thumbs-up. "Doesn't hurt to capture a moment of happiness even during a loss. I'll send it to you, Eli."

Sage turns to me and asks, "What are you going to caption that one?"

A smile lifts my lips. "'Home.'"

THIRTY-SEVEN

SAGE

IF THERE WAS a way to snap my fingers and remove my clothes, I'd have done it by now. However, Elias drives slowly, allowing some old country song—that no doubt is from Aiden's playlist—to float through the car as if I'm not going to spontaneously combust in the passenger seat. Every word he said to me in that hallway plays on repeat, but him saying I can *taint* him takes the cake.

Though I'm not going to be the one to bring it up. Even though he asked me to be his, I don't know whether that includes my body too. I really hope it does.

By the time we're in the elevator, he's watching me with a predatory gaze and I watch him right back.

Take me, my eyes say.

Don't tempt me, is his reply.

"You scared of me, Elias?"

The elevator dings open to a lower floor, but no one enters. Elias crosses the small space to stand before me, towering, smirking, mocking. "Should I be?"

The deep rumble of his voice zings a shot of electricity to my core, and I know then that I won't survive tonight. Whether he takes me or not, I'm completely ruined by this hockey rookie who bakes me sweet treats and supports me like no one ever has.

Grabbing the collar of his shirt, I yank him close, just inches from my lips. "Why don't you find out?"

Pillowy lips brush over mine. Sexual tension drips off the elevator walls, and it's so hot in here, I wouldn't be surprised if I find condensation blurring the mirror.

Ding.

I jolt back but Elias stands there, watching me, *devouring* me with just a look.

My eyes flick to the elevator doors drawing open. "This is our floor."

The corner of his mouth lifts, as if my words somehow satisfy him. Moving out of my way, he allows me to exit first and follows, making my back tingle with awareness. The deafening silence is almost suffocating. When he leans forward to unlock the door, the bolt twists and we stand there, back against front, just breathing.

Elias's lips brush against the shell of my ear. "Open the door, Sage."

My hand shakes so much you'd think I was the one who hasn't had sex in four years.

When I open the door, I expect him to tear my clothes off and take me on the nearest surface, but instead he drops his gear bag by the entryway and heads to the kitchen. He opens the fridge and takes out a carton of orange juice.

"Thirsty?" he asks.

Yes. I don't answer, and he looks over his shoulder to see my blank expression. It's like he's moving in slow motion. The sound of liquid filling the glass, the slow slide of it against the counter before he gulps it down. When he moves to the sink to wash it and put it in the dish rack, it's entirely too much.

"Are we gonna have sex?" I blurt.

His body begins to shake, and when he turns around, I realize he's laughing. At me. I watch him with annoyance fizzing on my skin.

"Sorry," he says, wiping a nonexistent tear from his eye.

Not caring for his pitiful apology, I pivot in an attempt to storm away, but I don't get anywhere. He grabs my wrists and pulls me back.

I bump right into him. "What?"

He tuts at my sharp tone. "You've waited months. Where did all that patience go, baby?"

Oh God, I love the way he calls me baby. There's something about the smooth timbre of his voice that makes it sound so hot yet gentle. My thighs squeeze together and he tracks the movement with a faint smirk.

"If I haven't made it clear already, Sage, I want you. All of you. In every way that I can have you." His hands move down my body to cup my ass. "Tell me what you like."

My patience is running thin. "You know what I like. You had proof of it all over your thigh. And your face."

He chuckles like I'm a one-woman circus. Elias draws closer and slips his hand between my legs. "You like when I touch you like this," he rasps. "When I kiss you like this." His lips capture mine, then move down to my neck, teasing and biting. "But show me what else. Let me make it good for you."

This man is about to break a four-year vow, and he wants to make it good for *me*? I'm not one to complain.

"I want to taste you," I say honestly.

"*Fuck*," he mutters, pressing his forehead against mine. "You can't say things like that. It's been a really long time and I want this to last."

"I don't care if you come the second my tongue touches the tip, I just want you."

He moves away from me to lean against the counter and stare at the ceiling. "I don't deserve you."

"Yeah, you do."

He swallows, bringing his gaze back to me, and it's like I've flipped a switch. "Then show me," he says. "Show me how much I deserve you, Sage."

In one swift move, I pull off my top and greet him with my bare breasts. They're nothing more than a handful, but he stares like they're the best pair of tits he's ever seen. It's the first time that I've been with someone that I haven't cared how my body looks. I don't itch to check if I'm bloated or hesitate to reach for the button of my jeans. Elias stands still, eyes on fire and hands still gripping the countertop. I remove my jeans next, tossing them beside me, but when I go for my panties, he stops me.

"Keep them on," he says, pushing off the counter. "Now, get on your knees."

Holy shit.

I drop in an instant, and when he undoes his belt and unzips his pants, I think I'm running out of air. It's like the trailing suspense in a thriller when you know someone's going to die. It's going to be me.

He pulls off his shirt next, and the drool practically dribbles down my chin. I can't focus between his ripped torso and his boxers that tent with his thick erection. But then he pulls his boxers down and tosses them away. When his cock springs free, I stare at the shiny gray metal stud at the base of his length, and the one on the tip. My stomach tightens. Elias is so reserved and introverted that the sight of a piercing is still shocking.

"Open your mouth."

I don't hesitate, and Elias eases between my lips. The second my tongue touches his shaft, he groans so loud, I'm worried I've done something wrong. But his eyes squeeze shut and his head tips back, and I realize he's trying not to come. The metal hits the back of my throat and heat pools in my core, making me hum in pleasure. As I wrap my hand around his cock, I lick the underside, all the way up to the tip, which leaks precome.

His grip tightens in my hair. "Just like that."

Elias shivers when I twirl my tongue around his shaft. His reactions are so instant, I don't want to stop. I want to make him feel good. I want to prove to him that this right here, with me, is worth it. That his vow wasn't for nothing, and he deserves the pleasure he's deprived himself of for so long.

With a newfound purpose, I take all of him. I use my hands to cover what my mouth can't, and revel in how warm and smooth he feels in my mouth.

Elias grips my chin, his eyes shining like he believes I hung the moon. "Come here." He pulls me up to his lips, and he kisses me.

"I wasn't done," I mumble against his lips.

"Me neither," he replies.

I open my mouth to protest, but he slips his fingers between my lips, making me suck them. As he slides them out, he traces a wet trail down to my hard nipples, flicking and pinching them until I'm a moaning mess.

"Take me to your room," I pant.

Elias lifts me in his arms and takes me straight to his bedroom.

Kicking the door closed, he gently drops me on his bed and kneels in front of me. Parting my legs, he uses his thumb to rub the wet scrap of fabric between my thighs. He leaves a trail of kisses along my skin. Then Elias pulls the fabric tight, straining it between the wet folds and watching me writhe with unadulterated lust.

"Touch yourself. Look at how wet your pussy is from having my cock in your mouth."

I hook my fingers beneath the waistband of my panties and drag them down my legs. Elias helps me, and the stringy thing rips with just one tug before he tosses it away. Plunging one finger inside, my head falls back in pleasure, and Elias curses. When I show him my wet finger, he takes my wrist and sucks it clean.

"You taste better than I remember."

I giggle like a schoolgirl. Clearly, I'm out of control. "You've been thinking about this?"

"Every fucking day," he says, roughly yanking my hips to the edge of the bed. "Now make my dreams come true, Sage."

His hot mouth seals over my clit, and my back arches. The swirl of his tongue and then the suction of his lips mix to send a high-pitched sound ringing in my ears. I'm electrified and floating all at once, my body sizzling like a hot grill.

When he pushes two fingers inside me, I fist the comforter. It was one thing having him touch me in the bathtub, but here, without the soapy water, the sight of his touch is intoxicating. His rhythm quickens and every muscle in my body contracts. His fingers scissor inside me, and there's a flutter wreaking havoc in my stomach. Elias builds my orgasm to a crescendo.

This man should never have been celibate. Those four years were a step back for women everywhere.

"Please. *Please* make me come."

"Too polite," he rasps. My orgasm hangs in the invisible space between us, and I'm desperate for it.

"I need to come," I barely whisper.

He shakes his head as he slows the moment to a torturous pace. "Try again."

"Fucking hell, Elias. Make me come!"

His fingers curl in acquiescence, and I'm off to space on my little rocket ship. I hear him chuckling, but I'm too spent to care if he finds my stamina laughable. We might both be athletes, but nothing could have prepared me for this. For *him*.

Lifting onto my elbows, I crawl back toward the center of his bed, wanting every inch of him on me. He doesn't need me to ask, because he follows me to where I want him, right on his back. I climb on top, and his eyes go wide, both of us just inches away from finally getting what we want.

I'm grinding on him, lost in the feel of him between my legs. Hot, thick, and hard. His handsome face watches in awe and his Adam's apple bobs. "I want to feel you inside me, Elias."

His guttural groan reverberated between my legs. "Please, Sage, just—*fuck*," he moans. "I need a second, j-just give me a second, and then I want you to sit on my cock," he stutters.

I nod, loving the tortured look on his face as he composes himself. His sweat-damp skin and tousled hair aren't helping my patience, so I rub myself over his length. He grips my waist tightly, forcing me to stop but then pushing me down harder to grind on him. Like he can't decide between wanting me to stop or continue.

"You're too perfect. Fucking irresistible," he says, cupping my face to bring my lips to his. He kisses me gently, sweetly, as if he isn't harder than a pipe under me. As if I'm not close to whistling like a pressure cooker.

"Elias, I need you," I whimper.

The four simple words seem to click everything in place for him as he shifts to give me exactly what I want. He releases my face to grab my waist, and I can practically taste the pleasure of having him inside me.

But he freezes, completely.

"Condom," he grits out. "*Fuck*, I don't have a condom."

My disappointment is that of someone finding coal in their Christmas stocking. "None?"

He looks up at me like I should know the answer to that. "If I did, they'd have expired about four years ago."

Right, celibacy.

He runs a hand through his long hair. "I'm sure Aiden probably—"

"I'm on birth control. And I'm clean if you want to go without one," I say. "But no pressure."

"No pressure?" he chuckles breathlessly. "Sage, if you want that, I'll give it to you. I'd give you anything. But if it's about not having condoms, I'll run to the store and get some."

"No." I shake my head, letting my hands fall flat against his chest. "It's not only about that. I want to feel you. I want you exactly how you are, Elias."

He groans, and if I'm not mistaken, there's a pink flush on his cheeks that makes me suppress a bright smile. Elias Westbrook is *blushing*.

"Are you sure?"

"It would be a shame not to feel your piercings inside me."

When he kisses me, I feel sparks all over. Confidence emanates from him, and if I ever said he was shy when it came to sex, he's proving me wrong in every way he can.

"Then fuck me how you want, Sage, and I'll make sure you feel everything."

THIRTY-EIGHT

ELIAS

THE FOUR-YEAR WAIT is worth every second.

There's no hesitation when Sage lowers herself on me, but my entire body roars to life and simultaneously hums to a stop. The two sensations pulsing under my skin are an impossible combination. Sage moans and the sound of it snaps me back to reality. She squeezes around me so perfectly, I moan.

"It's too much," she cries. Her head hangs and her curly hair fans her face. She looks at me through her lashes, brows furrowed, but she's only halfway down.

"Not for you," I rasp. "You take my cock so well. We can make it fit in this perfect pussy, right, baby?"

Her eyes glow at the challenge. I draw slow circles on her swollen clit and watch as her arousal coats my fingers. She slides down my length easily until I'm buried to the hilt. The moment the piercing at the base of my shaft hits her clit, she gasps and curls her fingers on my chest.

Sage drops her forehead to mine, and I hold her hips to rock them. We stare at each other, and when she caresses my face, thick cords of something massive and foreign knot around my heart.

"Are you okay?" she whispers.

These words cut off my air supply. I'd expect nothing less. But at a moment where I'm taking so much from her, I can't have her worrying about me. Even if it feels damn good.

"Don't worry about me, baby." I drag her over my piercing, making the stars in her eyes reappear. "You like that, Sage? Like the way it feels on your clit?"

Sage nods quickly.

In the cloudy haze of her grinding on top of me, I let my hands roam her body. I watch my wet dreams personified with pure satisfaction.

It takes a second for me to look up again. "Good. It's only for you."

She rides me harder, like those words mean everything to her.

"You like being the first to take my pierced cock in this pretty pussy?" The words grind out, and I shouldn't be asking when I'm this close to coming. I search for a rhythm that keeps her moaning loudly. Her pussy squeezes so tightly around me that I clench my jaw to hold back.

She whimpers. "Yes."

"Then get on your back and let me watch your eyes roll."

She's flat on her back in one swift movement. I take my time kissing all the way up her body until I take one puckered nipple into my mouth and release it with a pop.

"*Please*, Elias," she whispers desperately. Her nails dig into my shoulders, and her fingers slide into my hair and pull me to her mouth. I'm situated between her legs, and it feels like heaven when she squeezes them around my waist, urging me forward. I slip my tongue into her mouth and play with her tits until her nipples are hard peaks under my thumb. I pull away to kiss along her neck, and her vanilla scent gives me a head rush.

"Want me to keep going?" I whisper as my hands travel to where her hips buck.

"I've wanted you to keep going since the moment I met you. I've made that pretty damn obvious, Westbrook."

The mouth on this girl. I'll never get tired of it. Never get tired of her.

Kissing her is the only thing keeping this slow and at a pace that I can follow. With Sage, I know she won't care how long this lasts, but I'm determined to make this good for her.

"We can go slower," Sage offers.

I kiss the considerate words off her lips and let my fingers slip between her wet folds, playing with her clit until she's so far gone her eyes are rolling back.

"Elias, it's too much. It's too good." Her nails dig into the strained muscles of my back, and I'm sure there will be marks on my skin. As long as they're from her, I don't care.

"Take what you need, because I'm about to fuck you exactly how I want."

She makes a grateful sound. "This is so much better than just imagining you touching me."

Jesus. She wants me to take it slow, but if she continues saying shit like that, I won't be able to. Especially when her hips buck as I grip the base of my dick and press the head to her slick core.

But I'm a glutton for punishment. "What do you usually think about?"

She slides her fingers down my abs, which are working overtime right now. "This is pretty damn close." Then she pauses. "But it's usually me in the shower, and you on your knees."

I choke back a groan. "We can arrange that."

She straightens her strong, toned legs to rest them on my shoulders, showcasing her insane flexibility. I nip the inside of her thigh, making her yelp before I soothe the area with open-mouthed kisses.

Sage moves her hips as if she's desperately searching for my cock to fill her again. I use the tip to spread her arousal all over her already soaked pussy.

"Look at you, baby, you're so pretty. Dripping fucking wet for me." I spread her legs wider to get the perfect view, and Sage lets me push them further than I thought possible. She doesn't strain, and that's from years of ballet. When I sink into her, her eyes squeeze shut like she's in pain. When I'm about to stop, she opens them, and it's like the sun has risen.

I'm barely holding back, trying to get her where she needs to be. Closing my eyes is the only way I can delay my release now, because looking at her flushed face isn't helping slow anything down. She squeezes around me and I try not to burst. My heart keens, and Sage gasps.

"I'm coming," she pants.

"Thank God," I grunt.

Her arms sling around my neck, and she watches me move in and out of her, and when my piercings hit the right spot, she screams my name. I fucking love it. Then, when I put my lips to her ear and tell her to come again, she does, pulling my release too. Once again proving her idea that she's difficult is wrong and reminding her when she's with me she'll never not be satisfied.

My release feels violent. It contracts every muscle in my body and wrings out every last ounce of pleasure from me. My chest heaves and I shudder in the aftermath.

I climb off Sage and fall on my back. She nuzzles my neck when I pull her closer.

"You're clingy after sex? Who would've guessed?" Her chuckle is short-lived, and when she looks up at me, I know what she's thinking.

"Real," I say. "It's all real."

"And this is all of you?" she asks softly.

"Yeah, baby. It is."

Sage runs a finger along my abdomen, tracing the curves of each muscle. "And it's mine?"

"If that's what you want."

"Then why haven't you asked me to be your girlfriend, Elias?"

I turn to face her, lifting her chin so she looks at me. "If you think I'd fuck anyone other than my girlfriend like that, you're mistaken."

She continues to look at me expectantly. Not budging. My stubborn girl.

I sigh. "Will you be my *real* girlfriend, Sage Beaumont?"

It sounds ridiculous to ask. She's mine. She's been mine from the very beginning, and asking her to be my girlfriend? It sounds like a weak title compared to how she makes me feel.

Sage rolls a shoulder. "I'll get back to you on that."

I drag her underneath me again, and she giggles uncontrollably. Holding myself up on my forearms, I watch Sage brush her curls away from her face and pucker her lips to suppress a smile.

I kiss her. "Say it."

"Fine," she relents. "I'll be your girlfriend."

I flip on my back to pull the comforter over both of us, and she smiles contentedly into my chest. Sage lies right on top of me, over the steady beat of my heart that sings the same song whenever she's with me.

THIRTY-NINE

SAGE

AS I STEP into the kitchen on a Saturday afternoon, I'm wrapped in a stomach-growling aroma. It's been weeks and we've been stocked with fresh baked goods. When he sees me, Elias lifts me onto the counter. He hands me a bowl of strawberries, as if to keep me occupied, like I'm some annoying child who would distract him. It makes me smile anyway.

"Do I get to help?" I ask.

He pipes frosting onto a batch of cupcakes. "Sit there and be a good girl, Sage."

My thighs squeeze involuntarily. He called me that over and over this morning when I dropped to my knees in the shower. But the way he pulled my hair and urged my head further down on him did not make me feel like a good girl at all. Quite the opposite, actually.

"Why are you making cupcakes?"

"Just trying something new." He places one on his palm and turns to me with a boyish smile. Like a student showing the teacher their finished artwork. "Open your mouth."

"And you say *I'm* inappropriate."

"Just do it, baby."

I comply, savoring the cupcake as he feeds me the first bite. I hum out a grateful sound. He chuckles, handing me the whole thing before tending to the rest.

"That is so good. It tastes different, what did you put in it?"

"They're sugar-free," he says.

A fist grips my heart. "Why?"

Elias doesn't look at me, but I know he hears the hitch in my voice. Once he's finished with the cupcakes, he trails his hands up my thighs and pulls me to the edge of the counter. "Probably been a while since Sean's had a good cupcake."

My heart explodes into a mini fireworks show. But Elias doesn't let me say thank you. Instead, he kisses me, and those fireworks burst in my mouth too. He tilts my head up and slips his tongue between my lips. I let him kiss me however he wants, and I enjoy the taste of him mingling with the vanilla icing.

When I tighten my legs around his hips, the fabric of his jeans rubs along the inside of my thighs. He breaks the kiss abruptly.

"Easy," he warns, reminding me of Sean's proximity.

I reluctantly let him pull away.

My little brother is a few doors down the hall in the shower. Sean is with us this weekend because he wanted to make up for missing my birthday. He stays at school all year long, and never complains, but it must be torture.

We picked him up from school this morning, and after Elias made us lunch, Sean drilled both of us about our relationship like an overprotective father.

"You have an excessive number of cherry-scented candles in your bathroom," Sean says when he walks into the kitchen in a fresh T-shirt and basketball shorts.

Elias offers him a cupcake and he's about to refuse before Elias says, "Sugar-free."

Sean blinks, staring at the white frosting for a long time. We watch him with anticipation, and I notice his glossy eyes. They mirror my own, because the way he looks at my boyfriend is the same way he looked at our uncle when he asked Sean if he wanted to try out for junior hockey. In awe.

He doesn't say a word when he takes a bite, but his eyes sparkle. "Is there anything you can't do?" he says through a mouthful.

"Don't inflate his ego." I roll my eyes even though I know those cupcakes are damn good.

"Ah, never mind, there it is. You can't make my sister shut up," Sean remarks.

Elias's laugh is muffled into his fist. When I gasp in offense, he clears his throat. "Yeah, but I'm not a big fan of the silence anymore."

I narrow my eyes at Sean. "You would be bored out of your mind without me."

"Doubt it," he mumbles, still chewing. I chuck an oven mitt at him; he catches it effortlessly. Damn athletes and their stupid reflexes. "I'm kidding!"

Aiden's voice echoes from the living room, and Sean hastily stuffs the entire cupcake into his mouth, giving Elias a muffled thanks. The lively sounds of a cheering crowd emanate from the living room. It's the newest NHL video game that was released this month. This one features a mix of new and classic players, including Summer's dad, Lukas Preston.

When I turn back to Elias, he lets me take the bag of icing and pipe some onto the extra cupcakes. Another batch comes out of the oven, and I help with those too.

Elias's phone pings on the counter, and when he glances at it, his expression drops.

"What's wrong?" I ask.

His shoulders tense. "It's the wire transfer text for the money I send to my biological dad."

"Oh." I try not to involve myself more than I should. But I can't help it. "I don't know how you do it. You shouldn't have to give him your hard-earned money because of a lie. It's not fair, Elias."

"I have no choice."

"You do," I assure him. "The girl who your dad paid came clean, and your parents would do anything to protect you. Nobody will fault you for being manipulated."

"I don't want anyone else getting involved in my mess after all these years. I have you now, and I'd hate for people to question your character because of rumors about me. I won't let that happen."

I cross my arms over my chest. "Do I look weak to you?"

"Not at all."

"Then stop worrying about me. Decide for yourself if you want to live your life with the feeling you just had after reading that text." I press my hand on his shoulder. "I'm here for you. Every step of the way."

After a long, tense minute, he nods. "I'll think about it."

It's frustrating watching him endure his dad's rhetoric, but I recognize this isn't the moment to intervene. "Cupcakes for dinner are perfect," I say, changing the topic. "But I'm kind of a responsible guardian, so I have to feed that kid something nutritious."

Elias chuckles, his shoulder relaxing. "We're going out to dinner. It'll be a little celebration for you securing *Swan Lake*."

I agree, only because Sean will love it. But if it were just us, I'd much rather have Elias cook dinner, watch *Dirty Dancing* on the couch, try my new face masks, and spend the night in his arms. And maybe on his thigh.

When the evening sky dips into a pretty midnight blue, we head out. Aiden stayed at home because he has a virtual date with Summer. Something about a special episode of their favorite show airing tonight.

For the most part the car ride to the undisclosed restaurant is silent, aside from Sean's music playing on the speakers.

"I've decided I'm going to Dalton for college," Sean announces.

My head whips to him. "I thought you were aiming for a hockey scholarship to Yale?"

"Haven't you heard? Yale is the enemy." He sounds dead serious. It seems like him hanging with Aiden and playing video games with the rest of the guys online has resulted in a successful brainwashing. "Besides, Dalton beat them, and I want to carry on the legacy."

I snort. "They were ahead by one at the Frozen Four. I'd hardly count that as a victory."

Elias gives me a sidelong glance. "Oh yeah? You wanna say that to my face?"

Rolling my eyes, I look over my shoulder to see Sean laughing. Ignoring the two Dalton cronies, I stare out the window as we approach the CN Tower.

"Is that . . . ?"

"We're going to the revolving restaurant?" Sean asks in excitement.

It's the restaurant where Elias and I had our first date. The memories hit me instantly, and my mind skips to the two of us standing by the water, settling in the comfortable silence.

Elias smiles. He's so nonchalant, it's like he's taking us to a fast-food chain. The restaurant is primarily haute cuisine, and usually after big showcases, this is where dancers like to go. I'd always opt out and heat up a frozen dinner at my apartment instead.

"It's a special day," Elias says. "I thought we'd celebrate properly."

ELIAS

INSIDE THE RESTAURANT, Sean stares out the floor-to-ceiling windows. The building completes a rotation almost every hour, giving us a 360-degree view of the city. When Sage excuses herself to go to the bathroom, Sean nudges me.

"I never got to say thanks for the jerseys. And for making Sage's birthday a good one. I know she told me it was okay for me to hang out with my friends, but I still feel guilty."

"You don't have to thank me, Sean. I wanted to do it."

He holds my attention as he finishes off his fried appetizer. "I know I should ask what your intentions are with my sister and all that, but considering everything you've already done, I'm not sure it's necessary." Sean pauses as if collecting his thoughts. "But just in case you haven't figured it out yet, Sage is a people pleaser, and she'll work herself to the bone to make sure everyone she loves is cared for, even if that means neglecting herself."

That is not where I saw this conversation going. Sean loves his sister, that much is obvious, but knowing he sees behind the curtain where she hides her problems tells me he worries about her a lot more than he lets on.

"I'm her younger brother, so Sage doesn't let me take the burden off of her. Sometimes I don't even realize that I put it there, because I end up relying on her for everything. So, I want to make sure that at least with you, she doesn't have to do that."

If Sage were listening to this, she would be crying right now. "Your sister is my priority. If she wanted to shut off her brain and lean on me for the rest of her life, I'd happily support her. But I know where her passion lies, so I'll do everything I can to make sure she fulfills it."

He bites into his truffle-buttered baguette, and the crunch accompanies the thoughtful look on his face. "Damn. I was kind of hoping you would be an asshole so I could continue not being a fan." He lets out an exaggerated sigh. "It was easier when the only stuff I knew about you was your shitty stats and the articles online."

His words remind me of how far I've come from those tabloids. "You know that stuff in the media is almost always a lie, right?"

"I know, I know. It's gossip made by miserable people with no lives."

Those words are straight out of his sister's mouth, and I can tell she's been feeding that to him for a while. Probably ever since she was pictured with me.

"And my stats were never bad, you little shit."

He scoffs. "Yeah, *now*, thanks to my sister. Before she came into your life it was like you hadn't seen a puck. My uncle said so himself."

He's exaggerating, but Marcus probably did say that. "I still hold the record for the most assists in the season."

What I lacked in goals, I made up for through assists. Not exactly impressive, but it's still something. Why am I defending myself to a fifteen-year-old?

"Right." He drags out the word, but then cracks a smile as he digs into another appetizer. "I'm kidding. Everyone's saying you're one of the reasons we got that far in the playoffs. Crawford's still my favorite, but you're a pretty close second."

"Guess I'll have to try a little harder to change that."

"This"—he gestures to the food on the table—"is a pretty good start."

FORTY

SAGE

I FEEL LIKE it's my first day of high school and I'm a nervous twelve-year-old with no friends. After we took Sean back to school this morning, I dropped Elias at his morning skate and went home to get ready for my first rehearsal.

It's a few hours later when Elias rushes into the room, dropping his gear bag to head straight to the shower. I offered to pick him up when he was done, but Aiden drove him back.

"Five minutes and we can go. I'm going to grab a quick shower."

I watch him strip out of his clothes in the bathroom. "You're not even going to ask me to join?"

"The door's open, baby," he replies, the shower muffling his chuckle.

It isn't long before he's out again with a towel around his waist. I'm shameless when I map his happy trail. Elias pulls out a gray Henley and dark-wash jeans to change in front of me, and I don't do a damn thing to give him any privacy.

In the car, I double-check my bag four times, running through a mental checklist. We arrive at the front entrance of the downtown theater, and when Elias opens my door and presses a kiss to my forehead, I don't move. He doesn't say a word as he stands next to me outside the car.

"Your mom called to wish me luck," I tell him, trying to distract myself.

He gives me a knowing look but indulges me. "She was very excited."

"Have you decided what you're going to do about your dad?" I've been hoping he's realized none of what happened at world juniors was his fault and that he can stop paying for it.

He stiffens with discomfort but responds anyway. "I don't want to worry about this anymore, and I hate that you worry about it too. So, I'm going to figure out a final payment."

I pull him into a hug and wrap my arms tightly around his waist. Elias has been beating himself up over giving his birth dad money behind his parents' back, so this decision has to give him some relief. But deep down, I can tell he's been worried over what might come next.

"Whatever happens, I'm proud of you."

He hugs me back before he whispers, "We can't stand here forever, Sage."

"I'm nervous," I admit.

Elias pulls away, reaching for his wallet. My curiosity mounts as he extracts a small square from one of its pockets. He flips it over, revealing a Polaroid. Eight-year-old Sage wearing a bright smile and a blue tutu at her first recital.

"That's mine," I say, reaching for it, but he snatches it away.

"Mine now." A soft smile plays on his lips as he looks down at the picture. "The first time I saw this at the studio, all I could think about was how determined you are. You put your everything into this, and now you have exactly what this eight-year-old girl dreamed of."

"But what if—"

"No ifs. You promised her the world. Now, go make sure she gets it."

With my facade of confidence—one that ballerinas have ingrained in them—and Elias's words keeping me afloat, I walk into the building. The walls are covered in pictures of famous ballerinas and awards. In the distance, there's a hushed whisper of anticipation as other dancers head inside. I follow the signs, and the elevator takes me up to the highest floor. The doors open, and the familiar scents of rosin and hardwood fill my nose.

When I step into the studio, it's everything I imagined. Soft, gentle light fills the space, dousing the polished wooden floors and mirrored walls in a warm glow. Ballet barres line the perimeter, and speakers are fitted into the walls. The air hums with excited energy as dancers flit around the room, and I feel a sudden rush of belonging.

When our choreographer, Adrien Kane, introduces himself to the room, everyone quiets.

"Good morning, company. Let's get started."

We're immediately told to line up by character, and of course with my name being first on the call sheet, I stand first. All eyes lock on me, and a lash of insecurity bites at me.

It doesn't budge when we move on to the rest of the cast. Adam, who will play Prince Siegfried, is my scene partner. He's not towering over me; he's probably just shy of six feet with a lean figure. His black hair and symmetrical features make him appear every bit a prince.

He only gives me a nod in acknowledgment. I chalk up his standoffishness to nerves, maybe the same ones winding through my gut. My alternate is Ashley. Her piercing blue eyes lock on mine like a predator to prey. There's an unsettling coldness in her gaze that trickles down my spine. I push the feeling aside. She'll have to pry this role from my cold, dead hands.

Playing Rothbart is Jason, who welcomes me with a crushing embrace. The heaviness coiling my lungs eases a little. "No one expected a newbie to bag the principal role," Jason says.

"I guess I got lucky," I say.

He chuckles. "Zimmerman doesn't do luck, and we all heard about your audition. That kind of reaction from the three of them is almost unheard of."

The words are so matter-of-fact that I don't bother thanking him. For the first time, I actually agree that I earned this.

"But watch out for those two," Jason whispers, nodding to Adam and Ashley, who are tucked away to the side. They're engaged in conversation, but even as they talk, their eyes dart around the room in assessment. "They're envy personified, and no one wants that around."

I pry my eyes away from them. "Envious of who?"

"You."

His words reveal the target on my back that I was too blind to notice.

"She's my alternate. She has to be talented to score that role," I offer.

"She is. But she's also the daughter of a trustee."

In an instant, I sense the role of the swan queen slipping from my grasp. Yet, before I can dwell on the weight of that realization, we're thrust into a test rehearsal of the pas de deux between Adam and me.

As Adam lifts me according to the choreographer's directions, his hands are steady. I'm relieved to not be paired with someone who struggles to lift me. It's never fun to have a partner who complains about your weight or height—I've experienced both.

We stumble through the routine, making more mistakes than I'd care to admit. I assume we'll have ample time to iron out the performance, but my hope dwindles when Zimmerman enters. His presence throws me off-balance. A whispered exchange between Adrien and him leaves me with a sinking feeling, and when Zimmerman exits, disappointment gnaws at me.

I can't shake that feeling, and nerves make me cling to the sidelines, hesitant to fully dive in and embody my role. Adrien isn't happy with the progress of the performance. After our third hour, he gives us a fifteen-minute break.

Jason catches me in the corridor. "Don't focus on the end goal right now. All that matters is that you're improving. You're good. Don't doubt it."

"You're awfully nice for someone who just met me."

He shrugs. "Why waste time? We're going to be seeing each other's faces all year."

Despite his reassuring words, a lingering sense of dread clings to me like a shadow, and sticks around until the end of our first rehearsal.

Sweat dampens my skin, and exhaustion drapes over me like a heavy cloak as I head to Elias, who's already waiting for me by the car.

When we're driving home, I lower my seat to lie back. But I can't relax because my sore muscles contract with every movement. My feet are in more pain than they've ever been, and my neck is as stiff as a board.

"My parents asked us to visit next week. Do you want to come?" Elias asks.

I turn, despite my stiff bones. "For what?"

"To meet them."

The weight of a bowling ball settles in my stomach. I'm sure this is a big deal, and I should say yes immediately, but I can't. Not when I'm reminded of just how unimpressive I am. I had to use their son in order to get somewhere in life, for Christ's sake.

"You can say no. Don't just agree because you think that's what I want," he adds.

"I want to," I blurt out, surprising myself. He looks at me, his eyes searching. "Because knowing them is going to bring me even closer to knowing you, and I'd never miss that."

There's a long pause before he chuckles. "A yes would have sufficed."

"Right, 'cause I'm sure you didn't like me blowing your ego."

"I loved it. A lot. But now that we're talking about blowing . . ."

"Oh God, where did my sweet Elias go?"

"He has this girlfriend who can't speak a sentence without throwing in a dirty joke. She's bound to rub off on him."

I snort. "And rub off I do."

FORTY-ONE

ELIAS

FAMILY DINNERS HAVE always been an important part of my life. Whether it was with my parents or at our off-campus house in college, I've made it a point to eat with the people I love.

"So, what's off the table?" Sage asks.

She dozed off the minute we boarded the plane to Connecticut. Now, as we're driving to my parents' house in Greenwich, she's awake and stressing herself out.

"Just be yourself. They already love you," I reassure her.

"They love the Sage they've seen online and spoken to over the phone. This is Sage in the flesh."

"Arguably the best version." I glance over at her. "You won't say anything wrong."

"So sex talk is a go? I'll tell them about the time we almost broke the showerhead."

I clear my throat. "Okay, maybe some things *are* off the table. We can make a list."

She sighs with relief. "Thank you. I'm not good with parents, Elias. If I don't have a filter, I'll terrify them."

Flipping open the mirrored visor above her seat, Sage fixes her hair. She applies gloss, and her lips move like she's memorizing something. Then she pulls out her phone to take notes. "Okay, so no sex talk, and I'm assuming that means no dirty jokes either."

"How about we just avoid anything we wouldn't talk to Sean about?"

"Oh, that's good!" She types it into her phone. "But what about telling them we're perfect for each other because we both have terrible birth parents?"

"Let's leave my bio dad out of it. They don't know about the money, and I want to keep it that way."

Sage puts her phone away, and her hand finds mine. "Are you sure you're okay with doing that today?"

I turn to her at a red light. "I don't want him dictating any part of my life. It's not fair to me or my parents. Or you." I've been mulling this over for weeks, but when Mason found Elias Johnson's address, I knew it had to be done.

There's no room for clouds over my head when I have a ray of sunshine in my hands.

Sage draws a soothing pattern over my knuckles, but when I pull into my parents' estate, she gawks out the window. The wrought iron gates swing open, revealing the long driveway flanked by meticulously manicured lawns. The air is heavy with the scent of freshly cut grass and the blooming magnolia trees. My mom's favorite. And based on Sage's candle collection, hers too.

Sage chuckles nervously. "I don't think I'm dressed for this."

Her floral summer dress makes her look innocent and nothing like the girl who had me pinned under her last night. "Should I remind you how much I like your dresses?"

She gasps. "This is not the time to be saying things like that!"

We approach the front entrance, where I park. The golden sun reflects off the floor-to-ceiling windows on the front of the house. When I'm rounding the car to open Sage's door, my parents descend the front steps to greet us.

My parents bypass me and engulf Sage in a sandwich of a hug. I'm watching in shock as they giggle with glee. Sage stares at me wide-eyed.

"Okay, you two are going to crush her," I say, pulling them away.

"I don't mind," Sage pipes up, still looking stunned.

My dad steps back. "Apologies. We're usually more sophisticated."

"Not true." I interject. "The first game of mine they went to, they managed to piss off an entire section of parents. The bright green poster board they brought to cheer me on blocked everyone's view the entire game. By the time someone told them, the game was half over."

"Some children appreciate their parents' support," scolds my mom.

"I always appreciate you guys." I pull her in for a tight hug. Jane Westbrook is short, only five foot two, so when she hugs me back, her face barely comes to my chest.

My dad slaps a hand on my back. "Our friends came over to watch your final."

I shake my head. "Sorry to disappoint."

"Are you kidding? You played a hell of a game, son. The commentators even said so."

"Exactly. You don't score three goals on a fluke," adds Sage.

My mom is beaming so wide I'm sure it's hurting her face. "It's so nice to finally see you in person, Sage. How long are you two here?"

"We head out tomorrow," I answer. With Sage's rehearsals we only have one free night.

My mom doesn't approve but waves us inside quickly. The patio is arranged in their backyard for an outdoor dinner. The long table is decorated with flowers and candles. My mom made a huge roast chicken dinner like we're having a Christmas feast. I have no complaints because her food is my favorite. She's the reason I enjoy cooking.

As we help bring out the food and set the table, Sage appears lost in thought.

"You okay?" I ask, pulling her from her daydream. The only sounds out here are the quiet clinking of utensils against plates and the soft hum of my parents' conversation.

"Yeah," she replies. "I'm just acclimating. I've never sat at a table like this before."

One would think she's referring to the food or the patio, but I know she means family.

My lips graze the side of her temple. "Guess I'm taking a few of your firsts too."

"You're taking a lot more than just a few," she whispers.

We pass around the side of roasted vegetables, and my dad cuts into the chicken. "So, how long have you two been together?" he asks.

"A few weeks."

"Months," I correct. "We've been together for three months."

"Right." Sage laughs awkwardly, hiding her face behind a long gulp of water.

"Who keeps track anyway?" my mom says. "I can't tell you how long it's been for us."

My dad feigns offense. "Thirty years next month."

My mom plants a kiss on his cheek in a silent apology. The rest of our conversation mostly revolves around Sage, and I love it. She looks happy here. But when the conversation pivots to my teenage years, I grow stiff.

"You've come a long way, Eli," my mom remarks. "I didn't like how you became after the world juniors."

"Jane," my dad admonishes.

"I'm sorry." Her voice trembles, and tears well in her eyes. "If someone messes with my kid, I can't help but feel angry."

"Mom, you don't need to carry that anger," I assure. "But I am sorry that I've caused—"

"Why would you be sorry? If anything, it's our greatest regret that we ever doubted you," she interjects.

I had no clue my mom carried that day with her as heavily as I do. The weight of disappointing them has always burdened me, but realizing it affects them just as deeply releases something in my chest.

"It's okay," I offer, but her expression remains somber.

Sage squeezes my hand. "I would be angry too, but Elias has come so far that I'm in awe of him every day. You two did a great job."

Her words work like a balm, smoothing away the tension from my mom's face.

For the remainder of dinner we skirt any conversation about my recent past, and my parents regale Sage with stories from my childhood instead. Embarrassing, but they make her laugh.

When we're finished with dinner, we head inside. "Eli, your room is exactly as you left it. I've stocked the bathroom with some toiletries," she says, turning to Sage with a warm smile. "Let me know if you need anything."

When my parents head to the living room, I pull Sage toward the opposite side of the house, to my room. Halfway down the hall, she hops onto my back, and I swing open my door and playfully deposit her onto my bed. My room has always been a slate gray color with a king bed and an en suite. I was never the type to decorate with posters or have colorful bedsheets.

Sage floats around my room, her gaze wandering from the vinyls gifted by Kian, to the stack of books on my bedside table, to the pictures of my family—the guys and my parents.

She smiles at the picture of younger me and my parents wearing custom T-shirts with a picture of the three of us and the words "The Westbrooks" printed on them. "Do you want kids?" she suddenly asks.

The question surprises me but not nearly as much as I would have expected. "Do you?"

She laughs. "You can't just copy my answer."

"Well, if we're having them together, I think I'd want your input," I say.

"This is probably a bad time to tell you about my husband, then." She glances over her shoulder to catch my unamused expression. "I think I want to adopt."

"Yeah?"

She nods. "I was so scared of Sean having to go through foster care, but seeing your parents tells me there's some good out there. And I'd like to be a part of it someday."

I didn't think Sage could get any more perfect. But she proves me wrong every day. She moves on to twirl the blue nylon of my World Junior Championships ribbon between her fingers before holding it up to me. "The big moment?"

"Huge."

She puts it back. "Do you keep it as a memory?"

"Not a fond one."

She moves toward my dresser and looks through the drawers like she'll find something. Her fingers run along the neutral shirts and pants. "You know other colors exist, right?"

I follow to where she stands. "I think you wear enough for the both of us."

She glances at her yellow sundress, beaming.

"You done, warden?" I say.

Sage collapses onto my bed and looks at me like I'm supposed to know what she's thinking. I think I have a pretty good idea when I take a step forward and her eyes flare. Enjoying her thrumming anticipation, I pivot and lean against the dresser instead.

We stare at each other for a long beat.

"What's your move?" she asks, lifting onto her elbows.

"My move?"

She runs a hand over the gray comforter. "Yeah, like in high school? How did you get the girl?"

My face must show my confusion.

She sits up. "If I was a girl you wanted—"

"You are."

"What would you do?"

"You're already in my room, I don't think I need to try any harder."

She doesn't seem satisfied with my straightforward response. Sage makes a move for the door. But I intercept her before she can reach it, allowing my lips to trail along the side of her neck. Brushing her hair aside, I press my nose against the curve of her throat, inhaling her sweet vanilla scent. "Tell me what you want," I murmur.

She turns so her back is against the door. "I want you to pretend."

When Sage asks for what she wants, it always makes my heart race. I can never predict what she'll ask for, but she knows I'll give it to her no matter what.

A shiver rolls through her when I allow my warm breath to fall on her sensitive skin. "First, I'd ask if you would want to go somewhere quiet."

Her sigh of pure pleasure escapes when she grips my forearms. "Yes. Take me somewhere quiet."

I slip my hand over the curve of her ass, slowly lifting the fabric of her sundress. "Then I'd make sure you were sober."

"I am." Her answer is shaky and breathless.

Our mouths brush, and her breath hitches.

"Then I'd ask if I could kiss you," I whisper right against her lips. I don't hear her answer. Instead, she raises herself up to meet my lips. Her mouth is hot and needy, her nails digging into my wrists, telling me she wants this—*me*—now.

She pulls back. "You're not going to ask if I'm single?" she purrs, playing along. She moans when I lift her dress to her waist. Letting my hand slide over the bare skin.

"No." I pull her bottom lip between my teeth. "Because I don't care."

"Oh, you should, my boyfriend is huge. We need to make this quick." She tries to move me to the bed, but I don't budge.

"I'm taking my time with you. Your boyfriend can wait." I trail kisses along her collarbone, pulling her dress over her head. The perfect view of her breasts makes my blood heat. I take her nipple into my mouth, squeezing a handful in my palm, and enjoying the way she writhes against me. With a flick of my thumb, I hook it into the waistband of her panties and tug them down until they slip off her hips. My kisses trail lower, descending her trembling body, and I can feel her pulse ricochet against my lips. She yelps when I pull her leg over my shoulder and press her firmly into the door. The house is large enough that my parents won't hear, and Sage must know it, because she moans loudly when I push two fingers inside her.

"More," she cries. "I need more."

Listening to her breathy command, my mouth seals over her clit as she shakes. "You look so pretty spread open. Is this all for me? Just from the sound of my voice?" I whisper against her slick pussy.

Sage's eyes squeeze shut, her fingers tangling in the long hair at the nape of my neck.

"You want more?"

She moans in pleasure. "*Yes*. Give me more."

With two fingers already inside her, I increase my speed to match her moans. When the languid strokes of my tongue accompany the movements, she gasps and arches her back.

I curve my fingers at the perfect angle, and within seconds her toes curl and her orgasm comes crashing. She's loose limbs and quick breaths when I move back up to her face.

"Can your boyfriend make you do that?"

"I don't know," she pants. "You should do it again, so I can really compare."

I lift her and drop her on my bed, her curly hair bouncing. If I wasn't so fucking hard right now, I'd spend an eternity staring at every inch of her, committing it to memory.

With a hand to the back of my head, she pulls me in for a desperate kiss. Her hips grind against mine and I pull back to remove my clothes, tossing my shirt, jeans, and boxers into a messy pile. I line up my cock between her legs, slipping the tip between her slick folds. Sage's eyes light with the same fire I feel inside.

But then her gaze softens when I kiss her forehead. "Hi, Elias," she whispers.

"Hi, baby."

Sage is so outspoken and confident, but when I show her the smallest amount of gentle affection, she's practically a shy girl again. Then she tightens her legs around me, urging me forward, and feeling like I can't take another second, I sink into her.

She squeezes around every inch of me and takes what she needs. And I give her all of it.

"ONE LAST PICTURE!" is what my mom said before she made us stay an hour longer to pose in front of every tree outside our house. My parents love Sage. I know that because those pictures are going on the mantel.

But even as I feel lighter seeing my parents after so many months, it's a blood relative that's been on my mind. The check in my pocket was burning a hole in my pants all throughout lunch. Since Sage has to head back for rehearsals, our flight is tonight, and I had to schedule some time to finally wipe my hands clean of the mess that is my biological father.

Now, knocking on the metal door of the neglected house in Parkville, I'm aware this could have been the place I called home. Or it was until my parents stepped into the merry-go-round of foster care to adopt me.

I glance over my shoulder to where Sage sits in the car. It took a lot to persuade her to stay put and not accompany me. The neighborhood is not safe, so I made sure to lock the doors. Yet, from the way she peers through the window, I know she's poised to leap into action at a moment's notice.

The front door opens, and it's like looking in a fucking mirror.

Elias Johnson stares at me through hooded eyes. He's wearing a stained white tank top and sweatpants, holding a beer in his hand as his aged brown eyes survey me with disdain. His angular jawline and a straight nose strike a chord of familiarity. Despite this, nothing about him makes me feel nostalgic.

His gaze flickers over to the rental car, easily spotting the Beamer in the quiet street. I know he sees Sage, and I'm sure she's staring right back, so I take a step to my left to block his view. We're virtually the same size, but I have a few pounds of muscle on him, and his sluggish movements tell me he'd be out cold with a single hit.

I hold out the envelope, and his eyes finally drop to the white paper. He snatches it from me, ripping it open with one hand. He withdraws the check and scans the amount I've written on it. When his gaze meets mine, his eyes bulge in astonishment.

"What's this for?" His deep voice is strained, like he's been smoking. It sounds different, deeper than the last time I heard it. Four years ago.

"This is it. That's the last check you'll get from me. If you are careful, it should be enough for your . . . lifestyle," I say, taking a step back. "Don't ever contact me again."

Looking at him now feels like staring at a fragment of myself that got lost along the way, and yet this reunion leaves me feeling nothing.

His eyes dart to the car again, like he's realizing something.

"You think this is enough? You're makin' ten times this."

I release the tension in my jaw. "Because I put in the work. All you did was blackmail your own kid. So, you can spread your lies to the media, I don't care, but this is the last time I'll ever see you."

The lines of anger deepen on his forehead, and he wears an expression I can't quite pinpoint. I'm not sure I care to.

"Oh, the media will care a whole lot. You walk away, and I'll make sure of that."

I shake my head in pity. "You do that."

There's no anger anymore. There's nothing. I only feel resignation when I step away from his look of displeasure. I walk straight back to the car, where everything good is, and I don't look back once.

The scent of vanilla fills the air, bringing a smile to my face as I savor the quiet moment.

"You want to talk about it?" Sage asks softly from the passenger seat.

"Not right now, but I'm okay."

Her presence alone is enough to ease the tension in my shoulders. As I'm removing my wallet from my pocket to drop it in the center console, Sage points to my hand.

"What's that?" Her gaze fixates on my wrist.

I follow her finger to where my thin sweater bunches on my forearms, revealing the freshly wrapped tattoo under the clear bandage. I had planned to surprise her with it later.

"Elias, what is this?" Her voice wavers when she pulls my wrist toward her, dusting her fingers over the reddened skin where the fresh tattoo sits.

"It's a plant," I reply. The stems intertwine to curl around my wrist, their multiple branches covering the surface of my skin in a meticulous design.

Her eyes dart to mine. "What plant?"

"Sage."

"Sage? Is . . . is this why you disappeared earlier?" Her voice shakes. "Your mom said you were helping with groceries."

"I was," I confirm.

Her disbelief deepens. "And a tattoo just happened to be on the grocery list?" she deadpans. "Why?"

"You know why."

She shakes her head. "No, actually I don't."

"Because I love you, and I want you with me all the time, even on the days you can't be."

A moment of quiet lingers, thick with unspoken thoughts.

Then Sage bursts into tearful laughter, a sound that feels infectious. She wipes her eyes and sits there like she's not sure how to grapple with the information. For a second, I think it may be too much, but in the next heartbeat, she releases her seat belt to face me.

"You got it for me?"

I give her a blank look. "I don't know anyone else named Sage."

She laughs. "You could just really love the herb."

"No, I think I really love the girl."

Then Sage climbs over the center console, and I catch her on my lap. She hugs me. She hugs me like she needs me, and it's more than I could ever ask for. The embrace is a wave of bliss, a flood that momentarily helps drown out the knowledge that we'll be apart soon. In this instant, all that matters is the warmth of her presence and the reassurance that she's here with me.

"Let's go home," she whispers into the crook of my neck.

I nod, but she doesn't know that I'm already there.

FORTY-TWO

SAGE

TENSION BUBBLES ON our last day of rehearsals until it reaches a boiling point. Things have been stressful, and I'm sure Elias has noticed how quiet our drives have been lately. Though he never makes me talk. Instead he laces our hands, and we listen to his music the whole way.

While I'm breaking in my pointe shoes, Ashley sits by me without a word. As my alternate, she's been glued to my side from day one. It's her job, but her intensity is almost too much. There's a palpable level of irritation I can feel from her when she sees me performing with Adam. Turns out Jason wasn't kidding when he said she was livid when I secured the part of the swan queen, because Ashley's parents have been donating to the theater for years to score her a principal dancer role.

However, Aubrey Zimmerman doesn't care about that. He doesn't care for anything other than finding the best dancers. It's the theater as a whole that pushes the social media front. They seem to think ballet is a dying art that can only be preserved through the new wave of virtual entertainment. They may be right, because as of last week, we've sold out of tickets for *Swan Lake* for the entire month we're performing in Toronto, and we're booked solid for the next year in several ballet theaters across the world.

It's a lot of travel, and the Sage from a few months ago couldn't be happier. But now when I've found my home, it's bittersweet knowing I'll be away from it. Away from Elias.

As I run through the choreography in my head, the orchestra begins playing the introduction for act one. I have about thirty minutes to drink something so I don't pass out onstage. Rehearsal or performance, the adrenaline is just the same.

Our stage manager taps me on the shoulder, talking into her headset as she flashes a smile. I head toward the stage, seeing Adam on the opposite side, waiting to make his entrance. He looks nervous, as in "pale face, just vomited backstage" nervous, but Ashley whispers into his ear and he nods like he's okay. Still, when he meets my eyes, his harbor a dark cloud.

The White Swan pas de deux echoes through the theater, and when we transition into our positions, Adam's confidence from earlier doesn't translate.

"You're both too stiff. Like fucking planks! Relax," Zimmerman shouts, his voice growing more frustrated with each move. "Attack it, Sage! Capture the room."

Taking in his critique, I try to do exactly that. But when Adam lifts me, it feels all wrong. I try to straighten his hold, but his hands wobble, and I feel the drop before I even hit the ground.

Everything happens in slow motion. My dreams practically flicker on a piece of film in front of me when I land on the ground with a thud. There's a collective gasp of horror from the room. As the scream escapes my throat, a shooting pain sears through my leg and up my spine.

I'm frozen in fear with an uncomfortable pulsating in my ankle. The entire theater hushes when the orchestra comes to a crash ending, enveloping us in an eerie silence.

Adam curses and clutches his wrist.

"Give her space," Zimmerman shouts, his panicked voice making my anxiety skyrocket. My heart is so loud, I can barely differentiate between the burning in my lungs and leg. "Can you stand on it?"

This can't be how it ends.

I can't form any words to answer Zimmerman, but I don't have to because the company's first aid attendant rushes to my side. She pokes and prods my ankle to test my reaction. There's a soreness, but the earlier sting has dampened. I'm looking to her with desperation, when she smiles. With her arms around my torso, she lifts me to stand. I'm terrified to put weight on my ankle, but when I finally do, I almost collapse from relief. Now that I'm on my feet, the pain is only a dull throb that I've encountered countless times, and when I rotate my ankle, to feel for pain, it doesn't come.

I exhale. "I'm okay," I announce. "It's not broken."

There's an audible sigh of relief from the room. Jason gives me a comforting pat on the back. But all I can focus on is the one frustrated huff, and it belongs to Ashley, who storms out with Adam running after her.

Note to self: Watch your back.

FORTY-THREE

ELIAS

FINDING MY GIRLFRIEND on my bedroom floor with a lighter and a shoe might be a weird situation for anyone else, but I'm dating a ballerina.

Sage singes the ends of the ribbons on her pointe shoes with the flame while mumbling something to herself.

"Starting another fire?" I ask.

Sage startles. She rolls her eyes and chucks one of her shoes at me. I catch it before joining her on the floor.

Watching me, she finally laughs, and I realize I've missed the sound. She's been so in her head about her big performance that we haven't been able to just relax.

"Did you sleep?" I ask. My nightmares have been less intense, and I owe it to Sage. But I know her insomnia isn't getting better with the stress from rehearsals. The tired creases under her eyes confirm that much.

"I feel rested. But I probably shouldn't have gotten used to sleeping with you," she says.

I don't like that. The long distance is inevitable for us, but its reminder isn't welcome. "It's only for a year."

She glances at me. "But after that I'll have other productions. The schedule is relentless."

I give her the pointe shoe, brushing my hand over hers. "We'll figure it out."

Sage focuses on cutting the ribbons on her other shoe, singing off the ends. She doesn't speak for a long time, and then she sighs. "I don't know if I can do it."

Her words crash in my ears, and I don't know if I heard her correctly. "Do what?"

"The production."

My head rears in shock. Those words never would have come out of her mouth a month ago. I fucked up by letting her get lost in this world. She needs to find a balance. It's the first thing we learn in hockey.

"What are you saying?"

"My whole life, I've been running. From people, from my past, and from my reality." Her voice is shaking. "But now, with you, I don't feel the need to run. I'm okay with staying right where I am. I think I wanted to join the NBT because it gave me another reason to keep running. I'm chasing this perfect version of myself, and it feels like I have been for years."

This isn't the reason she gave me on our first date, and I know that one was the truth. It's the one thing that's given her purpose. You don't give up on that because of one setback.

"You were never meant to keep running, Sage. You were meant to grow, and you have. The Sage who told me her goal was to become as good as Misty Copeland isn't the same Sage saying she'll let go of her dream because of one bad day."

"But it's not just one bad day," she argues. "That Sage didn't see her entire career flash before her eyes when she almost injured her ankle during a rehearsal for the biggest show in her career. My scene partner dropped me for the first time, and I think it was on purpose. I know they don't want me there and they're hoping I crumble under the pressure. I'm risking everything to be the principal ballerina, but it's like there's a target on my back."

"What do you mean he dropped you on purpose?" Disbelief runs a line of fire down my back. After I picked up a limping Sage from her last rehearsal, I was worried. It took some icing and rest, and some self-care nights to help the soreness. Knowing someone may have dropped her on purpose lights a rage inside me. "We have to talk to the director. That's unacceptable."

She dismisses the notion. "That's not how it works. I'm not going to accuse them of something without any proof. I've been training for weeks, and something always goes wrong. Zimmerman can see that, and he doesn't accept anything but the best."

Slowly, the real reason behind her decision becomes clear. She's never wanted to quit, she's just afraid she won't be good enough. "They're not going to give up on you, Sage."

She drops her shoes and stands to walk over to the window. "What if they already have?" she whispers.

I follow her. "Did the league give up on me?"

"No, but that's because you proved yourself."

"And you don't think you can do the same?" She doesn't answer, so I push. "Did you believe in me, Sage?"

This time she turns with a new fire in her. "I've always believed in you."

"And did you wait for me?"

She stares at the floor and murmurs, "Very patiently."

I hold her waist and press a light kiss to her temple. "So patiently. And look where that got us."

"In a great roommate arrangement?"

When I nip her ear she chuckles. "It got us something we never thought we'd have."

I reach for her hand, flipping it over to kiss the inside of her wrist. Her pulse gives away her feelings. I linger—one, two, three kisses in a row.

"If anyone gets it, it's me. You don't have to pretend that you're okay, but I'll never let you doubt yourself. There's nothing that can dim your light, and if you think there is, I'd crush it before it ever touched you."

She turns in my arms to face me. "But I'm serious about not running anymore, Elias. I want to stay with you, and with Sean. I don't need any of that other stuff."

I caress the smoothness of her cheek with my palm. "That's the thing about having your people. We'll always be right where you left us. Still loving you, and still cheering you on."

"But I would be happy with you and with teaching at the studio," she urges. "There's nothing I want more than to show you exactly how much by staying."

"If I could handcuff you to myself, I would. But you're a star, Sage Beaumont, and you're too precious to be kept a secret." A stray tear slips down her cheek, but I wipe it away. "The studio will be here when you get back, but right now, you know what your heart wants."

"Wow, you really want to get rid of me, huh?" Sage jokes.

"Go be a star, Sage." I hold her face in my palms. "I'll still be here when you get back."

TEACHING MY GIRLFRIEND how to cook is harder than I anticipated. Sage is talented in a lot of things, but she needs to stay far away from the kitchen.

After Sage prepped her shoes for tomorrow, she let me practice a few lifts with her because she was worried she may be too heavy for her partner, Adam. Fucking ridiculous. I offered to remind Adam there are consequences for dropping my girlfriend, but she refused. Our practice session quickly turned into a *Dirty Dancing* reenactment. We nailed it on the first try.

Now, we're on our second attempt to cook tonight's chicken

dinner because the test piece I gave her burned. She says she's too impatient to cook.

When I hear a sizzle, I look at the pan to see a cloud of smoke. "Too hot!" Rushing over, I take a tea towel and pull the pan away from the heat. "When it smokes like that, it means the oil is burning," I explain.

"Isn't it supposed to be hot?" Sage pouts, holding the tongs in her hand. "I'm not good at this, Elias. The last time I cooked, I reheated a frozen lasagna, and it lit on fire," she admits.

I flick off the stove heat and stop her from burning the chicken again.

"It's a work in progress, and I like teaching you. But you don't have to learn how to cook, baby. I can cook for us." That would be for the benefit of everyone in this building. Or the firefighters' biggest nightmare won't just be her candles.

"No, I want to learn. I'll cook the next time your friends come over."

I give her a tight nod. There are worse things than food poisoning.

Then the front door bursts open, and Aiden barrels into the kitchen. "Living room, now."

His hair is disheveled like he just ran up the stairs rather than taking the elevator. I glance at Sage before we follow him to the living room, where he turns on Sportsnet.

That's when I see my face. Well, my biological father's face.

"What is he doing?" Sage asks.

Elias Johnson stumbles onto the screen. His eyes are glazed over with intoxication, his white button-up is stained and wrinkled, and his hair is long and greasy. He's drunk out of his mind, and it's obvious from the way he sways at the podium.

I should have expected this—I *did* expect this. However, seeing him on television makes my fist tighten. He's using this platform to smear my name, and I find it ridiculous that this outlet would even allow it.

This just solidifies that the media only sees us as monkeys that are expected to perform. Aiden stands by the TV, his jaw clenched in anger. I move to sit on the couch, and Sage sits next to me, pressing her hand into my palm. I hold it tight.

"I can't fucking believe he's actually doing it."

My phone rings somewhere in the apartment, but I don't go to answer it.

Aiden's phone rings next. "It's Mason," he informs before placing it on speaker.

Mason's voice is level with a hint of suppressed panic. "Eli, I am so sorry, I wasn't aware of any of this. It's unacceptable. We're trying to cut the broadcast, but—"

"Mason, let him talk. If not now, he'll find another way."

"Eli—"

"It's long overdue."

"My son isn't who you think he is," Elias Johnson starts. The word *son* from his mouth makes my blood bubble with rage. "Those rich folks you all know as the Westbrooks. The ones he's calling his parents. Yeah, they hid his scandal—" He stops talking abruptly, leaning forward on the shaking podium with a grunt.

The reporters throw out questions behind the camera as he pulls himself together. There's a sheen of sweat covering his pale face, and his hands are shaking as he readjusts the mics.

"It started at world juniors. They hid Elias's habits and he paid me off," he continues, his speech disjointed and erratic. "I've seen it all with my own eyes, and as his father, I worry. My son is using dr—"

I wait for the lies to spill from his mouth and poison the airwaves with his drunken accusations. None of this makes me fearful, but knowing my parents will have to relive it and feel guilty angers me. But then, just as quickly as he started to speak, he clutches his chest and falls forward. His legs must give way beneath him because he tips off the stage and crashes into the reporters in front of him.

"Did he just . . ." Sage wonders aloud.

Aiden scoffs. "I think he passed out."

For a moment, there's stunned silence on the screen, then chaos erupts as the reporters scramble to help him up. But I can't help but feel a sense of grim satisfaction as I watch his pathetic display.

The broadcast suddenly cuts to a commercial break, and Aiden turns off the TV. I expect anger, sadness, resentment—but nothing comes. I'm not sure if he had a heart attack or the alcohol made him tip over, but I don't think I care to know.

"No one's going to let him back on TV after that," Aiden comments.

Sage rubs a hand on my back. "Are you okay?"

I look to Aiden, then at her hand in mine. "I expected it, and if he wants to get on TV again, which I'm sure Mason will do everything to stop, I'll deal with it."

"*We'll* deal with it," corrects Aiden.

He's right, because I know through it all, I have my real family, and nothing anyone does or says can take that away.

FORTY-FOUR

SAGE

IT'S OPENING NIGHT, and my three favorite guys are seated in the third row, right in the center like I told them to. My uncle, Sean, and Elias are flipping through the program and talking happily with each other. I do a double take when my former instructor, Madame Laurent, holds my uncle's hand in hers as he brushes his lips along her knuckles. A strange thumping fills my heart, unlike the usual nerves. Just as I'm going to slip backstage, Elias waves to someone behind him, and I freeze.

His friends—*our* friends—Aiden, Summer, Dylan, and Kian shuffle into the row to take their seats. The family in the seats behind them watch with wide eyes as if just now recognizing the giant hockey players. Then, Jane and Ian Westbrook descend the steps of the theater to their seats. My eyes sting so badly, but with the powder on my face, I can't ruin it with tears.

Our orchestra plays Tchaikovsky's "Introduction." As I'm watching act one from the side stage, I run through the choreography for act two in my head.

"Sage." The stage manager taps my shoulder. "White Swan entrance in thirty."

As I make my way back to my private dressing room to check for any final adjustments, I notice Adam's door cracked open along the noisy hallway. Voices emanate from behind it, and when I approach, I realize he and Ashley are arguing.

"I asked you to do one thing for me! What are you so afraid of?" she says.

Adam exhales loudly. "I can't do it, Ash. It's unethical."

"It's unethical how I've been working my ass off to get here yet I'm forced to watch from the sidelines! If you can't do this for me, Adam, we are done."

Then the door swings open, and I'm frozen in place. Ashley stands before me, dressed in the White Swan costume identical to mine, as my alternate. Not happening.

"Sage?" Adam says, rushing to the door. "W-what are you doing here?"

I look away from a fuming Ashley. "I was hoping we could talk."

Adam shrinks under Ashley's glare before she storms out and Adam ushers me inside.

"Sorry about that." He sits in his makeup chair to fix his hair in the mirror. "So, what's up?"

This is the most attention he's given me since we met. I'm immediately suspicious.

"I know we've been struggling with that lift. But we did it right for weeks, and something's been off since the past few days. I think our focus is shot, and that's what throws us off. But if we focus on each other, we can do it. I know it."

He eyes me through the mirror, and the smallest flicker of pity flashes through his eyes. "Yeah. You're right, I'll do that. Bring back my focus and all."

That doesn't sound convincing, but I nod. "By the way, I understand that being an alternate is challenging, so whatever Ashley's feeling is valid. But don't let that change how you perform your principal role."

I stride out to my dressing room to prepare for the next act. It's when I'm going to head out that I notice the flowers on my vanity—peonies, in pink and white hues. A white square of cardstock protrudes from the bouquet, catching my attention. I pull it out to read what's written on it.

> Keep the black swan outfit. I want to watch you take it off tonight. —Elias

I'm laughing, trying not to let the tears stain my cheeks. I think I found my favorite flowers. When I'm using a tissue to pat my eyes, I hear the announcement for act two.

"Time to shine, Sage." The stage manager signals for me to head to the side stage. I spot Adam and Ashley on the opposite side, arguing again. Then Adam exhales and nods, kissing her gently. I don't let that distract me, and fall away from my body to let the white swan take over.

Immediately, I move to center stage, where it's our first lift, and Adam executes a wobbly hold, and it sends a pang of panic to my chest. The spotlight beams right at us and I keep my composure, letting my eyes stray only for a minute to find my family in the center row.

Then he lets me to my feet not at all gently, and I lose my balance. It's an obvious misstep but I recover quickly. When he spins me in his hold, I glare at him.

"What are you doing?" I whisper through a tight smile.

His eyes betray a shadow of uncertainty that sends a shiver down my spine. Our movements through the remaining sequences falter, disjointed and out of sync. As the curtains draw closed once more, a simmering rage boils beneath the surface of my skin.

"Looks like you're all out of that beginner's luck," Ashley quips, moving past me to join Adam, a sinister smile dancing on her lips.

"What was that?" Zimmerman yells, staring at Adam and me.

An eerie silence replaces the chaos backstage.

Ashley comes by his side. "Aubrey, if you need me to step in—"

"Enough," he interrupts sharply, lifting his hand as he pivots toward us. "You've ruined the first lift. We have an entire routine left to execute. What in the world is happening?"

"I'm trying, but she's off-balance," Adam interjects.

I glare at him.

Zimmerman jabs a finger in Adam's direction. "Take responsibility for your weak hold. Fix it, or I'll fix it for you." Then he turns to me. "You're in your head. I saw what you can do at the audition. Give me the version we came here for. Give me that, Sage."

I nod. "I can do it."

"Good. Because you have no other choice."

Zimmerman storms off, and a breath I can't seem to release catches under my rib cage.

"Adam is fucking with you," Jason says, coming to my side. He's dressed in all black to represent the evil sorcerer, Rothbart. Our routine is next, and I know at least with him it'll be a good performance. "Zimmerman needs to put in Adam's alternate."

I can't speak. I squeeze Jason's shoulder and head to my dressing room to change into the Black Swan costume for act three. The makeup artist is quick. She sprays my hair, adds the black crown and dramatic black eyeliner. When she's gone, I can finally pace the room like a lunatic. I'm doing breathing exercises and imagery, but none of it calms me. Tears threaten to spill from my eyes just as a knock sounds at my door.

"One second!" I shout, quickly dabbing my eyes with a tissue.

"Sage."

The voice almost breaks me. I open the door and slide my arms into Elias's strong hold. He doesn't hesitate to hug me, and we stay like that for a beat.

"Did I suck that bad that you had to come check on me?"

He pulls back. "You took my breath away. But I came here because I think you were right. Adam's messing up a simple lift. I've done it with you, and I know it's not supposed to look like that."

I blink to keep the tears from falling. "I don't know what to do. I can't perform like I'm supposed to. Like I've been training to."

"No one can dim your light." He says it with so much intensity I have no choice but to believe him. "Tell me what you need me to do, and I'll do it."

I pull him close, and he pours his warmth into the touch. "This is enough."

I know Elias would do anything for me, but this time I have to do it for myself.

The announcement for the second act in ten sounds around us.

"You're okay?" Elias asks.

I nod. "Thanks for the flowers."

"You decide on your favorite ones yet?"

"Yeah, but I kind of like letting you guess."

He smiles into the kiss he plants on my lips, and when he pulls away, I drag him to my mouth again. The simple connection eases the cord of panic that chokes my heart. "Finally got that good luck kiss, huh?"

"I think I'm going to need another," I say. "You know, to make up for the one you didn't give me."

With this kiss, he lets me take. Allows me to pour all the emotions flooding my mind into him to take his calmness instead. With a warm swipe of his tongue against mine I feel a contentment swim through me.

Elias lifts my chin. "You think you'll be okay?"

Opening night hasn't been anything like I've dreamed, but I know I wouldn't trade it for anything. "Yeah, I just need to let go."

He smirks mischievously. "I can help with that."

"Get out of here!" I push him. "You're going to miss the big finish."

"I can stay another thirty seconds and see it right here." He taps his thigh.

"Shut up, Elias." I'm laughing as I walk him out of my dressing room, and he shoots me a bright smile before heading down the hall. My smile drops when I look at Adam's door, which reads Prince Siegfried.

I take a deep breath. I'm going to figure this out. I won't be complacent this time.

Rap, rap, rap.

As Adam opens the door and catches sight of me, he begins to close it again. But before he can shut it completely, I swiftly insert my pointe shoe between the gap.

"I don't know what your deal is," I start. "But if this is your way to sabotage me, it won't work. Even if I break my damn leg out there, I'll still perform. You can't take this away from me, Adam. So, figure out whatever you're doing, or I'm going to request that Zimmerman have your alternate perform the last act with me."

As I turn to leave, he halts my movement with a firm grip on my wrist. I instinctively pull away.

He sighs. "I fucked up. There's just so much pressure from my parents, from Ashley's parents, from the entire fucking company. I don't know who to please anymore."

He runs a frustrated hand through his hair, and that's the first time I notice the bags under his eyes. They're dark and creased, like he hasn't slept in a while. His tired face pulls at a sympathetic string in my chest.

"Black swan in five," the stage manager says as she walks past us.

As if I'm embodying Odile herself, I let go of the need to tell Adam it's okay and what he did wasn't his fault. But those words never make it out.

"Look, we're on the third act, and if you can't figure it out by the end of it, that's not my problem. But it's time to choose who you're doing this for, and whether they're worth it."

"Sage—"

"It's your choice, Adam," I say, cutting him off. I head onstage for act three. My and Jason's scene goes perfectly. He reads my every move and pulls a darkness from me that sinks me into character. Adam has a small role where he watches us perform. When the curtains draw again, the crowd roars with applause.

"Now, that's what I want to see," says Zimmerman. "Nice job."

The praise has Jason and me squealing all the way to my dressing room. I quickly change from the Black Swan and back into the White Swan. When my makeup artist heads out, I hear yelling from Adam's room across the hall.

As I cautiously peek out from my door, his swings open forcefully, revealing Adam standing there with the door held wide. Ashley stands behind him, her chest heaving with visible rage.

"We're done," he declares, his voice firm and resolute.

The intercom interrupts their heated stare down. "Five to last act. All dancers . . ."

"I'm tired of this. Tired of you," Adam persists, his frustration palpable. "Get out."

"But, babe—" Ashley attempts.

"Enough, Ashley!" Adam cuts her off sharply. "Leave, or I'll tell everyone the truth—that you wanted me to sabotage Sage, just so you could have her role."

My heart thumps slowly, the weight of Adam's revelation sinking in. I had suspected as much, but hearing it confirmed ignites an angry heat in my face. There's a satisfaction rumbling through me when Ashley shrieks and storms off down the hall.

A sudden flurry of black rushes past me, heading straight for Adam. It's Jason, still dressed as Rothbart, charging forward with determination. Adam staggers backward, caught off guard, and is pushed into his dressing room by the force of Jason's advance.

"You asshole!"

"Jason," I call, rushing inside to pull him away from Adam. "It's not worth it."

Jason's eyes flare with red-hot anger. "He's disgusting. Did you hear that?"

Adam sobs, his voice thick with remorse. "I'm so sorry, Sage. It was making me sick. I never should have agreed to do it. Please believe me."

The tension is exacerbated by another announcement. "Two minutes to curtain up."

I hear a distant angry voice boom through the halls. "Where are my leads?" Zimmerman's voice carries a threat that has me stumbling out of the room.

"We have to tell Zimmerman," Jason urges.

I shake my head. "We have to perform."

"Sage."

"No, Jason," I assert firmly. "Everyone's worked way too hard to get here, and I won't let him disrupt this production."

Elias was right; no one can dim my light, and I'll be damned if I let Adam make it flicker. With that thought echoing in my mind, I stride purposefully toward where Zimmerman paces the wood floors. Relief washes over him when he spots me, and he gestures to stage left. "Go, go, go!"

And I'm off.

Emotion takes over my body, and I float with the music. Adam dances like perfection embodied. There's not even a hint of the disarray I saw in his dressing room on his face. He pours the emotion of his performance into mine, like he's letting go and somehow doing the same for me. I can't help the smile that shines through when he completes a perfect lift. Not a single tremor in his hands as he executes it with elegance.

In Zimmerman's version of *Swan Lake*, the lovers don't meet their demise in the last act. Prince Siegfried frees Odette from the curse of the evil sorcerer, and she sheds the darkness of Odile to become her true self.

With each sweeping lift, I feel a sense of freedom wash over me.

The panic from earlier dissipates, replaced by a serene confidence. The orchestra descends into the finale, and we complete our pas de deux. The spotlight shines down on me, highlighting our final move, and for a moment, time seems to stand still.

Like drops of water, contentment falls on my skin and cascades from my head all the way down to my toes. It's like a wash of victory that settles deep in the crevices of my mind that constantly tell me I'm not good enough. It feels like proof. Like a lawyer who just won a decades-long court case, or a person lost at sea finally being rescued. Those emotions curl like a ribbon around my mind and my heart, and I can practically see the years of hard work emanate from my body.

I've waited my whole life for someone to tell me I'm worth it. Worth choosing, worth staying, worth loving. To tell me my dreams are attainable, and I wouldn't be another fallen star with no way back. Elias has said that every step of the way, but it never truly clicked until this moment. Until *I* decided that I'm worth it.

The music stops and we remain frozen in place. The crowd erupts with applause, their cheers echoing through the theater. When the roses fall at my feet, a single pink peony lands at center stage. Its delicate petals seem to glow amid the sea of bloodred flowers.

Although I can't see him, my smile grows wider. Because I know then that no matter how far we might be, there will always be a piece of my heart that Elias Westbrook is holding on to.

Note to self: When one door closes, smash the window.

FORTY-FIVE

ELIAS

"WHY DO I have to wear a blindfold? Is this a new kink?" Sage asks.

She's limping but never once says anything about how sore she must be. I'll let her pretend for now, but I'm dying to get her into one of our self-care baths.

Our. I've been waiting so long to be able to say that and not have any flicker of doubt that it's true. Right now, I know there will never be another flicker of doubt.

It took hours to get out of the theater after her performance, but I'd stay all night if it meant I'd get to see Sage smile like that. I was going to record her, but I was so entranced by her that I couldn't pry my eyes away.

Everyone insisted on flying in for the show, especially my parents. Our friends and family alone took up an entire row, and seeing Sage's reaction made the chaos before the performance all worth it. When she met us in the foyer, she was overjoyed to see our friends.

Now, the smell of smoke and a mixture of an earthy scent surround us. The light from the moon and its reflection off the water light the path to her surprise.

"You'll see. Just a minute," I say as we walk through the secluded parking lot.

"Is this punishment for making you sit with my uncle for three hours?"

I chuckle. "We had Sean as a buffer. It was fine."

The talk I had with Marcus weeks ago comes back to me. Despite everything, I know from that alone that he recognizes how much I care for Sage and has to like me at least a little bit because of that.

When Sage's feet touch the sand—because she refused to wear shoes—she gasps and squeezes my hand even tighter. I'm sure she hears the crashing sounds of the waves and the rustling of the trees surrounding us. There's a crackling from the glowing fire, and the group of our friends trying to stand quietly as I stop in front of them. "Okay, ready?"

Sage nods, and I pull the blindfold from her eyes.

"Surprise!" everyone shouts.

Seven chairs. A campfire. A table full of takeout. And all the people we love.

She gapes at them. Then turns to look up at me, her eyes twinkling from the reflection of the fire and the tears overflowing her pretty hazel eyes. It's the look that makes me want to wrap her in my arms and never let go.

"This is for me?"

"It's always for you."

The last time we were here, I was certain that whoever ended up with Sage Beaumont would never be bored. The girl is a star, and as much as I denied it then, I wanted to be the one she shone down on—the one she broke out of the sky for, and the one that caught her.

Sage's eyes fill, and when she blinks, a single tear rolls down her cheek. She's still in shock when I dust a kiss over her knuckles.

Summer comes up to us with Aiden right behind her. "We're so proud of you, Sage. You were ethereal!" She pulls her into a hug and guides her over to where Dylan, Kian, and Sean are waiting for us.

Sean is next to hug her. He's getting taller now, and makes Sage look small in comparison.

"Would you say it's worth it?" Aiden asks.

My best friend stares at me with a smug look. Like he knows if I had chickened out, I would spend the rest of my life regretting every moment I wasn't holding on to Sage's hand.

"Worth every fucking second."

No matter how many times Sage and I might have to sleep away from each other, I know that when she's finally next to me, none of it will change how we unravel one another.

As we eat and talk with our friends, Sage's smile is infectious. At one point Kian suggests karaoke and makes Sean hold his phone to show the lyrics for some love song. I'm watching Sage laugh with our friends from my seat across the fire. It might be a little creepy, but she's impossible to look away from.

When she glances at me, I don't bother looking away. A smirk plays on her lips, and she narrows her eyes before walking around the fire to my chair and dropping right into my lap. Her hair flutters in the wind, sending the vanilla scent to drown my senses.

"Summer is really invested in how many piercings everyone has," Sage says.

I groan. "Give it up, Preston!"

After Aiden let it slip that he got a tattoo because of the hat of consequences, he mentioned that one of us has a piercing. Ever since then Summer's been trying to find out who has it. Thank God she doesn't know Aiden and I aren't the only ones who had to pick a dare from that hat.

Summer sticks her tongue out at me.

I roll my eyes and adjust Sage so she's sitting comfortably across my lap. She pokes my chest. "I have a complaint against you, Westbrook."

"Yeah?"

She digs her phone out of her pocket and shows me the screen. "You broke every rule."

It's the list of all the rules we made that day in her apartment, and she's right, I broke every single one, including the last one she put there as a joke. *No falling in love.*

"Me? I think I recall you in a similar position, breaking those rules one thigh at a time." I bark out a laugh, but her glare quickly sobers me. Sage tries to move off my lap, but I tighten my hold. "You're right, it was all me. Guess that means we have to make some new ones. But this time there's no expiration date."

That answer satisfies her because she nuzzles into me. "I don't deserve you."

I lift her chin and force her to meet my gaze. "First rule. You don't get to say that, ever."

She rolls her eyes but kisses me anyway.

"Gross," Sean mutters when he passes us to grab a drink from the cooler. He acts disgusted, but I know he's never been happier to finally see his sister have something for herself.

"Girls don't have cooties anymore, Sean," I tease him.

He glares. "You just bumped yourself down a few spots. I think I like Dylan and Kian better."

Of course, Aiden is still reigning in the number one spot. "Try living with them for four years, that'll change pretty quickly."

"Hey!" Kian shouts from the other side of the fire. "You loved it."

"It's true. Eli got the chance to play daddy," says Dylan. "But Sage probably knows all about that."

Sage gags. Summer takes the marshmallow from the s'mores Aiden is trying to make and chucks it at Dylan.

He catches it in his mouth. Idiot.

Sean rolls his eyes—like his sister—and scampers to where Kian tells him about the time he fell in the ocean.

"So, is PDA still a no?" Sage asks, taking in our position.

Our friends are only a few feet away. Not once have I looked around for cameras in the bushes. I want to keep her like this, in my bubble. "It's definitely a yes. Lots of it."

"I guess I can work with that." She beams. "What about flowers?"

"Different ones every week for the rest of our lives."

I can tell she likes that answer when she takes my hand and drops a kiss to the inside of my wrist, where the ink darkens the skin. "What about long distance? What are the rules?"

"No rules. Just the truth," I say. "Anything that bothers us, we talk about it."

Sage lifts her pinkie. "Elias and Sage unfiltered?"

I smile, intertwining our pinkie fingers. "Yeah, Elias and Sage unfiltered."

When she burrows into me, the light from the campfire bounces off her skin and embeds itself inside my chest. A feeling of relief sinks into my entire body.

Because I know that no matter where I am, I'll always be home as long as I have her.

EPILOGUE

SAGE

Three years later

I'VE TRIED TO put on my gold pearl drop earrings six times. Today is one of those days that tests you until your only option is to cry in a secluded corner. First my hair didn't cooperate, then my dress had shrunk in the wash—courtesy of Elias teaching Sean how to do laundry before he has to leave for college—and now I've poked my earlobe enough times that it's throbbing.

"Elias," I call from our en suite, hoping he's still only down the hall and not lost in the sugar-free cake he's icing for tonight's celebration. The kitchen is his sanctuary, and after my many failed attempts of trying to learn how to cook, I've finally let go of the possibility. Everyone was much too elated by that decision. Now, I only step into the kitchen when I'm putting my flowers into a vase. This week, Elias bought me pink dahlias.

These days, my time at home is spent practicing in the studio of our apartment building. We're still in the same building as Aiden, only a few doors down. Sean made it a point to visit us every weekend, so as soon as Elias found an available three-bedroom, he bought it.

With a frustrated sigh, I attempt for a seventh time to wear the earring. My arms are tired, and my fingers feel raw from being poked by the earring. I need a massage.

Elias and I have updated our self-care night to include massages. That means he gives me a massage, and I fall asleep before he can get one. He never complains and I think it's because I've finally curbed my insomnia.

After my first year with the company, it was worse than ever. But pretty soon, I found a hack to sleep even in stuffy hotel rooms. The secret is to sleep with Elias on a video call. My phone's battery life deteriorated pretty quickly, but my performances were much stronger. Strong enough that I just completed my third and last year with Nova Ballet Theatre. After consistently performing principal roles in *Romeo and Juliet*, *The Nutcracker*, and of course *Swan Lake*, the long days, the injuries, and the emotional toll of the ballet that fired me up only make me want to slow down now. I want to be still for a little while.

I haven't told Elias yet, but I bought the ballet studio on Brunswick.

Clutching the small earrings in my palm, I resist the urge to toss them aside in frustration. It's then that strong arms envelop me from behind, pulling me close. Elias presses gentle kisses along my neck, his warm breath sending shivers down my spine as he finds that sweet spot where my neck meets my shoulder.

"Help me," I whine.

He takes the earring, the ones he gifted me when I completed my last *Swan Lake* performance, and it takes him less than a second to put them in each ear.

I let my head fall against his shoulders when I exhale.

"What's wrong?" he asks, slipping his arms around me.

"No one talks about how hard it is to watch your siblings grow up," I confess quietly.

"I know," he whispers into my hair. "But you raised a great man."

"I did, didn't I?" I gaze up at him. "But that teenage phase was brutal."

"Sixteen-year-old Sean was possessed by the devil." Elias shudders. "But all that hard work paid off. Now, he's following in his brother-in-law's footsteps and heading to Dalton."

The day Sean rejected his offer to Yale because he was accepted on an athletic scholarship to Dalton, all of our friends were overjoyed. Safe to say, Yale is still the enemy.

"I don't know if I like the influence the guys have on him."

He laughs. "I turned out fine, didn't I?"

I make a noncommittal sound, and he squeezes my waist a little tighter.

"What was that?" His lips draw closer, just inches away from my glossy ones. "I'm pretty sure you were screaming about how godlike I am just last night."

I did. Because no matter how many times he touches me, he lights up every nerve of my body like it's the first time. Only someone with omnipotence can pull that off.

"I think I need a reminder."

He raises his brows, and happily leans in. The pressure of his kiss feels like home.

"It'll take two hours with traffic. Can you guys kiss later?" admonishes Nina when she pushes open the bathroom door.

Nina Beaumont-Westbrook, our uptight tween, stands at the threshold of the bathroom, already dressed. Her hair is done up in a neat bun with tiny gems all over. She's wearing the dress Elias bought her, the flats that I did, and the ballerina necklace Sean brought back from one of his hockey games in Montreal.

Three years ago, I met Nina, the eight-year-old girl in my ballet class. It turns out my inkling that she came from a broken home had been correct. After one particularly hard night just two years ago, Nina's parents dropped her off at my studio, and they never came back.

It broke my heart.

The moment I locked up after a solo session, there she was, in pink pajamas, quietly asking to sleep in the studio. When Elias arrived to pick me up and saw the two of us—her with her lost hazel eyes, and me with my teary ones—he didn't need to ask any questions. Without hesitation, we simply went home, called our lawyer, and took the necessary steps to ensure Nina would always have a home. Once she was cleared to travel with me, we spent most of the year checking out popular ballet when I had the odd performance. She loved meeting everyone, and the light I saw in her eyes was a reflection of my own. Sometimes Elias wonders how we're not blood related. For months, we fostered her, granting her the freedom to decide where she wanted to stay. The day she chose us to be her parents was the best day of my life; our wedding day is a close second.

"Come on, people, we have a graduation to attend," she says.

Elias and I laugh and salute our punctual eleven-year-old.

We rush out after her, piling into the Bronco and straight to York Prep. It's June, so the green leaves dance in the distance, and the sun beams down on us. My thin pink dress blows in the wind as we walk over the gravel and to the back of the school.

Banners with the school's black and crimson colors flutter in the gentle breeze. The scent of freshly cut grass mingles with the fragrance from the flower beds lining the pathways. Groups of family members chat excitedly, clutching bouquets and gifts for the graduates.

When we find our seats, Uncle Marcus and Amy Laurent—Smith-Beaumont now—come to greet us as the ceremony is already starting. All the seats in our row are reserved, and we get disapproving looks from the parents who try to snatch a seat. Elias sits easily, blocking off half the seats, and Nina glares at anyone who tries to slip into one.

Our friends finally arrive, noisily walking down the gravel path toward us.

"Why do they have outdoor graduations when the sun is trying to kill us?" Dylan says as he shuffles past us to find his seat.

"Yeah, I thought Canada was supposed to be cold," adds Kian.

Summer snorts. "Sorry to break it to you, but our igloos melt in June."

Nina waves excitedly when she spots her uncles, and plants herself in the seat right between them. They shower her with compliments, and she blushes, brushing a curly strand that falls loose from her bun. Like mother, like daughter, I guess.

When the names are called, we're all ready to cheer for Sean. Elias slips his fingers through mine, his thumb brushing over the diamond band on my finger before he intertwines our hands. I haven't taken off this wedding ring since we got married on a random Wednesday in April, two months ago, at Lake Ontario.

"Sean Beaumont," the principal announces. Our group explodes with cheers and applause, shouting, and Kian jingles a tambourine and Dylan blares an air horn as Sean walks across the stage. His gown is black and the sash is crimson. He does some silly fake-out to his principal before shaking his hand.

"Sean will attend the prestigious Dalton University on an ice hockey scholarship. He thanks his amazing friends and family for supporting him throughout the years. But most importantly, he dedicates this achievement to the one person in his life who has always been a constant: his sister, Sage."

Like Elias knows the tears are going to fall, he hands me a handkerchief and pulls me close. I burrow into the space he creates for me, the one I've occupied for the past three years. Nina comes to us, and I kiss the top of her vanilla-scented hair. Elias scoots over to let her sit with him, and we watch the rest of the commencement, cheering again when Sean's best friend, Josh Sutherland, dances across the stage. Soon, the grads toss their hats in the sky. It's a flurry of black and crimson tassels.

Sean shouts my name and runs right to us.

Aiden and Summer engulf him in a hug first and hand him a small blue box. "Open it!" Summer urges.

Sean glances at my smiling face before pulling off the cover on the gift box.

"Keys?" He turns the silver keys in his hand.

"They're the keys to the off-campus house. We want you to stay there when you head to Dalton."

When Aiden told me he wanted to pass down the keys to Sean, instead of selling the house his grandparents bought him when he started at Dalton, I didn't know what to say. Instinct made me want to refuse because we've never had a place to call home, but knowing Sean can have that without relying on another institution for housing made my heart crack in two before it bound itself back together.

Sean blinks rapidly in an attempt to stop his flow of tears. Aiden laughs and pulls him in for a hug that we all join in on. An overwhelming feeling of belonging pokes at my heart. Because this is how I like it.

Just us, and our little family.

ACKNOWLEDGMENTS

Sometimes in life, you meet the type of people who make you wonder where the heck they've been your whole life. I've had the privilege of meeting those people through my author journey.

Nina, your belief in me is the only reason I made my deadline for this book. Thank you for keeping up with my sounding boards, even when I developed insomnia and would wake you up at ungodly hours to talk about this book. It was all worth it when you cried reading the epilogue. You're a once-in-a-lifetime friend, and I'm so glad I met you in this one. In case you didn't already realize it yet, Elias is for you.

Peyton, our invisible string will always be my favorite part of this publishing journey. I'd like to think there isn't a universe out there where we don't meet. It would truly be a tragedy if we weren't friends in every single one. We've lived a dozen lifetimes this year alone, but I'm eternally grateful that I got to do it all with you, even if it meant watching our teams tank in the playoffs while we finished (read: procrastinated) our drafts. Thank you for saving me from *spiral*-ing, and here's to saving each other from more in the future.

Carlyn, for sending me daily screenshots of your favorite scenes from *Collide*. Hopefully, this one will tide you over until Dylan's book.

Shayla, can you believe this?

Kristine, Mary, and the amazing editors at Berkley, thank you for transforming this book from an incoherent brain dump into something I can be proud of. Jessica and Stephanie, thank you for your hard work in making sure I get to see my books everywhere. Darcy, Anna, Beth, Grace, and Maisie at Bloomsbury, thank you for rooting for me since day one. Deborah, Natasha, and the team at PRH Canada, thank you for making this series feel so special. Jessica and everyone at SDLA, thank you for making this all possible.

Last, because you all deserve to close out my first fully traditional release, thank you to my readers. I don't think you even realize what an impact your words have. There are days when imposter syndrome fights to win, but then a sweet message from you makes it all flutter away. You are the only reason I get to do this. I'd go through all the hard parts of this journey over and over if it meant that at the end of the day, I still had all of you. Thank you. Like, a lot.

Keep reading for a preview of
Summer and Aiden's love story in

COLLIDE

available now!

ONE

SUMMER

SHE'S HOLDING A gun to my head.

Well, figuratively at least.

The gun in question: hockey. The woman holding it: Dr. Laura Langston, Ph.D.

"Hockey?" I repeat. "You want *me* to do my grad school application on hockey?"

Langston has been my grad school advisor for the past year, but I've been working under her wing since I started at Dalton University.

She's everything I want to be, and I've obsessed over every academic paper she's written. She's kind of my celebrity crush in the nerdiest way possible. With her Ph.D. in sports psychology, countless papers published, and experience with Olympians and athletes around the world, she's inspirational.

Until you get to know her.

When they said *Don't meet your heroes*, they were talking about Laura Langston. She's the human equivalent of an angry swarm of wasps. There are plenty of professors who treat their students like total garbage and think their fancy piece of paper means they can be tyrants, but Langston is a different species. Her brilliance is undeniable, but she is patronizing, dismissive, and purposely difficult when she knows you need her help.

So, why the hell did I choose her as my advisor? Because her success rate in getting students into Dalton's prestigious master's program is too enticing to ignore. It's the number one program in North America and students vetted by her are guaranteed acceptance. Not to mention she chooses who will be eligible for co-op—a competitive program that allows one student from our cohort to work with Team USA. It's been my dream from the age of eight, so I'll suffer through her monstrous dictatorship if it means I'll soon have my own master's degree in sports psychology.

"You need to start using your resources to your advantage, Summer." She surveys me above the rims of her glasses. "I know you hate hockey, but this is your last chance to submit a solid application."

The word *hate* slips past her lips as if my aversion to the sport is completely fabricated. Considering she's one of the few people who know why I stay far away from the icy rink and the similarly icy men skating on it, I barely keep my composure. Sticking me right in the center of that blue circle with an empirical research study that determines the fate of my future is pure evil. An evil only Dr. Langston and her molten heart can manage.

"But why hockey? I'll choose football. Basketball. Even curling. I don't care." Does Dalton even have a curling team?

"Exactly. You don't care. I need you to do something you care about. Something you feel strongly about. Hence, hockey."

I hate that she's right. Sweeping aside her overall ominous nature, she is a smart woman. I mean, she didn't get her Ph.D. for nothing, but being her student is a double-edged sword.

"But—"

She lifts a hand. "I won't approve anything else. Do this or lose your spot. The choice is yours." It's like the universe sent me my very own *Fuck You* in the form of my professor. Years of working my ass off in undergrad only to be told hockey is my saving grace. What a joke. Clenching my fists, I swallow the urge to scream. "That isn't much of a choice, Dr. Langston."

"If you can't do this, then I overestimated your potential, Summer." Her voice grows sharp. "I have four students who would kill to have your spot, but I took you under my wing. Don't make me regret this."

She didn't exactly choose to take me under her wing. I had a 4.2 GPA and killer reference letters. Not to mention the extremely difficult advisor's exam she implemented last year to pick out the best students. I got food poisoning from the campus cafeteria that week, but I still dragged myself to the exam. I beat every student, and I'll be damned if they take my spot now.

"I understand what you're saying, but as you know, I'm not very fond of hockey. For good reason, might I add, and I doubt my research will be an accurate representation, considering that."

"Either you get over your apprehension or lose what you've worked for."

Apprehension?

Ignoring the pointed jab feels like trying to ignore a bullet lodged in my sternum. "There's no reason why I can't choose basketball. Coach Walker would happily let me collaborate with one of his players."

"Coach Kilner has already agreed to allow one of my students to work with his players. Get me your completed proposal by the end of the week or forfeit your spot, Ms. Preston." Her dismissal is clear when she twists away from me in her chair.

If I could commit one crime and get away with it, I have a feeling it would include Dr. Langston.

"Okay. Thank you," I mutter. She's typing aggressively on her computer, probably making another student's life a living hell. I imagine she goes home and crosses off the names of students she has successfully tormented. My name and the doll she sticks pins into are at the top of that list today.

I've successfully avoided everything to do with hockey for the past three years, only for it to be my front and center for the next few months. I'm beyond screwed, and I have to suck up my distaste for the sport of my Canadian ancestors.

I use all my willpower to not slam her door on the way out.

"You look pissed." The voice comes from the hallway leading to the advisor's lounge. Donny stands against the wall, dressed in cashmere and his brown eyes focused on me.

I've made a few mistakes since I got to college. Donny Rai is one of them.

An exhausting two-year relationship later, we have no choice but to see each other every day because we're both getting the same degree and applying to the same post-grad program. It doesn't feel like a competition between us, but I know Donny wants that co-op spot just as bad as I do.

He falls into step with me. "An ultimatum?"

"Exactly." I look over at him. "How did you know?"

"She gave one to Shannon Lee an hour ago. Shannon's thinking of dropping out now."

My eyes widen. Shannon is one of the smartest students on campus. Her work in clinical psychology was sent for review, making her the youngest student considered for publication.

"That's ridiculous." I shake my head, knowing how screwed I am. "You're so lucky you submitted your application early. The rest of us are stuck completing this new requirement."

He shrugs. "It's only a conditional acceptance."

"Right, like you would ever let your 4.0 drop."

"4.3," he corrects.

Donny is at the top of the dean's list every year; he's in every club and committee imaginable. He is the poster child for the Ivy League, so it's no surprise he managed to carve his way into this competitive program. I like to think I'm academically gifted too, but I might as well wear a dunce cap in comparison.

"I have a meeting right now. But I'll help with your application; we both know you'll need it."

The insult stings, but Donny just smiles and peels away to head to his meeting with the Dalton Royal Press. Yeah, he works on the school paper, too.

When I finally stomp into my dorm, I fall flat on the living room couch. "If I gave you a shovel, would you hit me over the head with it?" I ask Amara.

"Depends. Am I getting paid?" I groan into the throw pillow, but she pulls it away. "What did she do now?"

Amara Evans and I have been roommates since freshman year. Luckily for me, being best friends with a tech genius means getting perks from the university for her contributions. The most important one was securing Iona House. The only student living complex with two-bedroom and two-bathroom units. It's still cramped, but anything is better than the communal bathrooms where athlete's foot lurks in every corner. "She's making me do my application on hockey," I tell her.

Amara drops the pillow. "You're kidding. I thought she knew about everything."

"She does! This is what I get for sharing my secrets with her."

"Can't you find another advisor? She can't be the only one who gets students accepted to the program."

"No one has her success rate. It's like she's rigging acceptances, or something. But maybe she's right. I should put aside my *apprehension*."

Amara gasps. "She did not say that!"

"Oh, but she did." I sigh, rolling to a sitting position. "How come you're back so early?"

"Sitting in that lecture hall with a bunch of sweaty dudes isn't how I want to spend my first day back."

Majoring in computer science means ninety percent of Amara's class is dudes. Which isn't something Amara's used to, coming from a family of five sisters. She's smack in the middle and says she's never known a moment of peace. Stuck between the impossible position of being the older and younger sister, and simultaneously having to deal with teenage hormones and adolescent tantrums. As someone with twin sisters who were born when I was already a handful of years older, I can't relate.

"Are you going to the party tonight?" she asks.

Being surrounded by hundreds of drunk frat dudes sounds like a nightmare. "I have way too much to do."

Her exasperated look tells me I'm in for a lecture. "Last semester you said you'd loosen up and enjoy your senior year. You said you would go out more, Summer. If I have to drag you along, I will." I did say that. To be fair, it was after I cried over a particularly difficult assignment and Donny's perfect score sent me over the edge. That's when I vowed that I'd let loose, because only focusing on school wasn't making my grades better.

I shoot her a sheepish look. "But I have to start that proposal, and I have readings to do."

She huffs out a breath. "Fine. I'll go with Cassie, but you have to promise to take a few breaks."

"Promise. I'll even go for a run later."

Amara's head hangs in disapproval. "Not the type of break I was talking about, but I'll take anything if it gets you out of here."

TWO

AIDEN

SHE'S WATCHING ME sleep.

Drawing away from the last remnants of my dream means I'm hyper-aware of my current surroundings. Either she's enjoying the view, which I wouldn't blame her for, or she's planning on ripping off my skin and wearing it later.

The latter seems more likely, because I fell asleep on her last night.

The welcome party at our house had gotten a little out of control. By a little, I mean *extremely* out of control. When Dalton University's left-winger and one of my best friends, Dylan Donovan, is in charge of a party, it's meant to turn into a rager. Mostly because I decided not to be the one policing it. We had just come back from break, so it was the only time I'd let myself drink before the season starts up again, and I'm not sure how much I'll regret that decision until I've seen the aftermath.

Opening my eyes means having to deal with the aftermath.

When Aleena, a smoking hot redhead, picked me out of the crowd to do body shots last night, it was only right that we found ourselves in my room, naked and all over each other. Though that didn't last long, because sleep debt is real, and I am its latest victim.

I train every day and take a full course load, and when I'm not doing that, I'm keeping the guys out of trouble. So, as I laid her on my bed and kissed my way down her stomach, I fully knocked out. It would have been embarrassing if I was conscious, but the sleep was so great I had no complaints.

"Morning." I stretch my arms out and under my head, opening my eyes to see exactly what I expected.

Red hair pools on my chest and full pouty lips are trapped between white teeth. "Good sleep?" she asks. "I hope you're not feeling too lazy this morning."

Anyone else would have been emasculated by the comment, but I couldn't be. Not when practically every girl on campus knows that *lazy* and *Aiden Crawford* have never been used in a sentence together. This was a one-off, and judging from her darkening blue eyes, she knew I'd make it up to her.

I chuckle. "Great sleep, actually."

"Well, if you're awake now"—she runs a red fingernail down my chest—"we can start the day off right."

What kind of host would I be to turn down that offer? When her hand trails lower, I flip her over and make up for last night.

By the time Aleena finishes up in the shower, I'm already downstairs making breakfast. Turns out women are big fans of steam showers, and I am the proud owner of the only one in the house. Rightfully so, because my grandparents had bought the house when I got accepted to Dalton. But that didn't stop Kian Ishida, the team's right-winger and our roommate, from fighting me tooth and nail for it. The captain card never failed to win a disagreement, but now he's across the hall with his loud music and constant pounding on my bedroom door.

I offer Aleena breakfast, but she only shakes her head in response before walking out the front door. I smile to myself. There is nothing better than a one-night stand who doesn't try to be your girlfriend after.

Eli watches the exchange with raised brows. "That's a first."

"What is?"

"It's past ten. You've never had a girl stay that long. Did you finally find the one?" His eyes widen with a grin that I'd like to punch off his face.

"I fell asleep last night before we got to do anything. It was only right."

"How chivalrous," he says dryly. "You've been exhausted lately. Think you need to cut back?"

Now it's my turn to laugh. Elias Westbrook, "Eli," as everyone knows him, and I have known each other since we were in diapers. His worry doesn't irritate me like everyone else's because I know he says it with great caution, and I must really be cutting it close with practice and school if he's saying something. "I'm fine. I've made it work for this long; what's a few more months?"

He doesn't seem to like that answer, though he only nods and plates his eggs.

"Sick party, guys." An early-morning straggler walks out of the house wearing just boxers, the rest of his clothes dangling from his arm. The pin on his jacket tells me he's one of Dylan's fraternity brothers.

Dylan is the only one out of us who is part of a frat. Kappa Sigma Zeta treats him like royalty, and although he lives with us, he could easily have the master suite in the Greek Row house. But according to him, having to be in the same house as the "ass-kissing freshmen" is the last thing he wants.

I eat a spoonful of oatmeal. "Where are the rest of the guys?"

Eli scrolls through his phone and shows me the screen. It's a picture of Kian passed out on the grass at the front entrance of our campus. Behind him, the monument of Sir Davis Dalton is trashed. I squeeze my eyes shut, hoping there is a simple explanation for this. Maybe a really good Photoshop job. "Who took that?"

"Benny Tang."

I pause mid-bite. "Yale's goalie? What was he doing here?" Having Yale come here after we slaughtered them in a game before winter break would be the worst possible scenario. The last thing I remember before heading upstairs was telling Dylan to shut it down soon. Clearly, he didn't listen.

"Might wanna ask Dylan. I wasn't here."

Of course he wasn't. If Eli, the only other responsible one, hadn't been at the party, that means the two overgrown children, Dylan and Kian, were in charge.

This all started when they lost a bet last semester that has us throwing the majority of the parties on campus. The parties we don't throw, we have to provide the booze. When I found out, I had both of them benched for two games straight.

Despite everything, I'm hoping this is a nightmare and I'm still in bed with Aleena. "And do I wanna know where Dylan is?" I ask cautiously.

When Eli picks up his phone again, I groan.

He chuckles. "I'm kidding, dude. He's passed out in the living room."

"IT WAS ME."

Every eye in the room zeroes in on me, and I regret ever learning how to speak. The pounding in my head persists because Coach wanted to torture us with practice before we gathered in the media room for a mandatory meeting. The bright white of the rink had sent my headache doubling in pain. I don't drink often, and my body never lets me forget when I do, so today was no exception. Everything was intensified, including Kian's loud voice, which spewed paranoia about why Coach called a meeting. The kid woke up with grass stains on his body and still wondered what was happening.

When Coach Kilner entered, he was fuming, his pale skin glowing red. He even knocked the hats off the heads of the juniors, who immediately cowered to the back row, and I began regretting my decision to sit up front. Kian and Dylan were way in the back too, hiding behind our goalies.

"A fucking party that trashed campus?" Coach yelled, and suddenly everything made sense. "Is this a fucking joke to all of you? Never in my twenty-five years of coaching have I had to deal with this kind of blatant disregard for the school code of conduct."

That part wasn't all true. I know for a fact that Brady Winston, the captain from the year before mine, threw a house party that landed a yearlong ban on Greek Row. The dean's car went missing, the swim team's pool was trashed, and all extracurriculars were canceled. So I'm pretty sure trashing the campus and vandalizing the monument of Sir Davis Dalton isn't the worst thing to happen to the school.

"When I became a coach after years in the league," Coach started as Devon muttered, "Here we go," beside me, "never did I think I would be giving my senior players a lecture on throwing parties."

"Coach, the party—"

"Shut it, Donovan," Kilner scolded. "We are in the fucking qualifiers that will get us to the Frozen Four and you are messing around with other colleges. At this stage?"

"Yale came here. Shouldn't they be getting the brunt of this?" asked Tyler Sampson, our alternate captain, and one of the smartest guys on the team. He's headed to law school instead of following in his hockey superstar father's footsteps.

"They are not my problem, you idiots are! I should have every single one of you suspended," he says, rage pouring out of his sweat-covered forehead.

"But then we wouldn't be able to play the Frozen Four." Kian's chiming in didn't help the rest of that speech, and now he's stuck with laundry duty for a month. It was originally a week, but Kian kept protesting, and everyone knows if Coach gives you a punishment, you shut your trap and take it.

After that, no one interrupted, except when I opened my big mouth to incriminate myself.

"What do you mean?" Coach asks, staring daggers at me now. I've seen that sharp glare too many times, and it should scare me enough to sit my ass back down, but I don't.

"I'm the one who threw the party."

Eli curses behind me, but he doesn't say anything else because he knows when I make a decision, there's nothing anyone can say to talk me out of it.

Coach runs a hand over his mouth, muttering something under his breath. Most likely about how much of a dumbass I am, and I'd have to agree. "This is how you wanna play it, Crawford? You sure it wasn't a collective mistake?"

He's giving me an out. More out of desperation than anything, because when the school gets wind of this, I will be punished. My only hope in putting myself on the line is that they'll check my academic standing and my hockey career before shelling out anything too severe. My fate will be better than anyone else's on this team.

"It was all me. I let Yale attend." Kilner nods, and I can't help but notice the minuscule flash of respect that flickers through his features before it's replaced by the usual anger. "I'll report to the dean. If someone has a different story than your captain, speak now."

The atmosphere in the room shifts, and I know the team wants to have my back, but the expression on my face must convey what I hope, because they reluctantly sit back in silence.

"Then why the hell are you still here!" he shouts, forcing us to shuffle out of the media room. Coach pulls me back. "My office after you've showered."

The locker room is eerily quiet for the first time ever, and when I step out of the shower, I'm greeted with Kian's sullen face. "Cap, you didn't have to do that," he says, looking guilty.

I run a towel over my hair. "I did. I fucked up last night; I shouldn't have let my guard down."

Eli sits beside me. "If that's your takeaway, you're looking at this all wrong. This is everyone's fault, mine too."

The locker room murmurs in agreement.

"I know you guys want to have my back, but it's on me to be a good example, and last night I wasn't. This isn't a united front kind of thing. The dean's involved, which means he'll see to it that everyone gets punished. We can't have that going into the season. If it's just me, the consequences can't be too bad," I say confidently.

My confidence withers when I enter Coach Kilner's office. It's never an exciting event to be here, but today it's especially grim. He's at his desk, tapping the mouse with a heavy hand. When he finally decides to give me his attention, he gestures for me to sit. He continues torturing the mouse until he chucks it at the wall.

It clatters to the floor in two pieces.

I swallow.

Kilner leans back in his chair, squeezing his stress ball tight enough to burst. "Where were you the last Friday before the end of semester?"

The question throws me off. I just confessed to a pretty heavy account of reckless abandon, and he's worried about last semester? I barely remember what I had for dinner last night, let alone what I was doing two weeks ago.

Except the memory hits, clearing the haze of my lingering hangover. "After practice ended, I headed to the house," I say.

"The boys?"

"Same thing."

"Party?"

Fuck. Why does he look so pissed? The only thing I remember from that party was a pretty blonde. It had started to get a bit out of hand, but I trusted the guys to handle it. It's the only reason I let myself relax last night. However, I've never lied to Coach, and I won't start now.

"Yeah, a party."

"So, you're telling me a party—mind you, one that you boys have multiple times a week—is the reason you missed the charity fund-raiser?"

Oh, crap. The charity game.

In an attempt to pacify Kilner, I signed everyone up to coach the kids before their charity game. Spending two days a week with unfiltered children takes its toll, and it didn't help that it was finals season. So, when I stopped showing up, so did everyone else.

"Those kids were waiting on that ice, and you didn't show. What about the weekend before that? Same thing?"

I nod. Dalton parties never eased. If you can't find one, you're looking in the wrong place.

He lets out a derisive laugh. "You missed the mental health drive that the psychology department put on specifically for athletes. The hockey team didn't show, and neither did football or basketball."

To be fair, I don't pay attention to campus events. "How is that my fault?"

"Because instead of knowing where you had to be, there was a party all you idiots were at! If my players don't honor their commitments, do you know what I do, Aiden?"

"Bench them," I mutter.

He's fuming now. "Good, you're paying attention. And do you know why I called you in here?"

"Because I threw last night's party," I answer, "and I'm the captain."

"So you know you're the captain? I thought maybe you're too hungover to remember!" he shouts.

I wince. "I'm sorry, Coach. Next time—"

"There will be no next time. I don't care if you're my star player or Wayne fucking Gretzky, you will be a team player first." He releases a deep, agitated breath. "You should be leading your team, not partaking in their stupid games. Those boys respect you, Aiden. If you're at a party thinking with the wrong head, so are they. Smarten up, or I will have no choice but to put you on probation."

My face contorts with confusion. "What? There's no chance I get academic probation."

"We're not talking about your classes here. The party is being investigated."

Ah, fuck. Remember when I said I wouldn't know if I regretted drinking until I saw the aftermath? I regret it now. Probation is bad, like tearing your ACL bad. If the news gets to the league, they'll send agents out here to assess me as an eligible player. I had just signed with Toronto, because draft didn't mean shit until you put pen to paper. Making a mistake now would be fatal.

"I can't be on probation."

Coach nods. "You're in luck, because before the dean went on sabbatical, he informed the committee that anyone involved in the trash fiasco is to be dealt with. Since you have taken on that very stupid responsibility, your name is first on the list."

I am going to kill my fucking teammates. "What does that mean?"

"That they gave me the option of probation or community service."

An air of relief fills me. "That's great. I'll do community service. I will single-handedly scrub every inch of Sir Davis Dalton."

Coach gives me an unsettled look. "As great of a mental image as that is, it's not that simple," he informs me. "A lot goes into eligible community service hours, and since we don't have a precedent, it's going play-by-play."

I snort. "Like a prison sentence where I get out on good behavior?"

"You're in no place to be a smart-ass," he reprimands. "I would have been forced to put you on probation if it wasn't for her."

"Who?"

ABOUT THE AUTHOR

Bal is a Canadian writer and booklover. Before she decided to jump into the romance pool, she spent her time gushing about books on social media. When inspiration strikes, she is found filling her Notes app with ideas for romance novels. She loves reading about love, watching movies about love, and now writing about it herself. There really isn't much else that gets her heart fluttering the way HEAs do. She fell in love with writing and hopes to continue living out her romance author dreams.

VISIT THE AUTHOR ONLINE

AuthorBalKhabra.com
AuthorBalKhabra
AuthorBalKhabra

Ready to find
your next great read?

Let us help.

Visit prh.com/nextread

Penguin
Random
House